PALADIN

PRAISE FOR FIREBRAND

"A well-drawn and important read… with emotionally
high stakes, *Firebrand* is a moving, expertly written, and
entertaining work of young adult fiction."
Self-Publishing Review, ★★★★½

"An intriguing, fresh look at an important period of
American history… the story speaks to the heart."
The BookLife Prize

"A novel rife with tension on every page."
Kathleen M. Rodgers, author of the award-winning novel of
'Johnny Come Lately'

PALADIN

Firebrand Book Two

SARAH MACTAVISH

Dove Hollow
BOOKS
Roanoke, Texas

Image Credits

Pages iv, ix: Sarah MacTavish; Page 111: Library of Congress, Prints & Photographs Division, Civil War, LC-DIG-ppmsca-32992; Page 180: Library of Congress, Prints & Photographs Division, Civil War, LC-DIG-cwpb-01560; Page 202: Library of Congress, Prints & Photographs Division, Civil War, LC-DIG-cwpb-00133; Page 310: Library of Congress, Prints & Photographs Division, Civil War, LC-DIG-cwpb-01099; Page 339: Library of Congress, Prints & Photographs Division, Civil War, LC-DIG-cwpb-04351; Page 406: Library of Congress, Prints & Photographs Division, Civil War, LC-DIG-ppmsca-32890

Dove Hollow Books
PO Box 831
Roanoke, TX 76262

Cover design by Julie Keller
Editing by Stephen Parolini and Justin Cartlidge

978-0-9969383-5-8

10 9 8 7 6 5 4 3 2 1
First Edition

To all of my sweet 'Scribblers' at the library.
I can't wait to see your stories come to life, too!

"I could only thank God that I was free
and could go forward and work, and I was
not obliged to stay at home and weep."

Sarah Emma Edmonds
2nd Michigan Infantry

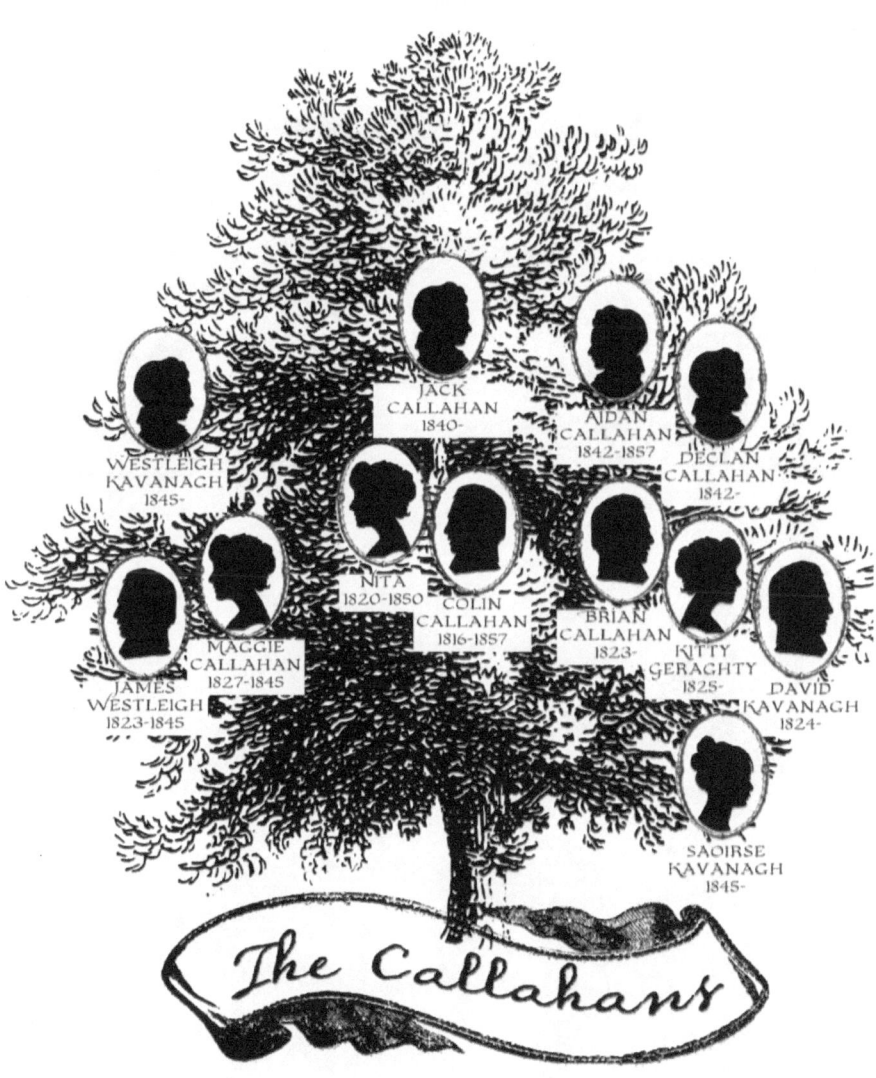

The Callahans

A NOTE ON PRONUNCIATION

Saoirse's name in this story is pronounced *SEER-sha*, but
SER-sha, SAIR-sha, or SOR-sha are also acceptable,
depending on the dialect of Irish.

1

SAOIRSE

Dove Hollow, Pennsylvania
April 12, 1861

Some memories are so strong, they hurt. You're just walking along one day, minding your own business in the present, so, when out of nowhere the past comes up and whacks you right between your eyes. Near takes your breath away, it does. Makes your bones heavy.

"Níl aon tinteán mar do thinteán féin."

There's no hearth like your own hearth.

My brother Aidan said this to me the night he died. Before he tried to run away, to go back to Ireland. I suppose he was trying to explain why he needed to leave, but I didn't understand it then. Four years now, and I hadn't given it much thought—it all stung too much.

But confound it if it wasn't stuck in my head now, in his

voice, along with the memory of his sad eyes. The words echoed incessantly as I stepped off my father's front porch, bag on my shoulder, hat on my head. I wore my skirts this time. Needed a quiet exit, it being in the middle of the day and all. No sense drawing attention to myself traipsing about town in trousers, even if they did make traveling easier.

I suppressed the urge to look behind me as I put distance between myself and the sweet little house at the end of the lane. Once the road crunched beneath my feet I let go a long-held breath and increased my stride as best I could, with that cumbersome petticoat twisting 'round my ankles. I aimed for the top of the hill that overlooked our little valley.

Beyond that...

There's no hearth like your own hearth.

Sure, and that's grand, Aidan, but you mind telling me which hearth is *my* hearth? You can't? Well, then be quiet with you, now.

He didn't listen. I shook my head to rattle the voice loose. Tried to hum a song or two to drown him out, but 'twas no use.

"I'm going this time," I said through clenched teeth. "And nobody can stop me. Not even you."

I knew better. The only person stopping me was my own self. Ever since the night I came to Dove Hollow, since I found my father, my spirit was fidgety. But I stayed for

David—my da—and I am glad I did. The past few months had been full of more comfort, and joy, and love, than ever I'd known in all my sixteen years.

But my feet itched something terrible.

I focused on the road in front of me, lest the sight of Dove Hollow or any of its residents produce in me any longing to remain. 'Twas a lovely little town, quiet and content, like a sleepy sigh. After all the troubles I left behind in Texas, I needed the rest, to be sure. But now the time for resting was done.

The dairy farm lay before me at the bottom of the hill, and I saw a figure sitting on the fence, leaning forward on his knees, hat tipped down. There was a bag on the ground below his feet.

I swallowed the lump in my throat and increased my stride, even as my knees gave a little quake. I wouldn't lose my nerve, not this time.

As I neared, the hat tipped up, revealing a wry smirk on a handsome Cherokee face.

"Well, now," Jack drawled as he slid off the fence to lean against the post. He eyed me with poorly masked amusement. "We really leaving this time, or not?"

I stopped and adjusted my bag as I straightened my shoulders. "*I* am. You don't have to go anywhere."

Jack shrugged. "I already told you. You go, I go."

My heart went a bit mushy. Jack Callahan—the boy I thought was my cousin but who became something closer than a brother—how did I ever think he would let me leave without him? But I forced a frown. "And how did you know I was—?"

"Saoirse, don't you know by now I can read you like a book? It was all over your face this morning at breakfast."

I cringed. I hoped David hadn't noticed.

"So," he said, picking up his own bag. "Where are we going?"

I groaned and leaned against the fence. "I don't know…"

Calloused hands gently pulled mine from my face. Jack pushed his hat back and drilled me with eyes the color of Connemara marble. Earthy green, just like Aidan's. Though Jack's were full of so much more pain. "Talk to me. What's the matter this time?"

"I don't belong here."

"Saoirse," he said softly. "Come on, tell me."

I learned a good while ago it was useless to lie to Jack. But I couldn't look him in the eye, all the same. "I dreamt about Abigail again," I whispered towards my toes. His hands left mine cold. "The—the house was on fire. And I could hear them all calling for us—"

Jack drew a long, ragged breath, and I felt terrible now for bringing it up. But they haunted me. Brian and my mother. Abigail and all of the other men and women still living in chains down there. We abandoned them in Texas. And how I've been able to get a spot of sleep since, I have no idea.

4

"I thought—" my voice cracked. "Thought if there was a chance, some tiny sliver of hope, we could—"

"Saoirse." Jack tugged at the chain around his neck and pulled out her wedding ring that had been dangling over his heart. The one plucked out of the ashes of what was once our home...

Jack's eyes were wet. "Abigail is gone."

"But what if—"

"You know what she would say if she heard you talking like this? You forget, you're still wanted for killing a man."

A shiver snaked through me. "I didn't want to kill him." I hardly remembered firing my weapon. It was all such a terrible blur.

Jack cocked an eyebrow. "Yeah, and I'm sure they'll understand if you just explain to them how you didn't *mean* to shoot the man while you were interrupting their lynching."

I glanced at the fading scars that wrapped around Jack's neck and shivered again. "So you're wanting me to stay, is that it?"

Jack shook his head. He picked me up by the waist as if I weighed nothing at all and set me on the fence before climbing up next to me. "I'd be a fool to try and make you do anything, you know that." He started scraping mud from his boots against the rail beneath us. "I just want you to think about what *you* want."

I kicked my heels against the fence for a minute. What

did I want? I wanted to fix everything, that's all. Bring Abigail back. Bring my family back together. See slavery's end.

Although when I thought about those last two, I wasn't sure which task would prove more impossible.

"You know what I want." I squinted at him. "Same as you."

He nodded and stretched his arms above his head. "Well, before we both go hell-bent into I don't even know what kinda trouble, I want you to consider a thing or two."

My shoulders drooped.

Jack held up a finger. "We're wanted."

"You said that already."

"And I thought it was worth mentioning again, considering they'd likely shoot us on sight."

"Fine. Next?"

Jack crossed his arms over his chest and his eyes traveled back down the road from where I'd come. "Your pa would be heartbroken, seeing as he's just started getting to know you. Sixteen years, he thought you were dead. And then you hang around for barely six months before running away?"

I scowled. "Too much, Callahan."

"Just being honest. And it's not just David you'd be hurting. But if you left without telling Westleigh goodbye, you'd crush that poor boy."

I rolled my eyes. Westleigh Kavanagh, my new step-brother—or was he my *adoptive* brother? My half-brother's cousin? I wasn't so sure exactly what he was to me, but I knew I was just fine with skipping town before he returned from Pittsburgh.

My cheeks burned as I thought of him at university, meeting new people, studying new things, making plans for a bigger and better life beyond this little valley. But Jack was right. After all he'd gone through getting me home to my father, I'd likely break his heart if I left now.

I grabbed my skirts and jumped back down onto the road, turning to face Dove Hollow. "All right, are you happy, then? I'm staying."

"Don't do that to me, it's your choice."

"Ah, sure it is," I muttered.

Jack shook his head. "Well, before you go home, you figure you ought to tell me why your knuckles are all cut up this time?"

I glanced down at the scabs on my right hand and blushed. "I... might have broken them on Jonas Horner's teeth."

"Again?"

"Could've been one of his brothers, I can't tell their stupid faces apart."

"Saoirse—"

"He called my mother a whore," I spat. I wasn't surprised the whole town knew my story. How else did they explain the sudden appearance of David Kavanagh's long-lost daughter? Even if they didn't know the details, they would cast whatever judgements they'd like. But the loss of my mam was still so fresh, I don't even remember hitting Jonas 'til David was pulling me off him.

Just another day of me making a fool of myself in front of Dove Hollow and bringing shame to my father. But sure 'twas satisfying to see Jonas with his lip all busted.

Jack pulled me into a hug. "I would've hit him, too."

"See, I'm taking after you," I said. "Giving my mouth a rest and let my fists do some talking for a change."

Jack frowned at me.

"What?" I shrugged. "Ah, I told you I don't belong here, didn't I?"

He gave me a peck on the cheek. "Maybe. Or maybe those boys need a busted lip now and again. Just let me watch next time."

"You'll have a front row seat, you will."

"All right, you little hellion." He pulled away and slung his arm through mine. "Let me walk you home, keep you out of trouble."

"Fair enough." I laughed and set my head on his shoulder. At least no matter where I went, there would always be Jack.

I kicked a loose stone down the road as we walked, silently cursing myself for failing to leave. I could almost hear Aidan's stifled laughter. The cheeky devil.

A familiar ache spread through my chest. Oh, how I

missed him. It made staying in Dove Hollow that much harder, thinking of the promises I'd made before he died. I was supposed to protect them. Take care of them. Mam, Brian, Declan. And what a grand mess I made of that.

My fists curled at the thought of my remaining brother. No, 'twasn't my fault about Declan. If he'd just stayed away from Reeves, and the vigilantes, and their fires, they might have left us alone. But Declan sold his measly little soul to those slave-owning tyrants. And Abigail—sweet Abigail—paid the price. I would never forgive him for that. And I doubt even Aidan would've, either.

Rattling wagon wheels brought me out of my brooding. Dove Hollow's unlikely physician, Lucy Bischoff, sat atop a wagon. She waved at us.

"There you two are," she called out, stopping her horse. She motioned us to her. "I've come to fetch you, Jack. They're waiting for you at the church. We've got a bigger crowd than we anticipated. People are anxious to hear you speak."

Jack groaned, and I elbowed him in the ribs as I leaned in to whisper. "Remember, I did try to get us out of here..."

He elbowed me back and nodded at Lucy. "We were just on our way into town."

Lucy's smile was sympathetic. "You don't have to do this, you know," she said as we climbed into the wagon. "If you aren't ready, I'll tell my brother to leave you be."

George Bischoff, known around the county for the

parties he threw at his tavern, had gotten it into his head to throw a fundraiser for a local anti-slavery society. And he somehow cajoled Jack into talking about what happened in Texas. I shivered. Even I wasn't ready to relive it, though I would've done so to spare Jack in a heartbeat.

I felt Jack tense next to me, and watched a small battle being fought in his spirit as he worked his jaw. He fiddled with Abigail's ring, and my heart wrenched. It was too raw, too soon...

Finally, he cleared his throat. "Don't think anyone's gonna want to hear me," he said hoarsely. "But if it helps the Cause, I'll do it."

"If you're sure," Lucy said. She snapped the reins, sending us back down the road to town.

Jack gripped his knees and let out a long, slow breath.

I leaned in, searching his eyes. "Are you certain, Jack?"

"It's for Abigail," he said, staring at his feet. "Of course I'm certain."

I reached for his hand, and he gripped mine tightly.

For Abigail.

I couldn't hear Jack's words from my spot across the church yard, but I could hear his deep voice breaking as he struggled through our story. I could feel his anguish all the way from my post, stuck behind a table of baked goods.

I scowled at the back of the heads in front of me. Most of Dove Hollow and dozens from all over the county were gathered on the lawn. One boy turned around and waved at me wildly, his grin visible across the yard, and I couldn't help but smile back. Allison Horner, Westleigh's friend, was the only decent lad in his family. He was a foolish sort, never quite serious even when he ought to be. But he never stopped trying to make Jack smile, and for that I loved him.

I studied the rest of the crowd. George's idea seemed successful so far. If only the people were as generous as they were curious, gawking at the Cherokee man on the church steps.

"Jack shouldn't be up there," I whispered to Lucy next to me.

"He's doing fine, love," she said.

"He wasn't ready," I protested. "I told George I would speak—"

Her hand found my shoulder, and I tensed. I didn't take my eyes off Jack to look at her. I felt like a coiled spring, ready to run up and rescue him at any moment.

"I don't like it any more than you do," she said, voice rough. "But we wouldn't have half this crowd if a woman spoke."

I spat on the ground.

Lucy sighed. "Agreed."

I bristled. "Then why don't we tell them to—?"

"Now's not the time, Saoirse," she said firmly. I opened

my mouth to protest, and she cut in. "Why don't you tell me why you had your bag packed earlier instead?"

I clamped my mouth shut.

Her eyes softened. "Is everything all right? You know I'd lend an ear if ever you need it."

I shook my head. "Don't worry, Jack's already talked me out of it. Again."

Lucy put her hands on my shoulders and smiled sadly. "But that doesn't fix why you wanted to leave in the first place, does it?"

I felt stinging tears gathering behind my eyes. "It doesn't."

Lucy wiped my cheek. "You're restless. You have been since you got here, I know. And it only got worse when Westleigh left for school, didn't it?"

She was a shrewd woman, the smartest I knew. I'd only known her for a short while, and already she understood me better than my own mother. Reminded me a lot of Abigail.

"I feel utterly useless," I mumbled. "Jack and Da try to include me, but it's not the same."

"Thought you liked learning your papa's trade?"

"It passes the time." I didn't mind carpentry, but I'd much rather be running around on horseback with my da when he did his sheriffing. That was a firm *no*. "But I don't want to be *occupied*, I want to do something important."

Lucy rolled her eyes with a small laugh. "Oh, little one, I understand more than you know."

I gawked at her, the only woman physician in the whole of western Pennsylvania, as far as I knew. What could she mean?

"Understand what?"

We looked up to see my father limping carefully towards us through the crowd, which started to break up and mingle about the yard. David favored his right leg, which twisted oddly at his ankle, having injured it several times in his boyhood. Usually he tried to mask it, though today it seemed he would need that walking stick he kept in the parlor. But it appeared the stubborn man had left it at home, from the look Lucy was giving him now.

"How maddening men can be sometimes," Lucy quipped, lifting her chin. "Present company not excluded."

David only winked at her, and I swear I saw her knees weaken. He was a handsome charmer, with his dark hair, boyish grin, and pale blue eyes that always held a spark of mischief. He and Lucy had been sweethearts for years, though they would never admit it.

Westleigh said it was because of some promise my da made—to God, to himself, I'm not quite certain—but David swore that until he had my step-father's forgiveness, he wouldn't move on with his own happiness. Rubbish. What about Lucy's happiness?

I didn't like to think about it, since it reminded me of what I was. Little bastard child, the result of a betrayal between David and my mother, who was inconveniently married at the time. Never knew myself until just a few months ago, when Westleigh came blustering into Texas on the autumn wind and knocked my feet out beneath me. But, if I were being honest with myself, I'm grateful he did.

"How's my sweet cailín?" my father wrapped an arm about my shoulders and pulled me in to give me a loud kiss on my cheek.

I melted against his side, letting him hold me, and feeling like a rotten heel for thinking of leaving again. "Grand," I lied. "How'd Jack do, then?"

"Brought more than one tear out of some of the toughest in the crowd," he said proudly. "Should've seen the way Mrs. Horner kept using her handkerchief."

I folded my arms. "Tears don't mean anything if they don't loosen their purse strings."

David's brow arched and he stifled a smile. "Ah, be patient with them. D'you know what a miracle it is to have them all stop and listen to Jack's story in the first place?"

"It ain't enough," came the gruff voice over my da's shoulder. David pivoted, and Jack pushed through the crowd towards the table. I blinked. He looked angry, not sad. He gripped the edge of the table, glaring at pastries while he spoke. "The tears. The good intentions. Even their damn money. None of it will—"

He coughed, unable to finish.

My heart twisted in my chest.

Jack dropped his head, his hair falling into his face.

"Sorry." He sighed shakily. "I'm sorry. Just—Saoirse, help me get outta here? I just want to go home."

"Go on," my da said, giving me a little push. "I'll help Miss Lucy here."

Jack nodded gratefully, and I grabbed his hand to lead him through the crowd.

There's no hearth like your own hearth.

Right, so, Aidan. Home seemed like a grand idea. But I took one more glance over my shoulder at Lucy, who fussed over my father's crooked tie, and I couldn't help but wonder what she meant, about understanding my restlessness.

It made my feet start to itch all over again.

WESTLEIGH

Dove Hollow, Pennsylvania
April 14, 1861

I woke with a start from a finger prodding my shoulder. Towers of books surrounded my head, laid upon my desk. My face was stuck to the pages of the Iliad. A warm Sunday afternoon and Homer made a perfect recipe for a nap.

I groaned and sat up stiffly.

My roommate, Ted Mitchell, tossed a small card onto my lap before stretching himself out on his bed across the room. "That came for you while you were 'studying.'"

I turned it over in my hand. There was an advertisement printed on one side, and a time scrawled in hasty handwriting on the other. "A barbershop? Who brought this?"

"Don't know why you even bother," Ted said, not hearing my question. "Lectures will likely be cancelled tomorrow, since there's a war and all, now. The fort's surrendering, they say."

I turned away before he could see my face. "I hadn't heard…"

"Because you've been hiding all day," he laughed. "It's all over the papers. All the fellas were talking earlier about joining up, soon as the opportunity comes. Heck, even our professors are leaving. Won't be a school left to go to."

I stared out the window as a heavy dread settled on my shoulders. "Maybe."

"But not little Westleigh Kavanagh."

I ignored him, inspecting the card again. A barbershop? In Pittsburgh, at least. Six o'clock? "Is a barber even open on a Sunday?"

A pillow struck my head. "Hey, runt! I'm talking to you."

"No, I'll not be joining up," I grumbled, throwing the pillow back. "I don't believe in war." I stood and inspected myself in the mirror. My short blond hair was still neatly trimmed, and even at sixteen, I had not a single whisker on my chin. I certainly had no need of a barber.

But anything to get me out of this room, away from his questions.

When I turned around, Ted was studying me. He gave a disapproving grunt, rolling his eyes. "Army's better off without you, anyhow. Takes a… tougher sort, you know. To be a soldier."

I could've told him all sorts of things, what I'd done, the dangers I'd faced in the past year. But I let the matter drop. "I'm going out."

I stomped towards the door. He wanted to goad me into a scrape, I knew. He and half of my classmates had been trying, since I first arrived at the beginning of the term. Didn't seem to be any rhyme or reason to it, their singling me out. Just could tell I was the coward, I guess. Like sharks smelling blood.

Or like being in a whole school of Jonas Horners.

"Out? Out where?"

I let the door close between us and took a deep cleansing breath. I checked the address on the card. A few months in the city now, and I knew most of the streets, though I rarely frequented this one. Still, it was daylight, and I had plenty of time to make my way there. Enough time to doubt my sanity along the way.

"You don't even know who sent this," I muttered to myself, rubbing the card between my thumbs. I kept my eyes glued to the pavement, moving quickly through the streets. Walking through the city made me nervous, no matter where I was going. Every corner I turned, I half-expected to see that charlatan of a marshal and his wicked grin. The thought of him almost stopped me short. Could he have sent this card? But he didn't know I was in the city, did he?

I kept walking, mostly because I was closer to the shop

now than my dormitory, and I was anxious to get out of sight again.

I came upon the front stoop and squinted at the door. It was locked.

I checked my pocket watch. A quarter to six. Perhaps I was simply too early...

"There you are, lad!" A harsh whisper came from the alleyway next to the shop. A tattooed arm reached out from the shadows and motioned me closer. "Back door, come on!"

I breathed a sigh of relief. Eoghan. Of course. I would recognize that old sailor's tattoos from a block away. I followed my father's friend around the corner, and he paused to let me past him through the back entrance.

I stopped on the step. "Why all the hush?" I whispered, looking around. "You haven't seen the—"

"Not a sign of that rogue." Eoghan nudged me forward. "We just don't want anyone to think we're open for business right now."

I stumbled through the door. "We?"

"Ah get inside, you'll see, you will."

A floorboard creaked under my shoes and voices in another room abruptly stopped talking.

Eoghan called out. "Just me lads, and I've brought a friend."

They stayed quiet 'til we stepped into the front of the shop. A man my father's age with a neatly trimmed mustache stood next to a chair holding a razor. His customer was a black man with his face lathered up, ready for a shave. Two others stood by the counter, one inspecting his face in the mirror. I nearly knocked the third one over, tripping across the room to embrace him.

"Timothy? You're back!" He helped me to my feet. Last I'd seen my friend, he was fleeing that wretched slave catcher. I stammered, all too aware of the other eyes in the room on me. "I didn't hear from you—I mean, I knew you made it out of Dove Hollow, but—It's good to see you."

Timothy laughed. "You too, kid." He held me out at arm's length for inspection. "Look at you! You get taller?"

I blushed. "If only," I mumbled.

"Well, something's different about you." Timothy winked. "Maybe you're just walking tall now. Heard 'bout what you did. Going to Texas, rescuing your cousin. That was very brave of you."

I shrugged and looked away. Foolish, maybe. And I would've done it again in a heart-beat, but I never would have called it brave.

"Who's the kid?" the barber asked, going back to his work, scraping the whiskers off the man in the chair. He spared a side glace at me. "He that sheriff's boy?"

"Sure and I've told you about Westleigh," Eoghan waved him off. "He's a good lad, you've nothing to be fretting over."

I nodded. "I promise, I won't say a word about... whatever it is we're doing here."

Timothy grinned. "We're fairly proud of this place. Met Jones there— " he pointed at the barber, "when I came back down from Canada, just before Christmas. He had this idea, helping runaways through his shop, get 'em trimmed up, new clothes, help them start a new life here in the city. There's a whole growing neighborhood of free blacks up a ways."

"That's amazing! I—wait, Christmas?" I asked, feeling a sting. "Have you been here, this whole time? And didn't send word you were safe?"

Timothy exchanged a glance with Eoghan. I saw him struggling for his next words before he shrugged. "I'm sorry to let you worry," he said. "You and your pa took me in when no one else would. I meant to come back, send a letter, something. But I got word about my family, and I had to leave."

"Your family?" My heart leapt for him. "And did you find them?"

Timothy shook his head, staring at his feet. "I... no."

"Not yet," Eoghan corrected, gripping Timothy's shoulder in encouragement. "We've not given up hope though, have we lad?"

Timothy offered a weak smile, but I saw no hope in his eyes. He cleared his throat. "In any case, I only just returned. Eoghan caught me up on you and Dove Hollow, all your adventures. Then we set up this meeting."

"Meeting?" I said, looking around. The other men stared

back at me, and I realized I wasn't there to just come calling. "What's this about?"

The barber looked up from his work again, glancing at Eoghan and Timothy before drilling me with an unreadable stare.

Timothy folded his arms, leaning forward to whisper as though there were ears in the walls. "We're going back south, Eoghan and I," he said. "War's on our doorstep. Nobody up north's all that keen on actually honoring the Fugitive Slave Act. Up here, runaways are more likely to find safety. But the ones down south—"

"How deep south?"

Timothy chewed on his words, glancing at the others again. "Deep. Can't say much more, you understand."

"I do," I said, though all this talk was making me fidgety. "But why have you brought *me* here?"

Timothy stifled a smile. "We want you to come along. You and your pa, if David would join us. We could use you. Help us get more folk to freedom, Westleigh."

There was a familiar fire in Timothy's eyes, like I saw the night before he left, when he told me of his plot of revenge and blood. The hairs on my arms stood on end. When I spoke, my voice was hoarse. "Surely you don't plan violence, do you?"

Timothy's mouth went flat. "Lord and I been wrestling a lot with my plans as of late. But I won't lie to you. I mean to do everything in my power to protect those we're trying to save. Does that answer satisfy you?"

I nodded, even though a memory flashed in my mind's eye—my cousin, pointing a gun at my face—and my knees started quaking.

"Can't say much else," Eoghan said, sitting down on the windowsill across from me. But we'll need an answer soon. We're leaving in a few weeks."

"You are stronger than you think, Westleigh," Timothy said, grasping my shoulders and watching me expectantly. "Will you join us?"

I froze. The underground! They waited silently for my answer, but all I could think about was that gun inches from my nose, the slave catcher's hands around my throat, the mass of scars that tore Jack's shoulders...

"I—" I stammered. I wasn't brave. I was a coward. Saoirse was right—I was no abolitionist. I swallowed, and finally grasped at a few pitiful words. "What was my father's answer?"

Timothy leaned back to study me. "Haven't asked him yet. But even if he says no, Westleigh, our offer still stands for you."

"He'd never let me go without him, and he'd never leave Saoirse," I managed, trying to avoid the look of disappointment in Timothy's eyes. "And there's school—"

"If war comes, your school will be empty by the end of the week," Timothy declared, pacing the room. He suddenly stopped in front of me. "And just what will you do then?"

"I don't—"

"It's all right." Eoghan tossed an arm about my shoulders. "It's a lot to think about."

He must have said something to Timothy with his eyes, for my friend sighed and paced to the other side of the room. Eoghan spun me about to face him.

"Listen here, you just take time to consider it," he said cheerfully. "The moment you change your mind, you send a letter to Jones here, and we'll get you sorted. All right, then?"

"Grand," I said, sighing shakily. "I'll pray over it. Just don't mention it to Da, yet? Let me think it over, first."

"There's a good lad." Eoghan slapped my shoulder again, nearly knocking me to the floor. "Enough of this, I'm famished. Let's all head down the road for a bite and a drink, then we'll take you home."

I paused. "You mean my dormitory."

"No, boy," Eoghan said, looking apologetic. "Don't figure they'll be many lectures for you this week. It's time to get you back to Dove Hollow, don't you agree?"

I didn't want to admit it, but I felt a huge surge of relief. "Yes. Yes, I think I'm ready to go home."

April 15, 1861

I awoke late the next morning to one hundred pounds of fur sitting atop my chest and my dog licking my ear. I groaned and tried to shove Wilberforce off, but he only gave a low bark, and stuck his paw on my face.

"Pfft!" I swatted him away. "Missed you too, boy. Get off!"

Wil rolled over next to me, presenting his pink belly, a gleam of mischief in his eyes. I knew the look—I'd better commence with the petting before he decided to run amok and knock over the furniture.

I sat up and scratched him with one hand, fishing for my spectacles on my nightstand with the other. Blinking away the remains of sleep, I looked around my room, and smiled. Everything right where I left it, as if I hadn't been gone a day. My dog at my side. The smell of breakfast wafting up the stairs. The sound of my father's boots on the floor below me. It was good to be home.

I hurried downstairs and into the dining room, the last one awake, as usual. It was long after midnight before I arrived back in Dove Hollow. Saoirse and Jack were asleep, but David was up, waiting for me in the parlor. Eoghan came in for a pint, and we all stayed up talking until it was almost dawn.

Just before he departed, Eoghan stood as if he were about to leave us with one of his infamous speeches, sloshing his whiskey about in his glass. But instead he sang a song, one that stole the very heat from the room. It was a song of emigration, of leaving Ireland, the sort that Lucy refused to let my da sing at parties. But the words meant something different to us that night.

MACTAVISH

Kind friends and companions come join me in rhyme
Come lift up your voices in chorus with mine
Come life up your voices, all grief to refrain
For we may or might never all meet here again.

We hardly spoke while we made our goodbyes, or when David and I parted to go to bed for a few precious hours of sleep. And now my da sat at the end of the dining room table, eating breakfast in silence while he stared unfocused ahead.

At the other end, Saoirse and Jack quibbled over the morning paper. She looked even lovelier than I recalled, though she hardly gave me one glance when I entered the room. She wore a yellow dress, and her black hair was styled in ringlets, which bounced by her ears as she reached across the table to try and snatch the paper out of Jack's hand.

"Give it here, you've had it long enough!"

"You'll have it when I'm finished."

"Ugh, but you're a slow reader." She sat back and drummed her fingers on the table.

"And you're too impatient," he muttered from behind the pages. "I'm trying to see if there's any more details in here…"

"Maybe we should see if anyone has a copy of the *Times*," she said. "Sure and they would have a bit more, it's a bigger paper."

"More about what?" I asked, sitting at my place. I glanced at David, but he hadn't even blinked. "What's going on?"

Saoirse jumped up and finally wrestled the paper away and began to read frantically.

"Sumter," Jack said, scraping the knife across a slice of toast. His eyes were brighter than I'd seen them yet. "The fort is fallen."

"I heard yesterday, at school," I said. David's chair scraped, and I turned to see him limping out of the room. I swallowed. "What does that mean?"

But I knew. A heavy cloak of dread settled about me.

It meant Timothy and Eoghan, even my roommate were right. It meant war.

It meant everything was about to change.

3

SAOIRSE
Dove Hollow, Pennsylvania
April 21, 1861

I didn't hear a word of Reverend Bischoff's sermon, staring down at my tapping toes, thumbing through my Bible over and over. My mind was in a haze ever since Jack told me he meant to enlist. After the news of that fort in South Carolina surrendering, Lincoln called for volunteers to put down the rebellion. Seventy-five thousand soldiers. And Jack would be one of them it seemed.

He'd go, all right, and with Allison and all the Horner brothers likely to follow. Westleigh would stay behind of course. He'd already got himself teaching back at the little schoolhouse on the hill, doing at least some small something with his life. I would be trapped here. Aimless, useless, and bored. Jack would leave me alone.

Or so he thought.

I didn't care two bits what he said. If he went away to war, I'd be on his heels no matter how hard he fought me. And so I spent most the morning in church attempting to go over the particulars in my head. But it was difficult to concentrate, seeing Jack twisting Abigail's ring between his fingers.

I blinked away the water in my eyes. I knew why he had to go. 'Twas why I was so desperate to join him. Together we'd fight, perhaps even die in her memory, and for all of those still in bondage. For freedom.

It was the very *least* we could do.

I caught Westleigh staring at me. I quickly turned my head aside to hide my tears. Ever since he came home he'd been on my own heels like a lost puppy, and I tried my hardest to avoid him. The last thing I wanted right now was his sympathy. Or worse, having him talk sense into me with those big, sad eyes of his.

The church-folk stood to sing and to pray, and I breathed in the trepidation of those around me like factory smoke. It set my lungs and throat on fire so that I could only whisper along. Even Allison, near the front with his family, seemed disquieted.

As we dispersed, the usual hum of conversation and laughter was subdued. Families went home, with few lingering about on the lawn. Allison dragged Westleigh off to who-knows-where. But Jack and I stood with my da and the Bischoffs, waiting for the reverend to finishing shaking hands so that we could go to the tavern for our Sunday afternoon meal. I say we stood together, but 'twas more the men were gathered in a tight huddle, with Lucy and myself on the outside. Jack had his back to me, whispering. As if I didn't know what they spoke about.

"Don't think there will be a regiment formed around here." George shook his head. "Likely the boys around this area are heading to Pittsburgh to enlist."

David gripped Jack's shoulder. "You're sure about this?"

Jack's head dipped as he nodded. "Absolutely. Leaving first thing tomorrow."

I folded my arms and ground my heel into the dirt.

George glanced up and saw me over Jack's shoulder. His mouth flipped into a grin. "You'll have to take it up with Saoirse, from the looks of it."

Jack half-turned towards me and sighed.

Lucy touched David's elbow. "Let's get on to the tavern, and let these two talk."

Don't know what they expected us to say. Jack couldn't convince me to let him go and I couldn't convince him to stay. But maybe they thought our shouting match would make for a good spectacle.

David squeezed my hand. "See you both at the tavern, then. Don't be long." He kissed my cheek, like he always did, before following after Lucy and George.

I watched them retrieve the preacher and leave the churchyard before I even opened my mouth.

Jack cut in first. "I know what you're going to say, all right?" He turned to face me fully. "And the answer is *no*."

I narrowed my eyes. "Who said I was asking for your permission?"

"Saoirse—"

"I'm coming with you, Jack. You can't stop me."

Suddenly he was in my face, jabbing his finger at my collar bone. "This ain't a joke," he hissed. "And it's not a game I feel like playing with you."

I pushed him back. "I'm serious. And you're rude."

Jack squeezed the bridge of his nose. "Do you realize how long I've been wrestling with this? We've known it for a while now, that war was coming. I don't *want* to leave you—"

"Then don't do it. Simple as that."

"But I have to!" Jack dropped his arms at his sides in a helpless gesture, and his voice grew small. "It's—I couldn't do anything to save her. And that eats me alive. But this—I won't be able to live with myself if I don't go, if I don't fight. Please understand."

"I understand why you have to fight," I said softly. "What I don't understand is why you won't let me come with you."

"Too dangerous."

I smiled weakly. "I did just fine saving your backside in Texas, didn't I?"

"From a handful of drunken vigilantes, sure," Jack said. "You're talking about an army."

I threw up my arms. "Why is it so different for you?"

"Because *I* don't have anything else to lose!"

The yard was quiet, but I didn't look about to see if we had any other spectators. I was too busy trying to pick my heart up off the ground. A breeze blew across my wet cheeks, making me shiver.

I leaned in towards Jack. "You have *me*."

Jack's shoulders wilted, but his eyes were hard as ever.

The thick silence that hung between us was torn asunder when Allison, arms full of wadded up clothing, suddenly plowed straight into us. His face was red and he could barely speak.

Allison shoved a pair of shoes at Jack, gasping. "Hold these." Then he took off towards the great oak in the center of the churchyard, dropping a sock as he ran.

Bewildered, Jack stared at the shoes. "What in the—?"

I grabbed Jack's arm and pulled. "Come on!"

We followed, catching up as Allison struggled to climb the tree, a pair of trousers slung over his shoulder.

Westleigh arrived on our heels, bent over with his hands on his knees. "I tried—I tried to stop him—"

Allison paused his climbing to look over at us, grinning like a madman. "Jonas skipped church. I just found him down by the pond, skinny dipping with Liza Verner."

My eyes widened. "Are those—are those your brother's trousers?"

Jack dropped the shoes on the ground in disgust. "I ain't taking part in any of your shenanigans."

"Just toss up the shoes when I get up, and you can go!" Allison grunted as he pulled himself up on the first branch.

Westleigh frowned. "And on a Sunday, too…"

Jack scoffed. "I'm going to the tavern."

"Aww, but you'll miss the fun." Allison winked over his shoulder.

I matched his grin and turned to Jack with a shrug. Terrorizing Jonas would be a service to the community. "We're in."

Jack rolled his eyes. "Oh, nuh-uh. I'm not—"

But I grabbed his hand and pulled him back towards the tree.

We needed this.

Allison's foot slipped as he hoisted himself higher still, dropping another sock on Jack's head.

"Allison!" Westleigh called out. If anyone could stop his foolishness, it would be him. "You're going to break your neck! And that's nothing compared to what Jonas will do to you."

Jack scowled up into the branches. "Get your ass out of that tree, Horner."

"I'm almost there!" Allison regained his footing and stretched carefully, hugging the trunk with one arm. He lashed out with his brother's trousers and successfully snagged them on a branch high above his head. He grinned down at us. "All right, toss up a shoe!"

Jack shook his head as he bent for the first one. "You're gonna break—"

Allison yelped at the same time Jack and Westleigh shouted, and my heart stopped as he fell. But his ankle had caught in the crook of a branch, and he hung upside down now, at least ten feet in the air, with his coat fallen down around his face. I laughed so hard I tripped back and sat hard on the ground.

Allison flailed, crying for help, and I clutched my aching sides.

"Al!" Westleigh ran up underneath him, hands on his head. "Are you all right?"

"Sure, meant to do it." Allison struggled in vain.

I cackled from the ground. "Your face, it's so red!"

"I have half a mind to leave you up there," Jack grumbled. But he started climbing anyway. The tree was old and its branches were thick. They didn't even budge beneath his weight. Jack rose to stand on the largest, with Allison's face at his feet, and he squinted at the boy's trapped ankle. "I'm afraid I'm going to drop you on your head if I even touch it…"

Westleigh shifted nervously next to me. "Jack, be careful…"

Jack stared down at him. "Do I have to?"

I stood up and moved beneath them. If I reached, I could barely touch Allison's outstretched fingertips. "I could catch him."

"And you'd both break your necks." Jack grunted, climbing higher. "I can try and pull him up instead—but you gotta hold still, boy!"

Allison relaxed, letting his arms dangle by his head. "You sure you know what you're doing?"

"I could let you hang here 'til your face bursts instead."

Westleigh paced beneath them. "I cannot watch this..."

After a bit more swearing, Jack pulled Allison up to sit on the branch beside him.

"Thanks," Allison panted. "Let me—let me sit here for a second, I'm all dizzy..."

"Sit as long as you want." Jack swung his leg over the branch. "I'm getting down."

Allison swayed where he sat and grabbed for Jack's arm. "Wait!"

"Let go!"

Allison slipped again, still clutching Jack's arm. Jack lost his footing, and both came tumbling to the ground in a tangled heap. Jack hit the ground first with a sickening crack.

Allison landed atop of him and rolled off, shaken but unharmed.

"Jack!" I threw myself beside him as Westleigh helped Allison to his feet. "Jack, are you all right?"

He flipped over on his back and groaned. Sweat beaded on his face. He raised a shaking finger and pointed at his leg. I didn't know much about bones, but it sure looked broken to me.

Allison inched forward and grimaced. "That doesn't look good."

Jack reached up and snatched Allison's collar. "Your face ain't gonna look so good when I'm through with it!"

That's when we heard Jonas bellowing from the creek.

Allison wrenched free and scrambled back. "I um, I'll go and get Lucy, shall I?" He pointed in the direction of the tavern as he stumbled to his feet. He winced down at Jack again. "Just—just don't move."

"Al!" Westleigh called after him, but he sprinted away before Jack could threaten him again.

Jack certainly wasn't going to be soldiering anytime soon. But Allison would sure wish he was, because Jack would make his life a living hell.

"Well," David said, nodding at Jack's bandaged leg before tapping his own, "welcome to the club."

Jack moaned and let his head drop back against the pillow.

Lucy sank into a chair nearby, looking just as exhausted. Setting a bone, it seemed, was even more horrible than I imagined.

Jack himself had even passed out for a bit, and I wish I had. Those sounds...

"How long?" Jack croaked, covering his face with his hands.

Lucy gave a half-shrug. "Depends on how fast it will heal, and how well you listen to me. A couple of months, probably."

Jack groaned again. "I'm gonna kill him."

"Not 'til you're back on your feet, you're not," Lucy said dryly. "We'll let you rest. Do you need anything?"

Jack didn't answer.

I touched his arm, and he flinched, moving his hands to scowl at me. I forced myself to speak patiently. "What can we bring you, Jack?"

"Coffee."

"You should be lying—"

"Coffee!"

"Coffee it is," David said quickly, ushering me and Lucy out of the room. "You just rest here."

Jack's glare followed me until I was in the hall and the door closed between us.

"You two wait in the parlor," David said. "I'll fetch it for him."

Lucy and I collapsed on the parlor sofa. She twisted around to look at me. "What's he so sore at you about?"

"Probably for dragging him into Allison's antics in the first place."

"Hmm," Lucy said with an angled brow. "A word of advice—you may wish to avoid such activities in the future."

I rolled my eyes. "Oh, I'm certain 'twas the talk of the town. I'm used to the evil eyes and whispers, you know. I don't care a whit what they say about me."

"I know," Lucy said gently. "And though I admire you for that, you should probably try to care a little. For your father's sake."

37

"So you say I'm shaming him, is that it?"

"Not at all!" Lucy grasped my hands, eyes shining. "Oh sweet girl, your father cares as little for what they say as you do. You're both stubborn that way."

I relaxed a little, but a coal of indignation still burned in my stomach.

Lucy lowered her voice. "It's your father's business. He won't tell you this, but he lost another customer this week."

"What! Because of me?"

"Shh! I don't know, dear. But all the same, do try to be a little more careful."

I nodded, staring down at my fists. Seems like there were just as many no-good gossips and meddlers in Dove Hollow as there were back in Brookfield. Why can't everyone just mind their own business? And why did I bring such whispers and scandal when it was Allison doing all the mischief? Never mind the fact Westleigh was there, too. And did they even care about everything Jonas does?

But all I have to do is sneeze in church and I'm Jezebel.

That coal burned hotter.

"Now, tell me about Jack," Lucy said, breaking me out of my dark thoughts. "You were having words earlier."

"Maybe he figures I paid Allison to give him a bit of a push out of the tree."

"Ah," Lucy said, nodding. "Yes, he won't be enlisting in anything for some time. I take it you were asking him not to go?"

David's footsteps echoed down the hall, and I waited until I heard the door to Jack's room creak before I answered. "Sure, and I know *you* know 'twas more than that."

"You want to go with him."

I hugged my arms to my chest. "He said he'd go wherever I went. Why can't it be the other way around?"

"Saoirse," Lucy said softly, her eyes sad. "You can't be a soldier."

"Shush!" I glanced at the hall. David was coming down the hall again. I frowned back at her. "I know. But I can't be apart from him, either."

"I don't think you'll have to worry about that," David said from the hall. He limped into the parlor and sat in his chair across from us. "This war will likely be over before Jack can join it. This conflict will be short-lived, they say."

"Which is why I want to do something *now*," I blurted. All the frustration bubbling up over the last few months was beginning to spill over. "I'm going mad, sitting here at home, night after night, doing nothing at all."

I tried to ignore the wounded look in my father's eyes as he spoke. "It won't be so bad as that," he said softly. "There are plenty of ways folk at home will be able to help."

I kicked up the edge of the rug. "Home," I echoed to myself.

Lucy reached over and squeezed my hand. She drew a deep breath. "I know how she feels, David," she said softly. She pointed at his ankle. "And so do you, I think."

David and I both winced together. I hadn't thought of just how miserable he might have been, thinking of himself trapped here, too, while other men went away to fight.

Lucy straightened her shoulders. "On that subject—well, I reckon I should just be out with it. I received a letter from my brother Andrew last week." She swallowed, hesitating. "He's asked me to come to Washington with him. All those soldiers means more physicians, and nurses, and Andrew has assured me they won't turn away any help, female or not."

David's brow furrowed, but he stayed quiet.

"I've given him my reply," Lucy said softly, "and I'll be leaving in a fortnight."

I wilted. Now even Lucy would leave me? This was too cruel.

But what if—no. I couldn't handle broken bones, much less bullet wounds. But Washington? A chance to do something important? It gave me pause, at least.

I almost begged Lucy to take me, too, right there. But seeing my da's face, I stayed silent. His eyes hadn't left the pretty doctor next to me. His jaw was set tight, and I wondered if that was the same face I was giving Jack in the churchyard earlier that day.

4

WESTLEIGH
Dove Hollow, Pennsylvania
May 7, 1861

Allison smacked me hard in the arm. "Just ask her!" he blurted, spitting part of his lunch on me.

I ignored him, staring down at the letter in my hand. Timothy and Eoghan were about to leave Pittsburgh and had extended their invitation for me to join them once more. My hand trembled as I unfolded and refolded the paper a few times, lost in thought.

"Look, she's right over there."

"I know where to find her, Al." I kept my eyes down at the letter in my hands, pressing the creases together, as we walked through town square. "We live in the same house."

Allison made a grab for my letter. "What'chya got there?"

I dodged him and shoved it in my pocket. "Nothing." I hadn't said anything about meeting Eoghan and Timothy

41

in the city, or the offer they made. I didn't want the thousand questions I knew would follow.

"Westleigh." Allison grabbed my head and forced me to look in Saoirse's direction. She was sitting on a bench, laughing and talking with his sweetheart, Ellen Moore.

I tried to wrench myself free as she frowned at us, but Allison caught me by my neck and locked his arm around my head. I stumbled under the weight of it.

"I know you want to," he declared, "so if I have to light your trousers on fire, you *will* ask Saoirse Callahan to the church picnic next week."

I gave him a shove and stumbled away. "You're mad," I muttered, daring to cast another glance in Saoirse's direction. She paid no attention to us. She'd hardly spoken to me at all since I'd been home. I shook my head. "She's like my—well, I'm not sure what we are—"

"Nothing! I did the figuring myself." Allison fished a small notebook out of his pocket, suddenly looking very proud of himself. He flipped it open and pointed to some scribbles on the page with a puffed-out chest. "All right, so she's the daughter of David, who adopted you. Your mother was Maggie Callahan, whose brother was Brian Callahan, who married Saoirse's mother. You've not even grown up together, so…. you're really nothing at all. Not by blood, anyway. Got it?"

I rubbed my temples. "What's your point?"

"My point *is* nobody's gonna give a fig if you kiss her."

I hid my face behind my hands. "Please, leave me alone."

"Allison!"

I peeked through my fingers to see Ellen running toward us, with Saoirse on her heels. My heart dropped to my toes.

"There you are." Ellen Moore stopped in front of Allison with her hands on her hips. "I've been looking all over for you. You weren't at David's shop."

Allison held out the remains of the sandwich he had picked up from George's place. "Lunch."

Ellen's brow arched. "For two hours?"

He only shrugged, taking a large, sloppy bite of his food.

"Could you be more disgusting?" Ellen rolled her eyes. "Don't answer that. Come on then, and stop troubling Westleigh. I need to speak with you." She grabbed his free hand and began to pull him away, but not before throwing a wink over her shoulder at me and nodding at Saoirse.

Did the whole town think I was infatuated with Saoirse? I tugged at my collar. They weren't wrong, but was I so conspicuous? Did Saoirse herself know? Perhaps that was the reason she avoided me…

But here she was now. Alone. With me.

She watched Ellen drag Allison away.

I cleared my throat, and my voice still came out as a squeak. "What—what's all that about?"

"Hmm?" Saoirse turned, and regarded me as if she only just noticed my presence. "Ellen's talking to him about Washington."

"Washington?" I watched them as they walked across the square. "She's not going with Lucy, is she?"

"You didn't know?"

I shook my head. Poor Allison.

Would this war end up tearing us all to pieces?

I felt a headache start to bloom behind my eyes, and I tried to massage it away.

"Well," Saoirse said, "I think I'll be on my way home—"

"Wait, I um, have a question for you," I blurted out. She paused, her brow gathered nervously. Words failed me, and I felt my face heat up. Judging by the look in her eye, she knew what I was going to say. And I was certain she was going to decline. "Next week, after church, there's a—"

There was a clatter on the tavern steps behind us, and we turned to see Jack stumbling down on his crutches. One slipped out from his arms and fell to the ground. Saoirse rushed to help him.

"I'm fine," Jack grumbled, hobbling as she handed the crutch to him.

"How's your leg?" I asked.

Jack reoriented himself with a huff. "Not healing fast enough."

Saoirse rolled her eyes. "Ah, don't be so dramatic, now. You're mending just fine, Ellen says. And there'll be war enough left over by the time you're on two feet again."

She kicked a stone across the lane. Silence hung in the air as it skittered.

I shifted on my feet. "It can't last past summer, can it? I mean, the rebellion surely will be put down soon, won't it?"

Jack's brow rose. "I think you're underestimating the resolve of the rebels. You were down there. You were chased with the rest of us halfway across the country."

I removed my spectacles to pinch the bridge of my nose. The ache was sharpening into a migraine.

"That was just one slave owner in Texas." Jack spat on the ground with a curse. "You think the rest would give up so easily? No, I don't think we'll even see the end of this by Christmas, not by a long shot."

"Jack," Saoirse said, and I glanced up to see her shove an elbow into his side. She nodded at me.

Jack's expression softened. "Sorry Westleigh," he said quietly. "You heard any more news from your school? Are they resuming classes next term?"

"I don't know." I held half a breath tight in my chest, trying to keep my voice steady. "Guess it all depends on the fighting. Just about everyone there enlisted. Even the dean."

"But not you," Saoirse said, squinting at me. I couldn't interpret the question in her eyes, but it made my face hot all the same.

"No," I replied. "I—well, war is… I mean—"

Jack shook his head. "Don't think poorly of yourself for not joining, Westleigh. Not everyone is meant to be a soldier." He gave a pointed look at Saoirse, who scowled.

"Well," she said, glaring at him before turning to me. "What will you do now? Keep teaching?"

I fiddled with the folded paper in my pocket. "That—yes, that's the idea."

Saoirse tilted her head, studying me. "You can't stay in Dove Hollow forever, Westleigh. You don't want to."

"What about you?" I blurted. "Will you be following Ellen and Lucy?"

Saoirse gave Jack another glare. He muttered something in his mother's language, swinging his crutches out to storm away.

Saoirse rolled her eyes again and stomped after him. She didn't even glance my way as they left me at the tavern, arguing down the road as they went.

I sat down heavily on the steps, trying to ease the pounding in my head before I ventured home. I tried to shut out the noises around me, but that left only the jeers of my roommate and the other boys at school, echoing whispers of contempt passing back and forth in my mind.

Coward. Gutless. Yellow-belly.

But their insults didn't afflict me half so much as what I truly feared.

What did Saoirse think of me?

Saoirse pulled me aside into the hall before supper, and I

couldn't even look at her. We waited for Jack and David to go into the dining room, and I stared at her hand on my elbow.

She leaned too close. "Whatever you do, don't go mentioning the war around David."

I inched back. "I wasn't—"

"Grand." She dropped her hand from my arm and knotted her brow. "And don't mention Lucy. Or Washington, either."

My tongue felt three times larger in my mouth. "Washington? Oh, so, are—are you…"

"Later. Let's not keep them waiting on us."

Saoirse whisked into the dining room, leaving me to collect myself before I could follow.

David finished setting out our supper and smiled at me. "Take your seat and we'll pray for the meal. It's going to need it." He threw in a wink with his old joke—he made it every time he did the cooking—but he couldn't mask the weariness in his eyes.

I sat beside Jack, across from Saoirse, and bowed my head.

"Lord, thank you for your blessings today…" David's deep voice took on a soothing softness whenever he prayed. "Please bless this food, and our time together. Give us wisdom to guide our decisions during these trying times. In your Son's precious name, we pray—"

"Amen," we murmured together.

David dove straight into the potatoes and wouldn't meet any of our eyes. No one knew what to say. Saoirse tried to ask me more about school, but I couldn't say much without mentioning the current conflict. I started to ask her about her afternoon, but she only gave me a quick shake of her head and resumed picking at her plate. David had even forbidden newspapers at the table, so Jack concentrated on his food as if it were saying something profound.

I shifted in my chair and grasped for something—anything to speak about. I never really minded silence, but this sort was too heavy. "Have you—" My voice startled poor Wilberforce, who ran off barking towards the front door. "Um, Saoirse, have you read the latest chapters of Great Expectations yet?"

Her eyes widened. "I haven't! Have you the latest edition of Harper's? Allison won't give me his. And don't say anything, I don't want it spoiled."

"Wouldn't dream of it." I smiled, feeling the tension in my shoulders ease for the first time in weeks. "I have a copy in my room, I'll fetch it for you after supper. So, you are enjoying it?"

Saoirse nodded. "Other than Pip frustrates me to no end. He is so blindly in love with Estella and he can't even see she doesn't feel the same about him, the poor idiot."

Jack coughed beside me, and I wanted to crawl under the table. Seemed even he knew about my failed attempts to court Saoirse.

She didn't seem to notice. "Oh, I'm sorry Jack—are you reading it, too?"

Jack wrinkled his nose to hide his smirk. "I tried, it bored me."

Their conversation overlapped and muddled together as I took out Timothy's letter under the table. I tried to focus on the words, but too many voices knocked about in my head.

It takes a tougher sort than you to be a soldier.

You're stronger than you think, Westleigh. Will you join us?

You can't stay in Dove Hollow forever. You don't want to.

So what will you do now?

"Westleigh!"

A pea bounced off my nose and rolled off the table, where Wilberforce lapped it up happily.

Saoirse giggled. "Good aim, Da."

My father grinned at me across the table, and I lost myself for a moment, just glad to see his smile. He nodded at me. "What're you reading that's got you so lost to the world, then?"

I blanched. The letter.

David sat up a bit straighter, his grin fading. "Is something wrong, lad?"

Saoirse bristled. "Is it news of Declan?"

I blinked out of my daze. "What? No, it's not that…" I reluctantly passed the letter across the table to my father. "It's from Timothy. He and Eoghan have asked me to go with them."

"With them?" David frowned at the letter. "Where? Not down south, surely."

Out of the corner of my eye, I saw Jack stiffen.

I cleared my throat. "They're leaving tomorrow. They've asked you to come too, Da. To help. With the... underground."

David read the letter, frown deepening.

Saoirse smacked me in the arm. "When were you planning to tell us?" Her eyes were blue slits. "And what about me? And Jack? Or did you want to keep your own little adventure all to yourself?"

"No! I mean, I didn't—"

"You were going to hide it from us?" Saoirse dropped her silverware with a clatter on the table. "Afraid I couldn't handle it, were you?"

David sighed. "Now, Saoirse—"

"That's not it at all!" I protested. "I hadn't even—"

"So when I asked you today at the tavern what you were going to do, this just slipped your mind?" She scoffed, shoving away from the table. "I've got a headache. I'm going to bed."

She stomped from the room.

I dared a glance around the table. David was examining the letter again. Jack pushed his fork across his plate, staring at nothing. He worked his jaw. No doubt he was thinking of Abigail.

I groaned. Stupid, stupid Westleigh.

"Jack," I whispered. "Jack, I'm sorry—"

He offered a tight smile, but reached for his crutches. "Don't worry about it."

I slumped. "You're off to bed, too?"

"Oh, my leg is just bothering me." He tried smiling again. "Don't worry about me, kid."

Jack bid my father goodnight, and then it was just the two of us.

David propped his elbows on the table and put his head in his hands.

I couldn't eat any more, either.

Why do I bother trying to speak? Nothing good ever comes of it.

After a few moments of silence, I slid out of my chair to stand next to my da. He didn't lift his head again until I put my arm around his shoulders.

"I'm sorry, *Athair*," I murmured. "I didn't mean to ruin supper."

David snorted. "I ruined it before we all sat down, remember?"

It was enough to make me laugh, and I was glad for that. I reached for the letter. "I wasn't planning on leaving," I said. "Especially without telling you."

"Not twice, eh?" His mouth tipped in a half-grin, but I still winced at the reproach in his eyes.

I slumped. "No, sir."

"Good." David nodded. "You know, I understand what

you're feeling. You want to do something. Anything but sit here night after night while the world falls to pieces."

"Yes."

"So do I. And so does Saoirse. And Jack." David rubbed his face. "It's right maddening, isn't it? We're all caught in the same place. All of us, left behind..."

He stood to clean up the table. I helped by giving bits of scraps to Wilberforce, who'd wandered lazily into the room, ready to beg.

"It's why I cannot blame Lucy for wanting to leave." David paused to lean against the table, resting his weight on his fists. "Or Saoirse."

"She really is going to Washington, then?"

"I don't know. You'll have to ask her. She hasn't had the courage to tell me yet."

"I'm not sure she wants to speak to me right now."

David rolled his eyes. "She's too much like her da. Give her a bit to cool that head of hers."

We carried the dishes back to the kitchen in silence, but a more comfortable one than before.

I paused in the doorway. "Da, you don't have to worry about me. I won't be going anywhere."

David smiled sadly. "You will, one day. You can't live here forever. Well, perhaps you could, but—"

"I mean with Eoghan and Tim. Or—or enlisting."

He folded his arms. "You sound almost disappointed about that."

"It's only, the other boys were calling me things—I—"
My words died in my tight throat.

David crossed the room and put his hands on my
shoulders. "Tell me. Why did you really not want to tell me
about Eoghan and Tim?"

I stared at the buttons on his shirt. I couldn't look at him.
"Because I don't want to go with them." I grimaced. "And I
was afraid you would. And that you would think me a
coward."

David squeezed my shoulders, bringing my eyes up.
"How could you ever imagine I would think such a thing of
you?"

"Everyone else does."

"Ah, and why should you be listening to them?" David
dropped his hands and poked me in the chest. "And what
do they know about your heart? You've got courage and
conviction to put them all to shame, you do."

Courage? If only. I couldn't even tell Saoirse how I felt
about her. All I could think of was Dickens and poor love-
sick Pip. I couldn't bear that sort of humiliation.

"Now then," David said, sighing. "Why don't you want
us going with them?"

I startled. Was he seriously considering—?

"Saoirse," I said quickly. David's mouth tipped in a grin,
and my face burned. "I mean—how could we leave her
behind?"

He shrugged. "Who says we would? Next reason?"

I swallowed. "It's dangerous work."

"Aye, that it is. But...?"

But it was worth it, risking our lives for others, I finished for him silently. And he was right. I stood there in our kitchen, wrestling with myself, until my da gave a heavy sigh.

"Whatever you decide to do, Westleigh, I will support you with all of my heart. Just as I would Saoirse."

"I don't want her to leave," I croaked. "I care for her, Da."

"Then tell her that, lad."

I don't believe he understood my full meaning.

"Why don't you get some rest," David said, nudging me toward the door. "It's been a long day. Sleep will clear your head."

But when I retired to my room that night, I could not sleep. I sat upon my bed, my mind anything but clear. Saoirse. David. The underground. The War. I couldn't make sense of anything and I felt more lost than I'd ever been in my entire life.

Oh, Lord, what was I supposed to do?

I crawled off my bed, and my knees found the floor. I pressed my forehead against the mattress and clasped my hands tightly together at my chest.

"Please, God, tell me what to do. Give me an answer, Athair..." If I could but know the Lord's direction for me, I would at least have peace. No matter the reply. I whispered aloud, begging Him for wisdom, until my knees ached and my head grew numb. And still I had no answers.

If that wasn't bad enough, thoughts of Saoirse threatened to distract me—my mind wandered to ways I might confess my feelings for her. But I would shut them out and force myself to concentrate on my prayers again until my thoughts were utterly incoherent.

Just as I was about to drag myself back into bed and let sleep give me the only peace I would find, I thought of Saoirse again. Her name cut through the muddy drowsiness to fill my heart until I thought it might literally burst, and I was overwhelmed by one desire... to follow her *anywhere*. I buried my face into my pillow to muffle a growl of frustration. Why couldn't I hear Him?

The door creaked open behind me.

SAOIRSE

Dove Hollow, Pennsylvania
May 8, 1861

I paced outside Westleigh's door, listening to his reverent whispers, though I could hardly hear the words. My bare feet didn't make any noise, and I was careful not to step on that one creaky plank by the landing. I lost track of time waiting for him to finish praying.

The Lord may not have any limits on His patience, but I did.

While I waited, I contended with myself. Go back to bed, Saoirse. Don't even bother him with the mess.

I could already hear Westleigh's arguments in my head.

You're a girl, Saoirse.

Why did they continue to think I didn't know this somehow?

You're only sixteen.

Well, I imagine if I was going to lie about my sex, what was a little fib about my age?

But then there were the other arguments that I had fewer answers for.

You will break Da's heart.

You could get hurt.

Or worse, you might have to kill someone.

Again.

Westleigh hated guns. Hated war more, I'm certain. So how could I even ask this of him?

As much as I hated it, I needed Westleigh Kavanagh's help.

If only he would stop praying for a bit and let someone else say a few words.

I finally heard his *amen,* and I let myself inside. "Can't sleep either, can you?"

Westleigh twisted around and squinted at me. His eyes were puffy. "I um, I was praying." He pulled himself up and sat on his bed. "Come in. Did you—was it a nightmare?"

I shook my head, stepping farther into the room. "Couldn't even get my mind to rest long enough to sleep in the first place."

His head *thunked* against the headboard. "Me either."

I pulled my dressing gown tightly around me and sat at the foot of the bed. Wilberforce leapt up between us and flopped over, inviting me to scratch beneath his chin.

Westleigh cleaned his spectacles with his handkerchief. "What's troubling you?" he asked almost hesitantly. "What's on your mind?"

I gave a weak laugh. "I'd be here all night long telling you that."

Westleigh simply shrugged and replaced the frames on his face. "I'm listening."

"Even after my snapping at you at supper like I did?"

"I didn't mean to keep a secret from you," he said. "I've had quite a bit on my mind—"

"Are you going with them?" I asked a little too sharply.

Westleigh pursed his lips. "Are you going to Washington?"

"I'm not," I assured him. "I can't say I didn't consider it. But that's Ellen and Lucy's path. Not my own."

Westleigh picked at a loose thread in the quilt. "So, what's keeping you awake?"

I stared until he lifted his eyes to meet mine again. And the way he looked at me... I felt as if I could tell him a whole world of secrets. But that wasn't the reason I hesitated. 'Twasn't just secrets I was about to burden him with.

I took a deep breath and let it all come out in a rush. "I'm joining the army, just as soon as Jack is well enough."

Nothing about his expression changed. He didn't try to tell me how foolish I was, or talk me out of it, or laugh as if I were telling a joke. He was simply quiet for an unbearably long moment before whispering a simple question. "Why are you telling me this?"

"Nobody else would listen, or understand—" I paused. "Well, perhaps Allison would, but then the whole town would know it, wouldn't they?"

Westleigh laughed. "I think you can give him a bit more credit than that."

I leaned forward. "I need help. Someone on *my* side. Help me prepare. To convince Jack, if that's even possible."

"You want to fight in the war…"

"You disapprove?"

"Not because you're a girl, if that's what you think. War itself."

I bristled. "Even if such a war would bring freedom to those in oppression?"

He rubbed his red eyes. "There just has to be another way. A peaceful way. One without killing."

"And just how do you expect to bring freedom your way?" I scowled. "Ask the rebels nicely? How many people in bondage would suffer while they wait for your peaceful resolution?"

"Surely we can find a way to reason—"

"I've lived among those monsters." The blood in my veins boiled. "You recall them setting fires in Texas just to create a panic, don't you? My own *brother* was one of those arsonists. And they're the same sort of men who try to justify owning another living being! They won't give up their slaves without a fight. They're vile, wicked, dishonorable—"

"Shh! You'll wake the house."

"Sorry." I cringed. "But you must agree, they cannot be reasoned with."

Westleigh tugged at the collar of his nightshirt. "Perhaps you're right…"

I took a deep breath, struggling to calm my pounding heart before it started fluttering. "I'm sorry for troubling you. If it bothers you so, you don't have to help. I'll manage, just—don't tell anyone."

He could no longer look at me. "You—you're certain about this, are you?"

"Absolutely! If you only knew how lost I've felt since we left Texas…"

"I have a bit of an idea," I barely heard him mutter.

"This is my chance to do something important." And to make amends for abandoning Abigail, but I couldn't say that aloud even if I wanted to. "I'm nothing but a burden to David here—"

"No." Westleigh's head snapped up. "You are a *gift*."

"Even still." I blinked away the mist in my eyes. "I have no purpose. I must find it."

His brow knotted. "I cannot fault you for that."

"Will you help me, then?" I inched forward. "I know I shouldn't even be asking, but I don't know what else to do."

Westleigh grimaced and folded his arms across his chest. "I'll help, but on one condition. You must tell David."

The boldness I felt a moment ago fled. "Westleigh... this would kill him."

"He's stronger than that," he said. "Believe me. But what would hurt him more is for you to keep it a secret. That's my condition, Saoirse. You have to tell him."

I lifted my head to see him holding out his hand. I sighed, and took it. "When I'm ready, I will."

"Deal." Westleigh's smile was forced. "First things first. We need to figure out how to make you into a boy."

I sat up straighter. "I already have a pair of trousers!"

Westleigh arched an eyebrow. "Um, I think it'll take a bit more than that." He pointed. "You'll have to cut your hair."

I tugged at a tangled strand. "It's bothersome anyway."

He pursed his lips, studying me. "There's also your voice. And the way you walk. All of your mannerisms... and this." He lifted his chin and pointed to the little bulge at his throat.

I wrapped my hand around my smooth neck. "Well, I've seen boys that barely have an Adam's apple," I said. "Yours isn't so noticeable either. Are you trying to tell me this isn't possible?"

"Not at all." Westleigh scratched his head. "It will be some weeks before Jack is anywhere near to being on the mend, we have time. But all the same, I think I may need some help, too."

I groaned. "Not Allison."

"He's a better secret keeper than you think," Westleigh insisted. "And he'd never discourage you from this. It isn't in his nature."

Allison would likely consider the entire endeavor a game. But I would rather that than Jack's stubborn opposition. "Fine. But only Allison. And I have a condition of my own."

"What is it?"

"Take care of David," I whispered. "He'll already be so lost without Lucy. Promise me you'll take care of him."

Westleigh's eyes were sad now. "I promise."

"Grand." I beamed. "So, shall we start with this tomorrow?"

He nodded towards the clock on the mantle across the room. "You mean today?"

I glanced behind me. "Ah, right."

"But yes. After breakfast, we'll catch Allison, let him in on your plans. In the meantime, we ought to try and get some sleep."

"Agreed." I slipped off the bed, and paused, studying Westleigh's face again. With his spectacles back on the nightstand, I could see the puffiness of his eyes. "I'm such a selfish clod, talking about myself all night. Something's eating at you too, what is it?"

Westleigh shook his head, pulling his legs under the quilt. "Just praying for direction."

"Oh." I shifted my weight, not ready to accept his evasive response. "Well, did God give you any answers?"

Westleigh laid down, his back to me. I almost thought he fell straight to sleep before I heard his quiet, enigmatic, "Yes."

May 12, 1861

The coach that was to take Lucy and Ellen away from us waited in front of George Bischoff's tavern while we said our long goodbyes. I sat on the porch steps with my arm slung around Wilberforce's neck, watching Allison as he ground his heel into the dusty road. He nodded at something Ellen said, then shrugged his shoulders and looked away.

Ellen touched his arm, and he drew it back, shifting on his feet. She lowered her head sadly. Allison bent forward, gave her a quick kiss on her cheek, and hurried away. When he hit the edge of the square, he took off at a run.

I waved at Ellen. She shuffled over, taking a seat on the porch, on the other side of Wilberforce. Her face was downcast, but she didn't cry. That didn't stop Wil from laying a paw upon her knee in canine sympathy.

I leaned over. "Did he beg you to stay?"

She blew out a sigh. "He didn't."

"Did you want him to?"

"It would have been nice if he tried. But it wouldn't have worked, anyway." Her eyes danced. "Nothing could keep me from going with Lucy."

I threw my arms around her, squishing the dog between us. "We'll miss you so!" Ellen wasn't Abigail, but she was the only girl my age in Dove Hollow that had been welcoming to me when I first came to town.

Ellen squeezed me tight before releasing me. "Oh, I'll miss you too! And I will write, I promise."

I bit my lip. "Well, I have a confession to make," I said, and she leaned in closer. I dropped my voice to a whisper. "I don't know how much longer I'll be in Dove Hollow myself."

Ellen stole a quick glance in David's direction, but he and Lucy were deep in conversation. "And just where might you be?"

"I think you already know."

Ellen's eyes finally widened. "Oh, Saoirse, if you're caught—"

"I won't be," I assured her. "Westleigh and Allison are already starting to coach me. And Jack will be there, though I'm not sure when I'll be breaking the news to him. He might kill me himself."

Ellen laughed. "You're absolutely mad!" She shook her head. "But I admire your courage. Yes, I'll write soon, so you shall have my address. And you must write me too, as often as you can."

I grinned. "As often as I can."

"And one other thing," she said, her face suddenly going very serious. "You must promise to take care of Westleigh."

I blinked. Westleigh? "But he'll be here in Dove Hollow, Ellen."

"Don't be so sure." She nodded ever-so-slightly towards the carriage, and I looked up to follow her gaze.

Westleigh quickly turned around and pretended to be interested in the dirt.

I scoffed. "You know how he feels about fighting."

"Yes," she admitted. "But I also know he's as brave and foolhardy as you are. And have you seen the way he looks at you? He'd probably follow you to the ends of the earth."

Lucy and David waved at us, and Ellen stood. But I remained on the porch steps, stunned. Surely Westleigh would never do such a thing to David. Not after promising to watch over him. My jaw tightened. No, he wouldn't dare. And especially not for *me*.

I made myself stand and join the others, catching a smile from Westleigh as I did. I returned a stern look of warning.

WESTLEIGH
Dove Hollow, Pennsylvania
July 7, 1861

Allison brandished the scissors with a mischievous gleam in his eyes. Saoirse shot me a worried glance, squirming in the chair.

"Are you certain you want to do this?" I asked for likely the hundredth time. We were hiding out in the barn behind George's, putting the finishing touches on our mad project. But this final bit would be the most drastic.

Saoirse took a deep breath. "Just get this over with, Horner. And mind my ears, would you?"

"Relax, I'm an expert at this! Now hold still—here goes nothing…" Allison held out a long, shiny lock of hair. We all held our breath. With a quick snip, the lock fell into Saoirse's lap.

She picked it up with a whimper.

"What are you going to do when Da notices your appearance?" I squinted through the cracks of the barn door, watching for movement outside. "Because he *will* notice."

"Lice," Allison said, snipping away.

I scratched my head and shuddered. "Jack certainly won't believe it."

"Which is why we need a *full* dress rehearsal," Allison insisted again, giving a snip of his scissors for emphasis. "Now sit up or you'll lose an ear."

"You did just fine last week in Butler," I reassured her. She'd donned her costume, pinned her hair up in a hat, and we took a short trip into a nearby town, where we didn't know anyone. Well, almost anyone. Allison had at least five cousins there. But we went in and out of a couple small shops, had a picnic in the local park, and no one was the wiser. "Besides, we're running out of time. Jack may be ready to leave any day now, especially now that Lucy's not here to fuss at him."

Saoirse sat up and slid her hands under her bouncing knees. She was dressed in her brother's old trousers, a shirt borrowed from Allison, and one of my old waistcoats. Her coat Allison snitched from one of his brothers'. It was a large, awkward fit on Saoirse, but it certainly helped to hide her feminine shape.

But with her long hair settled loose about her shoulders, she looked perfectly ridiculous.

I rubbed my eyes and shook my head. What in Heaven's name were we doing?

"Tell me the plan again," Allison commanded, looking uncharacteristically stern as he worked on Saoirse's hair. "You're to go into the tavern..."

"And I'm to willingly interact with Jonas." She pretended to gag. "Could we not find *any*one else to—"

"Jonas flirts with every girl he sees. You almost gave him a black eye for it, remember?" Allison cut another sizable chunk of Saoirse's hair, and we both cringed. "If you can pass as a boy in front of him, you'll do great."

Saoirse chewed her lip, and I didn't feel any more convinced than she did.

"Let's review your rules," I suggested, giving another quick glance through the barn slats. We were clear for now, but I still worried about George discovering us. I picked up a biscuit from the stash of food Allison had snitched for our lunches, and tossed an apple to Saoirse. "You have several *unmanly* habits you'll have to hide if you're ever to pass as a boy."

She took a deep breath. "I should be mindful of my voice, my laugh. Wear a handkerchief about my neck, just in case..."

I held one aloft and nodded. "And remember to pay attention to your gait, the way you walk."

Allison laughed. "Yeah, don't forget to swagger and spit."

"We don't all swagger." I frowned in disgust. "Or spit."

"Well, maybe Saoirse shouldn't be taking advice on how to be a boy from *you*."

Saoirse covered a smile with her hand.

My ears burned. "Hilarious." I pointed at Saoirse. "And never do that, either."

She shoved her hands back under her knees.

"Or that."

"Och!" Saoirse threw them in the air. "I don't even know how to sit properly!"

"I think it's rather the opposite, actually."

"Don't cross my ankles, don't sit on my hands, don't show my hands to anyone," she said in a forced, deep American voice.

I grinned. "Precisely. Although, I wouldn't change your voice all that much. You'll never be able to keep it up. And it doesn't suit you, at all. They'll know it's fake in an instant."

"Yeah, Westleigh sounds like a girl, so you could get away with it, too."

I lobbed the biscuit at Allison's head, but missed by an inch.

Saoirse ducked. "Sciss-*ors!*"

Allison dropped his head with a sigh. "You're right, this will never work."

Saoirse twisted around and grabbed a handful of his shirt. "Just. Finish." She glared at me. "And stop throwing things. I'll not be stabbed in the head by a couple of eejits before I have a chance to be shot at."

The hair stood on my arms, and I turned away. "Right," I muttered. "Sorry."

Allison went back to his barbering, and we were all quiet for a moment.

"When you're sitting," I said, leaning against the barn door, "just remember to relax. Don't close yourself off. Take up space. If you don't know what to do with your hands, place them upon your knees."

Saoirse slouched her shoulders just a bit—careful not to disrupt Allison's cutting—and propped her ankle on her opposite knee. She dropped her hands casually on her thighs. "Like this, then?"

I tugged at my shirt collar. Oh, what would Lucy say if she saw Saoirse sitting so? But I managed a nod. "That's a start."

"I figured you'd gotten this down by now," Allison teased behind her. "We've only been at it for weeks."

Saoirse scowled. "Sure, and you've only had practice at being boys all your lives. But of course, I should be able to perfect it in a month or so, right? Besides, it's been hard to get away and practice without David asking questions. Just finish already, I'm tired of sitting here."

The sight of her dark locks on the barn floor made my palms sweat. I tried not to look at Saoirse herself. And it wasn't her hair—whether she wanted it chopped off or not was none of my business, of course. But she was one step closer to signing enlistment papers. Which meant...

I turned away again, pretending to look outside, trying not to listen to the sound of the scissors.

A few more moments later, Allison declared he was finished. I forced myself to look.

Her hair was cropped and combed like ours. Straighter than Allison's, hers was far more obedient, and parted well on the side without the use of oil. Not that Allison ever bothered to use any. His was a wild brown mop sticking out every which way.

"Don't forget this." Allison plopped a slouch hat on her head.

An image of her standing in the hotel doorway, drenched and exhausted, flashed in my mind. The first moment I ever laid eyes on her.

I blinked it away, and still saw only Saoirse standing in front of me, not the boy she pretended to be. I handed her the handkerchief, which she quickly tied around her neck and tucked under her collar.

Allison kicked the dark hair into the hay to hide it. "All right, we need to work on your gait some more, so walk around. Let's see."

Saoirse took a tentative step, then caught herself, and tried her best to walk confidently up and down the barn floor. "How's this?" she called over her shoulder.

Allison tilted his head, watching her. Then he looked to me. "What's your opinion?"

My brow rose. "You're asking me now?"

"Oh don't be so sore." He rolled his eyes. "I was only teasing. Come on, what do you think?"

Saoirse stopped in front of me, and I found myself blushing as I made myself study her carefully.

She must have noticed my discomfort, for she suddenly smiled. "Don't be so shocked, Kavanagh," she teased. "'Tisn't the first time you've seen me in trousers."

I tugged at my collar again. "I reckon she could fool someone else," I said hesitantly. "But she's still too beautiful." The words left my mouth before I could stop them. Maybe it was time to just cut out my tongue.

Saoirse blinked in surprise, blushing.

Allison guffawed and slapped his knees. "Just—imagine Jack." He wiped his eyes and swallowed another laugh. "Walk—walk like he would."

Saoirse grinned. "All grumpy and stomping? All right, then." She hunched forward with an exaggerated scowl and plodded about, making the horses twitch.

"You forgot the limp," a deep voice said behind me, and we all jumped.

Jack stepped past the barn door.

"I should have known you were up to something with all your sneaking around lately." His gait was still uneven, but fairly steady for not using his crutches. "But just what in blazes do you think you're doing?"

Saoirse marched straight up to him and lifted her chin. "What does it look like I'm doing?"

Jack crossed his arms. "You *look* like you're fixing to make a fool out of yourself."

"I knew you wouldn't understand." Saoirse's stare hardened. "But it doesn't matter. You cannot stop me from following you."

He leaned into her face. "You wanna test me on that?"

"Jack, please." I crept into view. He slowly angled toward me, and I swallowed. "Please, she has as much right to fight for her country as anyone. Can you not give her a chance?"

A tired sigh escaped him. "I can't believe she dragged you into this, too."

"She didn't," I said softly. "I was glad to help."

"Help?" Jack snatched the hat from Saoirse's head and jabbed a finger at her shorn hair. "You call this helping? Don't you realize what you're doing?"

"Yes." I took another step towards him. "I'm letting her make her own decision. Jack, you know she'd do this with or without our blessing."

Saoirse met my eyes, and a smirk tugged at her lips.

I laughed. "I'd rather not stand in her way."

Jack pivoted on his foot and with a frustrated growl, he hobbled away to glare at the corner. "It's never going to work," he said with his back to us. He turned back around and nodded at Saoirse. "Just look at her. She'll never pass."

"Shows what you know," Saoirse snapped. "I did just fine in Butler last week, didn't I, Westleigh?"

I nodded hesitantly, trying to avoid Jack's glare.

"We've got another trial ready for her." Allison slid out of the stall beside me, still standing well away from Jack. "Send her into the tavern. See how she does."

I nodded. "That way, if this fails—well, the worst thing that can happen is she'll be humiliated."

Saoirse scowled. "Sure, and that's nothing at all for you lot."

"But she won't fail," Allison insisted. "I think she'll make it. Let's put this to the test. Jonas is in there, he can spot a girl a mile away."

"Forget Jonas," Jack said, giving Saoirse a closer inspection. He grunted softly. "Your father is in there. If you can fool him, then I might—I *might* consider letting you come. Otherwise your ass is staying home."

Saoirse looked more dejected than ever. Close to tears, even. "I cannot fool my own father," she whispered. "And if I fail—I'll have to tell him what I've planned. I—I can't do that to him, not yet. I'm not ready."

Jack scoffed. "Then I reckon you shouldn't have cut your hair."

Allison touched her arm. "You can do this, Saoirse. Come on, you've got to try."

"We'll come with you," I added, though I didn't relish the idea of admitting to David what we'd done, either.

"Yeah, I'll say you're my cousin or something," Allison said. "No way David's met them all. Heck, I haven't even met them all…"

Jack glanced at his pocket watch. "Time's wasting. Get to it or go home."

He handed Saoirse back her hat, which she crammed down so low on her head she almost covered her eyes. She shuffled out the door, and the three of us called out to her at once in overlapping voices.

"Don't look so timid!"

"Straighten your shoulders!"

"Don't forget to swagger!"

Jack followed her out first, but I lingered. The knot in my stomach—the one that had been growing since she first asked for my help—tightened and twisted.

Allison passed me, pausing to press something into my hand. He winked and slipped outside the barn.

I opened my hand. It was a lock of her hair.

"Sit there, I'll get us some cards." Allison started to pull out a chair for Saoirse and stopped, flashing her a grin before sauntering up to the bar at George's.

Saoirse winced as the chair scraped across the floor. But no one else in the busy tavern took notice. She sat down and rested her clasped hands on the table in front of her.

I took the chair beside her and leaned over. "Just breathe. Relax, no one is even looking at you."

Except for Jack, who practically perched on a stool across the room to watch her, sipping his coffee slowly.

David was at the counter, laughing with George, when Allison strode right up to him. They exchanged words, but I couldn't hear what was said.

Saoirse shrank inside her oversized coat. I could barely see her eyes as she peeked out from beneath the brim of her hat. "This isn't going to work…"

"Shush," I said, trying to give her a reassuring smile. "You passed him a moment ago and he didn't even look up. That's a start."

"And a finish," she said, pushing away from the table. "I've had enough, I want to go home—"

"Sam!" Allison slapped Saoirse on the shoulder so hard he pushed her back into her chair. "Leaving already? But I just found the fourth player for our game!"

Saoirse inched back up to the table, head still down, as Allison beckoned my father.

I gripped the arms of my chair and held my breath.

David grabbed his tea and limped toward the fourth spot, directly across from his daughter. "I've only time for one game, my boy," he said to Allison, and smiled at me. "Westleigh. I haven't seen you since breakfast. Is Allison getting you into trouble again?"

I laughed weakly. "Oh no, nothing like that."

Allison kicked me under the table.

David was too busy concentrating on stirring his tea at

the moment to notice my terrible lying. Although I figure we were all equally guilty in the trouble-making part, this time.

Allison dealt the cards. Saoirse reached out for hers, and quickly drew back before David saw her hand. He still wasn't looking up.

Allison cleared his throat.

Seemed now was the moment of truth.

"Mr. Kavanagh, I forgot. This is my cousin here, Sam Horner. Sam, this is our sheriff, David Kavanagh."

David set down his cup. "Don't let the sheriff part scare you—unless you're like the rest of the Horners around here." He winked at me and stuck his hand out across the table. "Nice to meet you, S—"

Saoirse finally forced herself to raise her head.

David jerked his arm back, sending his tea crashing to the floor.

There was light clapping from somewhere in the tavern, probably a patron thinking George had dropped something in the kitchen. No one seemed aware of the young girl in male clothing silently begging for forgiveness from her father.

Allison and I slid down in our chairs and could hardly bring ourselves to look at him.

But Jack wasted no time getting to the table. "That's enough," he hissed, leaning in close. "I told you this wouldn't work. Let's get you out of here before—"

David held up a hand, his eyes never leaving Saoirse's. He studied her, brow furrowed, until he swore softly in Irish. Then in a choked voice he asked, "Do you mean to enlist?"

Saoirse could only nod.

David swallowed and finally looked away. We sat in painful silence. Then my father pushed himself away from the table, walked around to stand behind Saoirse, and clapped her on the shoulder as if she really were a boy. "I think," he said hoarsely, "you will do just fine."

Saoirse struggled to remain in character and gave another short nod. "Thank you, sir."

David glanced around to me and Jack. "I'll see you all at supper tonight. We'll… we'll speak then." He shuffled back towards the bar, looking quite a bit older than his thirty-six years.

None of us could move, or speak, for the next few minutes. It was Allison who first dared. "Come on," he whispered to Saoirse, who looked as if she were about to cry. "Let's get you back to normal before you ruin your disguise."

She nodded and stood, and I could see that she was shaking. But Jack and Allison were careful not to help her.

"You three go on ahead." I picked up David's forgotten teacup. "I'm going to check on him."

They left the tavern, Saoirse behind Allison and in front of Jack, and still not one head turned at the sight of her.

I gathered my courage and approached David with his now empty cup, sliding onto the stool beside him.

"Go home, Westleigh," he said hoarsely, starting at the bar. "We'll speak later."

"But Da—"

"Do as I say." He rubbed his eyes.

I slowly slid off the stool and fidgeted there for a moment. Finally, I began to shuffle away. He half-turned, but still would not look at me.

"Just answer me one question," he said, voice low enough I had to return to his side to hear him. He took a long, slow breath. "Do you mean to follow her?"

My heart shot into my throat and lodged itself there. "Of course not," I said, though I sounded less certain than I ought to have.

David didn't seem convinced of my denial, either. I saw the tears in his eyes as he looked up at the ceiling. "They're just children," he whispered heavenward. The ache in his voice almost destroyed me.

Deep in my gut, I felt like I was being pulled in a dozen different directions. So many promises, so many fears. All I wanted was to hold everyone close, keep them home, keep them safe. But I also felt a tug in my heart to follow her, even if my feet were stuck fast.

David recovered with a cough and waved me away. "Get yourself home, then."

"Da—"

"Please," he entreated, turning red eyes to me. "Go on. Just make sure she stays around long enough for me to say goodbye."

My eyes stung. "I will," I whispered, and left him. I only dared one glance behind me, but he hadn't moved. He sat slumped over the bar, both hands buried in his thick black hair, head bowed in prayer, shoulders shaking.

7

SAOIRSE

Dove Hollow, Pennsylvania
August 7, 1861

I kept my strides long as I could to put distance between myself and Jack's endless nagging, but even with that limp he was on my heels. I marched myself home, shame burning me from head to toe. The look on David's face... it was more than I could bear.

But my resolve was unwavering. David said I would do fine. I passed Jack's test. I would follow him to war and there wasn't a blasted thing could stop me.

Except for the nasty voice in the back of my mind that mocked me for daring to think I could.

Suddenly Jack grabbed my arm and yanked hard. "Are you even listening to me?"

I wrenched myself free. "Are you talking to me, now?" I quipped, not bothering to look behind.

"Don't sass me," Jack huffed, tripping to catch up. He caught hold of me again, with both of his great meaty hands pinched 'round my arms, and held me fast. "I need you to listen."

I stopped struggling and sighed. "Jack, I'm aching tired. You've said your piece. But you aren't my father, and—"

"Do you know what it would do to him if he lost you?" Jack's words were quiet. I nearly wilted again, and his expression softened. "Saoirse, do you know what it would do to me?"

"Same if I lost *you*."

"Believe me, I understand why you want to go," he said, reaching for my hands. I slapped them away. He frowned. "But this isn't your path! You're not meant to be a soldier, for obvious reasons you can't seem to accept."

A fire roared to life inside of me. "Nobody gets to tell me what I'm meant for." My throat burned. "Can't be a soldier. Can't vote. Can't go to a school like Westleigh's. Can't even speak to a crowd. I suppose you figure girls are good for nothing but making dinner and babies? Or to be kept like a doll in a house? Is that what I'm meant for, Jack?"

Jack looked embarrassed. "I didn't mean—"

"*They* don't know half of what girls are capable of! So I'll use their stupidity against them. And they sure as hell won't see me coming." I did my best to stand tall. Strong. Like a soldier would, though my knees were quaking. "I'll show them. I'll show *you.*"

Jack stopped, his hands dropping back to his sides. His green eyes glistened as he stared at me for the longest time. "Okay."

"Okay?" My heart began to swell, and abruptly went hard again. I crossed my arms. "I didn't need your permission, you know."

But Jack only laughed. "I say 'okay,' because I'm not going to stand in your way anymore." His smile disappeared. "Just so long as you promise me not to get yourself killed. You got that?"

I nodded, because I had no voice.

Jack dusted his hands on his trousers, looking around, then back at me. He studied me up and down before flicking the brim of my hat. "Gotta say, Wes and Allison did a better job than I care to admit."

I swallowed. "You think so?"

"Well, you're right about one thing. Nobody's used to seeing a woman in trousers." He circled around me. "Hmm. And plenty of boys your age are just as scrawny, and don't got a single whisker on their chin, either. But you can shoot and you aren't weak, even if you are a runt."

"This *will* work, Jack! For no other reason than they won't even believe it's possible."

Jack scratched his head. "Well, we'll find out, won't we? Trouble now is how to figure out how you make your exit. You've done gone and cut off all your hair, then you'll disappear without notice, and it won't take much for Dove Hollow to figure out what you've done."

I rubbed the back of my bare neck nervously. "I'm sure Da can handle all the gossiping." But I silently cursed myself, and the boys. Perhaps I could wear a bonnet to cover my shorn hair. And if Jack would wait a bit longer...

Then I saw my accomplices come running towards us down the lane. Allison's limbs were flying about as he raced ahead of Westleigh, waving his arms above his head. He was shouting something, but I couldn't make it out. By the time he arrived to us in the yard, he doubled over his knees, wheezing.

Westleigh caught up, looking red, but not from running. The conversation with David hadn't gone well, I figured. Oh, how I dreaded supper.

Westleigh pointed up towards the hill, where the schoolhouse sat. "There's a notice," he said as Allison coughed loudly from the ground where he collapsed. "A recruitment poster. Allison says there's a man trying to get a company together and go to Washington City."

"Reverend Henricks—" Allison rasped. Jack grabbed him by the collar and pulled him to his feet. "Thanks. The reverend's calling himself 'Captain' now. He's a big

Methodist preacher from the next town over. Fought in the Mexican War."

Westleigh nodded. "Peter knows him well."

Westleigh fidgeted about as much as I was. I reckon the thought of a preacher going to war upset him.

Jack glanced at me. "Did it mention a meeting place?"

"Tonight at the church," Allison said. He looked at me sternly, holding fast my gaze. "You're ready, Saoirse. I promise you."

Westleigh only looked at the ground.

"Let's get on home, lads," I offered. Maybe Westleigh would welcome the chance to excuse himself from our talk of war, then. "We can discuss it more there."

"Go on without me," Westleigh said, and pointed at Allison. "We'll—we'll go let Da know about the post. He might want to come home sooner."

Grand, I thought to myself. Jack's hand gripped my shoulder, but he said nothing this time.

Westleigh started dragging himself back down the lane to the tavern. Allison followed, but a few strides later turned and called out to me. "See you at the church tonight, Saoir—hey, what are we gonna call you now? Let's see, Sam? Sammy, Solomon, Stephen..."

I shook my head. That was one thing I didn't have to think about—I'd known from the beginning what my name would be.

"Aidan," I said, chest swelling with pride—or was it that longing ache again? Either way, I was almost too overcome to speak again, but I managed. "Aidan Kavanagh."

The church was packed more than ever it was on a Sunday morning. Just about every person in Dove Hollow, and some men from some of the smaller neighboring towns, had come to see the recruiter. They thought to move the folks outdoors, but a summer storm came blowing in out of nowhere and crammed us all inside.

A man in an old blue uniform that fit a bit too snug for him stood up near the pulpit behind a table. He kept beaming over the boys in front of him as he smoothed down his greying mustache, going on about the brave lads that have come forward to fight.

"Now, some told me I shouldn't waste my time on farmers' sons who weren't brave enough to join up when President Lincoln first called for volunteers," his voice boomed out over the mumbles of the crowd. More than a few faces looked at each other in confusion—never mind the reverend hadn't joined up in April, either. Still, the veteran puffed out his chest. "I say you boys are the smart ones, who know how to watch and listen, weigh their choices carefully."

"Or they got pushed out of a damn tree by the local village idiot," Jack muttered beside me. He glared at Allison, who ducked back into the crowd.

We stood at the back of the room where most of the older men and ladies stood, watching the boys jostle about in their excitement in the middle of the room. Three of Allison's brothers were there. They'd pushed their way to the front, more than eager to join up. There was a buzz about the place that eased my nervousness. I felt a tingle beneath my skin, raising me up so that I almost bounced on my toes.

David's hand was on my arm, lest I fly away. I settled back and looked up at him. His eyes weren't red anymore, but the mirth I usually saw there was dulled. He was watching the crowd, sniffing every so often like he had a cold. I knew better.

Jack stayed beside me, waiting. We figured it was best to let the other boys go first, have fewer eyes on me when I went up for my turn.

My turn. I suppressed a grin. This was it. My turn to have the same choices and chances as any boy. To do my part, to avenge Abigail, to show those foolish rebels the folly of their treachery. My chance for a grand adventure, on my own, without the stifling expectations of my 'weaker' sex, or the well-meaning protections of my family. For real freedom.

There's no hearth like your own hearth.

Aidan's words came to me suddenly, unbidden, making me shift on my feet. I slipped my hand under my collar to fiddle the chain around my neck that carried his ring, tucked under my shirt like Jack wore Abigail's. I wore it with me for luck. Not to have the ghost of my brother guilt me every step of the way.

"Sure, and home will still be there after the war," I muttered to no one in particular.

"Steady," Jack said beside me.

I bit my lip and willed myself to be still. Glancing to the left, I caught sight of Allison again. He was discussing something heatedly with Westleigh. I bent my ear to their conversation.

"Don't you see them?" Allison gestured behind him. "Look at my brothers—they're waiting for me. Do you know what my father would say if I—"

Westleigh's response was too quiet for me to hear, but I could see the anguish in his face.

Allison shook his head, and he smiled weakly. "I know. I know, but I *want* to go. I'm sorry, I should have told you sooner—"

I jumped as a brass band struck up a lively tune. The Horner boys cheered with the rest of the new soldiers. Most of the crowd began filing out of the church, and I overhead them talk of drinks at George's place.

Jack nudged me. "You ready?"

David gave my arm a reassuring squeeze. "I'll go up

with you, Love," he said in my ear. "You're too young, they'll likely need my permission."

"I'm already lying about my sex," I whispered with a weak laugh. "What's another about my age?"

"There's not a chance in Hades they'll believe you're eighteen, '*Aidan*,'" Jack said. "Come on, now or never."

They urged me forward, and I swallowed hard. Dozens of townsfolk still lined the walls, but nobody noticed the small 'boy' sandwiched between Jack and David. There were enough strangers mingling about that came with the reverend. I was simply another unfamiliar face.

Allison caught up with us, standing at my elbow in line. I looked at him, and he gave me a wink. "You'll be fine, Kavanagh."

I let go a rush of held breath. As badly as I felt for Westleigh, 'twas a relief knowing Allison would be with us, too.

"Where do I sign up?" Jack was saying to the preacher-captain. "Eager to shoot some rebs."

Captain Henricks blinked at Jack in surprise. "Well now, listen to you! You certainly came a long way to Pennsylvania, son. And just where did you come from?"

Jack didn't even flinch. "Texas. That a problem, sir?"

"Not at all." Henricks waved his hand. "I served with a few Texans myself. Just surprised to see one of you — well, especially one of *you* up in these parts."

Jack's jaw tightened, but he said nothing.

The old man laughed suddenly. "Don't look so grim, son. Just sign here—" he pointed to a list of names. "I'll be taking us all to Washington and get us enlisted in a proper regiment, once we get ourselves a company together. Glad to have you, boy. Sign an 'x' there—ah, good, you can write. Always fascinating to see an educated Indian."

Jack masked his anger, but I heard him mutter in his mother's tongue as he stepped aside, and I knew enough to know it wasn't polite in any language.

"Who's next?" the old soldier called out, and pointed at Allison. "You there! Are you eighteen, son?"

"I am," Allison said, pushing forward to stand tall. I gaped at him—sure, and he was eighteen, but he looked now ever so much older. I almost didn't recognize him. Henricks handed him the pen, and Allison started to add his name to the list. "I'd be honored to join you and my brothers."

"Another Horner," the captain said with a nod. "Lots of brave boys in that family."

"Yes sir," Allison said. I about expected the buttons to pop right off his waistcoat.

Henricks waved him aside, and finally saw me. My heart was knocking something fierce in my chest, and I could feel myself shaking as the man looked me over. Only David's hands on my shoulders kept me steady. I forced myself to lift my chin.

The officer squinted slightly, and I couldn't breathe.

Finally, he chuckled. "Well you certainly aren't of age. But I admire your courage—"

"He's sixteen," David said behind me, and I felt him hold me tighter. "But stronger and braver than most boys. I've come to give my consent." His words ended in a pinch, and he coughed.

"Ah," Henricks said, smiling at me. "Well, I figure we can get a letter from your pa there, can't we? We'll make do. And your name?"

I took a deep breath, praying my voice wouldn't give me away, but trying to remember not to alter it, as Westleigh counseled. "Aidan Kavanagh," I said, softer than I meant to.

"Aidan Kavanagh," the man repeated, handing me the pen. "Sign here, son."

I hesitated, afraid of my small hands, but only for a second. I grabbed the instrument and hurriedly scribbled my new name on the list. The recruiter didn't look twice at me, scanning about the room for other willing and able-bodied young men. I almost burst out in nervous laughter at my success, before Jack pulled me aside to safety.

"And you, boy," I heard behind me. "Is your pa vouching for you, too?"

I started to turn as David spoke up. "Oh, no, he's not—"

"Yes," came Westleigh's shaky reply. He dared a glance at me, and then turned his eyes to the floor. "I'd like to enlist."

My blood turned to fire. "No…"

Jack held me fast. "Don't you *dare*," he hissed in my ear.

"He promised!" I twisted around to beg him to stop it. "Jack, he swore—"

"You say one more word, and I'll tell them who you really are."

I shrank back. "You wouldn't."

His voice was like ice. "Try me."

I spun around to see Westleigh adding his blasted name to the list, just like Ellen warned me. Part of me knew all along that he would. But as I watched my father standing behind him, pale and dazed, anger choked my throat.

He *promised*.

Now David was handing the recruiter a short note, giving his consent for me—for us—to fight. Westleigh stood beside him, still staring at the floor, looking miserable, like he knew exactly what sort of a damned liar he was. And I hated the sight of him.

The band started playing again. Thunder shook the walls of the church. But none of it drowned out the roaring in my ears.

Jack pushed me toward the door, but I kept my glare fixed on the back of Westleigh's head as we followed them outside. Allison was jabbering next to me, something about a farewell parade in the morning, but I couldn't listen. I didn't even bid him goodnight as he ran to join his family for one last night at home.

Our ride back to the house was silent. David and Westleigh sat in the front of the cart with Jack and myself behind them. And all the while my temper stewed.

Inside the house, my da mumbled something that sounded like "tea" and disappeared into the kitchen. Jack urged me and Westleigh into the parlor, and it took every ounce of my willpower not to deck the little bastard right there.

I marched up to him. "How could you?"

He stumbled and fell back on the sofa.

"What the hell are you thinking?" I seethed.

Jack tried to pull me away. "Did you really expect him to do any different?"

I fought him off me, still glaring at Westleigh. "I *expected* him to keep his promises."

"I never intended on enlisting," Westleigh protested, fighting back tears. "Please believe me, I—"

Jack forced his way between us, pushed me back, and tried to calm Westleigh. "It's all right," he said. "You're doing the right thing."

"No he isn't," I spat. Not even Westleigh looked convinced. In fact, he looked like he was about to be sick. "Nothing's official yet. He's not coming, and that's the end of it."

Jack whirled on me. "You think you have a right and he doesn't?"

"He's a pacifist," I snarled. "Sure and he can't even see a gun without getting the shakes. He's not fit to be a soldier!"

"That's enough," my da's scratchy voice sounded from the hall. He stood in the doorway with a tray of tea and biscuits. "I'll not have this night end with all of you at each other's throats."

I winced and sank down on the other sofa, my anger washing away as guilt filled me instead. It left me feeling weak. My last night with my da, and I was finding ways to hurt him even more. His eyes were no longer wounded, but heavy and sad. He likely aged a few years in a single evening, with all that we were putting him through.

David passed around the tea, and Jack took his without making a face, but Westleigh didn't even raise his head. He sat bent over his knees, clutching his head in his hands, face cast down to the floor. I felt a pang of regret for yelling at him so. But I wasn't wrong. He had no business fighting in the army, and not because he was weak, but because he was *gentle*. Why couldn't anyone understand that?

David took his place beside him, and we all sat in silence for what seemed like hours, sipping our tea. Nobody reached for the biscuits or mentioned supper. Our appetites had been chased away.

Jack sat like a rock beside me. I tried to feed off his confidence and forced myself to sit straighter. I took a deep breath, reaching inside for that surety and strength I had before, in the church, adding my name to that list. But I couldn't even get my hands to stop shaking. Jack grabbed one and held it.

The silence in the parlor, after a time, became somewhat comfortable, just sitting there with each other. So of course Westleigh had to ruin it.

"I'm sorry."

My fingers curled into my palms, but a sharp jab from Jack's elbow kept me silent.

Westleigh raised his head. "I cannot bear to watch three of the people I love most march away to war while I am left behind," he croaked, his eyes boring into mine. "I just can't."

My jaw tightened. "And so this is what God told you to do, is it?"

Westleigh paled, and David waved his hand.

"I said enough." He sighed heavily. "You each have your reasons, and they are yours alone. I said before, and I meant what I said before—I will support you all, no matter your path. And I am proud of each of you. My brave knights."

David met my eyes and offered me a small smile. There was a sadness to it, he couldn't cover that, but for my sake he tried. And that choked me up the most.

"Now, since I am the one that must stay behind and watch my beloveds march off to war," he said softly, grabbing Westleigh's hand to squeeze it tight. "I have some requests for you. You will write me, as often as you are able. You will watch out for each other. And you will come home to me again, or I swear, I will go to Hell and back to find you."

I felt a sob rise in my throat and reached for my father as he opened his arms to me, and we met in the middle of the parlor, kneeling on the floor, embracing. He pulled Westleigh off the sofa and tucked him against his side. Jack moved too, wrapping his arm around our shoulders, pulling Westleigh and I closer together. We all huddled there, our heads bowed and our warm breath mingling together, as my father prayed.

"Ár nAthair, atá ar neamh, go naofar d'ainm..."

In the morning there would be a parade. Folk would cheer at us, handkerchiefs waving, the band playing again as we line up and march away to become a part of something greater. To defend our country, fight for those who couldn't, in the name of freedom and those who died before ever tasting it. It would be a moment of pride, one we'd carry with us all the way to Washington.

But the next morning, as we marched out of Dove Hollow, it was the memory of my da's voice, reciting the Lord's prayer in our native Irish, that gave me the strength to leave him. And I knew that same strength would bring me home to him again someday.

from the journal of Allison Robert Horner

August 21, 1861 — Arrived in Washington City. Westleigh and the others have suggested I make a diary in order to give them "at least five minutes peace and quiet a day," in Jack's words. I shall endeavor to capture within these pages all of the daily excitement and wonder which our current adventure in the army brings us, though I hardly believe that five minutes a day will suffice. Still, I will try.

August 22, 1861 — Today, we drilled and marched, marched and drilled till our feet were sore. Had a scare when our squad's sergeant pulled Aidan aside this morning, but it was to only enquire about his age. Westleigh had the foresight to hold a copy of David's permission for the both of them. Sergeant Kennedy was satisfied, though he grumbled about too many "wee lads" in the army.

August 23, 1861 — More drills.

August 25, 1861 — Review of the regiment. Saw a steeplechase.

August 27, 1861 — Drills, drills, drills.

August 31, 1861 — Guess what we did today? More drills.

8

WESTLEIGH
Washington City
September 23, 1861

frowned, trying in vain to tug my sleeves up to free my hands. I could have fit two of me inside my sack-coat. My trousers, too, were far too large. My shoes fit properly, but they were thin and poorly made. My feet still stung from marching the day before.

Allison propped himself up on his elbows in our tent with a laugh. "You look ridiculous."

"At least I'm awake and up," I muttered, cinching my belt around my waist as tightly as I could. Well, my suspenders would hold me together. Hopefully.

Allison let out a loud, obnoxious yawn.

I tossed a shoe at him. "Wasn't it your turn this morning? Mess?"

"Hmm?" He rubbed his face.

"Breakfast, Allison. I'm hungry."

He rolled his eyes. "I'm not so anxious to break my teeth on that stuff again."

"Ask Kennedy how he does it." Our sergeant had a way of preparing our hardtack in a sort of mush that made it more edible, even if it still tasted like wood. I wondered if the sutlers were selling something we could mix with it...

"All right," Allison said, pulling on his shoes. He stumbled out of the tent half-dressed. "Keep your kepi on. I'll take care of breakfast."

"Allison?" I heard Jack call outside the tent. "Where's my coffee, boy?"

"I'm *doing* it!"

I shook my head with a grin. Army life felt a little bit like the college in Pittsburgh, but with all the men gathered to train in the school of the soldier instead. Although there were far more tents and guns than I remembered. At least my "roommate" was tolerable, even if it practically took a bugle in his ear to get him awake in the mornings. To be fair, it was a struggle for me, too. My life, up to this point, had been more comfortable than I realized.

Since we arrived in the capitol, every day was spent in study. We rose early, we ate, we drilled, and we read, although some spent less time on that activity than others. I, for one, took the task of reading our soldier's manual very seriously.

Saoirse was right, I wasn't so fit to be in the army as the

rest. I was soft, weak, and I hated the very sight of guns. Firing them in drills left me feeling sick every time. Doing chores around the camp took me longer than the others, as my arms were more accustomed to carrying books than firewood.

But if there was one thing I could do, it was study. So I decided to memorize that manual. I would teach myself to be the best soldier I could.

Outside our tent, the rest of our mess—our squad-mates—emerged while the sun was still little more than a notion in the sky. Allison finally had the fire going. Jack was helping him, probably more out of impatience than kindness. Jack was an entirely different person before our morning coffee. I usually had the presence of mind to avoid him, and I imagine he appreciated it. Allison wasn't so astute.

I sought out Saoirse instead. She stood in front of the tent she shared with Jack, eyeing the other men with her arms folded across her chest. I moved to her side and mustered a cheerful smile. "Good morning."

She gave me a curt nod, hugging her chest tighter. She rarely spoke in front of the others, too worried about the sound of her voice. She spoke even less to me, but that was fine. I couldn't blame her for being sore at me.

Still, I didn't want her to be alone. So we stood apart, silent observers as the rest of our mess milled about.

Allison's three older brothers—Jonas, Thomas, and

Robert—heckled him as he went about his task. Jonas snatched the kepi from his head and began tossing it back and forth between the other boys, laughing as Allison ignored them. It wasn't anything he hadn't lived with his entire life, after all.

But Jack wouldn't have it. He jumped up and snatched the hat mid-toss and glared at the other Horners. They scattered, shouting insults over their shoulders once they were a safe distance away. Saoirse and I grinned at each other, but she caught herself and turned away again with a scowl.

Someone shoved past me, stomping through our mess to shout at the Horner boys. "This isn't a playground, you daft eejits!" Sergeant Liam Kennedy balled up his fists and glared down at Allison. "And what have you been at, boy?"

"Sorry, sir."

"Sorry isn't breakfast. Get a move on, we don't have all day!"

Kennedy was a factory foreman from Pittsburgh. Before that, Belfast. He was a short man with an even shorter temper, mid-thirties, with fiery red hair and a wiry beard. He reminded me of a younger version of Eoghan, which was probably why I couldn't help but like him, rough edges and all.

But his barking did some good. Soon we had eaten and were lining up for drills as the sun finally made its appearance over the horizon. We were weighed down with our knapsacks, sweating under our heavy uniforms, bumbling about as we tried to march.

"Dress left!" Kennedy shouted. "Left—your—that's your right, Haering! Your other—dress to your feckin' *left!*"

Allison nudged poor Josef and muttered Kennedy's commands in German, and the young farmer moved over with a red face.

He was getting better. At least he knew his left from his right. A few others weren't so fortunate. And they had difficulty remembering.

"Mary and Joseph! Connolly, if I have to tell you one more time—"

We spent the morning marching, though I was constantly skipping and stumbling to catch up. Saoirse, too. Our shorter legs could hardly keep up with the long strides of the men around us.

"Keep up, Tiny." The sergeant smacked Saoirse hard on the shoulder, nearly sending her to the dirt to be trampled. "I'll not be carrying you on my back to Virginia."

She gritted her teeth and increased her stride, staring ahead.

The marching was made harder by the awful beats coming from our musicians. They were about as well-trained as we were. Some of the men tried to help by singing little songs, but then Jonas started chanting the lines of some bawdy limerick and all semblance of discipline vanished.

Then came the order I dreaded every drill. Even before they finished shouting the command, I felt myself cringing, preparing myself for the disaster to come...

"Wheel left!"

By the time we'd picked ourselves up out of the tangled mess of limbs and reformed the lines, the officers looked ready to spit nails. Kennedy was so angry he couldn't speak anymore.

Thankfully, we had made it to noon. We broke for a quick lunch in the midday heat. Most of us were too tired to do anything but concentrate on our rations. If only the same could've been said about Allison's brothers.

They started rough-housing next to us as we ate, kicking up dirt in our faces and more than once nearly falling in the middle of our meal. Then an elbow flew back and knocked Saoirse in the head.

"Watch it!" she snapped, whirling around. Her face fell as she realized what she'd done. She hunkered back over her knees, turning her back to them, but it was too late.

I groaned.

"Watch yourself, 'Tiny.'" Jonas loomed over her, sneering.

Saoirse gripped her knees and kept her head down.

Jonas kicked over her cup, splashing her trousers with coffee. "What, you have nothing else to say to me?"

I leapt to my feet. "Leave—"

He gave me a shove before I could even finish, and I

tumbled back down to land hard on my seat. Jonas grinned down at Saoirse. "Pretty pathetic if you gotta have a mollycoddle like Kavanagh stand up for you." He nudged her with his foot. "What's that make you, huh?"

I held my breath, not even caring about Jonas' insult. Did he suspect her? We'd managed so far to escape their notice—Saoirse had a backstory ready if the Horners ever cared to ask for it—but mostly, they left her alone. There was plenty enough in the army to distract them. When Allison introduced her as my cousin on our way to Washington, Jonas had replied, "I don't care," and that was that.

"Back off," Allison snapped at his brother. "You're going to get us into trouble again."

"Then what?" Jonas stalked over to Allison. "You gonna write home to mama and cry about it?"

Jack slowly rose to his feet, and Jonas froze, eyeing him warily. He stepped back to sneer. "You think you're so tough, but just you wait. One of these days—"

"Shut up, the lot of ya!" Kennedy shouted as he stomped by. "Or I'll be beating all your hides straight back to Pittsburgh!"

I was never so glad to get back to drills. Nor was Saoirse, from the looks of her. Her scowl had deepened as the day went on, and she walked about sort of hunched, eyes glued to the ground, like if she tried hard enough she could will herself to be invisible.

I spent enough years around Jonas Horner to
understand the feeling.

The afternoon was spent in inspection and more drilling.
We were learning how to fix our bayonets, those long,
deadly slivers of metal, to the ends of our rifles. Over and
over we'd reach across our bodies, pull the blade from its
scabbard in one fluid motion, and lock it onto the end of the
barrel. Every time I saw the gleam of it in the sun, I felt a
small shiver. As if the rifle itself wasn't fearsome enough
before.

We practiced loading and firing them, with Kennedy
shouting at us the entire time to be quicker about it. But our
sluggish speed was nothing compared to the atrociousness
of our accuracy. Only a handful of our company hit their
marks. Jack was the only one to make all of them.

"Aim low," Kennedy muttered after I nearly fell back
from another kick of my gun. "You might actually hit
something that way…"

From down the line we heard the firing of a rifle,
followed by a startled cry, and our line fell apart as we
craned to see the commotion.

Private Connolly leapt back, practically dancing away
from the smoking weapon at his feet. The rifle was bowed
and blackened near the hammer, bent awkwardly.
Connolly was wringing his hands.

"Nearly took my face off!" he cried. "Did you see that?
Blasted thing—"

Captain Henricks sighed. "Did you have it double-loaded again?"

"No sir, it just blew *up!*"

The commotion rose to overlapping voices, some jeering, some laughing. The rest of us grimaced at our rifles with some uneasiness. My stomach felt like a seesaw.

"Get back in line!" Kennedy marched up to us, waving his arms. "Just get back!"

"What's the matter?" Jack called out to him. "Connolly all right?"

Kennedy shook his head. "Fool'll be fine. Damn shoddy guns. Some bastard trying to make a quick buck, selling slapped-together rifles to the army, I bet you that's what this is. Third one this week..."

Allison squinted at his weapon. "Should've bought them from my uncle. Jacob Horner? He's the best gunsmith in western Pennsyl—"

"We *know*, Allison."

We managed to make it through the rest of the day without another incident or giving Kennedy a heart attack. By the time supper came, we were dragging ourselves back to camp, almost too tired to eat. Especially with how much effort it took to chew that hardtack.

Jack whistled to us just outside the camp, jerking his chin up when we turned around. "A minute, fellas. Over here."

Allison and I followed him, Saoirse sandwiched between

us. Jack waited for the rest of our messmates to walk by before he spoke. "We gotta discuss what happened today."

"I know." Allison scratched his head. "But I've been fighting with my brothers for eighteen years, if I knew how to get them to stop—"

"That's the thing." Jack's brow gathered. "You can't keep standing up to them."

Allison blinked. "Pardon?"

"For Aidan," Jack said, pointing at Saoirse. "The both of you can't keep on speaking up, they already think sh—he's timid enough as it is."

"I am *not* timid," Saoirse growled.

Jack folded his arms. "You let them keep pushing you around, it's going to get worse."

"I'm not *letting* them do anything!"

"And when you two," he pointed at Allison and me, "keep trying to defend *Aidan*, what do you imagine your brothers will start to think?"

Allison snorted. "Thinking? You're giving them an awful lot of credit..."

"I can't say anything for myself," Saoirse hissed. "I—I can't speak up, Jack, or they'll hear me—"

"Is that what this is about?" he asked. "Your voice?"

"What if I give myself away—"

"Again," Allison chuckled, "*far* too much credit."

"I can already tell," Saoirse said, and swallowed nervously. "I think I can see it when Jonas looks at me. He might not know it yet, but he's going to figure it out sooner or later..."

Jack and I both grimaced. Allison was right, Jonas wasn't terribly smart. But even he could only be fooled for so long. How long could she keep up her charade?

Allison snapped his fingers. "I got it! I know how you can throw him off the scent."

"I'm afraid to ask," Jack muttered.

Allison ignored him, grabbing Saoirse by the shoulders and squaring her up in front of him. He lifted his chin and pointed. "Hit me."

Saoirse laughed. "Are you mad?"

"Let's fight," Allison said, putting up his fists. "Fight me, and they won't think you're a mollycoddle anymore."

"I feel I should be insulted."

"*They* said it, I didn't. Come on, let's do it."

"They aren't even watching."

"They will. It's a fight. It's like blood in the water to them."

"This is the stupidest—"

"Oh, shut up, Jack." Allison rolled his eyes. "Come on and hit me as hard as you can. I can fake the rest, it needs to look real."

Saoirse's brow rose. "You think I can't hit you hard enough on my own?"

I winced. Oh dear.

Allison shrugged. "Well, you are a—"

Saoirse swung out and clocked Allison right in the jaw.

"Whoa! See, now that's—" He rubbed his jaw, laughing. "You're almost there, but—"

She punched him in the gut, and I winced as he doubled over, staggering forward. He crashed into her. She shoved him to the ground and pounced.

That's when a small crowd began to gather, hollering and cheering as they watched the smallest soldier in our company wrestle Allison, whose gangly limbs lashed out as he tried to get away. Saoirse was quicker. She grabbed him by the hair and flipped him on his stomach, wrenched his arm behind his back before he could throw her off of him again.

"Ah!" Allison gave a half-laughing cry as she pulled his arm back harder. "Okay, okay! Uncle!"

Saoirse mushed his face into the dirt as she pushed herself to her feet. "You forget," she said with a triumphant smile. "I grew up with brothers, too."

"What in blazes is going on here?"

The spectators scattered before Kennedy could catch them, and I saw a glimpse of Jonas and the others as they disappeared behind the tents. At least Saoirse had her witnesses.

Allison picked himself up out of the dirt. His lip was busted, his hair was a mess, and still he grinned. "Nice job, kid."

"Horner! Kavanagh!" Kennedy marched up to them. He

glared at all of us. "I see any more of you boys fighting, and you'll be sitting in stocks for a week, do you understand me?"

"Yes sir," we all answered.

Kennedy stalked away, muttering to himself.

Jack shook his head. "This is going to be a long war..."

Encampment near Washington, D.C.

SAOIRSE

Washington City
6 October, 1861

The message came early morning, after our Sunday sermon, and it fluttered in my hand as I stared. It was a brief note, simply instructing me to report to the hospital in town that afternoon.

Signed A.C. Bishop, surgeon.

Allison took it from my hand to inspect it, while Westleigh leaned over to get a glimpse. Jack just stared at me.

My mouth was dry. "Someone's found me out."

"They could be requesting you to transfer there," Allison said with a shrug. "Maybe they need soldiers helping at the hospital."

"Why Aidan?" Westleigh asked. "Why not any of us?"

"I haven't seen anyone else getting transferred," Jack said, snatching the letter away to read it.

112

"What do I do?" I squeaked. "What—what happens now?"

Jack handed the letter back, his brow tilted. "You obey your orders, of course."

Westleigh stood. "I'll go with you."

Allison rose with him.

I held up a hand, getting to my feet while my knees knocked together. "I can't have you two following me everywhere." I tried to stand straight and tall—well, tall as I could—and lifted my chin. "I can do this on my own."

The boys exchanged worried glances, but I didn't give them a chance to argue with me further. I took the note from Jack and forced myself to walk in the direction of the hospital. I could feel their eyes on my back as I left.

My confidence faltered. What if I had been found out? What would happen to me, then? Would they throw me in jail? Or simply bare my secret for the world to shame me, and send me home? I shivered. What madness ever convinced me that I could do this? They would see it as madness, surely. Perhaps they would lock me away in one of those shrieking houses. I could already feel the creeping cold dark closing around me. I hugged my arms to my chest and sniffed.

I should have stayed home.

My feet brought me to the hospital about the time I considered running all the way back to Pittsburgh, and I stumbled up the steps.

Inside was a bustle of activity, and a dozen listless men crowded the main hall, sitting or leaning against the wall miserably. I inched away from them. A sickness was sweeping through the camp. Measles, Jack said. The four of us already got it as children, so we were in little danger, but it still made me nervous to be in a house with such illness.

The fever almost claimed me, as a child. I was already a sickly thing. I remember my mother was so worried, she didn't leave my side for two weeks. There were even nights I awoke to see Brian leaning over me, whispering soothing words as he mopped my forehead.

My eyes began to water with the memory.

A nurse saw me loitering by the door and marched over to me and scowled. "What is it? Don't just stand there."

I couldn't speak. I handed her my note.

She squinted at it. "Ah. You're late. He's left already, but he's instructed to send you to his address. I'll fetch that for you."

She bustled off, leaving me stunned in the hall. When she returned, I hardly could comprehend the directions she gave me. I muttered my thanks and stumbled back out the door. What in Heaven's name was going on?

The doctor's residence was nearby, and I somehow made it there without getting lost. By the time I arrived on his stoop, my head was buzzing and my heart was jumping in my chest. I raised my hand to knock, when the door flew open wide.

Ellen stood in front of me, grinning from ear to ear.

"You're here!" She threw her arms around me, nearly knocking me off the porch. She let me go just as quickly, looking around in embarrassment. She grabbed my hand and yanked me inside before slamming the door shut again. "Sorry, should have waited till you came in."

I made a noise that was something between a laugh and a cry. "What—are you mad? What is—"

"Sorry for the deception," she said with a shrug. "We thought it would seem suspicious if we just showed up in camp and asked you over to dinner."

"We." I looked around the house. I heard stomping on the floor above me, followed by children's giggles. "Dinner."

"I'll take your hat," she snatched the kepi from my head, and paused to look at me, still grinning. "Aren't you a funny sight! They certainly did a grand job, I'll give them that. I don't think I'd recognize you if I didn't already know it."

She hung the kepi on a hook by the door and pointed at the parlor. "Sit down in there, I'll be back shortly."

Ellen ran off upstairs, leaving me in the hall just as confused as ever. I went into the parlor, if only to have a place to sit before my legs completely failed me.

There was more giggling and shouting upstairs, and I could hear Ellen's voice join them. I looked around. It was a modestly decorated room, and cozy. Reminded me of

David's parlor. There were books overflowing on the shelves. A doll slumped over on one of the chairs, and a few toys were scattered near the hearth.

I pushed myself to my feet to inspect the messy library, when I heard heavier steps in the hall and froze again.

The man in the doorway looked to be in his forties, tall, with honey-blonde hair and spectacles perched on his large nose. There were squint-lines by his eyes, and his lips were pressed together tightly, but he smiled and nodded at me. "Sorry to alarm you," he said. His voice had a clipped touch of a German accent. He extended his hand. "I meant to introduce myself at the hospital earlier. I'm Andrew. Lucy's brother."

I nearly wilted as I laughed weakly. "Oh!" I shook his hand. "What a relief. But you call yourself 'Bishop?'"

Andrew shrugged. "People misunderstood me enough and it eventually stuck. And it is easier for them to spell." He stepped aside and held out his arm. "After you. They are waiting in the dining room."

I was nearly knocked over a second time as I came into the dining room and attacked by Lucy.

"My sweet girl!" she cried, kissing my cheek. "Look at you! Come, sit down, you must be exhausted!"

She led me to a chair and I practically fell into it, looking around the room in a daze. The table was full of food—Lucy's cooking, to be sure—and my stomach grumbled loudly at the sight. Oh, to have real food after more than a month of rations.

Ellen sat across from me, waving. A girl of ten and her two younger brothers, all little blonde things, sat on the other side with her, bouncing eagerly in their chairs. Lucy took a seat beside me. Andrew sat at the head of the table, but the chair opposite him was empty.

"My wife Polly is with her sister and her new baby," he explained, spreading a napkin over his lap. "She asked to extend her apology that she wasn't here to meet you."

"Thank you," I said hoarsely. I looked at Lucy. "This—I didn't expect—How did you—?"

She covered my hand with hers, smiling. "Ellen told me. And we wanted to give you time to get used to your new life in camp," she said softly. "But I couldn't bear going so long without getting to see you, check on you, knowing you were so close by."

I blinked back tears. "I'm glad you did."

"We'll check on our boys soon as well," Lucy said with a knowing look at Ellen, who blushed and looked down at her plate. "But we thought it would be nice to get you away, first."

"How is Allison?" Ellen tried to ask casually, spooning mashed potatoes onto the youngest boy's plate.

I resisted my urge to tease her. "Fine," I assured her. "Same old Allison."

"I should hope not," she said with a laugh. "That doesn't bode well for the army."

"I think they'll get used to him eventually."

"And Westleigh?" Ellen asked, brow arching. "How does he fare?"

I tried not to roll my eyes.

Lucy noticed. "I'm sure he's well, too," she offered as she filled my plate. "And Jack. Everyone fit and healthy?"

I nodded. "Yes ma'am." I swallowed a spoonful of potatoes and sighed happily. If only Lucy could cook for us in camp...

I felt a pair of eyes on me and looked across the table. Andrew's daughter was staring, her head tilted. Did she know—?

"You're a soldier?" she asked, squinting.

I sat up a bit straighter. "Yes, I am."

Her smile stretched up to her eyes. She leaned forward. "What's it like, wearing trousers?"

Her father spluttered. "Julia! Not at the table!"

"Yes, Papa."

I winked at her, and she giggled before going back to her plate.

Supper went by too quickly. Lucy and Ellen told me all about their work at the hospital. It was grueling, and at times heartbreaking, they said, but I could see by the light in their eyes that they felt the same way about nursing that I did about soldiering. I felt a swell of pride as we shared even the most mundane details of our daily activities. Because deep down, we knew, we had purpose.

After dinner, Andrew took his children upstairs for bed,

which prompted a good deal of protesting from Julia. But after I swore to come back and visit another Sunday afternoon, she relented and retired with her father. Lucy and Ellen took me back to the parlor.

"We have so many questions!" Ellen said, grasping my hands as we sat on the sofa. "I couldn't ask you much at the table, you understand."

I shrugged. "What do you want to know?"

"Everything!" Her eyes were wide. "How do you manage it?"

"Manage what?"

"All those men," she whispered, leaning forward. "Tell me truly, this is the first sensible conversation you've had in weeks, isn't it?"

Lucy swatted at her, laughing. "You're terrible." She sobered. "But I am concerned, Saoirse. Are you sure you're all right? Ellen told me how terrified you looked when you arrived. I'm worried for you."

It was her motherly gaze that made my throat tighten again. I felt a weariness sweep over me, like I'd been holding it back since we arrived in the city and could keep it dammed up no longer. I swiped at my cheek with a frustrated grunt, and Ellen wrapped her arms around me tight.

"I'm all right," I croaked. "I'm just tired."

She let me go, and I wiped my other cheek. They sat quietly, expecting me to talk. Maybe I needed to.

"Some days I wake up from nightmares about being found out," I whispered. "The boys try to help, but the more they look out for me, the less sure I feel about myself. It's hard enough trying to learn the drills, do the work, keep up my spirits like the rest of them, without being scared that I'll—"

I pressed a hand over my eyes. I felt the sofa shift, and Lucy came to sit on the other side of me. Her arm wrapped around my shoulder.

"What is it?" she whispered. "What are you afraid of?"

"Failing." My chin trembled. "And I feel like—if I fail, if they find me out…"

"You'd prove them right," Lucy finished for me. I looked up to see her gazing at me knowingly. "And it's not only yourself you'd be letting down."

For some reason I pictured little Julia's wide blue eyes looking up at me again. "Yes," I said in a small voice.

"For the record," Lucy said, squeezing me tight. "Even if they drummed you out tomorrow, I think you've done a marvelous, brave thing. And that's not a failure at all. Don't you know how proud we are of you?"

Ellen gripped my hand and nodded.

"Now, you tell those boys of yours to give you some space," Lucy said. "Especially Jack. He's the biggest mama bear I've ever met in my life."

I laughed weakly. "You have no idea!"

She let me go and shifted on the sofa to face me. "Now,

on to more practical concerns. And don't shy on me, this is important," she said, all business now. "Are you binding yourself?"

I felt my cheeks color, but nodded. "Yes ma'am, although I'm not sure it's necessary."

"Better to be safe," she said, "but careful you're not wrapping yourself too tightly. The last thing you want to do is pass out in the middle of drills, or worse."

I felt the itch of the bandages across my chest that I'd been ignoring all day, and grimaced. "Noted."

Lucy dropped her voice. "And what are you doing about your menses? Have you had to deal with that, yet?"

Ellen squirmed next to me, her whole face red. I felt my cheeks heat up, too.

Lucy straightened. "I told you now's not the time to be shy."

"Not yet," I said quickly. "Everything's been... out of sorts, for a while."

Lucy nodded. "That can happen, especially since you're so young. Be careful, and write to me if you need to. There are plenty of ways you can be discreet about it. That's something you'll have to make plans for, Saoirse."

I kicked myself. Something else I should've thought about before, but 'twasn't like it was a likely subject to come up during my "training" sessions with Allison and Westleigh...

I shoved all those thoughts at the back of my mind and

prayed I'd never have to figure out how to handle bleeding. In the army. Surrounded by thousands of men.

I shuddered. "Again, noted."

Lucy looked me over. She fussed with my hair, adjusted the kerchief around my neck, nodding to herself. Then she gave a small pinch of my cheek. "Hmm."

"What?" I rubbed the spot where she pinched. "What is it?"

She pursed her lips. "Well, hardly any of those boys you're with can grow whiskers either, but if you're there for an extended period of time, you may have problems. And even still, you look a bit too fair and clean..."

I rubbed along my chin and jaw, thinking. "I can't pretend to grow whiskers, they'll know it's false."

Ellen sat up. "I know! Put a bit of dirt on your face!"

"Dirt," I repeated flatly. "I'll just look like a street urchin."

"Not enough to look *dirty*," she said, moving to the fireplace. She dipped her fingers in the ashes and turned back to me. "Just to give yourself a bit of a shadow!"

I inched away from her sooty fingers. "What are you doing?"

"We all have a little hair on our face, it's just very fine and light. Hold still." She lightly brushed her fingers over my face, not smudging, but dusting the ashes along my skin. After a few minutes, she sat back and pursed her lips. "Hmm. Well, it might take some practice."

I reached up and she slapped my hand away.

"Don't touch it!"

I stood up to look at myself in the mirror above the fireplace. There was a light shadow that almost matched the color of my hair, dusted across my jaw and my chin, and above my lips. "The first time I sweat this is going to run down my face. That would be awkward."

"Ah." Ellen slumped. "I hadn't thought of that."

I rubbed at the ashes and accidentally smeared it across my cheek. "Ugh. Now I'm a chimney sweep."

"But you don't look like a girl!"

We all broke into a fit of giggles, laughing until tears made trails through the soot on my cheeks. By the time we finished, I sadly noted the dimness of the light in the parlor now. The sun was setting. Time to go back.

Lucy sent me packing with a basket full of goodies to share with the boys, baked goods, and even some tea for Westleigh and I. But it was her hug that I'd take back with me and share the most. I tried not to cry, letting her hold me as long as she could, a memory of my mother creeping back as I buried my face against her shoulder.

Would my mam have been proud of me, too?

Ellen and Lucy promised to come see us soon, and told me to tell Westleigh and Allison it was their turn for supper, next.

As I came to the edge of camp, struggling with the heavy basket, I felt someone staring at me. I tensed, and willed myself to look up. A soldier about my father's age leaned against a building, a cigarette between his fingers. I tried to walk on, but as our gaze met, my steps faltered. I stopped as we both squinted at one another, sizing the other up, like two cats meeting in an alley. Fear snaked up my spine, but curiosity held me fast. The other soldier was tall and slender, but strong, with a glint of roguish daring in his eyes. And something else...

He beckoned me closer. I found myself inching forward, until I gasped, just as the woman raised a finger to her lips and gave me a wink.

"Pennsylvania?" she asked.

"Y-yes," I managed. "You?"

"Ohio." She ground her cigarette under her shoe, still not breaking eye contact with me. "Kinda scrawny, aren't you? What are you, twelve?"

I frowned. "Sixteen, thank you."

She swore. "You're a child."

"So's half the army."

The Ohioan smiled at me. She nodded at my basket. "Got anything worth sharing there? Since we're neighbors, and all." She stressed the word, and I could read the meaning in her eyes.

I offered the basket and watched her as she selected one of Lucy's pastries. "How'd you know?" I whispered as I leaned close.

She looked over me again, and I felt nervous at her

scrutiny, wondering for a moment if I'd gotten it all wrong. Finally, she took a step back and started to walk away. "Watch yourself, that basket looks heavy."

My basket? How else was I supposed to carry it? I dropped it to my side, letting it hang awkwardly by one hand at my knees. *Like this?* I asked silently with a tilt of my head.

She shrugged. "Thanks for the treat."

"See you around?" I asked hopefully. Another woman in the army! We could help each other. What if there were others?

She shook her head and slipped back into the shadows.

My shoulders slumped. So much for a new friend. But still I smiled. Somehow, I felt a little less alone.

With a full heart, I returned to find the lads just finishing their own supper.

Jack jumped up when he saw me. "We've been worried sick!" he cried. "What happened? Where'd you go? What—what do you have, there?"

"Sit down," I said, shoving the basket at him with a grin. "It's from Lucy, she sends her love. And biscuits."

Allison and Westleigh almost knocked each other into the fire pit scrambling to get to the basket.

"Hey, Al!"

We all stopped as Jonas and Robert stopped by the camp. Allison looked up, scowling around the muffin in his mouth.

Jonas grinned wickedly, looking at me as he spoke. "Saw Kavanagh in town earlier, being sweet on your girl."

I felt my gut drop. Allison looked at me, wide-eyed.

"Shut up, Jonas," I snapped, but I couldn't help my face burning red. He must have seen Ellen hugging me when I arrived.

Jonas shook his head. "I saw it, clear as day. What are you going to do about that, little brother? You gonna let him go after your sweetheart like that?"

Allison swallowed a much-too-large bite of muffin and looked at me in confusion.

I mouthed where Jonas couldn't see. "Hit. Me."

Westleigh bowed his head. "Not again…"

Allison lunged at me, yelling, and I made a good show of fighting him off as Westleigh dodged our feet and fists, and Jack rescued the basket of treats.

From farther down the lane, we heard a shout. "Kavanagh! Horner! What have I told you—!?"

We bolted and ran in opposite directions before Kennedy could catch us.

from the journal of Allison Robert Horner

October 10, 1861—*Pay-day, thirteen dollars*

October 11, 1861—*I need to find a new partner for cards, Westleigh is terrible. (lost thirteen dollars)*

October 25, 1861—*For a change of pace, drills. I can now march and load and fire this weapon in my sleep. Jack says that's the idea. Doesn't seem a very bright one to me.*

November 1: *Little Mac sent some of our boys scouting over the river last week, to defeat and disaster. Word is many were drowned trying to escape the rebels in boats. Papers saying hundreds more were captured. Praying for their families.*

November 13, 1861—*Picket duty. Saw a squirrel who didn't know the counter-sign. Decided to let him live. I sure hope he wasn't a spy.*

December 25, 1861—*Christmas celebrations. Lucy and Ellen brought us new socks and some pudding. Jack stayed in his tent for most of the day.*

January 3, 1862—*New year, more drills. Rumors are going around that this army might move sometime before the war is* *over. Lies, I say. Least it seems like our boys out west are being kept busy, but we're not hearing much good news for the Union.*

January 19, 1862—Boring sermon. Rainy day. Westleigh reads too much.

January 29, 1862—Got our likenesses made in town from some man with a fancy contraption. I gave mine to Ellen. She cried. Didn't realize I was that ugly.

February 2, 1862—Rain and mud and drills.

February 14, 1862—Saoi Aidan's 17th birthday today. The captain helped us celebrate with more drilling.

February 20, 1862—Jonas has come down ill. Or he's shirking, hard to tell. Captain and a few of the others went to the hospital, too.

February 25, 1862—More rumors we might leave. I don't think it'll happen. I think Little Mac's strategy is to bore the rebels to death. If they could just surrender and spare us the monotony though, we could call it a day and go home.

March 1, 1862—Visited Jonas in the hospital, got to see Ellen.

March 5, 1862—Captain Henricks has died. Jonas is getting worse.

10

WESTLEIGH
Washington D.C.
March 9, 1862

The morning sun peaked over the endless row of white tents to shine directly in my eyes, so I tilted my head down ever so slightly to block the light with the short brim of my kepi. But the sunlight glinted off the dew, so looking at the ground wasn't any better.

I straightened up, adjusted the rifle against my shoulder, and tried to ignore every other discomfort that plagued me. My sore feet from endless marching. The scratchy wool of my uniform, still not worn in enough to be tolerable. The bead of sweat that was dripping down my spine towards the waist of my trousers, despite the cool wet air. The way my heart pounded when I glanced down the line as we waited for inspection. Saoirse stood at Jack's right shoulder, her chin lifted in defiance of the sunrise.

Allison elbowed me. "Stop that. You're making me nervous."

Jack frowned at us, but otherwise didn't so much as twitch a muscle.

A high-ranking officer rode by on his horse. After he passed, I dared another glance to my right.

Saoirse's face was a little too clean this morning. She'd started to keep a bit of dirt smudged across her cheeks, but not so much that she'd be accused of neglecting her hygiene. Her freckles were too pronounced in that sunlight...

"Stop staring," Allison said. "You'll cause more trouble than you're worried about."

"For every inspection Aidan passes, I grow more worried about the next."

"You'll be the one in trouble if you don't —"

"Attention, Company! Inspection arms!"

Finally, after months of repetition, we were beginning to move like the machine that we were being drilled into. I sighed in relief as I took the rifle from my shoulder and rested it on the ground. Bayonet and all, it was taller than me. Saoirse had it the worst, she could hardly clean her weapon without assistance. Her arms weren't long enough to get the ramrod down without a good deal of struggle.

They inspected our weapons, our uniforms, and our accoutrements. Our knapsacks were laid out with care and order while the contents were inspected, until we put it all together again and marched—always marching—back to our tents or our posts. But on Sundays, when we got a rest, we could go into the city.

As everyone dispersed to their various posts and chores, Allison and I caught up with Jack and Saoirse. "Where are you two off to?" I asked, trying to swallow the squeak in my voice.

Saoirse's eyes narrowed slightly before she turned away without a word and took off back to the tents.

Jack gave a half shrug. "Sorry Wes. Don't worry, I'll keep an eye on Aidan."

"That's not what I—"

"Keep Allison out of trouble," Jack said, and jogged to catch up with Saoirse.

I watched them go and tried not to sigh. More than six months in the army, and I still think Saoirse had said hardly a dozen words to me. Jack was right. She was raised a Callahan. She'd likely hang on to her grudge till the day she died.

Allison's hand on my shoulder startled me out of my moping.

"Now, you keep looking at her like that and you'll *definitely* get her caught."

"Aidan," I corrected sharply, but I couldn't help the

blood rushing to my cheeks. Every chance we got, we used her brother's name. It made us all feel a bit braver, like we were invoking his spirit, bringing him back to life. With all the stories she had told of him, back in Dove Hollow, I was sorry I'd never met him, and sorrier he wasn't with us now.

It also kept us from slipping, using her by her true name in a moment of forgetfulness, or ruining everything with a quick slip of a *she*, or *her*. So Aidan, always. So far, it worked. No one suspected a thing, and over the months, Saoirse's disguise became second nature to her. But the longer this war dragged on, the more chances we had to lose everything. And we hadn't even seen battle yet.

Aidan moved and spoke with confidence now, and we'd gone this long without anyone suspecting anything at all, so I tried to tell myself I had nothing to worry about. Still...

"I'm uh, gonna go see Jonas." Allison stifled a cough. "Come with me?"

"Of course," I said softly. "How is he?"

Allison shrugged, and I didn't ask for details. We'd see soon as we got to the hospital, anyway.

We walked in silence for a few blocks, passing the other clusters of soldiers, some with ladies on their arms, all milling about the city on their day of freedom. First one in a while we'd seen with no rain.

Allison broke the silence, his darker mood gone like the storm clouds, as if it'd never been there. "Heard the new captain is showing up this week, and some transfers, too. Their old company was all but in shambles after Bull Run. Half of them deserted."

I remembered reading about the battle last summer. It felt like an age ago. "Huh. Well, at least we get the ones who stayed."

Allison snorted. "Or the ones too chicken to run."

I winced. "Maybe... though I can't say I know what I would've done in their place."

"Give yourself more credit, Wes," Allison said. "You'd never run. And you've made a fine soldier so far."

I laughed. "Well we haven't done much have we? I'm used to routine, rules, and study. Though not so much the physical aspect." I stretched my sore muscles.

Allison grabbed my face suddenly and squished it. "You even got some color in that pretty face of yours."

I slapped his hand away. "Oh, shut up."

He skipped a few steps ahead of me, grinning, and we didn't speak any more on our way to the hospital. He was still smiling faintly as he bounded up the steps of the building, but I could see the weariness hiding in the redness of his eyes.

The 'hospital' was a converted asylum. Hastily converted, since the main hospital was full of actual wounded soldiers. But more sickness swept through our tents, fever and dysentery, in addition to measles and chickenpox. A good quarter of our regiment, Jonas included, got caught in the wave. And Jonas wasn't doing so well.

I could tell by how pleasant he was to me when we visited.

The once smug boy who made it a daily habit to throw my schoolbooks in the mud actually smiled and greeted me when we arrived. He was pale, his hair damp and plastered to his forehead, his cheeks pink with fever.

"How are you, Westleigh?" he asked, voice thin. The corner of his mouth curled up as he nodded at Allison. "You keeping an eye on him?"

"Always," I said, watching Allison fidget nervously beside me.

"Heard some murmuring, rumors you fellas might be leaving this sorry town soon."

"Ah, they've been saying that for months." Allison rolled his eyes. "Now I think they're waiting on you to get off your lazy rear end."

"Yeah..." Jonas said, looking away. "Well, you tell 'em I'll be up on my feet before you know it."

Allison shrugged. "What's the rush? You got a nice bed, no chores to do. Besides, first thing we're doing once you're up is catching one of those shows you've been wanting to see."

Jonas's laugh turned into a coughing fit, and I felt an arm start to pull me aside as Allison sat on the bed to help calm his brother.

I turned to the nurse who drew me away, and she pulled me into a tight hug.

"Oh, my boy!" Lucy exclaimed tearfully. "Every time I see you in that uniform..."

I kissed her cheek. "I'm sorry I haven't been around to see you in a while. Or you, Ellen," I called over her shoulder. Ellen gave a quick wave before she hurried to sit with Allison and Jonas.

Lucy pulled back to inspect me, suddenly all business. "Are you feeling well? Taking care of yourself?"

"Yes ma'am."

"Drinking that coffee like I told you? I know you hate it, but— "

I made a face. "Ugh, that I do. But I've been careful to follow your instructions to the letter. We all have."

"Good," she said, smiling, but there was a mother's worried look in her shining eyes. She started to say something else and stopped herself. She brushed her hand over the shoulder of my coat. "Well, you sure look handsome in that Union blue."

I shifted on my feet. "It's still a bit large. They didn't have many that could fit—"

"You look *fine.* Very noble."

I cleared my throat. "Have you heard from Da?"

Lucy's brow creased. "I was about to ask you the same. He hasn't answered my last two letters. I imagine he's still cross at me for leaving." She blushed suddenly. "But if you—well, next time you write him, give him my—that is, tell him I— "

I leaned in to whisper, "I'll tell him you're doing well and wish him the same."

"Thank you," she said with a laugh, dabbing the corner of her eye. "And how is—?"

"Aidan. Grand," I said with a nod. "Still doing just fine, so far."

"Good. Give 'Aidan' my love." She glanced over my shoulder, and her face grew sad.

I turned to see the physician urging Allison away so Jonas could rest. Ellen had her arm around her sweetheart's shoulders, and he dragged his feet as she steered him from the room. He hardly raised his head as Lucy pulled us both into another hug.

"If I don't see you again before you leave—" Lucy's voice broke. Her arms shook around us, but after a quick squeeze she pushed us away again and reached out to straighten the wrinkle in my uniform. "Don't forget what I've told you. Go on, boys. Send my love and prayers to Jack and Aidan."

"We will ma'am," I promised.

Ellen led Allison out of the building, but it took me

longer to turn my back to Lucy. Her brother Andrew called her name, and she swept away to do her duty.

I lingered in the hall a moment more, feeling heaviness all about me. Jonas, the rumors of leaving Washington, and now the silence of my father. I lifted a quick prayer before dragging myself toward the door. It burst open before I could reach it, and I scrambled out of the way as two soldiers came through carrying an ill comrade between them.

I backed into the room behind me as I waited for them to pass, and felt a sharp elbow jab between my shoulders.

"Oy, watch it!"

"Sorry!" I spun around to apologize properly, only to trip into the side of a bed, accidentally grabbing the occupant's foot as I righted myself. "Ah! So sorry!"

"'Least that ain't my injured one," a voice grumbled. "Watch where you're going, Private."

"Yessir," I mumbled, red face down as I backed away. "Sorry—"

"Private," the man said sharply. "Stand and salute as you ought to, son."

I straightened at once, brought my hand up, and as I met his eyes my knees almost buckled and sent me sprawling again.

"Olsen!"

"That's Captain Oliver, to you." The once false

marshal, Marek Olsen, now lay upon a hospital bed, wearing Union blue with captain's markings. He gave me a slick grin. "Well, I didn't believe the roster before, and I can't believe my own eyes now. If it isn't baby Kavanagh! How in the hell did you get into the army? You the regiment mascot or something? Declan, show me that list again…"

Still frozen in attention, I whirled to the man next to me and felt my jaw drop.

Declan Callahan stared back at me, just as stricken, ignoring Olsen's outstretched hand. His face was thinner than I remembered, and he sported a fresh red scar under his eye.

"Don't stand there gawking, fellas," Olsen drawled. "Go on, Kavanagh. You and I will be seeing plenty of each other soon enough."

I blinked at him, still speechless.

He laughed. "That's right. Go tell your little friends you've met your new captain." His eyes narrowed with a thought, and he beckoned me closer. "Come here, boy."

I crept to his side, feeling a tremble in my bones, and he still urged me nearer to him, until he could grab a handful of my collar, and yanked me towards his face.

"You tell anybody *else* who I really am," he hissed in my ear, "and I will find you at night, and I will slit your throat. We understand each other?"

My knees started to shake, but I nodded.

He tilted his head. "Pardon? Didn't catch that."

I swallowed. Fear, pride, anger, all burned my throat as I forced them down to stew in my belly. "Yes, Captain," I managed. Just the word on my tongue made me sick.

He started laughing again, releasing me, and I bolted from the room, this time pushing my way past the soldiers lingering in the halls, and stumbled outside. Allison was already gone.

I ran.

Halfway to camp, I found him standing outside a shop with Ellen on his arm. Saoirse and Jack were with them. Jack had his hand on Allison's shoulder. I tried to stroll up calmly, but I was breathing hard, and shaking, and Saoirse noticed. Her scowl silenced me before I even tried to speak.

Allison ducked his head and sniffed. "I know Jonas is, well, Jonas... but he's still my brother..."

"I'm so sorry, Al," Ellen whispered, kissing his cheek. "I'll go right back and sit with him. If anything changes—"

Allison nodded. "Sure, thanks." He looked up and saw me, and his red eyes widened. "Whoa, what's the matter with you? You look worse than me!"

I gulped, still feeling my heart racing in my chest. "I—I just ran into our new captain."

"Captain?" Jack echoed, shrugging. "Martin Oliver. Heard he just transferred in with the new arrivals, but he wasn't at inspection this morning. Fool got his foot stomped on by a horse, somehow."

"His name isn't Oliver," I managed. I could picture myself waking up in the dead of night with that monster hovering over me, blade at my neck, and I shuddered. "It's Olsen. It's that bounty hunter."

Jack kicked the post beside him, spewing a good half dozen swears before stomping a few feet away, muttering in his mother's tongue.

Saoirse shook her head. "No, no, no! He—how can he be a captain? He's practically a criminal, he— "

"No telling who he blackmailed," Allison said. "But I'll bet that's what happened. Now, why he's Union and not sesech is the *real* question..."

"He threatened to kill me if we told anyone else," I blurted. "But it's worse."

Jack laughed bitterly. "Of course it is. We're already gonna be marching into battle led by a man who'd rather have us all dead. Not to mention—" he gestured wildly at Saoirse.

"Shush!" She slapped at him and leaned closer to me. "What is it, Wes?"

I hesitated, and by the way her jaw tightened, I could tell she knew. And she knew what it would mean. Because if there was anyone in the army who would know Saoirse the instant he saw her, it would be her brother.

Finally, I grimaced. "Three guesses who Olsen's personal attender is?"

Jack slammed his kepi on the ground and kicked it into the street. "Son of a —"

The evening's sermon was less of a sermon and more of the old chaplain's speech against the evils of cards that would have rivaled Jonathan Edwards himself. I don't recall a word of scripture being recited. After the brief but intense raving we retired to our tents to sit around the fire and play Whist. Well, I say we played, but Saoirse spent most of her time darting her chin over her shoulder, eyes wide as she scanned every uniformed man that wandered by. We'd seen no sign of Declan or Olsen since the hospital. But that was little comfort to her.

After a few rounds of losing, Jack dropped his cards and sighed. "If you can't even keep yourself together for a card game—"

"I'm fine," she said through her teeth. But she kept fidgeting with the cards, bending and unbending the corners.

"The moment he sees you—"

"And it's too late now, 'tisn't it?" she hissed. "What do

you want me to do, Jack? Just pick up your cards, then, we're losing."

Jack grumbled and the game continued in tense silence. Allison and I won another round, and he jumped up and ran a circle around us, hollering in victory.

Jack reached out and yanked him back to the ground. "You wanna shut up before you bring the whole camp over here?"

"No one cares, Jack," Allison said, brushing himself off. "That's the beauty of this, remember? Nobody's looking for a you-know-what in the army, so nobody's suspicious, but if you all keep acting jittery, they're gonna start to wonder why."

He sat up and grabbed all the cards to reshuffle them. "As for Declan—he's probably going to be running errands for the captain so much, we won't have to worry. And as far as the captain—well, Olsen didn't get a good look at you that night in the barn, did he?"

Saoirse thought a moment. "No, he didn't see me at all."

"There," Allison started dealing the cards, "you can relax, because everything's— "

"Private *Aidan* Kavanagh?" a voice shook behind us. "How dare you use his name."

Jack leapt to his feet. Declan was faster, raising his pistol. He kept it close to his chest, but it was enough.

Still, Jack sneered. "You think that's gonna stop me from beating your skinny—"

"Sit down before you make a scene," Declan barked. He glared down at Saoirse. "You get up, we have to talk."

"Not a chance," Allison growled.

Declan's eyes narrowed, staring at each of us in turn. "Unless you want me to be dragging an officer over here right now, I suggest you do as I say."

He grabbed for Saoirse.

I lurched forward. "Don't you dare hurt her—"

Allison tackled me, hand over my mouth to muffle my foolish cry. "Shut up, you little idiot!"

Saoirse shoved Declan away, and stood shakily on her own. "*I* will be just fine." Her lips twisted into a dark smile. "But if I'm not back in five minutes, you can come and kill the bastard."

11

SAOIRSE
Washington City
March 9, 1862

Declan's bony fingers pinched into my arm as he dragged me past the tents into an ally behind the camp. "Aidan *Kavanagh*," he repeated again, spitting out my father's name in disgust. "How dare you pair my brother's name with that blackguard's? To use it to whore your way through the army!"

I stumbled behind him, heart in my throat, letting him pull me until we were out of sight. In the shadows of the alley, he dropped my arm and whirled on me, only to have his face meet my fist.

He gave a sharp cry and fell back against the wall, clutching his bleeding nose.

"I should kill you," I growled, grabbing a handful of his hair. I pulled it tight, wrenching his head back. He tried to shove me away, so I slammed his head back against the brick wall, dazing him. "I don't even care what they'd do to me. I should shoot you where you stand."

The tremble in my voice betrayed me. Gave Declan enough courage to sneer. "You don't have the guts," he spat. "Playing soldier? What the hell are you thinking? Do you realize what they'll do to you if you're—"

"I'm only going to say this once." I leaned in close, feeling every bit of fire and tears that I've shoved down deep inside me over the past year rise up, and relished the idea of finally letting them free. "You'll leave me alone, you won't say a word, or it won't be me that does you in. You got Abigail killed. Jack won't ever forget that."

Declan's sneer faltered, and I saw real fear flash in his eyes. But his mask of contempt fell again just as quick. "I'm no more responsible for her death than you are," he said coldly. "You were the one that couldn't keep your mouth shut."

My hands started to shake. "You say another—"

But he'd won, and he knew it. He struck out and shoved me away, growling as he wrenched his hair free. I stumbled back, ready to lunge at him again when he held up his hands in surrender.

"I don't care to fight you. I don't care that you're here, and I don't care why. I just want you to stay out of my way."

I scoffed. "Sure, and you won't be running straight to the captain, telling him who I am?"

Declan tilted his head. "I could've brought him with me, couldn't I?"

"Why didn't you?"

"And get myself caught up in your scheme? I'm not an idiot."

"Could've fooled me."

"Save your petty insults," he growled. "And go. You're dead to me. I hope there's a rebel bullet waiting for you."

"Because you're too much of a coward to put one in me yourself, aren't you?"

I didn't see his fist coming, but I did see a flash of white as his knuckles cracked against my face. I dropped to the alley floor, skull throbbing.

Declan loomed over me. "You're going to dress like a man, you should take a punch like one. Now get up." He kicked at me. I scrambled to my feet and tried to bolt but he grabbed me by my collar and yanked me close.

"One last thing," he hissed, spit stinging the welt on my cheek. "You screw this up, and it won't just be your hide that gets it. I'll go after them too, Saoirse. And I'll start with that little doe-eyed sheriff's boy. And you'll get to watch him suffer, do you understand me?"

I could hardly breathe, and nodding made everything go dim. I gasped what I'd hoped was a *yes*.

He dropped me, and I almost fell to the ground again. I tripped away from him, but he stayed behind, in the shadows, just watching me run.

March 10, 1862

My face was a swollen mess in the morning. I rolled over on my back and touched my cheek with a hiss. It felt twice the size it should've been. I'd be lucky if I didn't get punished for fighting. Maybe I could tell them I tripped and ran into a brick wall. Certainly felt that way.

I sat up groggily. It was still dark out, the faintest blue light filtering through the tent. I always tried to wake before everyone else so I could take care of personal business privately.

Jack snored loudly. His back was to me, so I slipped out of my shirt to adjust the strips of cloth wrapped around my breasts. Not that I needed to hold down much, but I didn't want to take any chances.

My stiff fingers stung when I bent them, and I inspected my scabbing knuckles. Damn Declan's nose.

I shivered, clutching my bare arms against my chest to keep my heart from bursting out, and tried to breathe. Declan was here. It wasn't a nightmare. Well, 'twas certainly that, but not the kind I could wake up from.

I gulped down air, recalling Allison's words from when I'd stumbled back into camp a blubbering mess last night. I didn't tell them everything. There wasn't much point. But they saw my face clear enough, and I relayed his threat.

Allison was unfazed. "You're still here, Saoirse. He's right, he could've brought Olsen with him."

And he still could...

Westleigh voiced the same concern. "Can we trust him to keep his word?"

"Trust him?" Jack spat into the fire. "That snake?"

"I trust him to be a coward," I said.

Allison nodded. "Exactly. That's all that matters, isn't it? He won't say a word so long as he thinks it'll get him skinned too, right?"

"So you're safe?" Westleigh asked.

"Nobody's safe," Jack reminded us sharply. "We're in the middle of a damn war."

One against two sides now, I thought now with bile rising in my throat. I pulled my shirt back over my head and rubbed my eyes. I'd hardly slept last night, and for the few moments I did, all I could see was Declan shooting me in the back the moment we got into battle.

I crawled out of the tent, Jack still snoring away. I left my coat on the tent peg and my suspenders dangling at my sides as I stumbled towards the latrines. A few men wandered the edges of camp, sentries just come off duty. None of them looked twice at me as I skulked away to do my business.

Thankfully, I found the privacy I desired, did what I came to do, and headed back to my tent about the time I heard the bugle call Reveille.

Jack groaned from inside the tent, and I pulled back the flap to let in a bit of light. "Good morning, sunshine."

He scowled. "You know the rules."

"Ah, right. No speaking before coffee."

He grumbled something I decided was *thanks*, and I finished dressing. Tucked in my shirt, pulled on my coat, and started weighing myself down with my accoutrements. By now I'd gotten used to them, the heaviness of the belt, the sling around my chest, the smack of the bayonet scabbard against my thigh and the cartridge box at my hip. Didn't have to wear my knapsack this morning though, and that was a blessing.

I was dressed and ready for the day before Allison or Westleigh dragged themselves from their tent, Allison stretching himself like a cat in the sunlight. Halfway into an obnoxiously loud yawn, he caught sight of me.

"Whoa! Look at your face!"

"Looks better than your mug on any day," I retorted.

He only laughed, lazily pulling up his suspenders. Westleigh adjusted his spectacles, squinting at me. "Do you think it needs seen to? The cut?"

"Yeah," Allison leaned into my face. I could smell his morning breath. "He clocked you good."

I shoved him away. "I'm grand, thanks. Get your coats on already, I'm starving." I turned around and yanked Jack's coat off the tent peg and threw it at his chest. "Up. Coffee. Move your arse."

I heard shuffling and muttering. He was up, at least.

Soon the four of us were sitting around our fire with breakfast—some mash of our rations that was made just a bit more bearable with the apples Lucy sent with Westleigh the day before. Westleigh was frowning into that stout tar that Jack called coffee, and Allison had his face buried in the paper. Occasionally he'd shake his head or mutter his opinions about whatever news he was gleaning. Now and again he'd start reading the headlines aloud, or, heaven forbid, the contents of the article. Jack glared at him when this happened, but Allison never took notice, too engrossed he was in his paper.

"It's too early for any of that, Al," Westleigh said this morning, trying to spare us.

"Can you believe this?" Allison said, hardly listening, and went back to muttering at his paper. "Buncha cowards, that's what they are…"

Jack rolled his eyes. "It's the *Herald*. What else d'ya expect from that rebel-lovin', copperhead rag?"

"It's all I could get my hands on yesterday," Allison said. "Still…"

Thankfully, the call for drills spared us any more political talk. 'Twasn't that we didn't care… but I didn't want my head full of any of that mess so early in the morning. I needed the quiet. Just for a few minutes, at least.

We fell in line and drilled away half the morning, marched away the other half. In between, rumors passed up and down the ranks, as they always did, about when the army might actually move. Fellows fought over who had the better source, but they were always wrong. Seemed this army was set to remain in Washington. Maybe the rebels would get so bored, they'd give up. One could only hope.

I only got one funny look about my face, from our squad's sergeant. He seemed keen on saying something, but I flashed him a sheepish smile, threw in a shrug for good measure, and he simply shook his head. Less trouble for me, less trouble for him, I figure.

Until our captain showed up.

I felt my throat close up when I saw him, my slimy brother on his heels. He hardly favored his foot, and I muttered my disappointment that the horse hadn't stepped on his face.

Jack elbowed me in the side. I was going to have an eternal bruise there by the time this war was over.

Captain Marcus Oliver, as he called himself now. Looking almost gallant in that blue uniform. You'd hardly know him for the slave-catching monster he really was. His chin was raised as he inspected the company, a handsome smile on his face while he addressed the men. Blood pounding in my ears muffled his words. Couldn't hear a thing till Jack leaned over just so to whisper a single word.

"Steady."

A nervous laugh burst past my lips and the captain's eyes found mine.

Bullocks.

The company was dismissed shortly after, and I felt Jack's hand at my back pushing, urging the four of us to get lost in the sea of blue uniforms before the captain noticed.

Too late.

"Private Kavanagh," Olsen called out behind us.

Westleigh and I slowly turned, while Allison and Jack flanked us, pressing our shoulders in together as we froze for another inspection. I forced myself to breathe, to ignore the sweat that soaked my shirt under the stifling wool uniform, as Olsen sauntered over, his brow creased as he studied my face.

He paused in front of me, and his lips curled into a smirk. "Two Kavanaghs? You certainly do look like that half-witted sheriff. What's the relation?"

I pried my tongue loose to answer, but I found myself mute. What if he could hear my secret in my voice?

Westleigh answered quickly next to me. "Aidan is my cousin, sir."

"Hmm," Olsen said, still smirking. "And about as intelligent as his uncle, seems like."

My face burned. I thanked the Lord for my dry mouth, or I probably couldn't have kept myself from spitting in the man's face. But I would defend my father. "Thank you, sir," I scratched out.

Olsen snorted, and inspected the rest of our small line. When Allison saluted him, he only glared. When he came to Jack, a wicked grin spread across his face.

"Well, look at you. Hadn't seen you since you were a

scrawny little savage running 'round your pa's farm. Surprised they'd even let one of you enlist in the army."

I could almost hear Jack's teeth cracking.

But how did Olsen know him so well?

The captain shook his head. "Shame what happened to that girl of yours. She really was sweet on the eyes."

I felt Jack tense next to me. Oh, no…

Olsen came closer, stopping at Jack's toes, leaning into his face. Jack stared through his skull.

"Maybe if you'd just minded yourself," Olsen growled, "you'd still be down there with her, wouldn't ya? But you had to stick your nose where it didn't belong."

I grabbed for Jack's hand before I could think, but he slapped it away. His voice rumbled in his chest. "Yes, sir."

Olsen leaned back, sneering now. He held Jack's stare for a horribly long moment, and finally backed away. He wouldn't get the fight he was looking for. Jack was too strong for that.

"Am I gonna have any trouble out of you radicals?" he barked at the four of us now, loud enough to turn a few heads wandering by. "The stunts you pulled before won't be tolerated in this army. This isn't about your sanctimonious crusade. You're here to follow orders. To put down a rebellion and restore the Union. Nothing more. That understood?"

Only Allison was able to manage a convincing *Yes, sir.* But it was enough for Olsen to see the fury in our faces.

There was the tiniest glint in his eyes after he waved us off, and I felt his eyes on me as we marched briskly away.

I almost collapsed when we returned to our tents. Sat down hard on a crate and buried my face in my hands.

"I'm going to visit the sutlers' tents," I heard Westleigh say softly above us. "Does anyone need anything?"

Nobody answered him. He finally shuffled away. A few moments later, Allison announced he was going to check after his brother, and left us too.

Jack sat across from me. I raised my head to watch him as he poured himself another coffee. A tear dripped off his chin.

"Jack…"

"He worked for Reeves," Jack said huskily. "Overseer. Long time ago. Till they got cross-ways and Marek took off with half of Mrs. Reeves' jewelry. Least that was the rumor."

Jack paused to take a drink. Then he stared into his tin cup, gripping it till I thought he'd burn the skin off his fingers. "He's the bastard that sold Abigail and her family to Reeves in the first place."

Felt as if a knife twisted in my chest. "Oh, Jack… why didn't you tell me?"

He shrugged. "For what purpose?"

"So you didn't have to carry this alone, for starters." I narrowed my eyes. "So that's why Declan sought him out, when he was chasing us down. Reeves must've sent him."

"Maybe."

"But that doesn't make sense." I scratched my head. "If Olsen and Reeves went cross-ways, then why'd they be working together at all? Oh! Back in the barn that night, Olsen mentioned a debt Reeves owed him—what do you figure it was for?"

"Nuh-uh, you stop right there," Jack said, kicking my foot. "Don't go using your head to get us into trouble again. Just let it go, would ya?"

"It doesn't bother you? Why they're here, in the army of all things? What Declan's doing following him around like a kicked dog—"

"Only things bothering me right now are bad rations, bad coffee, and this conversation." Jack stood and dusted off his britches. "I need to take a walk. You should too. In the other direction. Go check on Westleigh, before that fool buys anymore books."

I tried to protest, but Jack was already shuffling away, hands shoved in his trouser pockets. I picked myself up with a sigh. I'd rather do what he said than get caught alone at our tents by Declan or the captain.

I headed off toward Sutlers Row, where a fair number of civilians parked their wagons, pitched their tents, and sold wares to the soldiers (sometimes for outrageous prices). Thankfully Lucy took good care of us, with socks and fruit and the occasional sweet treat, so we didn't have to visit the sutlers much. But I did owe Allison a new sewing kit, after breaking his needle trying to fix my brogans. The blasted things were already coming apart. Cheap, shoddy work, our shoes were.

I caught Westleigh just as he was leaving a tent with a small armful of books and laughed. "You know you'll have to carry all of those wherever we go, don't you?"

Westleigh glanced down, shrugging. "I'll sort that out when we finally *go* anywhere. If we ever do."

"Well, you may have a point, there," I said, craning my neck to read the titles. "What do you have, anyhow?"

"Eh," Westleigh shuffled the books around, almost dropping them. "Some George Eliot, a Gaskell... and oh — Wilkie Collins, *A Woman in White,* have you read it?"

I snatched the book on top that he nudged toward me and thumbed through the pages.

Westleigh smiled. "It's a detective story."

"I might have to take this one off your hands," I said, flipping through. "If only to lighten your load."

Westleigh laughed. "Well, I might have to start a regimental library." He shifted the books again. "Do you — um, do you figure Declan might find any of them of interest? I remember how much you said he liked to read, and —"

I glowered at him. "Are you serious, now?"

Westleigh shrugged. "Well, I —"

"Save yourself the heartache, Wes," I moaned. I had a fleeting memory of a stupid girl trying to win her brother over with a book once, too. A lifetime ago. One that ended in flames. "Just leave him be. You know he had some less than flattering things to say about yourself, he did."

Westleigh looked away. "All the same," he said quietly. "I thought a gesture might…"

"Only antagonize him further," I snapped. "And sure, that's the last thing we need right now, wouldn't you think?"

Westleigh's shoulders sank. "You're probably right."

"Jack said our captain and Reeves have a history, did you know that?"

"Well, I think he mentioned something about that when—"

I rolled my eyes. Of course Westleigh knew before I did. "Never mind. Jack says we need to keep our heads down. Means I can't ask what in blazes Declan and that monster are even doing in the army, and you can't try and make friends with my weasel brother. Clear, now?"

"Crystal," Westleigh muttered. "This is going to be a disaster, isn't it?"

I scowled and tossed the book back up on his teetering stack before stomping away. "Guess you should've stayed at home then."

March 12, 1862

Dearest Allison,

My heart breaks to give you this news. Your brother Jonas passed last night, and Tom and Robert have come down ill, too. Their sickness has struck them quickly, and I fear they will soon follow Jonas to Heaven. I sit by their sides as often as I am able, lend them what comfort I can. They ask of you often. Jonas wanted me to tell you how much he wished he had been a better brother to you. He even said to tell Westleigh he wished him well. Oh, how the truth of our own mortality can soften the hardest of hearts. If only we could learn this grace before Death stands in our doorway. I gave him your love, and he was at peace in the end. I will write to your parents for you. I know you are busy with preparations to leave Washington with our army. May God give our boys a swift victory.

Know for now that you have my full heart, and that I pray for you constantly.

I love you, you brave, silly man. Come home soon.

Yours,
Ellen Moore

12

WESTLEIGH
Alexandria, VA
March 17, 1862

We topped the hill overlooking the town, and the sight at my feet took my breath away. Columns of soldiers snaking through the streets, throngs of men moving in one big blue mass towards the boats that sat waiting in the Potomac. Meanwhile, Alexandria's citizens milled about. Older ladies cast wary glances at us, while the younger girls blushed and waved. Didn't matter to the girls that we were the enemy occupying their town, and it sure didn't matter to the Union boys that they were rebel girls. Didn't stop any of the flirting.

Saoirse rolled her eyes. "Shameless," she muttered to me. A young girl, no older than twelve, waved her handkerchief toward Saoirse with a giggle as we passed her by in the street. Saoirse's jaw dropped. "Was that for me?"

Allison snickered.

Saoirse leaned out of the line to call snap back at the girl. "Does your mam know you're out here? Go on, away with you now!"

The rebel girls scattered, giggling as they ran.

We stopped in the middle of town, waiting for what felt like ages. Always waiting. The rest of the folk went about their business, trying their best to ignore us as they passed by. The tension in the air made my skin prick.

"Look at that steamer," Allison remarked, nodding towards the river. Through the alley, we could see one of the boats, covered in colorful flags that fluttered in the strong spring breeze. "The way it's all gussied up, you'd think we were going on a nice cruise down the river, not to war."

Jack shifted, grimacing. "Thought I signed up for the army, not the navy…"

"I heard they're shipping us down to Fort Monroe," Saoirse offered.

I nodded. Seems we finally got passed a rumor that was worth something. "But don't you figure they ought've kept this all a secret?"

Saoirse laughed. "And how d'you suppose they keep moving the entire army and all its supplies on this many boats a secret?"

"Yup." Jack swayed beside me. "This seems like a great idea."

I studied his face. "What's the matter, Jack? You look a little green."

"Never been on the water before…"

Allison tittered beside me. "You know what, you three are

like the beginning of a joke! 'An Indian, a pacifist, and an Irishwom—'"

Saoirse hit him hard. "Shut *up*, Allison."

We pitched our tents that evening on the edge of town, likely to strike them again in the morning, to load up on the boats. I feared I would hardly be able to sleep with all the noise and excitement moving through town.

I felt a pang of sympathy for the poor folk who lived there—even if they were rebels. The noise and the chaos of an enemy army teeming their streets, wagons filling the alleyways, the smell of the livestock (and to be fair, some of the men as well) had to have been maddening. I kept such thoughts to myself, though. Saoirse looked about ready to spit on every one of them, and I don't think Jack would have stopped her. The pair of them were in such a foul mood by the time we finally got our tents situated that I felt it best to wander the streets with Allison.

He'd been out of sorts since the news of his brother's death. Almost quiet at times. I was so used to his mirth and his carelessness, I wasn't sure quite what to say to him now. If it were me in mourning, Allison would try to distract me out of my grief. But I didn't have his humor. And so I stood silently beside him as we watched the boats in the river.

After a time, Allison sighed. "Damn Jonas."

I frowned, watching his face. "What's the matter?"

The corner of his mouth twisted in an attempt at a smirk. "He and I always fought over who'd have work with Pa, take over the family business. Neither of us wanted it. Guess he won. Least Ellen will be happy…"

I nodded, shrugging. "Robert and Tom never had a claim to it?"

Allison laughed. "Believe it or not, Pa trusts them less than he does me. Besides, Robert's apprenticing Uncle Jake, and Tom was supposed to start working in Uncle Christopher's office. Well, I guess none of that's going to happen now…"

"Al," I said softly. "I'm so sorry about your brothers. If you need—"

Allison nudged me with his elbow, smiling sadly now. "Ah, you've been more than a brother to me than they ever were. But thanks. Family is family, I guess." Then he squinted, looking over my head. "Speaking of family…"

I turned to see Saoirse's brother walking towards us, hunched forward with his hands shoved deep in his pockets, eyes cast down.

"Declan!"

He stopped short in the street, and I waved as he looked up. His expression turned from confusion to irritation, and he altered his course to avoid us.

I started to move after him, when Allison caught my sleeve.

"What are you doing?"

"I was going to introduce myself."

Allison's brow rose. "You've met, remember? He shoved a gun in your face. Pretty sure he clubbed you with it too. Must've knocked your memory loose."

"Well, a proper introduction this time, I meant." I shrugged. "Family is family, like you said. He's my cousin. I just figured, if I made an effort to be kind—"

"Not that one, Wes," Allison muttered, holding my elbow till Declan disappeared into the crowd again. "Jonas was a bully. Declan is something else entirely."

Mail came that evening after dinner. Allison had the most, letters from his mother, another from Ellen, and a few of his uncles. Lucy wrote to Saoirse and me, and even penned a few words of greeting for Jack. Peter wrote me as well, as he did on occasion, catching me up on events at home, or giving me a word from scripture for encouragement. Once he sent me a small prayer book, and I kept that in my breast pocket always.

But there was still no letter from my da. Lucy's letter didn't indicate she'd heard from him, either.

"I worry about him," Saoirse said, pausing in her reply to Lucy. I let her respond for the two of us—her handwriting was neater than my own. "Does Peter mention him?"

"Not at all," I said, squinting at my preacher's latest letter. "Now that you mention it, that's—"

"Curious," she finished. She bit her lip. "Perhaps you should ask him, pointedly. It's odd he makes no mention…"

"Do you think something's wrong?"

"I don't think David is in Dove Hollow right now," Jack said from behind his newspaper. He lowered it. "And I don't think he's told anyone where he's gone."

My hand clenched around my pencil. "Not even Lucy?"

Saoirse gave a small smile. "I'm certain he's fine. He's probably off with Eoghan? Maybe they're not able to get a letter out, wherever they are. Could he be back at sea?"

I shook my head. "I—I don't have a single clue. He's not left Dove Hollow since I was born..." His silence worried me more than I cared to admit. If he was all right, why hadn't we gotten word? Why hadn't Lucy?

"Hey Wes," Allison blurted. "How do you spell matrimony?"

"Hmm?" I glanced up from my letter writing, only half-hearing his question. "Oh, m-a-t-r-i-m-o-n-y."

Saoirse's jaw dropped. "Are you writing to Ellen?"

Allison grinned crookedly. "Maybe."

"Wait," I set aside my writing and leaned forward. "Ellen? Matrimony? Are you asking her—"

Even Jack looked up.

Allison's face was red—I don't really recall ever seeing him blush—and he gave a self-conscious shrug. "Well, I mean I'm not making anything official or whatever—I want to do that proper, you know—but I figured it was time to, well, bring up the subject."

"Past time," Jack muttered. "You've been making that poor girl wait far too long."

I rolled my eyes. "You have no idea…"

"Well, she'll have to wait a bit longer, won't she?" Saoirse said curtly. We all looked at her, and I was startled to see tears shining in her eyes. "We're at war, Allison. You—any of us—might not even make it home. Why write to her now? So she'll worry even more for you? Why torment her so?"

I flinched, thinking of Allison's brothers. "Aidan—"

Saoirse's face went white. "Oh. I'm sorry Al…"

"No, you're right." Allison's pencil wavered. "I hadn't really thought about that."

"That girl is already worrying," Jack said softly, stirring the coffee pot. "Nothing you can do about that. Least this way she's got something more to hope for."

"Is that really better?" Saoirse whispered. "Getting her hopes up?"

"Hope is always better," Jack said firmly. "Doesn't matter how hard it hurts when it's broken. Better than living without it at all."

I heard the strain in his voice, felt the pain in his words as if they'd come from my own heart. Nobody spoke for a while, until Allison's smile finally returned.

"Too bad she didn't come with us," he whispered, with a pointed nod at Saoirse. "The two of you could lick the entire rebel army together and have us home by summer."

Saoirse scoffed. "If women ran this *country* we certainly

wouldn't have us all squabbling about in the mud like children, that's for certain."

"Two of you keep your voices down, why don't you?" Jack muttered. "Coffee's ready, so shut up and drink up."

Saoirse and I held out our tins, and Jack passed another to Allison. I looked down at the dark, stout liquid, and grimaced again at the smell of it. But Lucy said it was for our health, so I forced myself to drink.

Allison suddenly sputtered across from me, cussing incoherently. "What in the—"

We all looked up to see him staring at his coffee as if it'd caused some unimaginable offense. He took another sip, and his face contorted comically. Then he started to gag. "Oh! Oh what is—"

He ran off, making horrible noises as he retched on the other side of the tent.

I heard a soft chuckle and saw a hint of a smile on Jack's face before it disappeared behind his cup.

Saoirse folded her arms. "Jack, what did you do?"

Jack's brow rose. "I don't know what you're talking about."

I grinned. There was nothing Allison liked better than a practical joke, even at his own expense.

He was laughing and spitting furiously behind us. "Oh my word, I'm never getting that taste out of my mouth…"

"Jack!" Saoirse chided.

Jack slowly sipped his coffee and went back to his paper.

13

SAOIRSE
Virginia
5 April, 1862

Not even half past 8 in the morning and I was soaked to the bone, and ready to shoot the first rebel I saw. I cursed their wretched hides. Cursed the generals that marched us up this wretched peninsula. Cursed the wretched rain. And the mud—caked all the way up my trousers to my knees, making me feel like my legs were made of lead. I don't even know if what we were marching along qualified as a road anymore. And when we happened upon fallen trees blocking what little road we had, I let loose such a string of blasphemies that Jack just stared at me, wide-eyed. Only he knew what I was saying, though I saw Westleigh flinch. I forgot that he'd learned a bit of Irish, too.

But the absolute worst was the raging monster knocking about inside my head, pounding so hard I had moments where my vision darkened at the edges. I wanted to run out of our little line, find a tree to huddle against, and nap there till the war was over. But we stopped, worked at clearing the road so the artillery and supplies could go through, and by the time we were finished I *really* wanted a nap. But we pressed on.

All while we marched, we heard little ripples of musket-fire in the distance that made us clutch our rifles tighter. We'd yet to come upon the enemy, but we knew he wasn't far. Some of the other brigades were seeing action as we trudged up the peninsula.

On towards Richmond! the commanders urged us. Why we hadn't marched straight south from Washington City to meet the rebels head-on was of much debate among us lowly soldiers, but it didn't matter. General McClellan had turned our rag-tag selves into a right decent military machine. The man had to have some wits about him to do so, I supposed, so his cunning was no less impressive. And so we marched up the peninsula in our columns, despite the miserable rain, on towards Richmond.

"War will be over in a month," Allison declared solidly that afternoon. I could hear a bit of forced cheerfulness in his voice. 'Twas the most he'd said since he got the letter about Jonas and his brothers. But he smiled all the same. "Guarantee you. We'll sweep right up to Richmond, send all those rebels back to their mamas, crying. I betcha one month from now you'll all be home in Dove Hollow watching me and Ellen get married."

'Twas a wonderful thought, even if it seemed too easy. But despite the weather, our spirits were high, so we didn't contradict him.

"One month from now," Westleigh added, "maybe I'll be going back to school, finish my education."

"How about you, Aidan?" Allison asked behind me. "What are you going to be doing when this is over?"

"Sleep," I said, rubbing my temples. "Sleep the summer away."

Westleigh nudged me with his elbow. "You feeling all right?"

"No," I snapped, and felt sorry for it almost immediately. "Thanks. I'll be fine."

He wasn't convinced, but he mercifully left me be, too busy trying to wipe the rain from his spectacles, only to get them wet again. Finally he took them off and shoved them in his haversack. I wondered how well he could see without them. Then he tripped over a branch and Jack nearly trampled right over him. He yanked Westleigh to his feet and kept a hand on his shoulder for the rest of the march to guide him, just in case.

Every now and again, I could hear the ripping sound of a bullet cutting through air and leaves over our heads— stray shots from skirmishes nearby. I flinched at every one, and hated myself for it. If I was already so jumpy, what would battle be like? Would I stand and fight, or run? Or worse—would I be a terrible soldier, discovered as a woman, and prove to them all I was as weak and helpless as they saw my sex to be?

A humming sound broke into my morbid thoughts. Jack was singing to himself in that low, deep voice of his that made my heart buzz in my chest. I smiled, even though I couldn't understand his mother's language. His singing always had a way of soothing my spirit.

Thunder clapped overhead and he got a little louder. Loud enough for someone to shout at him from behind us. His ugly words mocked Jack's song, his mother's people, and made Jack's face burn. I wanted to turn and shout back at the brute, but as I glanced over my shoulder, Jack gave a shake of his head. I stayed silent.

Allison cleared his throat behind me and took a big breath before squawking "Old John's body lies a mouldrin' in the grave—!"

The rest of us groaned, wanting to cover our ears, if it weren't for the muskets we were carrying. Still, just about the whole line joined in, with Allison screeching like he thought his voice alone could send the rebs running.

"They will hang ol' Jeff Davis from a sour apple tree…"

After a full day of marching, with our clothes soaked through, our feet covered in blisters, we were given orders to make camp. Thunder—or it might have been cannon fire—still boomed in the distance. But thank the good Lord in Heaven, the rain stopped. In no time, Jack and the others had our tents propped up, but nothing could be found to place beneath our gum blankets for bedding. It would be a difficult night's sleep on the ground. Not that I counted on much sleeping. My bones were jumpy with the thought of impending battle. I could hardly eat dinner that night, either.

The boys were talking low around the campfire as I gripped my head and moaned. Everything was swaying. I wanted to lie down, but the ground would offer no comfort for me.

I heard the murmurs of their conversation suddenly stop.

"Aidan?" Jack's voice broke my thoughts. "You don't look so good."

"My head," I mumbled into my folded arms, resting up on my knees. "It's agonizing. Just… shush…"

I heard shuffling and a frustrated grunt, and suddenly my canteen landed at my feet.

"Why is that thing almost full?" Jack barked. "You haven't been drinking on the march again, have you?"

I glared up at him.

Jack had his fists at his hips. "Well?"

Allison and Westleigh looked back and forth between us.

I felt my face color. "I told you why." I picked up the canteen and drank from it greedily now, almost weeping as I quenched my thirst.

"You're gonna make yourself sick," Jack snapped. "Is that what you want?"

"What do you expect me to do?" I wiped my mouth. "'Tisn't as easy for me to—you *know*—" I stammered.

Allison stifled a giggle, finally understanding.

My face burned. 'Twasn't anything for those boys to answer the call of nature on the march. Myself, on the other hand...

Jack just stared at me with his *'well I reckon you should've thought about that'* look. I'd lost count how many times he'd used it.

"Nobody's gonna go watch you relieve yourself," he said.

Allison burst into laughter.

Westleigh smacked him.

Jack sighed. "You do what you gotta do. But you're gonna drink that water. Understood?"

"Yes *mother*," I muttered into the canteen. Already I could feel my head getting clearer.

Jack sat down and we ate the rest of our meal in silence. By the time it was over, I nearly tripped getting out of the camp to find a quiet spot in the woods to take care of my business. And at that moment, I didn't much care if McClellan himself caught me with my trousers down.

I took my time in the woods, resting against the tree when I finished. I listened to the sounds of the army, and the cannons in the distance. They'd almost grown quiet, but for the boom of the guns on the ships in the river. Occasionally we'd hear a shell strike close by, but we were just out of range. For now.

When I'd stayed away long enough to almost send Jack into a tizzy, I decided to head back to our tents, only to hear a commotion before I even came to the clearing. Men were shouting and scuffling, and when I came upon our campfire, I saw a tangle of half-dressed soldiers pushing and shoving.

A large, scruffy-faced man from Pittsburgh—Schmidt was his name—was leaning in Jack's face, spittle on his lips as he shouted at him. Two of his buddies, the Glenn brothers, held his arms back. Jack stood still, one hand on Westleigh's shoulder, as if holding him back. The other was clenched in a fist at his side. He said nothing to the snarling private.

Allison shouted back from a safe distance. "Get on out of here you gap-toothed buffoon," he said through laughter. No wonder he stood so far back. "Nobody asked your opinion."

"I'm telling you he don't belong here," Schmidt snarled, yanking his arms free from his friends. He shoved a finger in Westleigh's face. "You either! No injuns, no abolitionists. Can't trust the lot of ya."

At this, Jack only laughed, which made the private lunge at him again, cursing wildly.

I ran over to Allison and spoke in his ear. "What happened?"

"Well, a Negro woman came through camp, looking for work as a washerwoman I think. Got harassed by Smitty here, and Westleigh stuck up for her—blessed little idiot—and the rest doesn't need much explaining…"

Schmidt took a swing at Jack and slipped, landing face-first in the mud.

Allison cackled, slapping his knees.

"Shut your trap or we'll shut if for you, runt."

"Listen, fellas," I said, stifling a laugh as the private picked himself out of the mud. "We're all fighting on the same side, here…"

"I'm fighting for my country," the younger Glenn snapped. "Not for any damned abolitionists in Washington or their negroes—"

"We're fighting for freedom!" Allison surprised me with the sudden anger in his voice. "The foundation of this Union and all it stands for. You saying that's not why you're fighting?"

The other boy rolled his eyes. "Pretty words, but we all know when it comes down to it, you'd sell out your own countrymen for black freedom. You and all those radicals, you're traitors to your own race."

"Better than a fella who'd rather kiss a slaveholder's ass just to end the war and get back to his mama." Jack finally spoke. "Like some coward."

I winced. Oh, Jack…

Schmidt came at him, screaming, when he got clocked in

the head by the butt of a rifle. We all froze, and our sergeant was standing there, looking more than peeved, but he spoke in a low, dry voice.

"Don't think I need to remind you boys what the army says about fighting," he said. "Get up out of the mud, private, and get back to your tent. Save that hot-blooded rage for the real enemy. Go on."

Schmidt and the Glenn boys glared at us. Allison waved with a smirk when the sergeant had his back turned. But the officer pushed them away before Schmidt could say anything else.

Kennedy whirled on Jack next, finger in his face. "Am I going to have to keep my eye on you, Private Callahan?"

"No sir," Jack replied simply. He offered no explanation, no protest of innocence. But Westleigh wasn't so quiet.

"Sergeant, sir, you didn't see what they—"

But the sergeant cut him off, still staring down Jack. "We got enough to deal with, don't need any Indian trouble on top of things. So I hear just one whiff of it from you, boy, I won't shed a tear when we send your hide home."

The muscles in Jack's jaw tightened.

"Yes, sir," he said.

The sergeant shook his head and stomped away, muttering under his breath.

Westleigh was shaking. "Those vile, despicable—"

Jack gave him a small push to sit down. "Calm down, little one."

Westleigh's eyes were wide as he looked up at him. "But Jack, what they said about your mother —"

"You think that's the first time I heard any of that puke?" Jack grumbled. Allison and I took our seats with him, and Jack rubbed his eyes with a groan. "Won't be the last time either."

Westleigh looked stricken. He seemed to wrestle with a question on his tongue for a few minutes before drawing it out painfully. "What happened to them, Jack? Your mama? Her people?"

I stared at my toes. I'd heard this story before, and it still made my heart weep.

"Well," Jack said, scratching his head. "My mama died when I was a boy. Nothing much to say there. She was here one night and gone the next. Her and my baby sister. A fever, Pa said."

Tears stung my eyes.

"Now, her people..." Jack poked at the fire. "From what Pa told me, the government came in, forced them out of their homes in Georgia at gunpoint when she was a baby. They settled in Texas after that. Then, not long after she married my pa, her family was killed in some bloody mess outside Tyler. Those that survived, the Texans forced into Indian Territory 'cross the river, north. I was born about a year later. She never saw them again. Never talked about 'em much, either."

Westleigh was quiet.

Allison shifted on his crate, frowning. "Jack," he said softly. "How can you even fight for this country? After what they've done."

Jack scratched his head again, chuckled dryly. "It's a complicated thing, ain't it? I kinda got a foot in two worlds, you know? My pa came here because his homeland was starving and sick. He found all that freedom and opportunity you say you're fighting for. That's all well and good, 'cept that my mama's people had to get run off to make room for that dream." Jack sighed heavily, so many years of heartache heavy in his bones.

"So, how can I fight?" He shrugged. "Can't do much about what's already happened, can I? I can only do what's to be done now. I reckon, just by being here, I keep on reminding them all. That this dream of liberty's not just for the free men, or white folk. It's for every single complicated one of us."

That night, lying on that gum blanket, thankful for the clean dry socks Lucy made snuggling my feet, I listened to Jack breathe and wondered at my reasons for fighting. Sure, I believed in every bit what Allison said, what Jack enlisted for. And every time I closed my eyes, I thought of Abigail, and Jimmy, and all those men and women the generals now called *contraband* as they fled in droves to the freedom they thought lay within our camps.

But this nagging voice that sounded a little too much like Declan told me all I cared about was myself. My guilt.

My aching desire to prove myself. And that at the first sign of real battle, I'd flee. Like the trembling child I was.

"What the devil am I doing here?" I breathed into the night, burying my face in my arms as I tried desperately to sleep.

I heard Jack shuffle on his blanket, and he turned to face me. "Don't you know every man in this army is asking themselves the same thing? Don't think so hard, you'll drive yourself crazy. And don't doubt yourself, little sis," he said in a gentle whisper. "I believe in you."

from the journal of Allison Robert Horner

April 6, 1862 — *We're outside Yorktown now, getting ready to lay siege. Confederates are across the river, pickets can hear their songs at night. The army celebrated Westleigh's birthday today by sending up big observation balloons. Of course the reports were more men and more cannons across the river, so Wes didn't appreciate that much. Told him it was the thought that counted, right?*

*Fair Oaks, Va. Prof. Thaddeus S. Lowe observing
the battle from his balloon "Intrepid"*

14

WESTLEIGH
Yorktown, Virginia
April 8, 1862

Whenever I'd pictured war, long before I ever donned a uniform, I never quite imagined the image before me. Men scurrying about in the dark, moving logs and rails, digging, and occasionally ducking as a shell burst overhead. We moved like ants, frantically trying to build a hill. Or in this case, rifle pits.

"Get down!" Sergeant Kennedy shouted.

Allison and I dropped the log we were carrying and crouched down low as a shell roared overhead and splintered a tree some yards away.

Allison whistled. "Well, that saves us cutting down another tree, right?"

"Get up, get moving," Kennedy urged us. "C'mon boys!"

My fingers dug into the mud to lift the heavy timber. Allison struggled with his end, but we both managed to lift it and half-run to the fortification we were constructing. Ahead of us was the river, and beyond that, Mulberry Island, where the Confederates were entrenched and shadows moved in front of their fires like ghosts.

Between us, sitting in the river, were the gunboats that shot at us.

Another shell burst ahead, sending a shower of splinters into the air as it destroyed one of the pits we'd just finished building.

"Hang those rebels," an officer shouted from his horse. "And hang the general—where are those guns? We could take that island—"

Another firing overhead silenced him, and he went riding off, cursing.

"Keep going, boys," Kennedy said, shaking my shoulder. "You're doing fine, keep going."

We dragged ourselves back to the pile of lumber and passed Saoirse and Jack on the way. In moonlight, I could see the steely look of blue fire in her eyes. She strained with the weight of the rail she helped Jack carry, but she did not waver. Mud caked her hands and her face, dark fringes of her hair were plastered to her forehead with rain and sweat... but her image struck me, and my heart skipped a beat. It reminded me of the night we met—when she stumbled into that Fort Worth hotel room, ragged with exhaustion but lit from a roaring fire within.

"Westleigh," Allison grunted. "Kinda hard to lift this thing on my own…"

I snapped back, doing my best to ignore the splinters in my fingers as I helped Allison with another rail.

We continued to work like this through the night, constructing the fortifications that our sharpshooters would use later. It was hours before we had any rest, but no sleep still.

My arms burned as I leaned against a tree, gulping down the contents of my canteen. My entire body felt like I'd been crushed beneath the weight of every log we carried.

The rest of our company were scattered about in the woods, taking cover from the rebel gunboats, too tired to think about the fact that their shells could still take apart our cover—and us with it. All that mattered in the moment was breathing. And water.

Saoirse rested on the ground next to me, her eyes closed as she leaned her head back against the trunk. She lifted her canteen to her lips and grunted as nothing came out.

I dropped down beside her and passed her my own. "Here."

She cracked open her eyes. "You sure?"

"Yes, please," I insisted. "You need it more."

"Thanks." She took a long, thirsty drink.

I grinned crookedly. "Guess you're taking Jack's advice, now?"

"Ugh," she said, wiping her mouth. "Don't tell him."

"Lips are sealed." I laughed.

She thanked me again and returned the canteen. She shut her eyes again with a long sigh. I studied her face, noting the tracks of dried tears that snaked through the mud down her cheeks.

My heart pinched. "Are you all right?"

She sat up. "I'm grand," she muttered. "Why?"

"Just—just asking, is all."

"Because I'm not so fragile as you think," she said crossly. "I'm—"

"You were crying," I whispered.

She stopped, and wiped at her face. "Oh."

"I'm sorry. I was just concerned—"

"It's fine," she said, looking at her knees. She took a long, shuddering breath. "I was just thinking about my brother."

I nodded. "I'm worried about him, too."

She made a face. "I meant Aidan," she hissed. I winced. She shifted to face me. "I have no other brother. Do you understand this, Westleigh?"

"Sorry," I muttered again.

"I cannot comprehend you sometimes." Saoirse rolled her eyes and fell back against the tree. "Why can't you leave things be?"

"He's family," I insisted, and stopped her before she gave another smart retort. "Despite everything, he's blood."

"David isn't your blood." She pointed at me. "Is he still family?"

"Of course, but—"

"So family isn't your blood," she said, "family is the people who love you, and you love in return."

"Or both."

Saoirse scowled.

"I've never had *blood* family." I swallowed the lump in my throat. "No parents. No brothers or sisters. Doesn't make David, or Lucy, or the Bischoffs any less important to me. But now that I've found where I come from, I—I can't let them go so easily. Could you?"

"If I found out I came from the Callahans," she said through her teeth, "Yes, yes I could."

I could see in her eyes she meant it. And it broke my heart. "I'm sorry. I'm so sorry they hurt you."

She parted her lips to speak, probably to snap at me, but she gave a sad smile instead. "Thank you."

A shell burst far too close, and soon the whole regiment was up and moving again. No lines or columns, just a quick scramble further away from the river. It was darker still, storm clouds rolling in to block out the sun.

As we ran, we could see the artillery dragging up the big guns towards the river. Preparing for a siege. Many of the men were confused—we thought for sure we'd be going to battle soon. But if the movement on the other shore were any indication, we greatly underestimated the rebel's numbers. Thank Heaven for the balloons yesterday, or we might have rushed to our deaths.

Now, we set to digging, building, and waiting.

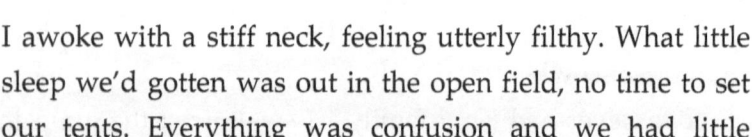

I awoke with a stiff neck, feeling utterly filthy. What little sleep we'd gotten was out in the open field, no time to set our tents. Everything was confusion and we had little notion to when and where we would be next.

Even breakfast was hurried, no time to cook anything… just grind down a bit of that impossible hardtack with our bare teeth and on we went, back to work.

Until the shelling started again.

We were caught off-guard—I thought we were out of range of those ships. So did the colonel, it seemed, the way he was hollering.

I don't remember feeling so much afraid as I was hurried. There was a panic of urgency that kept my hands steady though my heart pumped harder than I'd ever felt it. I only remember one moment of fear—when I couldn't see Jack, or Allison, or Saoirse, and I paused in my work to search frantically for them only to have Kennedy shout at me.

"Kavanagh! Pick that up and—"

The earth shook and suddenly I was flat on my back. Dirt showered around me. I stared up at churning grey clouds through the shredded leaves of the trees, fighting to catch my breath. I pushed myself up on my elbows. Then I heard the screams.

The pile of timber was obliterated, splinters everywhere.

Nearby lay Private Schmidt. There was a piece of wood as long as my forearm buried in his thigh. The younger Glenn boy, Stephen, lay facedown beside him, blood pooling around his head.

I scrambled forward. I made it to Schmidt the same time as another man, and we collided with each other.

"Steady there, Wes." Jack gripped my shoulder. His voice sounded faint in my ringing ears. He looked me over. "You wounded?"

I blinked in confusion. "I—I don't think so..." I patted myself down. I didn't see blood. Didn't feel any pain but in my aching head. "I think—I think I'm all right..."

"Good." He grunted as he moved to lift Schmidt by his shoulders. "Take his feet."

Everything tilted as I stood up, but Jack moved quickly and I had to follow, lest I drop the poor man's legs and send him into a new world of pain. I didn't pay attention to where we went. I just concentrated on my feet, on holding on to our charge, and keeping my eyes open. There was a warm sleepy pressure building in my head, and I wanted nothing more than to just rest my eyes.

"Almost there," Jack said, breaking me out of my daze. I stumbled, almost dropping the injured man, but I caught myself and kept going.

We arrived at a tree-line where other wounded men were brought, some from other regiments. There was little there for them, no field hospital tents or the like, but there were men buzzing about checking on the wounded, doing what they could.

"Whoa there." Jack's hand at my chest stopped me, and I felt my world tip again. He held me steady. "Sit down a second, let me take a look."

I didn't object, and with his help found the ground without sprawling on it. He sat beside me and inspected my skull.

"No bleeding," he said. "But you knocked it good. There's a nice knot there..."

I reached back and hissed, finally feeling the sting.

"No wonder you're staggering like a drunk," Jack shook his head. "You just take it easy here for a minute..."

"Saoirse," I blurted, and at Jack's expression, I felt cold. We looked around, but no one noticed us. I swallowed. "Aidan and Allison, are they all right?"

Jack wiped his brow, nodding. "Fine. I was running to get to you, but saw you were up and moving. Then I saw Smitty."

"Stephen is dead," I said softly. "Isn't he?"

"I expect so."

First casualty of the company, I thought with a shiver. "And what about—" I paused, catching myself as I noticed Jack's scowl. A wave of pain washed over my head, and I groaned, squeezing my eyes closed.

"I saw Declan running about on our way here," Jack said with a frown.

I nodded, and felt sorry for it afterwards.

"You know, Wes, I get it," he said. "I understand why you care. You think he can get better, that he'll have some miraculous epiphany and it'll fix everything. But sometimes bad people are just bad people, and they don't ever change."

His words hit my heart like a lead ball. I looked away, feeling hot tears well up and I didn't want Jack to see them. Finally, I found my words. "But God never gives up on us."

"I honestly don't know, Wes. But I know you ain't God. Eventually you're gonna have to let go and let Him deal with it, understand? Declan... you gotta let him go. And if not for your sake, then for hers."

I turned back to him. "Hers?"

Jack stared at me, searching my eyes for a long moment. "I saw the two of you talking last night."

"We shared water," I said quickly. I wasn't sure why I felt so defensive...

"Hmm," Jack said, staring at me again. He leaned closer. "I gotta ask, do you understand just what would happen if they found out who 'Aidan' really was? Truly?"

"What are you talking about?"

"There's no telling what they'll do," Jack continued. "But that's the scarier part, you know? They might send her home, and that would be a shame but that'd be the end of it. They also might decide to lock her up, you think about that? Or worse—if they thought she was a spy, well..."

My mouth went dry. "But how could they—"

"Someone gussied up in a uniform who shouldn't be?" Jack tilted his head. "What would be your first thought?"

"But… a woman…"

"Which brings me to my next point," Jack said, pinching the bridge of his nose. "If you can't keep your feelings more guarded, *you'll* be the one that gives her away."

"I don't—" I blushed. "Feelings, what feelings? I'm not… infatuated with—"

Good heavens I could barely swallow my own lie. They were right, of course. And it was all over my face, wasn't it? Oh, what had I done? Why did I ever join the army?

"And lastly," Jack said, starting to stand. He held out his hand and helped me to my feet. "If you really do care about her, you'll stay away from Declan."

"I never meant to—"

"I understand, believe me," Jack said, smiling softly. "You got a big soft heart, kid, but you need to understand one thing."

I waited, and Jack sighed.

"You keep pursuing Declan, you're going to push her further away. You can't have them both."

I felt that lead weight for the second time, and Jack nudged me.

"Come on, we should get back before they get all worked up and worried. How's your head?"

Worse, I thought.

Far worse.

15

SAOIRSE

Warwick Station, Virginia
April 28, 1862

You act like you never seen a chicken in your life," Jack hollered, laughing as I ran about the small farm. "Just grab the thing!"

"Sure, and easy enough for you to say," I retorted. I lunged for the fowl, only to trip and sprawl in the grass. I pushed myself up with a grunt. "We don't all have those giant hands of yours, now do we?"

Jack stood over me, grinning, holding chickens by their feet in each of his meaty hands. "You look ridiculous."

"Just give me those so *you* can catch us some more, will you?"

Jack laughed and passed them over. The poor birds threw themselves in a tizzy, and I almost screamed while feathers went everywhere. Jack gave me a look, and I shrugged sheepishly, trying to keep a desperate hold on the fowls. "I haven't, though."

"Haven't what?"

"Really been 'round chickens," I admitted. "I mean, we only had a few hens back in Brookfield. And I never had much to do with the livestock back in Ireland —"

Jack rolled his eyes and sauntered back towards the coop, passing Westleigh coming toward us. He held his haversack carefully, and practically tiptoed, grimacing.

I frowned. "What's the matter with you, then?"

"Are you sure we should be doing this?" He looked around the abandoned farm. "This — the army has strict rules about scavenging —"

The rebels that lived here fled the moment they saw the army coming. Good news for us, but Westleigh was conflicted. Which he mentioned often.

"You really want to eat hardtack and whatever we have passes for meat again tonight?" I wrinkled my face at the thought. "Besides, you heard the whispering. We didn't plan on sitting here, sieging for a month, did we? Supplies'll grow scarce."

"Especially since those crates went missing," he admitted. He stared at the eggs he'd collected with a grimly set mouth. "Still, doesn't feel right."

I shrugged. "Guess they should've thought twice before becoming traitors then."

"Guess so," he murmured, still looking down at his toes.

"Ah, cheer up then," I said. "You sure you're all right?"

He forced a smile, meeting my eyes for a brief second before a squeal broke the silence of the evening and both our heads snapped around, just in time to see a hog running fast as its little legs could carry it, and Allison stumbling behind.

"Ah," I said. "Eggs and bacon?"

"Don't worry!" Allison called out breathlessly, waving. "I got it!"

The pig barreled towards the trees as a figure emerged, looking startled as Allison shouted at him.

"Declan! Stop that pig!"

Declan froze wide-eyed as the pig ran straight for him, and he barely dodged out of the way as it ran by, knocking him to the ground. Both the pig and Allison disappeared into the trees, squealing and hollering fading into the distance. Declan picked himself up, looking mightily perturbed, and headed off back into the woods the other direction.

I broke into a fit of giggles.

"That can't end well..." Westleigh said, which only made me laugh harder.

"What's he going to do if he catches the thing?" I wiped my eyes, chuckling. "I'd love to see that scrawny boy try and drag that hog all the way back to—"

Suddenly I felt like I'd been kicked in the gut and doubled over with a moan. The birds in my hands fluttered, and I fought to hold onto them as pain twisted deep in my belly.

Westleigh turned to me, alarmed. "What is it?"

"Shush," I said through my teeth, trying to stand again. I felt the twist again and hissed. I crouched down on the ground, trying to hold very still, breathing slow as the pain faded. That's when it hit me. My cheeks flushed hot, and I stood, shoving the chickens towards Westleigh. "Hold these!"

The birds fluttered wildly, and we lost hold of one, but I didn't care. Westleigh managed to grab the other while I bolted for the trees.

"What? Aidan? Where are you going?"

Months, I swore under my breath. Months since I'd had to deal with the woman's curse. At first I'd been worried, after that talk with Lucy. But after the third month without any sign of bleeding, I praised the merciful Lord in Heaven. So of course it would seek vengeance on me now, out in the middle of the armpit of Virginia.

Thankfully, I was well prepared, as Lucy counseled. I found a secluded spot in the woods, took care of my business, and fashioned myself a bandage out of a handkerchief. 'Twasn't enough to protect my drawers, but I prayed I wouldn't bleed through my trousers at least. The trouble later would be how to take care of the soiled bandage out in the field. Not to mention the task of cleaning my underthings. We had a stream near the courthouse, if I could be discreet enough... Or else I'll just have to bury the bandage and find a new one.

I leaned my head against the tree and let myself weep at the pain and the unfairness of it all. Curse it was. As if everything we womenfolk had to deal with in this rotten world wasn't enough.

At least we'd be getting chicken for dinner. I couldn't bear to think of stomaching that salt-pork with my innards already in the state they were in.

Felt like I'd been bayonetted.

I let myself have a good cry and was cleaning myself up when I heard voices. I froze, crouched in the bushes, and listened. Whoever it was, they were arguing. That is till one got his mouth shut with a sound slap that made my own cheek hurt just to hear it.

"I told you I don't care how you do it," the other voice growled.

I sucked in a breath. It was Olsen.

"You gotta job to do, so find a way. Do I need to remind you—"

"No!" I heard my brother gasping like he was being choked. "I—I'll do it—"

There was more arguing that I couldn't quite make out—Olsen giving his orders, whatever they were—broken up by the occasional protest by Declan. His voice raised suddenly only to be silenced again by the striking of flesh. Even I winced.

The captain growled. "I don't know why I abide your incompetence. Just stop your sniveling and do as you're told."

"Yes sir," Declan rasped miserably.

Boots crunched the underbrush, and I waited until they were silent again to breathe. A few minutes later I allowed myself to stand. Finally, I took a hesitant step out of my hiding place.

Declan stood in front of me. His face was ashen, with dark smudges beneath his eyes and a bright red mark across his tear-stained cheek. There were red marks about his neck, too, and a fading bruise on his chin. He bared his teeth at me. "Of course you'd be snooping."

I scoffed, trying to ignore my pounding heart. What if the captain was still close by? "Not my fault you nearly stumbled on me answering nature's call."

Declan's face twisted in disgust, but it seemed to work. He sighed. "What did you hear? And you'd better answer honestly, or—"

"Just you getting knocked around by that bully," I snapped. "Honestly, Declan—what have you gotten yourself caught up in now?"

He didn't answer. Just stared off into the trees to try and hide how wet his eyes were.

I felt the slightest twinge of sympathy. "What are you even doing in the army?"

He glared at me. "I could ask you the same."

"Thought it was obvious?" I said with a laugh. "Being the dirty radical Lincoln-lover that I am."

Declan rolled his eyes. "If you keep playing these games..."

"Tell me what's going on, Declan," I whispered, reaching for his arm. He jerked it back. I swallowed. "This is Reeves all over again, isn't it?"

Declan glared at the ground. "'It was never Reeves," he muttered. "'Twas always Olsen."

"What do you mean?" I crept closer, mind racing frantically. "You're talking about the fires, aren't you? I know the captain used to work for Reeves. He said something about a debt. And the letter, the one that scared Reeves so bad, that was from Olsen, too wasn't it? What's all this about, Dec—"

He pushed me away and stuck his shaking finger in my face. "I've already warned you. You should be grateful I'm warning you again. Mind your own business, and try not to do something stupid."

"Yeah, and you yourself," I grumbled. Declan waved me off and turned to walk away, but I blurted out. "You could at least be kind to Westleigh! The poor eejit actually cares about you."

He paused, half-turning to look over his shoulder, brow furrowed. "Then he's like you say." He shook his head. "An idiot."

Jack hated those chickens. Must have, by the way he brought them to a swift end that night in camp. If the scratches on his arms were any indication, they'd put up quite a fight.

I elected not to tell him about my run in with Declan, especially since all I'd probably get was a lecture about keeping my nose to myself. But the problem ate at me all the more. Whatever Marek was wanting Declan to do—it couldn't have been good, if even Declan was protesting it. Or else he protested due to his cowardice—I couldn't follow a single thread of thought or theory without getting them all impossibly tangled.

So I sat folded up by the campfire, trying to keep my whimpers and grimaces at a minimum, holding my arms over my stomach while I waited for dinner.

Westleigh glanced at me sideways while he neatly arranged the eggs he'd foraged in a crate by our tents. "What's the matter?"

Damn his perceptiveness, even if he hadn't managed to look straight at me for weeks, now. I didn't notice it at first, but after a few days of him doing all he could to keep from making eye contact, I started to get curious. Now I was just annoyed. "Look at me."

Westleigh blushed as he looked up.

Jack paused in his cooking to watch us.

Westleigh shifted nervously and dropped his eyes again. "What?"

I shook my head. It wasn't worth it. "I'm unwell, that's all."

"Unwell?" His nose wrinkled. "Do you need to visit the sick tent?"

Jack laughed and turned back to his chicken, leaving poor Westleigh to figure it out on his own.

"*Unwell*," I said through clenched teeth. "I cannot say more, Westleigh."

He looked at me again, really looked this time, and I felt relieved. Why had he been so strange lately? We'd hardly spoken since that night the siege began, and I missed his company. Well, perhaps not at that moment, when I'd rather have crawled into my tent and not moved for days.

"I don't—" Westleigh's eyes suddenly widened. "Oh."

"Ta."

If he was finding it difficult to look at me before, he certainly couldn't do it now. It was almost funny, if I didn't feel like I'd been trampled by half the Army of the Potomac.

Allison suddenly came tromping back into camp. His hair was wild and had bits of twig sticking out every which way. His face was red and dirty, and he clutched a bundle in his arms. As he got closer, I heard it mew.

"That isn't a pig," I teased.

"Nope!" Allison sat down, presenting the cat. It was a

scrawny, scared looking thing with matted grey fur. "This is even better."

Westleigh's jaw dropped. "We are *not* eating that cat."

"What?" Allison looked horrified. "How could you even think such a thing! This is our new company mascot. I think I'll call her 'Virginia.'"

Jack frowned. "That thing's probably riddled with fleas, get it out of here."

"Don't you listen to the grumpy man, Ginny," Allison said, scratching behind her ears. She looked young, not quite a kitten anymore, not fully grown. And she started to relax in Allison's lap.

"What happened to the pig?" Westleigh asked.

Allison's expression soured. "I don't want to talk about the pig."

I snatched some of the chicken away from Jack and held it out to the cat. She started to purr as she ate it.

Allison grinned at me. "See, already making friends."

"We ain't keeping that damned sesech cat."

"She can't help all her humans decided to turn traitor," I said, scratching under her chin. She closed her eyes contentedly. "See, you aren't a rebel, are you, love? No, you're not, you're just a sweet, hungry little thing."

I pinched off another piece of meat and held it out to her.

"And stop feeding it my chicken."

"Well she can't eat the hardtack, now can she?" I took

her from Allison to finger-comb her fur. "But you can catch mice too, can't you Ginny?"

"Long as she isn't staying in my tent."

"Ginny will stay wherever she pleases," Allison announced. He stood. "I'm gonna fetch her a plate with some milk. Saw some of the boys in Company H brought a whole cow from a farm out east! Be right back."

The cat started curling around Jack's legs, begging for more chicken while Allison ducked inside his tent. A few moments later, he let loose a strangled scream, came bolting out of the tent, and he was gone quicker than you could say *Ginny the sesech cat.*

I caught Jack grinning as he poked at the chicken over the fire.

"What did you do now?"

He chuckled. "Don't know what you're talking about."

Westleigh sighed. "That's my tent, too…"

Jack shrugged and fed the cat. "Dinner's ready. Eat or starve, Kavanaghs."

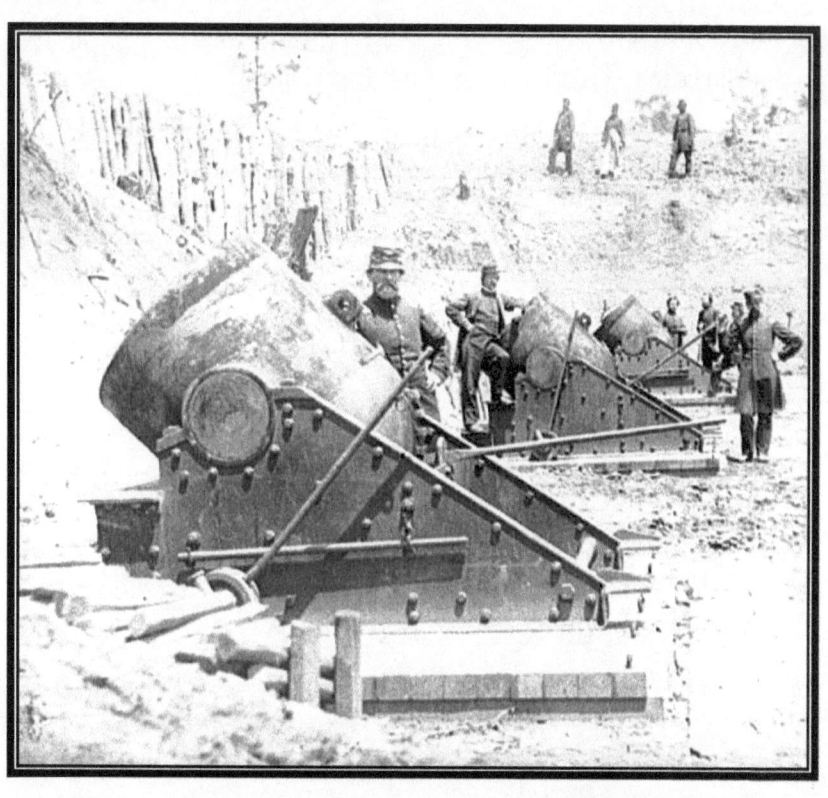

Yorktown, Va., vicinity. 13-in. seacoast mortars of Federal Battery No. 4 with officers of 1st Connecticut Heavy Artillery

16

WESTLEIGH
Yorktown, Virginia
May 3, 1862

I awoke with sharp claws in my back and the sound of Heaven rending to pieces above me in an explosion of fire and death. The ground itself shook, and Ginny fastened herself to my shoulders and would not be removed for anything.

"Westleigh!" Allison pried the cat from my back. "The rebs are lighting up the sky!"

I grunted and pushed myself up. "Is that who that is?" I fished for my spectacles and tried to calm the fear thrumming through my limbs. "Are we safe?"

"Can't reach us here." Allison handed me the cat. "It's got the boys down by the river ducking and covering, though. Come and look. It's a sight!"

He crawled out of the tent, and I put Ginny behind me.

She curled up in a tight ball against my haversack and stared at me with wide eyes.

"Stay there, girl," I said softly. Allison called to me, and I followed him. Saoirse and Jack were standing beside us, and the rest of our regiment was stirring, staring up at the sky as light flashed against swirling grey clouds. The barrage wasn't constant, just a few shells bursting every few minutes, and it seemed that the rebs were doing little more than making a terrible noise.

"What time is it?" Saoirse asked.

"Just past midnight."

She let out a loud yawn. "What the devil are they doing?"

Murmurs of a similar sort were going up and down the tent row as our company watched, like standing out on a summer's night to gaze on fireworks.

"Are we answering?" I asked, straining to hear. But there was no sound coming from the great monstrous guns and mortars set along the river in the fortifications we spent so long building. Never before had I seen such enormous machines, apart from a forge in Pittsburgh once. But that wasn't an instrument of death. And to see so many gathered in one place…

"Not yet," Jack said unnecessarily. "Heard we're about to do our own shelling tomorrow though…"

"About time," Saoirse muttered.

We watched the rest of the bombardment in silence.

Horses nearby snorted nervously, but everything else seemed still. Then, almost as soon as it had started, the Confederate guns went quiet. We stared at the sky for a little while longer, till one by one, we wordlessly crawled back into our tents to chase the few hours of sleep we had left, with uncertainty looming in the morning.

I let Ginny curl herself up in the crook of my arm, head nestled under my chin, and I scratched behind her ears until she sighed heavily and fell fast asleep. I jealously watched her, her little body hardly moving as she breathed, happy and content in my arms. Even Allison started to snore after a bit.

But all I could think of was that battle may loom ahead tomorrow. Finally, after almost a year in the army, we would fight. I would have to take up my rifle — that horrible tool fashioned for one horrible purpose — and I would fire it at a living, breathing, man.

I trembled, and Ginny gave a small noise of protest, burrowing further into my arms. I thought of Wilberforce, laying alone upon the parlor floor, and hated myself for leaving him. Especially knowing my father was still missing.

I shut away all thoughts of home, held tighter to Ginny, and let the sound of Allison's snoring lull me into a fitful sleep.

Cheers resounded around us — the whole brigade, likely the whole army, gave shouts and calls of triumph as we ran past our trenches, the guns, the fortifications, a great wave of blue crashing toward Yorktown.

And not a single rebel bullet fired our way.

The rebels, it seemed, had fled in the night. No one opposed us as we charged victoriously, bright regimental flags flapping with bravado in the sun as we claimed Yorktown.

Allison was beaming, chest puffed out. He nodded at me. "My grandpap fought here in the revolution," he said breathlessly, clutching his rifle with pride. "Fought the British in this very place. Isn't that something?"

He gave a shout as we topped a small hill, and suddenly an explosion sent us stumbling to our knees. Dirt showered into the air, men hollered in fear, and I saw a squad of soldiers crumble in front of us as a body crashed into them. Down the line, there were more shouts, more explosions, and dirt and smoke swirled around us. The commanders were hollering, forcing us all to stop. We crouched down, scanning the terrain for the enemy, and saw nothing.

Another line of soldiers pressed forward — our regimental color guard — unaware of the shouts around them to stop. The flag bearer ran hard, waving our colors high — until the ground at his feet erupted, and he was blown backwards. When he landed, the flag was gone, as well as the lower half of his leg. The rest of the guard were fallen around him, and I didn't know if they were stunned or dead.

My insides lurched.

Kennedy swore. "What in blazes—"

There was a flash beside me, and someone was running towards the fallen flag. Jack shouted loudly in my ear.

"STOP! Aidan!"

I watched in horror as Saoirse, rifle slung across her back, dove for the fallen flag and pressed forward, to the scattered cheers of the regiment. We followed, though slower than before, eyes glued to the ground to try to spot the danger that lurked beneath—though none knew what to look for.

Saoirse reached the crest of the earthwork where the others stopped, planting the flag in the dirt, unharmed. I stared in awe at that tiny soldier in a baggy, rumpled uniform, standing proudly by the colors as she wiped her dripping brow. Allison ran up behind her and clapped her on the shoulder.

I came up behind them and looked over the Confederate trenches. The earthworks were empty, the rifle pits unmanned. Only a few dozen grey-clad men were about, and none were armed. Wounded and sick, abandoned by their army.

Kennedy came shouting behind us. "Damned treacherous bastards!" He looked behind him from where we'd come. "Buried torpedoes in the ground, the cowards."

My mouth went dry. Where else had such cold, inhuman inventions been buried? How many men did we lose to such a callous scheme?

Jack smacked Saoirse in the arm. "You coulda got yourself blown up!"

"But I didn't," she panted, grinning. "I'm sorry Jack, I don't know what came over me…"

"Well done, Private," Kennedy nodded at her. "That was admirable."

"Yes, well done," I heard Olsen drawl behind us.

Saoirse flinched and turned to salute. "Thank you, sir," she said curtly, her other hand gripping the pole of the flag until her knuckles turned white.

The captain chuckled. "Least one of you Kavanagh's ain't completely useless," he mocked, glancing sideways at me. He shrugged. "But admirable? Guess we'll see how you do in a real battle, first."

Two blue flames burned in her eyes as she met him with a cold stare. "Suppose we will. Sir."

Olsen's smile faltered, and a look of pure hatred twisted his features. But he quickly dropped his mask over them again and turned away to bark orders at his lieutenant.

Allison muttered beside me. "Maybe he'll find one of those torpedoes…"

Saoirse just kept scowling at the back of Olsen's head, holding onto that flag as if she'd like to spear him with it.

Yorktown was abandoned. Seemed the rebels had used their bombardment at midnight to cover their retreat. The word going around the ranks was they'd retreated to Williamsburg, and we wouldn't be in Yorktown long.

The deserted rebel camp was in disarray. Crates tipped over with supplies spilling onto the ground, a few scattered arms that had been left behind. Even a few books with stained pages, fluttering like leaves in the wind. I could smell rain on the air that blew in. We'd have a storm again soon.

The officers dispatched men to round up the rebels that had been left behind. Those that couldn't stand were loaded on carts and sent away, off to the hospitals, before they'd be sent to a prison camp.

Those that could move were dispatched with sergeants to oversee the removal of their torpedoes. I felt a chill as I watched them, some lumbering about with fever, others dazed by wounds and hunger, prodded forward by bayonet to search out all the places they buried their devices.

"Better them than our own men, Wes," Jack said before I could open my mouth. "I know that sounds terrible, but that's the truth of it. At least they might know where they were buried."

"What are those awful things?"

"Shells," Allison piped up. "Saw one of the colonels inspecting one. They rigged it up to explode when you stepped on it."

Saoirse whistled. "That's—"

"Ingenious," Allison said.

Her eyes widened. "I was going to say heinous."

"Oh, well yeah, that too," Allison shrugged sheepishly. "But you gotta admit, clever—"

"No," I said sharply. "Don't think we have to admit that at all, thank you very much."

All the while, the camp buzzed with movement. Colored men, women, and children came pouring in from the countryside. Some had been camp followers already, washerwomen and the like, doing duties around the camp. The others had mixed looks of relief and fear, like they'd run straight to our camps from a plantation. Half of them were clothed in threadbare rags, many with no shoes. All of them hungry. Jack and I were already figuring how we could make our rations stretch and share, when the captain got up to address the company about our new arrivals.

He stood on Allison's crate to make himself look bigger, hands on his hips. Rain poured off the wide brim of his black hat. All that was missing was a whip at his side.

"I don't want to see any of you men fraternizing with the contraband, you hear me?" he bellowed. "This is a reminder to all of you. They are still *slaves*. They have been seized from the enemy, and are now property of the United States government."

His eyes found our little huddle, and even through the rain I could see the smirk in his lips.

"So don't go getting any ideas. You are not here for them. You will not give any of the army's supplies to them, or I'll have you locked up for thieving. You will keep to your duties, and prepare to leave in the morning. Now, eat up, and get some sleep."

After dinner we all huddled in the rain and mud, but our spirits were high. Allison took his turn up on a crate to regale the company, with an embellished air, the story of how Private Aidan Kavanagh braved a field of torpedoes to save the colors. Didn't matter much that they'd all seen it with their own eyes. They still cheered, and everyone decided 'Aidan' should lead us all the way to Williamsburg.

Saoirse for her part only smiled shyly and had to be nudged by Jack in a warning. She sat up, straightened her shoulders, and shrugged. "I'm not even a corporal, can't be part of the color-guard, boys. I just picked up the flag is all. Didn't want it to be blown to bits."

"Maybe they should give you a promotion, put you in the color-guard," Connolly said. "Seems only fitting."

Saoirse tried not to grin. "I'm just fine where I am. Let someone else have the honor."

Indeed, I thought with trepidation. I couldn't bear to

imagine her as a color-bearer, the target of rebel guns, no matter how honorable the position was.

But nothing else was said of Saoirse's heroism, and we spent the rest of the evening singing songs before the officers ordered us to sleep.

Just before we turned in, a small girl passed us by, one hand clutching her mama's skirts. In the other arm, a small grey cat was tucked snuggly against her body, trying to shield itself from the rain. Can't say for sure it was Ginny, but I'd like to think so. In any case, we never saw our sesech cat after that night. I hoped she'd found a little girl somewhere to be held by.

The small family came to a rifle pit and settled in, at least partially blocked by the wind and rain. I looked about for sign of the captain, but neither he nor Declan were anywhere to be seen. At the back of my mind, I realized I hadn't seen Declan for a few days since, but in the haste and confusion of the bombardment, and siege, and the rush of men, I reckon I missed him.

I gathered an abandoned rebel tarp we'd found abandoned by the rebels, and a wool blanket—a bit tattered, but better than nothing—and approached them. The father thanked me, and the little girl stared at me, wide-eyed. She whined and huddled against her mother, squeezing the little cat with all her might.

I tried to comfort her. "You're safe now."

Her parents nodded their thanks to me, though we all

could read it in each other's eyes. No one was safe. But at least, for the moment, our lies brought a little girl some peace.

I snuck back to my tent before I was caught.

I couldn't sleep, so I prayed. I prayed for every single soul huddled in that mud. But mostly I just prayed for a little girl and for the freedom that she hoped so hard for. I didn't care what the captain, or Sergeant Kennedy, or any of the other men in the army said. When next I'd see battle, it would be the image of that little girl and her cat I'd keep burned into my heart. If I was fighting in this war for anyone, I wanted it to be her.

17

SAOIRSE
Williamsburg, Virginia
May 5, 1862

Musket-fire rippled down the line and smoke billowed out in front of us, masking our view of the enemy, so you really didn't know if you hit anyone. Not till the smoke cleared, and you saw the line of rebels look a little thinner than before. But only if you were really looking. We were too busy being the machine that our general made us, finally getting a chance to fire our weapons in battle. It almost felt like another mindless drill, but for the bullets flying back at you.

"RELOAD!"

Cartridge. Powder. Ball. Ramrod. Cap. Hammer.

Wait.

"FIRE!"

I grabbed another cartridge from the box at my hip, tore it open with my teeth. Time and practice kept the powder out of my mouth now, though I remembered the coppery taste well. In the beginning it would coat my lips, staining them black, till I learned to tear and spit proper. I poured the powder down the barrel, placed the ball, shoved it down with the ramrod. Once I almost forgot to take the rod out again, nearly firing the whole metal bar at some poor rebel bastard and then rendering my weapon useless. I replaced it now, dug a tiny percussion cap from my pouch, placed it so, cocked the hammer, and waited again.

"FIRE!"

"Fourteen," I muttered under my breath, keeping count of the shots. I blinked through the blasted never-ending rain, tried to peer through the haze of smoke and fog to see if I found my mark.

The rebels answered us almost immediately. Minnie balls cut through the air with a spine-chilling sound, striking wood and flesh and dropping men around me. My heart beat hard, but my hands were steady. I was aching tired—we marched straight from Yorktown to the outskirts of Williamsburg to relieve General Hooker's men, who cheered at the sight of us. They looked worse for wear, their battery had been lost, but we came in the nick of time. The brigade held firm our ground, spanning 'cross the road in a heavy wood, and poured our fire into the charging rebel lines.

"Steady boys, here they come again!"

Crouched low, we ducked as artillery bellowed through the woods, shattering trees and raining leaves and splinters down on us. Then, from across the way, came that ungodly noise. It made us all shiver, the shrill way those rebels yelled. 'Twould've frightened a banshee.

We reloaded our muskets, and the butt of mine slipped in the mud. I reached out to catch it instinctively and gave a sharp cry as my hand closed around the hot barrel. Blast it. I scrambled, barely reloading it in time to fire. We held, waiting for the order, waiting for the rebels to come close enough to cut them down....

"FIRE!"

Fifteen.

This time I saw the bodies fall. Each one that dropped made me breathe a little easier, though I tried not to think hard on the matter. I simply reloaded my weapon.

"How's your hand?" Jack, crouched at my left shoulder, smirked.

"Ah, quiet, you." But I winced as I flexed my fist. "Going to sting later, it is."

"Let me look at it when this is over."

The lightness of our conversation made it easier to keep going, though we'd already been fighting for ages. All sense of time fled. It could have been hours, could have been minutes. All I knew is we had to keep those grey devils from coming any closer. We had to hold fast.

We fired a few more rounds, and another wave came, louder and fiercer than before. I could almost feel our line wavering.

Allison called out down the line to my right. "Easy now, they're just a bunch of noise, fellas."

We were firing at-will now, while rebel reinforcements arrived and the rain poured harder. I watched Allison out the corner of my eye. He was becoming a decent soldier, quick with his rifle and steady with his hands. But he chirped up now and again, even cracking jokes just to get a nervous laugh or two out of the men. Once he tried singing, but the sergeant shut him up. I think Kennedy underestimated the potential use of such a weapon as Allison's terrible singing on the advancing rebels.

At that point, Allison was too busy helping Westleigh. I heard a startled shout to my right, and Allison grabbed the rifle from his shaking hands.

"Wait, Wes! You've already loaded this. Thing'll explode in your face if you aren't careful—" He took the gun and fired at the rebels before handing it back and squeezing Westleigh's shoulder. "You good?"

Westleigh nodded, but I could see the tracks of tears down his dirty cheeks. He twisted around for a cartridge, but the box had shifted behind him out of reach, and he panicked. Bullets zipped by, and he huddled behind the fence rails, squeezing his eyes shut tight.

I ducked and reached over to move his box for him, sliding it around to his hip where he could grab it.

He met my eyes and tried to thank me, but cannon fire drowned out his words. I had no time for them anyhow. I reloaded my weapon and fired into the smoke again, and again, till I reached one more time into my box and found it empty.

Forty.

About that time the captain called for us to cease fire, and the line slowly quieted. You could hear the hushing sound of the rain over the field as the smoke slowly drifted away, and the setting sun reflected in it, casting about an eerie orange glow. The rebels had stopped firing, too. After a few moments, a cheer began building up and down the ranks. Men raised their hats in the air, their hoarse voices crying hurrah, and I squinted through the haze. The rebels had retreated. We held our ground through onslaught and fire, and came out victorious.

I raised my voice too, then turned to Jack in my excitement. He merely nodded, face grim. His hands still gripped his rifle, every muscle in his body taut, and I could see he was fair shaking with rage. I swallowed my exultation. This was far from over. But thank the Lord, we lived.

I glanced to my right, but Westleigh wouldn't look up at any of us. His head was bowed, and Allison was trying to rouse him. His gun lay at his knees, likely still loaded. I laid my hand on his shoulder, and he shrank further in on himself, but I leaned down to force him to look at me.

"You're here," I said softly. "You held the same ground we did. You live."

Brow furrowed, he finally nodded.

"We're all right," I said, smiling gently. "You're all right. That's all that matters, right so?"

"Yes," he whispered, wiping his cheek with the back of his hand. He straightened. "I—I'm good."

"It's evening now," Allison commented, nodding west through the trees. "Day's done, so should the fighting be."

The sun was almost gone. The smoke had thinned, and we could see the rest of the regiment. Men moved to take wounded to the back of the line. I saw two privates lift the body of their companion, fallen over the rail they fought behind, to lay him down. I couldn't see much, but from our vantage point, the regiment seemed more or less whole. Was our first true battle a victory?

I glanced around me, taking in the faces of the rest of our company, and didn't realize I was looking for the captain's until our eyes met. I gave a salute. He stood there, arms folded imperiously over his chest, and stared at me till I felt a chill in my bones. I shuddered and turned around. When I dared a glance over my shoulder again, he was gone.

A panic seized me, and I looked over myself, desperately inspecting my appearance. Did he know? Had I done something to reveal myself? I checked every brass button, smoothed back every strand of my short black hair, adjusted the kerchief at my neck. My fair freckled skin was still covered in mud, my uniform, soaked as it was, still bowed out in odd places with all the baggy extra material lumped around my small frame. Nothing was out of place.

But why had he looked at me like he *knew* me?

Jack nudged my arm. "What's the matter with you?"

"He knows, Jack," I squeaked, looking at him with wide eyes. My heart skipped now. In battle the blasted thing had been steady as a clock. Now it went wild, scampering like a three-legged dog.

"Who knows what?" Jack said, rolling his eyes. Then he froze. "No."

"I—I don't know," I said breathlessly, pulling my kepi down further over my ears. "He just looked at me, and his eyes, I could just see—"

"Calm down," Jack said, gripping my arm. But the way he looked around, I could tell he was nervous too. "Where'd he go?"

"I don't know—" I craned my neck.

"Stop it. You're gonna draw attention to yourself."

"Is that him?" I saw a couple officers talking. "No, that's the lieutenant…"

"Take a breath. Better yet, get yourself a drink."

I grabbed for my canteen and drank greedily. Jack waited for me to finish.

"Better?"

I wiped my mouth. "Yes, thanks."

"I see him now—don't look—he's talking to the colonel."

I groaned. Jack gave me a little shake, and I swallowed hard, trying to calm down.

"There he goes again," Jack said. "Colonel's rode off. Likely just gave him orders. You're fine, kid."

I put my head in my hands. I wanted to cry. Jack gripped my shoulder and gave me another shake. I didn't come up.

"Listen," he said, shaking me again. I peeked through my fingers. Jack laughed. "You did good, you know that? I'm proud of you."

My heart swelled. I raised my head, and I couldn't help the stupid grin from spreading. "You are, really?"

His eyes shone, and the corner of his mouth lifted in a smile. "I really am," he said softly. "And I'm glad you're here. I can't imagine you not being by my side."

I don't know why I ever sought out the blasted captain for approval. With Jack, I felt like I could conquer the whole rebel army. The pair of us.

Nothing could stop me now.

18

WESTLEIGH
Williamsburg, Virginia
May 6, 1862

I only ever saw death once in my life before the war. I'd seen funerals, I'd known some who passed on, but I only ever saw it up close once.

When I was twelve, Peter took me with him to visit an old shut-in who lived just outside of Dove Hollow. She'd been a friend of his wife's when she lived. Mrs. Nussbaum. Every Christmas, until she became too frail to leave her home, she'd bring my da and I a whole basket of German pastries. I always meant to visit her more often than I did. Whenever I came by, she had me sit and read to her. Never stopped smiling for a moment while I was there. Until the last time, and she passed on, right there with Peter and me by her side. I remember how much it bothered me, knowing there was no breath of life, no soul in that tiny old body. Those empty eyes, sweet as her face was, gave me nightmares for weeks afterwards.

Now… now…

I couldn't tear my eyes from the sights along the road as we marched into the town, chasing the Confederates at a slow, steady pace. Bodies littered the ground, blue and gray alike. Some were twisted into painful shapes and some had fallen mingled together, still grappled in the fight that killed them, killed not by bullets, but speared by bayonets. Faces stared up blankly at the morning sky, blood washed away by yesterday's rain. Others were half-buried in the mud. And all of them were *empty*. Husks of men with their souls violently taken from them.

The sights of all these terrified me, but I was relieved that I knew none of those faces, and I felt a flood of shame for thinking so. Someone knew them. Someone grieved. And I felt it should grieve me.

Allison wasn't having any of it. He was singing right along to the band that played *Yankee Doodle* behind us as we marched into town. I frowned at him, and he paused to lean over to me. "If I stop for a moment to think about any of it," he said, face suddenly serious, "I'm not sure I could move forward again."

I resolved to shove the images from my mind. At least for now.

Williamsburg was a small town with old brick houses, not a bustling port like Alexandria. Fewer civilians stood on the sidewalks as we paraded by, mostly just men and nurses helping to move the wounded.

A small group of ladies, smartly dressed with their wide ruffled skirts and crisp bonnets, stood in the doorway of a large building. They waved their fans furiously and scowled like they wished they could send us straight to Hell with just a look. I swallowed and looked away. Had they husbands or brothers lying dead in the fields behind us? They mocked us, shouting taunts as we marched by. A few of the boys behind me jeered them back and were sharply reprimanded by the sergeant.

"I don't care they're sesech, they're still ladies!"

Saoirse stifled a giggle at this and winked at me.

I started to return the smile, but I suddenly saw myself again, crouched behind the fence rails, cowering before the rebel onslaught as she bravely fired again and again.

I hadn't shot a single round during the battle. For three hours, I pantomimed, or froze completely, just praying hard for it all to be over.

Saoirse saved my life. Saoirse, Jack, Allison, the whole line. And I hadn't lifted a finger to save theirs.

I turned to the front and ignored her worried look. I couldn't face her. Not now.

We set up camp a mile outside town before going back in. Saoirse and I were attached to a detail rounding up wounded and getting them to a little church turned into a hospital. It was hard, heartbreaking work, but the blood didn't bother me as much as the dead did. Wounded meant hope. Where there was life, there was a chance.

Saoirse wasn't so at ease. We worked in silence, lifting rebel men onto carts so they could be taken away, and once or twice, I thought she might become ill. We came across one poor soul who couldn't be moved. Shot in the stomach. Even I had to turn my head. Saoirse stumbled to the alley and bent over, hands on knees, leaning on the building for support. I gave her a moment, and we went back to work.

Other soldiers were knocking on doors, checking buildings for wounded. We came to one, and a lieutenant held up his hand, forcing us to wait on the stoop. They knocked on the door. No answer.

Finally a voice shouted from inside. "Get outta here, you damned blue devils!"

"You will open this door or we will break it down, ma'am!" the officer bellowed.

Saoirse and I tensed, both backing away as the other men tightened their grips on their guns. The officer held up his sidearm level with his face, cocking the hammer.

Suddenly the door opened, and a shot rang out. The officer swore loudly, grabbing his shoulder, and the other soldiers rushed in. A woman screamed, furniture and china crashed, and another door slammed against a wall. We heard shouts outside. The officer whirled around to Saoirse and me, pointing.

"Get to the alley! He's getting away!"

We bolted, our worn-down shoes sliding in gravel as we halted in the mouth of the alley. Come running straight toward us was a towering man in a tattered gray uniform, eyes wild and brandishing a pistol.

A shot rang out, smoke stung my eyes while my heart leapt in my throat, and the man fell dead just yards in front of us.

Saoirse lowered her smoking rifle, looking a bit shaken herself. She laughed nervously. "That was close."

I coughed.

The rest of our detail came rushing around the corner. The lieutenant glared at the dead Confederate in the alley, holding his shoulder. He spat on the ground, swearing, and staggered off to get himself patched up now, too.

I stared at the fallen form, hearing the muffled sound of weeping in the house beside me.

"Westleigh!" Saoirse called to me. "Let's go, he won't need the cart."

I winced, and followed.

Back out of the alley I heard more shouting and froze at Saoirse's shoulder as we stared down the street. No soldiers were beating down doors, but another woman stood on her steps, waving her arms and yelling hoarsely.

"Rose, you get back here right now!"

A young colored girl with a small child on one hip and a basket of belongings on the other was walking as swiftly as she could in the other direction, like she couldn't hear a word the woman said.

"Get back here or I'll catch you and whip you raw!"

The girl didn't flinch. The woman kept on screaming, shouting obscenities in the wind, and the girl just followed the road out of town, heading towards our camps, until she disappeared beyond the trees.

I let myself smile, a held breath rushing out of me with a shaky sigh.

"Come on, then," Saoirse said, nudging my elbow. "Still work to do yet."

We helped take the cart full of wounded to the church, but already there were lines of men waiting outside, lying or sitting on the ground in various stages of distress. Most of them at least sported bandages, from wrapped head-wounds to arms in slings or bits of shredded shirts wrapped tight around wounded limbs.

The smell of blood was overwhelming. Saoirse reeled a bit as we came close.

A nurse rushed by with a pail, nearly knocking us both into the street, muttering under her breath.

I turned to see Saoirse staring down at her hands. They were stained with blood. She was shaking.

"Hey," I whispered, taking her aside. I showed her my hands, stained red from our work. "Mine too, it's all right."

She looked around us, at the hurting men, and her face pinched. "I might have shot some of these men, Westleigh." She tried wiping her hands on her trousers and swallowed hard. "I killed that man in the alley—"

"You did what you had to," I whispered. But I felt the same pain as I heard the moans of the wounded. Despite all they were, they were human first. Bullets didn't belong in humans. This whole thing, war, it wasn't natural. And the notion crawled under my skin like spiders.

Saoirse wasn't calming down. Her breath came quicker, and I pulled her to the side around the building. Tears were flushing down her cheeks. "I—I keep seeing Aidan," she whimpered. "Holding him, that night he died. Bleeding in that alley—"

I gently took her hands and lifted my canteen, pouring water over them, cleaning away the blood. I held them until they were still, not realizing I'd pulled her closer to me until she looked up, her freckles blending into her red cheeks.

Someone coughed behind us, and Saoirse nearly bolted to the other side of town.

Allison laughed. "Boy, aren't you two glad it was just me?" he said a little too loudly, throwing a wink my way.

I scowled. "You scared me half to—"

Saoirse shook her head, and I bit off the rest of my sentence with a groan.

Allison waved me away. "You're too jumpy. I was only kidding. Jack and I are finished, we're being sent back to camp. You two coming?"

"I promised I would stay and help a while," Saoirse murmured, looking away.

"Go on back with them," I said softly. "I'll take your place."

She looked up at me, her blue eyes shining. "Thank you, Westleigh."

Allison waved her over, and she quickly followed, throwing one quick glance over her shoulder at me before they headed down the road.

I stared at my hands, at my fingertips that were now clean, and marveled at the way her hands had fit inside mine...

The rattling of a cart scattered my thoughts. I shoved them all aside, rushing around the corner before someone came looking for me.

And I ran straight into Olsen. Oliver. Whatever the scoundrel called himself.

The captain loomed over me, hand on his saber hilt. "Where are you running to?"

"I—" I pointed to the church-hospital. "I was assigned—"

"Did I just see our other Kavanagh leave here?"

"Yes, sir, I took his place."

"What for?"

I hesitated. If I were to say Saoirse was feeling ill, would he think she was shirking? I waited too long to answer, but Olsen had other questions on his mind.

"I need you to tell me more about your cousin," he said. "When did he arrive from Ireland?"

I blinked. "Pardon?"

Olsen smirked. "Battle muck up your ears, boy? I asked when Aidan arrived in America. He wasn't around a couple summers ago."

"No sir," I said quickly, recalling the background Saoirse and I had concocted long ago, when Jonas had first started asking about our relation. "Left Galway a few years ago. He was living in Philadelphia until last spring. Came to Dove Hollow because my father offered him a job."

The captain grunted. "Sheriff's doing better for himself, is he?"

I didn't answer. I didn't want to give him any more cause to say terrible things about David.

"And what about you?" his eyes narrowed. "You're supposed to be in college with your books."

I swallowed. "Semester was cancelled."

"So you turned soldier instead of scholar." He chuckled dryly. "A piss-poor soldier at that. Never expected to see you have the guts to join up. Just what are you doing here, really, Kavanagh? You, your cousin, that Injun fugitive. Say, whatever happened to the girl? You just left that pretty thing all by herself?"

My fingernails dug into my palms. I scowled. "I'm fighting for my country sir, same as you," I said through my teeth. "May I be dismissed to my duties, please?"

Olsen smiled victoriously. Whatever he'd wanted from me, he got. He took a step back. "By all means, little Irish, go and be useful for a change."

I suppressed the urge to throw my shoulder at him as I passed by. I hurried into the church, where I ducked out of the way and mopped my sweating brow. I looked up at a cross on the wall, and begged God to end the war soon. Because I don't know how long we could survive the captain if He didn't.

Camp was quiet that night. Saoirse went to sleep early, while Allison and Jack played a game of cards outside her tent, hardly a word spoken in conversation between them. We were all too tired. But at least it wasn't raining, the first night in days. I pulled out a book to read. I'd stuffed my knapsack with as many tomes as I could before leaving Washington. Jack was kind enough to hold the rest of my necessities in his own so I'd have room, since he hardly carried anything anyway. But my knapsack was getting harder to carry, now that we were moving from here to there. Some men had chucked theirs along the road before the battle, with the hopes of returning for them. They were still there.

With a sigh, I reckoned it was time to lighten my load. I came across the Wilkie Collins novel. I'd read it already, but hated the idea of parting with it. I looked up. "Jack, Allison, do either of you think—"

"Not carrying any of your books, boy," Jack mumbled, shuffling a deck of cards.

Allison shook his head. "Nope, sorry Wes. Not interested."

I stood and looked around the camp. "Maybe I ought to see about redistributing some of them."

They didn't answer, already engrossed in a new round of their game.

I shuffled off, wandering around the campfires with my knapsack. It wasn't that the other men couldn't read or didn't like to. But I imagined most wouldn't care to haul around any extra weight, either.

Then I caught sight of Declan.

He sat hunched over outside of his tent, alone, trying to light a cigarette. It was the first time in days I'd seen him, and I was relieved to see that he lived. My next thought was that Jack would surely box my ears if he saw me going anywhere near him. But I took a deep breath, and casually strolled over to his tent.

"Declan," I said cheerfully, though my voice cracked. He slowly looked up, scowling. I cleared my throat. "I um—it's good to see you. I mean, I'm glad to see you're all right. After the battle, today, I didn't know—"

Declan flicked away the spent match and took a long drag from the cigarette. He blew out the smoke and his lips twisted in a cruel smile. "Saw *you* today. Tell me, how many rounds did you fire off?"

I gritted my teeth and thought about turning away. I shook my head and caught sight of the open book in

Declan's lap. It was wide and flat, with blank pages, and a pencil tucked in the middle. I smiled. "Do you like sketching?"

He slammed it closed. "None of your business."

"Fair enough," I said, forcing my tone to be light. I shrugged my knapsack off my shoulder and set it at our feet, crouching down to dig through it.

"What are you—"

I held up the Wilkie Collins novel. "Aidan says you like detective stories. Have you read this one?"

Declan scowled at his brother's name. "Go away."

"I've already read it," I said, continuing as though I hadn't heard him. I fished another out of my bag. "What about Dickens, are you fond of his work?"

"I'll give you to the count of three—"

I dropped the other books in my bag, but left the Collins at his feet. I pointed to it as I stood. "It was really excellent, I think—"

"One."

I held up my hands. "Fine, I'll go. Just..." I paused, chewing my lip. "I really am glad you're all right, Declan."

"Two."

I spun on my heel and hurried away, not even daring to look over my shoulder and see whether he picked up the book or not. But he didn't throw it at my head, so that was something.

Corporal Hastings stopped me on the way back to my

tent. "Jack says you're looking to give away books," he said. "Whatcha got?"

I grinned, holding out the open knapsack. "Take a look…"

19

SAOIRSE

Fair Oaks Station, Virginia
May 30, 1862

Blasted wind nearly took my kepi from my head. I held onto it for dear life while we moved double-quick towards the horrendous sounds of battle. But the regiment wasn't the only thing doing the quick-step.

"You sure you shouldn't be in a sick tent?" Jack asked Allison as the boy stumbled in the march and nearly toppled over.

"I'll be fine," he said, and whined. "Just fine."

"Told ya you shouldn't have eaten that old meat."

"You sure you didn't put something in my coffee again?"

"How dare you," Jack said dryly. "I resent the implication, Horner."

"Are we not even yet?"

Jack just laughed.

Allison hissed, grabbing his stomach. "I'm tired of jumping at every turn, checking my bedding for bugs, making Westleigh test my coffee."

"I told you I'm not doing that again," Westleigh called out.

I looked over at him and grinned. He returned a tight smile. So far, he seemed in good spirits. Though I worried for him, for what lay ahead.

General Peck himself led us and another regiment of Pennsylvanians straight into the thick of things, once again supporting the division's flank. We came to the field of fire and lined up sharply. Westleigh and Allison were on either side of me now, with Jack at Westleigh's right shoulder.

"You're gonna be fine," he was saying to Westleigh while we loaded our rifles. "We're all right here. Just pretend this is drills. Don't even think about what's on the other side of that field. Just keep loading and firing till they tell us not to. Got it?"

Westleigh nodded, though his hand shook as he poured the powder down the barrel.

Jack's deep voice had worked on me, at least, and I felt a strange sense of calm as the rebels advanced. I aimed with the others, watching Westleigh raise his weapon out the corner of my eye—and saw him lift his sights just a little higher right before the order came to fire. Flames and smoke and bullets poured into the rebels with that now familiar popping down the line. I saw Westleigh's rifle kick, knocking his shoulder back, and heard him as he gasped for breath afterwards. Jack kept encouraging him as we reloaded for another volley.

But soon that coolness I felt was shattered with the ear-piercing rebel yell. The rebel lines started rushing toward us with ferocity.

"Steady!" came the cries behind us, and we stood our ground, even while the very air was torn by bullets.

I will never forget those sounds. That terrible ripping or the soft thud as they punched into flesh. Men dropped all around us, and we hardly had reloaded and fired again before another volley shredded our ranks.

All the while, our leaders urged us forward. We gained ground by inches, only to lose them again in another wave.

Allison cursed under his breath. I knew we weren't doing so well whenever Allison started swearing.

I glanced to my right, and saw Westleigh starting to shake apart again, fumbling with the ramrod as he frantically tried to remove it from the barrel. I expected Jack to assist him at any moment, but when I saw the look on Jack's face, I was startled so that I nearly dropped my gun. 'Twas a different man who stood there, one I'd never seen before, and should hope to never see again.

There was death on his face. Not the vacancy of a corpse, grey and lifeless, but the spirit of Death itself. His eyes were almost otherworldly, his expression one of ice-cold rage.

He was a god of vengeance, come for a reckoning with mankind, and nothing on Earth or below it could stop him. He fired with a deadly speed, and I was in awe.

Westleigh finally loosed the ramrod and managed to fire another shot without aid.

But we'd lost the inches gained again. Our line was tattered. A few men had broken off and run for the safety of our guns bellowing from the trees behind us.

The rebels yelled again. Our line broke apart.

I hardly heard the commanders call for retreat as more bullets rained around us, hailstones zipping through the air. I felt one so close that it moved my hair. It struck a man behind me, and I dared not look. But I heard him fall.

Westleigh stumbled in front of me, and Jack paused to help him. "Come on! Get—"

Jack's arm jerked back and he cried out in pain. My heart stopped.

Allison grabbed for Westleigh and dragged him along, and I screamed for Jack. He met my eyes, and that spirit which possessed him before was gone. In its place was Fear.

I reached for him and he for me, and together we made it across the road to the woods. We ran. We'd failed. But none of that mattered. Jack was bleeding.

"I'm all right," he grunted, trying to push me away as we all huddled low in the trees. He showed me his arm. "Look, it's just a graze."

"I'm sorry," Westleigh's small voice came brokenly. "Jack, I'm—"

"You don't belong here," I said through my teeth. "We can't keep looking after you! Now look what's happened! You're going to get us all killed, you know that?"

I regretted the words soon as they left my mouth. Westleigh looked stricken, and he scrambled to get to his feet, despite the shelling that was going on overhead. He hurried away, deeper into the woods. Allison followed, calling his name.

"I said I'm fine," Jack grumbled. "Wasn't the kid's fault. Did you see that mess back there?"

I groaned. "I know. I'm sorry..."

"That boy is one of the bravest here," Jack said. "Shaking in his brogans, and still he holds the same ground we do. Does the same work we all do. Not a shred of complaining. Not a hint of shirking. He's not a soldier. But he's got guts. And there's got to be a reason he's here."

"I know, I know," I said, wiping my eyes. "It just scared me so badly, I thought—"

"I'm still here." Jack gave a shaky smile and pinched my chin. "Gonna take more than a bee sting to get me, you know."

I looked over the remains of our regiments. "Lots of bee stings."

He grunted, looking around. "They tore us up pretty good."

"I hope the rest of the brigade has done better. We're so close to Richmond." I looked at Jack. "This—it has to all be over soon, hasn't it?"

Jack's eyes darkened. "Don't think it will be," he muttered. "Least not in the way you're hoping."

"Oh, Jack, don't talk that way—"

He covered his eyes with his hand and bowed his head. I bit my lip, waiting for him to heave that deep sigh of his, and say a word of encouragement, or fuss at me to go check on Westleigh. But then his shoulders started to shake.

"Jack!" I laid my hand upon his back. He bent over on his knees and began to cry harder. I leaned over to whisper in his ear. "Jack, please, you're scaring me."

He raked his hands through his hair and sat up, sniffing. "I'm sorry." He tried to dry his face, but the tears kept coming. He fought for composure, and failed utterly, furiously wiping at his eyes in vain. I moved my arm around his back and was surprised when he leaned against me.

Jack took a shuddering breath when he finally found his words. "I'm just—I'm so weary. Some days, I..." he trailed off, and looked away so I couldn't see his face before he whispered. "Some days I wish the next battle could be my last, just so I could see her again."

His words took the wind out of me, and I leaned just as hard against him, swallowing my own tears. I held him a bit tighter and pressed my forehead against his shoulder.

"You know what she would say to hear you speak so," I whispered.

Jack sniffed. "Yeah, I do."

I didn't have to say it aloud. How he still had *us*. How we still needed him.

"I'm not going anywhere yet," he said. "But I'm so scared. Scared to death of losing you, or Westleigh—even Horner. Every waking moment, I worry... I've lost so much. I don't know what I'd do if I lost any more."

I wanted to stay there and hold him more, but he gently pushed me away, and straightened my cap.

"Enough cryin' now," he said softly, handing me his handkerchief. "Don't want to give anyone any ideas. Tears aren't very manly, you know."

I used the kerchief to wipe his face first. "That's absolutely idiotic."

Jack sniffed. "Yeah, yeah it is."

Westleigh wasn't anywhere to be found that evening for dinner, and for a moment I panicked that he'd deserted. But Allison assured me, with a well-deserved scolding glare, that Westleigh was strong enough to endure my petulant insults.

Still, he had no idea where Westleigh had run off to. Worried he might have gotten cornered by the captain, or

Declan, again, I offered to go and look for him. Neither Jack nor Allison tried to stop me. Westleigh might not have shirked off and run home, but it was clear they blamed me for him missing. I blamed me too.

We were back at our fortifications near Seven Pines, the regiment tasked with guarding, but after checking with the sergeant, I confirmed Westleigh wasn't on the picket duty. I moved through the tent rows, searching him out among the other small huddled groups of tired men. I caught a glimpse of Declan outside the captain's tent, but Westleigh wasn't there, either. Much to my relief.

I thought to check the sick tents, then hesitated when I remembered the blood and the noise and the smells from the hospital in Williamsburg. I leaned against a tree just outside of our tent row, waiting for my nausea to ease, when I saw him standing at the end of the road. He faced towards the contraband camp that sat at the bottom of the hill, watching the men and women there build what was starting to look like a little town.

"There you are."

He startled and sighed when he saw me. "Oh. Hello." He turned back around.

I came to his side. "Allison was looking for you."

"I went for a walk," he said curtly, still not looking at me.

For hours? I frowned, but I let it pass. "You missed dinner."

"I wasn't hungry." He hugged his arms to his chest and

continued to watch the people in the makeshift village below. "They need rations. There's more and more of them coming in every day. Half of them barely have clothes on their backs. I don't think the army has enough to feed them."

"The army doesn't even have enough supplies to feed us properly," I grumbled. Westleigh's jaw tightened, and I added quickly, "but I heard some Quakers have come to Yorktown, help with the contraband camps set up there. They're likely to help here, too."

Westleigh finally looked at me, eyes sad. "Maybe that's what I should've done," he muttered. "I wouldn't get anyone killed that way."

I looked at my feet. "I—I didn't mean that, Wes—"

"You're right," he said sadly. "I don't belong here. I'm a terrible soldier, the captain says. I'm only going to get you, or Jack, or Allison hurt, and I cannot bear the thought of—" He gave a small gasp. "Oh! How is Jack's arm?"

"He's fine," I waved my hand to put him at east. "Barely a scratch. So you aren't the perfect soldier. Doesn't mean you don't belong here."

His brow gathered. "Do you believe that? Or did Jack tell you to say it?"

Never did get used to how well that boy could read me. And it didn't make me feel any better that he seemed fond of me anyway. I gave a shrug. "Doesn't matter. Do *you* believe it?"

Westleigh looked away. "I'm really not sure."

"Well," I said slowly, "would you believe me that I'm sorry I was such a beast to you earlier today?"

The corner of his mouth lifted in a soft smile. "Of course I do. You were frightened."

"Doesn't mean I should've snapped at you." Tears stung my eyes. "You could yell at me, you know. Don't make it so easy on me all the time."

Westleigh tilted his head. "I'd be a pretty poor friend if I didn't give you grace for things like that."

"No, but I *want* you to yell at me!" I threw up my hands. "For heaven's sake, Westleigh. Fight me back. If I'm being an ass, I want you to tell me. Jack does all the time."

Westleigh laughed. "You—you want me to fight you?"

"I want you to stop being afraid of me," I blurted. "You say you're giving me grace. I'm calling you on your lies."

"My—my lies?" he sputtered. "But—"

"You want to be my friend?" I asked softly. "You start being honest with me. Stop hiding what you're feeling because you think you'll frighten me away."

Westleigh stared at me, his grey eyes glistening. He seemed to struggle for words.

I let myself edge closer, hoping to draw them out, not sure why I cared so much that he share his so carefully guarded heart with me. "Why *did* you join the army, Westleigh?"

I already knew, but I wanted to hear it from him.

I could see the lump in his throat as he swallowed. His smile was shaky, this time.

"Same as you," he said with a forced lightness. "I couldn't bear to be left behind. You understand that, don't you? Why I couldn't be left behind?"

I looked away. He was still hiding.

"I understand," I murmured. "Of course I do."

"I'm sorry I broke my promise," he whispered. "I'm sorry I left David. I feel like—like it's my fault he's missing."

The thought had crossed my mind, as well. But I couldn't hold that against him. Not anymore. Not when it was just as much my fault, too.

"I'm sure he's fine," I said. I smiled ruefully. "Besides, if Lucy couldn't keep that stubborn goat from running off who knows where, what makes you think you could've?"

"Maybe," Westleigh murmured.

The bugle sounded in the distance, calling us all to sleep.

"I'm surprised Jack hasn't torn apart the camp looking for us," I said, nudging Westleigh to come along. "Let's go before he starts hollering."

Westleigh kept his feet rooted to the ground, his brow puckered. "I still have a question," he said grimly.

I stiffened. "What is it?"

"How often should I fight you? Do you mean, all the time, or just pick one day a week? Should I inform you which day I chose, warn Jack, or just surprise—"

I punched him in the arm.

"Ow!" He rubbed it, laughing. "What was that for?"

"I said fight me," I teased. "I didn't say you should expect to win."

June 8, 1862

Dearest Allison,

I hope this letter finds you and our friends well. Lucy and I sit together every evening to read the paper and follow the news of the army's activities in Virginia. We pray for a swift victory, so that our country can begin to heal again.

It is very busy here in Washington. Every day more wounded are brought to the hospitals, which are becoming too full. Some boys are sleeping on cots in the halls, and even those are in short supply. There are rumors that Lucy and I will be moved to a hospital farther south, but we have no details yet. Thankfully, wherever we go, Lucy has promised we will not be separated. Do not worry for us, for we are very safe.

I'm sending along a small package of treats. I managed to find some of those wafers you like so much. Share them with the others, especially Jack, for they need the comfort. And perhaps Jack will ease up on his teasing, though I'm certain you have every bit of it coming. As for my answer, I am grateful for your patience. Let us see what the summer will bring. Hopefully, you will be home in another month, and we can speak of the future then.

All my love,
Ellen Moore

WESTLEIGH

Seven Pines, Virginia
June 15, 1862

If anyone had told me how miserably hot it would be in Virginia, maybe I would have stayed home after all. And it was humid, to boot. I was drowning in sweat, filthy and miserable no matter the hour of the day. I believe I preferred the constant rain and mud to this, though Saoirse said I must have been in the sun too long to think so. Meanwhile, Allison lay out in front of our tents hardly wearing anything but his trousers, moaning about the heat as he emptied his canteen over his face.

Jack, of course, said we were all 'a bunch of babies.' And one Sunday morning he thought the best remedy would be haircuts. Not such a bad idea, as it gave us the distraction and a little bit more of a breeze over our heads. And Saoirse's hair was starting to get a bit long. She wouldn't let

Allison touch her hair again, not after the first time, so she and Jack took turns tending to their own locks, while Allison and I traded scissors with each other.

"Don't go snipping off the top of my ear," Saoirse said nervously as Jack lifted the scissors.

"Then you better stop squirming, shouldn't you?"

"I think we all need a shave, too," Allison said, rubbing a hand over his face as I snipped at his hair.

Saoirse tilted her head. "I don't think we have one whisker 'mongst the four of us to speak of."

I felt my chin. She was right. "Well, maybe we ought to give the pretense of shaving?"

"Whatever for?" Saoirse made a face. "Sure, and do any of you even know how to do it?"

None of us responded.

"Hmm. Then there isn't a one of you that's bringing a blade to my face, that's for certain."

By the time we were finished with our haircuts, Allison was whining again.

"I'm melting," he huffed, flicking away the little bits of stray hair from the back of his sweaty neck.

"Let's play Whist," Saoirse offered, reaching for her cards. "We can even switch up partners this time."

Allison stood up and started pacing. "I can't concentrate on cards..."

"Then go take a walk," Jack snapped. "Your fidgeting is driving me mad."

Allison shrugged and jogged away, ruffling his damp hair and whistling Yankee Doodle.

Jack stretched with a yawn. "Don't know what y'all are complaining about. This is a dream compared to a Texas summer."

"I remember," Saoirse muttered. "It's still hotter than the devil's armpit out here."

I wrinkled my nose. "Wonderful image."

She did a small bow, winking.

We settled into a comfortable silence. Jack napped with the newspaper he was reading spread 'cross his face. Saoirse borrowed my sewing kit and went to work mending some of our socks. I shuffled through my knapsack and pulled out a random book. Tennyson, *The Idylls of the King.*

"What are you reading about today?" Saoirse said, looking up from her sewing.

"Oh," I held up the book. "Arthur and his knights." I opened the book to the beginning. I'd read it before, probably a dozen times since David bought it for me, not long before the war began. He loved tales of Arthur. We'd read Tennyson together, Thomas Malory, translations of Chrétien de Troyes as long as I could remember. And not just Arthur, but the Greek myths as well, or histories of Charlemagne. But what I loved the most was when we'd stay up late in the parlor, and by candlelight David would tell me stories passed down from his father about the Fenian heroes of Ireland.

All those stories, all the romantic tales of these heroic exploits, they had filled my head and heart with such a different expectation of this war. Even as I'd struggled with enlisting, when the heaviness of dread weighted my hand as I signed my name to that paper, I remembered this fleeting feeling of elation.

Here was my heroic tale, like some knight of the Roundtable, or one of Charlemagne's paladins, I would fight for a noble cause. God Himself surely blessed it, for it meant the freedom of the oppressed.

And here we sat in the sweltering Virginia heat, over a year into a war, so close to victory, waiting.

"Well," Saoirse's voice broke into my brooding. "Are you going to read any of it to me, then?"

"Oh," I said, smoothing down the pages which had fluttered in a welcome breeze. "Certainly, I—"

"Let's all go swimming!" Allison leapt back into the middle of us. "C'mon, the whole company's heading down to the river."

Saoirse laughed. "No."

"Aww come on," he pleaded. "You'd be the only one sitting out—"

"Allison," she said through her teeth. "You're an eejit."

He stopped. "Oh." Then he wiggled his eyebrows at her with a stupid grin. "You could always just come and *watch*."

"Ugh. I'll sit with Aidan," I said. I didn't much care for

swimming. Never really learned how. And the thought of being so exposed in front of the other boys made me as uncomfortable as Saoirse.

"What about you, Jack?"

The paper moved, and Jack sat up with a shrug. "I could use a chance to wash away all this filth."

Allison hopped up and down as he ripped off his shoes and tossed them at our tent. We stood to follow, and he was practically stripped bare and leaping into the water by the time we got to the bank. Half the company was already doing the same.

Saoirse blushed and quickly turned away. "Oh my."

I stifled a smile. "Surely you've seen your fair share of bare skin in the army already."

"Not so much at once," she said, eyes wide. She pointed to the trees by the bank. "Let's go sit over there. Did you bring the Tennyson?"

I held up the book, and caught Jack's eyes behind Saoirse's head, his brow arched in warning. I made a quick nod, and he started to take off his shoes to join the others.

Saoirse and I found an old log to sit on. We could hear the laughing and hollering from the river, but the trees made for a more discreet screen between us and the buck-naked soldiers.

I read aloud as she mended the socks, and I almost forgot there was a war. It felt like a summer's day back home. The birds sang in the trees as if they hadn't noticed the tops had been sheared off by cannon fire. Men splashed about like they were boys celebrating the end of a school term. I had a book, my friends, and a lovely sunny day. I took my first deep, full breath since we arrived on the peninsula.

"Do you really think it's almost over?" Saoirse asked, dropping her mending in her lap to crack her stiff fingers. I would have wondered if she could hear my thoughts, if I didn't know that we were all thinking—hoping—the same thing.

I scratched my head to still the tremble in my hands. If it was to be over soon, it wouldn't end quietly. I gave a small shrug. "I pray it is."

"Hmm," she said softly, staring at the socks in her lap. Her voice was smaller next. "Do you wonder if it'll have made a difference?"

"Slavery?" I laid the ribbon in my book and closed it. "It will have to. Surely Lincoln would not accept their surrender without the release of their slaves."

"That's not what he's saying," she said. "That's not what any of them are saying. They say that's not what we're fighting for."

"Doesn't matter if they're not," I said firmly. "God will not let so much blood be spilled if not for the end of slavery."

She inspected her hands again. "Do you truly believe that?"

I have to, I thought to myself. It's the only way I can sleep at night. "Of course I do. I only wish... I wish it could be ended another way."

"'The crimes of this guilty land will never be purged away, but with blood.'"

I grimaced. "John Brown."

"I used to think he was mad," Saoirse admitted. "Not anymore. He was right, you know."

"Don't you think there could have been another way?" I whispered. "We could have fought them with the law. We could still. With words instead of bullets. If their hearts could be turned—"

"They are beyond reason, you know that," Saoirse said, somewhat impatiently. "Even your Mr. Garrison knows that."

"But so many lives," I said, heart wrenched, "so many lives lost, to be lost still..."

"If we stopped the war now, how many lives will be lost in bondage, waiting for you to *reason* with men who right now are willing to die to defend slavery?" She gave a small yelp as she poked her finger, and glared at it. "Those Copperheads in the north are crying for peace, like a bunch of self-righteous snakes. They don't care for the colored lives being lost. Just their own."

My cheeks flushed. "That's not peace they want, then," I said. "You know that's not what I mean. No peace is possible while people suffer such injustice, I know that."

"I know you do," she said gently. "I understand. I wish we could have it both ways, Westleigh. Freedom without bloodshed. But it's a bit too late for that."

We settled into silence again for a few moments, while she returned to her socks. I watched her as I thumbed idly through my book. But she didn't seem to be any more at ease than before, hunched over, her brow wrinkled, her lips pressed tight together. When she spoke again, there was a forced cheerfulness to her tone.

"What will you do after the war? Will you return to school?"

"I hope so," I said with a light laugh. "I will never complain about another dull book as long as I live, not after the army."

Saoirse grinned. "I wish I could go with you."

I coughed. "You-you do?"

"Sure, and why do you think I was so sore about you going?" she said, blushing a little. "I wasn't very nice to you, don't know if you noticed."

I gave a little shrug. "Jack warned me of your temper," I teased. "I paid you no mind."

She rolled her eyes.

"Still," I said slowly, trying not to sound so pleased at the idea of Saoirse following me to Pittsburgh, "You really wanted to go, too?"

"I wanted to do *something*. I suppose now I have... and I'm not sure where I'd go from here."

"I don't see why you couldn't sneak your way into school either," I laughed. "Though I think you'd be bored silly."

"We'll just see what comes, then," she said wistfully, smiling. "I feel like I could do anything, after this. I don't think I've ever felt so... so..."

"Free?"

"*Weightless.*" She bowed her head shyly. "Like, I've always had wings but I've been afraid to use them." She shook her head. "And I don't want to rest till we *all* have them."

"Wings," I repeated softly, and the image of Saoirse as an angel made my heart skip a beat.

She threw a sock at me. "Don't go teasing me, now, or I won't ever tell you another thing!"

"I'm not teasing!" I laughed, throwing it back. "I—I was just picturing it in my head, and it was—"

"Silly?"

"No. Beautiful." I winced. There I go, speaking words aloud again...

Saoirse blinked. "Beautiful?" she whispered. She almost looked sad. But before I could answer her, the call for dinner sounded. Men started splashing toward the bank, scrambled to dress, and ran back to their tents with their uniforms all askew.

"We should get back," she said, gathering her socks. But she dropped them again, her jaw hanging open and her face redder than I'd ever seen it.

Allison suddenly came rushing by, utterly naked, hands covering his privates and shouting as he streaked past. "I should have expected this!"

We were stunned into silence while she composed herself, but I broke into a fit of giggles.

"Did you happen to see in which direction Jack ran?"

"No," I laughed, "but wherever he is, I'll bet you all next month's pay he has Allison's clothes."

21

SAOIRSE
Malvern Hill, Virginia
July 1, 1862

I glanced over my shoulder as our gunships fired shells over our heads toward the enemy on the other side of the ravine. Westleigh was huddled with a few of the younger boys, praying. Which was a difficult feat, lying on our bellies the way we were in the grass.

"Beloved, let us love one another. For love is of God, and every one that loves is born of God, and knows God."

Westleigh had his eyes shut tight and gripped his kepi in his white-knuckled hands. His voice wavered, but he lifted it to be heard over the sound of the big guns, the shouts of the rebels, the firing from the rest of our brigade up ahead.

"He that loves not, knows not God, for God is love…"

Sergeant Kennedy piped up behind him. "Listen now,

Little Father. Those words are great and all, but can't you recite a psalm or something, like everyone else?"

Westleigh ignored him. "There is no fear in love, but perfect love casts out fear..."

I swallowed hard, trying to pull some calm from his words to still the heavy pounding of my heart. 'Twas causing a terrible fuss that morning, pitter-pattering the way it used to when I was a child. Made it hard to breathe.

We didn't make it to Richmond, and the Confederate capitol yet stood. McClellan's army, our beautiful machine of justice, was getting run off the peninsula with our tails between our legs.

Our gunships rained fire into their armies, protecting our retreat. We were to make our stand here on the hill, but all we would win were our lives. The campaign was a failure. The war would rage on.

Westleigh finished his prayers, and Jack urged him to get back in our line with us. He slid between Jack and me. Allison was to my left. We waited there on our bellies till our generals called us.

Jack looked over the three of us. "Y'all ready?"

Allison shrugged, chewing his lip nervously. I nodded, but I felt less confident than I let on.

Westleigh pressed his face into the grass and groaned. "No."

Jack gripped his shoulder. "I want you to listen to me, Coz," he whispered. "I know it's hard, but you gotta remember just one thing. Just keep remembering, every reb you take down is one less gun firing at you, or me, or Allison, or Aidan."

There was a hitch in Westleigh's sigh.

Jack straightened his cousin's kepi and gave his shoulder another squeeze. "Every bullet you fire is gonna help save a life. Just keep remembering that."

"By taking another." Westleigh's voice was muffled by the grass.

"Well, this is the way it is. You gonna do your part?"

Westleigh finally lifted his head. The turmoil on his face was unbearable, but his eyes were steady and dry. "I will."

Jack smiled tiredly. "Glad to know you got my back, little guy." He looked over at me and winked. "You too."

Allison craned his neck and looked over. "And what about—"

"There's a reason you're all the way over there, Horner."

"Now wait just a second, I—"

Shouts from our officers drowned out Allison's protests and our lines began to move excitedly. We were brought to our feet. The captain roared behind us, and his command made my heart pound harder.

"FIX BAYONETS!"

What a terrific sight that was, the whole regiment in one fluid motion unsheathing our bayonets from their scabbards and affixing them to our rifles. Up and down the line, the sun glinted off these terrible instruments. With a shiver I remember our drills, how they instructed us to use them in combat. Firing a bullet at a man dozens of yards away from me was one thing. The thought of striking them with this—designed just so to make a man bleed more, Jack said—made my stomach turn. Before now, we'd been using ours to hold candlesticks.

We were to charge the enemy, then.

Grand.

Our colonel was riding back and forth, making shouts to us to get up our spirits. The regiment was emboldened, and even I felt my blood run hotter as their moods lifted.

I felt that weightless feeling again, as a bit of pride swelled in my chest. We were powerful and unstoppable and *right*. It didn't matter we were being run off from Richmond. I felt like every one of us were thinking the same thing. The rebs have taken too many of our brothers' lives already. We'd be damned if they took any more.

This was our purpose, and it was glorious. And sure, we were a gallant sight.

Even Westleigh looked a bit more lively than usual. His hands were steady. His eyes, shaded by his kepi, were fixed straight ahead, and his head was high. Seemed Jack's talk had done him some good.

They marched us forward as fire rained overhead. Our gunships kept blasting while their artillery whistled, and we quickened our pace, dashing toward the rebel lines.

I swallowed down my heart again, wincing at the tight

little ache in my chest. 'Twas my anxiousness, was all, mixed up with exhaustion and worry. But as we ran farther, a bit of darkness crept into my vision, and my feet stumbled. I gripped my weapon tighter, staggered forward, and crashed into the ground.

I covered my head as feet trod over me. Westleigh shouted for me, and I realized with fear that he used my real name, just before everything went dark.

I awoke, spluttering, with cold water splashing on my face. I covered my face in shame and moaned.

"Saoirse!" Westleigh hissed above me. I felt him shaking my shoulder. "Come on, come on, please…"

An explosion shook the ground nearby, and Westleigh cursed, throwing himself over me as dirt rained down. He reached for my hands to pull them from my face.

"We have to go! Get up, please—"

I let him pull me to a sitting position, and my head was sorry for it. The whole earth seemed to tip, and I wanted to lie down again.

"No you don't," Westleigh said, pulling at me again. "Get up, I'm getting you out of here…"

My breath came in short gasps, but I managed to sling my rifle over my shoulder as he helped me to my feet. "What—what's—"

"Move!" Westleigh kept his arm around me, half-holding me up while we rushed back towards the farmhouse where we'd been waiting before.

I glanced over my shoulder. "The battle—"

"I heard shouts." Westleigh gulped down a breath. "I think we broke their line."

"Why aren't you—"

"I'm not leaving you out there alone," he said through his teeth. "They can hang me if they wish."

We stumbled together, ducking as another shell burst, and he half-dragged me towards a tree close to the house where we'd marched from earlier. I tumbled to the ground and he sat beside me, pulling out his handkerchief to wipe my face with wide eyes.

"Are—are you shot?" he stammered as he inspected, hesitant to touch. His face was pale. "Where are you—"

"I'm fine," I wheezed, pressing a hand over my wretched heart. "I—I just had a spell."

"A what?"

I drank from my canteen, feeling like I wish I could sink into the earth while my heart seemed to want to fly away. I shook my head. "My heart. It—it doesn't work proper sometimes. I think the heat, and being run ragged like we are…"

Westleigh's eyes widened. "I should get you a doctor."

"No!" I grabbed his collar, yanking him close to hiss. "What do you think they'll find if they start examining me, Westleigh?"

He went paler.

"Help me up," I gasped, pulling at the trunk. My arms were weak. "We need to get back—"

"Not you." He shoved me to the ground. "You can hardly breathe!"

"I'll be grand," I muttered. "We've got to get back before they think we've run off—"

"You're not well." Westleigh held me by my shoulders, jaw set sight. "We can't keep you safe out there."

He was right. I could barely stand. If I got them killed trying to help me...

"Go," I rasped. "I'll wait here."

Westleigh hesitated. "I—I cannot leave you alone."

"I'll be fine," I assured him with a weak smile. "Go. Jack and Allison need you."

Westleigh swallowed and nodded firmly. He gripped my hand. "Please be safe."

I squeezed it back, blinking away tears. "You too, Westleigh."

He stood, holding his Springfield 'cross his chest, and bolted back towards the sound of fire.

I curled around myself, drawing my knees to my chest, and I wept and prayed.

I awoke again some time later, unaware I'd drifted to sleep. The sky was stained with a bloody sunset, and I felt filthy with sweat and dirt. I straightened my cramped legs and fumbled for my canteen.

The sounds of battle still raged behind me.

I finished every last drop of water, and pressed my palm over my chest, breathing deep. Whatever spell had happened was past now. I hoped.

I drew myself to my feet, still feeling a bit shaky. But all I could think of were my boys, and I pushed myself towards the lines of battle, feeling strength fill my limbs again as I jogged toward them.

The sight ahead choked my throat, though that may have been the smoke of our rifle fire.

We'd advanced some hundreds of yards and were now pouring fire into waves of rebels charging the hill. Grey uniformed bodies littered the ground. Our lines looked strong, but weary.

I saw Captain Oliver still standing, shouting orders, and squinted beyond him.

Allison, Westleigh, and Jack were alive, firing furiously at the enemy.

"Get down, you idiot!" someone shouted near me, and I felt a hand yank me down to the ground.

I looked up into Declan's grim face.

He scowled at me. "Where were you?"

I pushed him off. "None of your business." His brow arched, and I sighed. "I had a spell," I muttered, loading my rifle somewhat clumsily. I felt his eyes on me, and my face burned. "I'm here now, all right?"

Declan swore. "Your heart. You stupid little fool—"

"I didn't ask for your opinion!"

"What did you expect?" he hissed. "You think you're invincible, 'cause you always got Aidan to look after you. Then Jack. Now that sheriff's boy. What'll you do when they're all gone? You're nothing without them, you realize that?"

I growled and crawled forward toward the boys.

Westleigh gaped at me. "What are you—"

"Say another word, and you'll regret it."

Jack looked over at me. He grunted. "Both of you cut your chatter, they're coming again."

"Merciful God," Westleigh breathed, "when will this end?"

Not until night fell. Our brigade had been under fire for twelve hours. But the rebels gave up, fled the field, and tired shouts went up and down the line.

Thunder clapped overhead, and the heavens unleashed a torrent on us, quickly snuffing out our fire.

We retreated.

The regiment lost another dozen men on the hill, Sergeant Kennedy told us the next day. A few dozen more wounded. Allison did the math. So far we'd lost one hundred and fifty men to rebel bullets, though I prayed some of the wounded would be fit to return soon. The surgeon's saws tended to take more souls than even the rebels did. But thank the Lord again, my boys were safe.

You're nothing without them, Declan's voice snarled in my ear. *You pathetic little fool.*

I ground my teeth together till I thought I'd shatter them, and hammered the tent peg into the muddy ground.

The army escaped to a place called Harrison's Landing, and we set up camp. It was a miserable, hot, and crowded stretch of godforsaken land. I hurried with Jack to put our tent together and tried my hardest to ignore him. But that wasn't going to happen that night.

"I thought you told me you were done having those spells." He hammered another tent peg with a bit more force than he needed. "Do you realize you scared the—"

"I thought I was better, too." I wiped sweat from my brow with the back of my hand. "I *am* better. 'Twas an aberration, that's all. This damned heat..."

Jack scowled, unconvinced.

Westleigh glanced over, biting his lip. "What is it?" he asked softly. "What's wrong with you?"

My face flushed. *"Nothing."*

"Aidan's heart is weak."

"I'm not weak!"

"Lay down your pride for five seconds," Jack snapped, finger at my nose. "You know it ain't right, and you signed up anyhow. That was stupid."

"It *was* better," I protested. I looked at Westleigh. "When I was born—"

"I know," he said softly. "I read Da's diary, remember?"

"Right." I swallowed. "Mam said 'twas since I was born too early. But I haven't had a spell in years, Jack. And I'm sure I won't again…"

Jack shook his head. "You're just lucky Westleigh was able to get you out of harm's way—"

"Jack," Westleigh warned, watching me sideways. I don't know when I stood, but I was glaring down at Jack, nostrils flaring, fists clenched tight at my sides. And my stupid heart flopped about in my chest again.

Jack reached up and grabbed my fist. "Sit down. I'm sorry. Seems that Callahan habit of shooting our mouths off is hard to shake, isn't it?"

I yanked my hand back, shaking my head. "He's right," I mumbled aloud.

"Who's right?" Jack scowled. "What did Declan say to you?"

Tears burned my eyes. "But you're right, too. I was lucky Westleigh was there—"

"Stop," Westleigh said, rising. "That's not—"

"But it's true," I whispered, looking at them all. "I'm nothing without any of you. I can't do any of this on my own."

Allison looked up at me and shrugged. "Who says you're supposed to? Who says any of us are supposed to?"

Jack and Westleigh stared at me, and I felt myself shrink. Jack pulled me down before my knees gave way.

"The only person who would try and make you feel

small for needing someone else," he said, "is the sad sort of soul who doesn't have anyone to lean on. Or a fool that thinks he doesn't need anyone. Don't be that sort of fool, kid."

I nodded, but Declan's words still haunted me.

What will you do when they're all gone?

22

WESTLEIGH
Harrison's Landing, Virginia
July 4, 1862

I'd never seen a more miserable Independence Day. The birthday of our dear country, the one we were fighting, bleeding, and dying for. And we were too downcast to celebrate it, not that we had much opportunity. The officers were cracking down upon discipline. Too many men crowded in too small an area for them to allow for any slacking on that front. Michael Connolly tried to have a boxing match—though it turned into rather more of a brawl—and spent the next day dragging around a cannonball chained to his ankle.

So naturally, Allison decided to organize a Base Ball game.

To his credit, he got permission from the officers. Sergeant Kennedy and Lieutenant Brown were both eager to join, having been members of clubs back home. But that set off an argument about whether we should play by the townball rules we and Kennedy were used to, or play the New York game that the lieutenant claimed to be the only 'decently regulated variation.'

"What?" Allison laughed at the men voting for the New York rules. "Underhanded pitching? It's weak!"

"Well I've had enough ducking and dodging things flying at me lately," Corporal Hastings said with a disgusted expression. "I'd rather go with the New York game if it meant not getting a ball lobbed at my head."

"Where's the fun in that?" Allison fussed.

Hastings shrugged.

"You don't even have a ball," Saoirse said, watching the arguments with a grin. She'd never played a game before. Neither had Jack. Apparently it hadn't really taken off down in Brookfield. Not that I ever had much of a chance to play back home. Allison's brothers had seen to that.

"Got that taken care of," Allison said, hopping on one foot as he started to unlace one of his brogans.

Jack groaned. "Not your filthy sock."

"I have a clean one in my tent, you know," I said.

But Allison had already pulled it off and was replacing his shoe. He held up the limp sweaty sock. "Anyone got a bullet?"

Saoirse gagged. "That's disgusting, Horner."

"You want to play or not?"

Kennedy passed him a minnie ball, and Allison wound the sock tight around it, and we soon had a makeshift baseball. Then the arguing over the rules resumed.

I saw Declan standing off to the side and slipped away. He didn't look at me as I approached, but nodded at the gathered players.

"What's this, then?" he asked.

"Base Ball," I said with a smile.

"I saw a game once in Pittsburgh," he said. "Reminded me a bit of cricket."

My brow arched. "Don't let Allison catch you saying that." I looked at the arguing men. "Or any of them, for that matter."

To my shock and elation, Declan chuckled, and not mockingly.

I braced myself and took a risk. "Would you like to join us? Soon as they stop fighting over the rules, I could try and explain them."

Declan finally looked at me, as if he just realized who he'd been speaking to. He waved me off. "Why would I run around in the mud when I could watch you fools do it?"

He shoved past me, slipping a bit as he went by. I grabbed his elbow to steady him, and he nearly sent it into my ribs before stomping off. Still, he sat on a barrel near our makeshift field, and I saw him pull out his sketchbook.

Saoirse came to my side. "What are you doing?" She saw Declan and rolled her eyes. "What did you expect? He's got an allergy to fun. Get over here. We need you to break a tie."

"Oh, don't make me decide…"

"It's an easy decision," Allison said, looking at me pointedly. "I mean, why would you ever vote against your closest friend?"

"You just want to throw the ball at people's heads."

"I do, I really do."

I sighed, and raised my hand. "Townball." At least I was used to those rules. Even if the New York game seemed like fewer opportunities for bruising.

We split up in our teams, our squad with Kennedy and Brown on our side, and Sergeant Clark's squad on the other.

We were up to bat. Allison went first, hit a wild but decent ball, which landed with a disgusting *thunk* in the mud at the edge of our 'field.'

"I'm beginning to see this wasn't so wise an idea," Saoirse leaned over to say. But Allison managed to get to the second base, and it was her turn next. Unfortunately she was too small, none of the pitches were fair, and the catcher caught them all before she could hit a one. With Allison's rules, one out was all out, so we switched.

The other team took up the bat, and the sergeant pitched after a coin toss with the lieutenant, while we spread out among the back of the field. Our sergeant was an excellent pitcher, but finally one of the young privates got a solid hit, and we scrambled for the ball.

Jack scooped it up and threw it in the opposite direction of the runner, pegging Allison in the shoulder.

"Ow! What was that?"

"Sorry," Jack grinned. "I don't know how this game works."

Thankfully, our pitcher struck out the next batter, so they gained no runs. It was Jack's turn to bat next. He took the paddle and inspected it before stepping up to the plate. But the other team's pitcher, one of the Glenn brothers, shook his head.

"Nuh-uh, I'm not playing with any Injun."

"Bite your tongue," Corporal Hastings snapped. "If you don't want to play then get off the field."

Saoirse grunted beside me. "Huh, 'twasn't expecting that."

"Me either."

The pitcher grumbled something else and glared at Jack. Then he threw the muddy ball as fast as he could, right at Jack's head. Jack ducked, and the catcher caught it.

Saoirse tensed beside me. "That isn't fair."

"Well, Allison did fight for the Boston game's rules, which are a bit more… violent."

"I'm sure that's not what he meant."

"No, it isn't."

Glenn pitched again, and again Jack had to dodge out of the way. Hastings and the others on our team were hollering, but the other squad just laughed.

"Can't take the game, get out of the den," they called out at Jack.

Jack shook out his shoulders and approached the plate again. A wicked grin spread across his face.

Saoirse's eyes widened. "Uh-oh…"

The pitcher had a fast arm. He lobbed Allison's sock at Jack a third time, but Jack was ready for him now. He took a step back and swung at the same time, connecting with the ball with a loud smack. Mud flew everywhere. The ball shot back towards its origins, catching Glenn right in the gut. He tumbled to the ground with an audible *oomph*, and Allison and Jack both scored runs.

We cheered, and the other squad hollered. But I paid them no attention as I took the paddle and shook the mud from it for my turn. I didn't notice the shouting had turned mean until the lieutenant started barking.

"Break it up! Break it up, boys!"

I looked up in time to see Glenn take a swing at Jack. Jack ducked, sidestepping out of the way, and all hell broke loose.

Both sides leapt in, some trying to hold Glenn back. Jack kept dodging the swings, doing his best not to fight. But then Allison threw himself in the middle of it all, shoving Jack away, fists flying. He caught Glenn square in the jaw, laying him out in the mud. Soon there was just a pile of men scrambling and kicking and fighting and you could hardly tell who was punching who.

Jack took a punch in the eye, and that's when Saoirse herself charged forward, but Declan appeared beside us, grabbed her by the collar and yanked her back.

"Are you mad?" he hissed. "They'll squash you!"

She glared at him but hung back, settling for cussing at the instigators instead. All the while, Kennedy and Brown tried their best to break it up.

Then Olsen came running over. "What in blazes is going on here?"

The mass of scrapping men fell apart, half of them collapsed in the mud. Glenn still stood, one fist raised and the other gripping a handful of Jack's shirt. He released him when he saw the captain and stepped back at rigid attention.

"Should have known it was you starting trouble," Olsen growled at Jack. "Been itching for a court-martial since you joined up, have you? Come with—"

"It wasn't him who started the row."

I turned with wide eyes to see Declan step forward.

"There's your man," he said, pointing at Glenn. "He's been after him from the start of the game."

Saoirse looked over at me, jaw slack.

"That's right," Allison panted, picking himself up off the ground. His hair was caked with mud and he sported a bloody lip, but looked as if he'd had the time of his life. "They came after him—"

"Shut your trap, Horner," Olsen barked. He squinted at

Declan, and his glare made me shiver. Then he turned to the lieutenant. "Is that the way of it?"

Lieutenant Brown shrugged. "More or less. Glenn threw the first punch, as Private Callahan says."

Olsen looked around, glared at Jack again, and shook his head before stomping away. "Pick yourselves up and get back to your tents. The game is over," he called over his shoulder.

"Bastard," Saoirse muttered. "Sure, he'd punish Jack, but not the brute who started the row in the first place."

I nodded and turned to Declan. "Um, thank you for that, I—"

Declan turned away started to stalk back to his tent when his foot slid in the mud again. He righted himself, dusting off his coat. But as he took his next step, he collapsed onto the ground.

"Declan?" I rushed to him, and Saoirse too. We grabbed him by the shoulders to lift him, and he moaned. It was then that I noticed how badly he shook, the sallow hue to his skin, the sweat beaded on his brow. I looked at Saoirse. "He's got a fever."

She swallowed and stood, backing away. "Put him down, Westleigh," she said softly.

"He needs to get to the sick tent," I pleaded, holding him. I looked around at the others. I can't carry him on my own."

Jack staggered past the crowd of onlookers. He had a cut

on his cheekbone and he'd likely have quite the shiner over his right eye in a few hours. But he knelt and helped me lift Declan to hang between our shoulders. Saoirse stayed back, worry etched in her brow.

"Malaria, I'd bet," Jack said softly as we walked to the sick tents.

"Dear Lord," I whispered, looking nervously at Declan's face. He looked even weaker now. "I hope not."

"Don't worry," Jack added. "Only way you'll catch it is if one of those buggers bites you too."

I felt a phantom itch at the back of my neck and tried to ignore it, focusing on carrying Declan. "Hard to avoid them out here."

He nodded. "Pray we leave this place soon."

"Every day," I whispered. I glanced over at him. "So Declan—"

"I don't know," Jack said, glancing between us. Our cousin was out now, succumbed to his fever. Jack shook his head. "I gave up a long time ago trying to figure him out."

"I want to stay with him," I said suddenly, feeling that little seed of hope bloom inside of me. "Watch over him, maybe—"

"Don't, Westleigh," Jack said tiredly. "Let the docs do their job and you just mind your own business."

I spoke no more about it. I also avoided Jack's eyes when I asked the nurses if I could stay and help.

Jack just shook his head and left, and I remained at

Declan's bedside, when I wasn't assisting with the other patients.

For the next few days, I awoke, did my chores, fell in for drills when we had them, and returned to the tents to be of service. Jack didn't speak to me. Saoirse didn't say much, either, but once asked how Declan was faring, and I thought I read concern in her brow.

"He's faded quite a bit," I said, heart sinking at the image of him lying on the cot, looking so small and frail. I forced a smile. "But I'm sure he's almost through the worst of it."

I didn't tell her that it wasn't malaria. The doctor said it was influenza. Then all I would have gotten was an earful of grief from all of them, Allison included, if they found out. I was careful, I washed thoroughly and I kept what distance I could.

I was at his bedside when he finally awoke and recognized his surroundings.

He looked up at me, and he sighed. "You."

"Of course *me*." I shut the book I was reading. "No one else in this army cares about you apart from your family. The captain hasn't been by once to ask about you."

Declan turned his head. "Do you think that surprises me?" he laughed weakly. "I don't suppose I can get rid of you, in my state."

"Not a chance," I said, smirking. "Guess we'll finally have a chance to talk."

"You talk all you want, if you must," he said, sinking

further down on the pillow. "I'm not going to listen. But if you could spare me the cruelty and shut up, I would take it as a kindness."

I pursed my lips together. His breathing was ragged, but the last nurse said he wasn't in any danger, so I figured it couldn't hurt to pester him with questions. "Why'd you stick up for Jack?"

Declan groaned and turned his face into the pillow.

"Hey," I said, poking him gently in the shoulder. "If you don't really care about any of us, why'd you do it? Especially since you've probably upset Olsen…"

Declan lifted his head to glare at me.

"Sorry," I winced, and corrected myself. "Captain '*Oliver*.'"

He shook his head. "You're going to get us all in trouble, I hope you know that."

"Why did you?" I repeated, softer this time. "If it meant getting crossways with him?"

Declan's brow furrowed. "To be honest, I wasn't thinking about that at the time." He chuckled weakly. "I guess I'll discover the consequences later. Blame the fever."

I shook my head. "I would, but I don't believe you."

"Ugh," Declan growled, running his hands over his face. "Why do *you* care?"

"I've already told you," I said, forcing a smile. "We're family."

"Right," Declan said with a yawn. "Aunt Maggie's son."

"Yes!" I said, glad that he'd remembered. "But I was

raised by David Kavanagh, and—" I noticed Declan's scowl. "Ah, you know that name."

"I remember him, you know," Declan said hoarsely. "A little. I was very young when he left Ireland. Now I know why he did…"

I looked away. I hadn't really thought about what the knowledge of Saoirse's true parentage meant to the rest of the Callahans. I shrugged. "I didn't know about it all until the autumn before last…"

Declan's brow arched. "When you came to Texas to get her," he said quietly. "Is that what you were really up to?"

"I didn't intend on causing trouble," I whispered. "Don't misunderstand me, David means the world to me. But once I found out I had family, blood relatives, I mean, I had to find you. I just wish I'd found you all sooner."

I thought about that trip to Texas, searching for my family, only to find them broken. Jack clinging to life, Saoirse's heart in shambles, Abigail dead…

"It's my fault," I whispered. "If I hadn't written that letter, gotten Jack in trouble…"

Declan swallowed, looking away. No wonder he didn't want to have anything to do with me. He must have remembered the letter, too.

"It's not your fault," he said hoarsely. "It's mine."

I leaned closer. "What do you mean?"

Declan laughed. "Don't play coy. Surely you know. Jack does, and I'm certain he's told the rest of you about those fires." He shook his head. "Whether you sent that letter or not, it wouldn't have mattered. They were after him from the beginning. They would've found a reason eventually."

"Oh."

"Is that why you're hell-bent on speaking to me?" he asked, squinting. "Guilt?"

I tilted my head. "Is that why you stood up for Jack at the game?"

Declan scoffed, lips twisted in a sardonic smile. "If I'd known it would get me this sort of interrogation, I would have left it alone."

"Right," I said. I heard that mournful bugle calling through camp, signaling we should turn in to sleep. I stood. "I'll be back to check on you tomorrow."

Declan rolled his eyes. "If you must." He frowned at me, and hesitated. "If you really must," he said slowly, "might you bring by your books again? I finished the Collins novel, it was quite good. I—I wouldn't mind seeing what else you had."

I grinned. "Certainly."

"If you *must* visit," he repeated, and turned over away from me. "To assuage your guilt."

My shoulders drooped. I turned to shuffle away and paused at the end of the bed. "I came to visit you," I said softly, "because I'm trying to put our family back together. And I don't aim to give up easily."

"I rather wish you would," he mumbled. "We aren't worth it."

282

from the journal of Allison Robert Horner

July 10, 1862—*Couple of fellas started harassing Jack again today, but thankfully they only got to name-calling. Ever since the ball-game, seems like the bullies have been out in force. Guess Jack got their attention. Aidan and I have been his shadow everywhere he goes, much to his annoyance. But we'll be damned if we let anyone think he's alone here. Especially him.*

July 22, 1862—*Declan is back up on his feet, unfortunately, but now Westleigh's gone and gotten himself sick. And here I thought he was supposed to be the smart one.*

SAOIRSE

Harrison's Landing, Virginia
July 25, 1862

Allison made a face, staring at the cup Jack just handed to him. "Why is it I don't trust you?"

Jack rolled his eyes. "How many times I gotta tell you? We're even. Swear on my mama's old Bible."

"It isn't here," Allison mumbled, lifting the cup to his lips. He paused again and held it out to me. "Would you—"

"Ah, you can forget that," I huffed. "I don't trust him either."

"Look, after Allison jumped in that scuffle a few weeks ago? We're square." Jack slapped Allison on the back. "Go on."

Allison lifted his cup and nodded. "Thanks, Jack." He took a sip of coffee, and immediately spit it out, spluttering.

Jack grinned wickedly. "All right, *now* we're even."

"You know Al," I said, handing him the rest of my own coffee. "The way you were scrapping in there, you ought to try out for some of those boxing matches the boys over in 'A' Company got going. Then you can wallop that smug look right off Glenn's face without getting in trouble."

"Maybe," Allison said, coughing. "But I'm afraid I'd break my hand on his hard head."

"Speaking of hard heads," Jack muttered, nodding toward the street.

I twisted around to Declan stalking towards us, his grim face shadowed by his kepi. He still looked sickly, gaunt and shadowy-eyed, but then, I wasn't sure if that hadn't started long before he came down with the 'flu. But he was on his feet again. He held a couple of books out to me.

"These are Westleigh's," he said hoarsely, and gave a slight cough. "See that he gets them."

Allison folded his arms. "You could give them to him yourself, you know."

"Sure, and he came to see you often enough," I snapped.

Poor little fool. Westleigh had finally started coughing a few nights ago, and the fever set in shortly after. He begged us not to stay at his side, though we each took turns checking on him during the day. But Declan couldn't be bothered with it.

Declan's cheek twitched. "Just see that he gets them." He dropped the books on the ground beside me and shuffled away.

Jack spat on the ground. "Weasel."

I picked up Westleigh's books and dusted them off. "I can't believe Westleigh got himself ill looking after the ungrateful brat." I slid the books back in his knapsack, shaking my head. "Why can't he just leave well enough alone?"

"Ah, but Wes is a Callahan too, remember," Jack said, standing. "He's as much a stubborn ass as the rest of us. It just looks nicer on him."

"You off to see how he's getting on?" I asked. Jack nodded. I passed him a letter. "Came in early, from Peter, thought you might help him read it."

Jack tucked it in his coat. "Still no word from your pa?"

"None," I said. "Don't worry Westleigh about it, though. Tell him we're praying for him to be better again, soon."

"We'd all be better if we escaped this mud hole," Jack muttered. He tipped his cap. "Back in a bit."

I watched him go, sighing. "I worry," I said to Allison. "About Westleigh, I mean. If Declan's warming up to him, I just think it can't mean anything good, you know?"

Allison didn't answer, chewing on the end of his pencil as he squinted at the paper on his lap.

I craned my neck. "Another letter to Ellen?"

He looked up, blushing. "I can't figure how to respond," he muttered. "She writes such... lovely things. I sound like a bumbling fool in comparison."

I chuckled. "I never knew you to be this unsure of

yourself," I teased. "I'm sure Ellen will love whatever you write, long as it's from your heart."

Allison wrinkled his nose. "Or," he said slowly, "you can help me write something pretty."

"What makes you think I could?" I scoffed.

Allison gestured vaguely at me.

"Ah, I see," I said, crossing my arms. "And that naturally makes me better at writing a love note than you, why?"

Allison closed his mouth, thinking. "I don't rightly know," he said, scratching his head. "All the same, I could use your help…"

"She hasn't accepted your proposal yet," I said softly, "has she?"

He frowned at the letter. "She says she needs some time to consider."

"There is a war on, Allison," I said gently. "That makes matters of the heart fairly complicated, wouldn't you think?"

"A war?" Allison looked around in surprise. "I thought we were just out camping."

"The bears have armed themselves," I said dryly. I held out my hand. "Give it here, then, I'll take a look. But I'll not be writing your love letters for you. That's just odd."

We agonized over the letter for a better part of the afternoon before I realized it had been some time and Jack hadn't returned.

"Go check on him," Allison said with a laugh after I'd

turned to try and catch sight of him for likely the fifth time. "I can finish this. You've been more than helpful."

"You certain?"

"Sure," Allison said. "Make sure Jack isn't spending too long in that sick tent, or we'll all be paying a longer visit soon enough."

"True," I said, and left him to finish penning his words to his sweetheart. I made my way to the sick tents, trying to keep my head down and not take in the sorry sights around me. None of us looked so well-off after weeks left rotting in this damnable place, but some faces were sorrier than others. 'Twas a wonder we weren't all sick already. Our regiment lost a few boys to malaria this week, but that was nothing compared to the boys from the next brigade over. If we didn't leave soon, the mosquitos could claim a higher body count than the rebels.

I peeked inside the sick tent, and Westleigh turned his head immediately. A bright smile spread over his pale face. But there was no Jack beside his bed. I almost ducked back out without thinking, till Westleigh called out weakly.

"Leaving so soon?"

"Sorry," I said, slipping inside and moving to stand at his feet. "I didn't want to disturb your resting. I was looking for Jack…"

"He left here a little while ago," Westleigh said, propping himself up on his elbows. He coughed. "Is everything all right?"

I shrugged. "You know me, always worrying about him. Especially after that row during the townball game." I pointed. "You shouldn't be trying to sit up."

"I'm feeling much better—"

"Don't you dare," I said firmly, stopping him. "If you push yourself too hard because you're feeling like we'll think less of you, I swear I'll give you a sound beating once you're well again. Allison will probably help."

Westleigh blinked. "'Aye, Cap'n."

"Shush," I scoffed. "Right, so I'm off to find Jack. I'd stay—"

"Don't," Westleigh said, settling back down on the pillow. "I'd feel terrible if you came ill on my account."

I smiled softly. "Get well, Westleigh."

"That's the idea," he said with a wink. He shut his eyes, groaning softly. "I believe I ought to sleep..."

No sooner did he say the words did he drift off, and I stood there a moment more, watching him rest.

"God," I whispered, throat tight, "You'd better make that boy well again, or else You and I won't be on very good speaking terms."

I searched half of camp before I found Jack. Of all places where he might have gone, the last place I expected to see him was at Declan's tent, digging through his stuff.

I gasped. "What in Heaven's name are you at?"

Jack swore, spinning around to see me standing there in the street, arms folded. "You shouldn't startle people," he muttered, turning back round.

I laughed. "Well you're a terrible sneak-thief if you're not watching out for them." I crouched down beside him. "Seriously, Jack, what are you doing? What if someone else saw you—"

He waved me off. "Declan's tent here is at the end of the row. All the others are out watching the cavalry do a horse race. Besides, you think any of them care? Nobody likes that snake."

"Declan might care," I snapped. "If he caught you—"

"Then shut up so I can finish," he said, rummaging around a sack. Not finding what he wanted, he tossed it on the ground again with a growl. "Nothing."

"What could you possibly be looking for?"

"I'll explain later," he muttered. "Not here."

"Oh, so now you're worried he might catch you?"

"Move and get on," he said, giving me a little shove. We hurried away from Declan's tent, and Jack directed me towards a group of trees. He made a show of looking around before he spoke again. "Figured you'd catch on sooner or later."

"I haven't caught anything yet, so you'd better start explaining." My eyes widened. "Wait! You cheeky liar. You're snooping cause you think he's up to something!"

"I never said that," Jack said slowly. He hesitated, rubbing his neck absentmindedly. A nervous habit I'd noticed he picked up after that dreadful night. It hurt my heart to see it. He shook his head. "I'm sure the captain is, though. Question is, what's he got Declan doing for him?"

My mouth went slack. "After you told me to—"

"Hang what I said," Jack hissed, and winced at his own words. "All right? I didn't go looking for trouble, I *saw* it. A while back, after we first arrived on the peninsula. Captain got in some supplies from the quartermaster—some new shoes, I think—only they didn't get distributed at all."

"That's hardly anything," I said. "No telling where that ended up. Could've been meant for a different company, or—"

"I've been tracking their comings and goings for three months in my diary," Jack said. At my expression, he groaned. "Look, I know, I know. After all that fussing I gave you—"

"This better not be like the fires," I said through my teeth. "You better tell me all you know, or so help me—"

"I don't know much besides the shoes," Jack said quickly. "Just my hunches. Something ain't right, and Declan's been running too many errands for what seems proper."

Jack ran his hand through his hair and laughed bitterly. "Maybe I'm just going mad. Got myself jumping at shadows, seeing conspiracies 'round every corner. Been spending too much time around you."

"How amusing," I grumbled. "But you aren't mad. I've seen something myself. Didn't want to tell you—"

"Now who's keeping secrets?"

I glared. "After the scolding you gave me before?"

"Right. Go on."

"They were arguing," I whispered. "Back at Warwick. Captain gave Declan a good wallop and told him to 'do his job,' whatever that was. Reeves was mentioned."

Jack froze. "What about him?"

"Only that Declan said it was never him," I said, "always Olsen."

Jack's brow gathered as he looked away, thinking. "You think Olsen was pulling Reeves' strings."

"Remember the debt? He had some hold over Reeves, we know that."

"Olsen helped orchestrate those fires," Jack said what I'd been thinking for months now. "But why?"

"That's the real question," I said. "And I think the answer is because he's not his own man, either."

"What makes you say that?"

"Why else would he be here?" I gestured around the camp. "I doubt that sort of man signed up to be shot at because he has some sort of code of honor he's living by. He's got no love for anything besides himself."

"Fair point. But who's pulling the captain's strings? And for what purpose? We don't even know they're up to anything."

"But we *do* know," I insisted. "We just don't know *what*."

Jack swallowed. "This is why I told you to stay out of this," he finally said. "These are dangerous waters we're wading into."

"You were the one I caught with his hand in Declan's knapsack."

Jack shook his head. "Forget about it," he muttered. "Forget about all of it."

"Like Hell I will," I scoffed. "You certainly won't."

Jack sighed. "Well, whatever we do, we need to keep a closer eye on Westleigh," he said. "If that boy asks Declan too many questions and makes Olsen nervous, no telling what he'll do to him."

July 31, 1862

Soon as Westleigh was well again, we gave Allison the duty of being his shadow, which he agreed to without question. While Jack and I didn't give him reason for our worry, Allison seemed to understand. And he was good enough at his assignment that he just seemed his usual charmingly obnoxious self, instead of the little spy we'd made him. He didn't have to shadow him much, however, since we were usually all together anyhow. And a right miserable lot we were.

"How much longer will they have us wait?" Westleigh asked, a tinge of an uncharacteristic whine to his voice. "Weeks we've been stuck here. What are they waiting on?"

"Maybe we'll be trying for Richmond again," I offered, trying to sound more hopeful than I felt.

"Doubtful," Jack mumbled, cleaning his gun. "After giving them *weeks* to gather more forces?"

"How did it come to this?" Westleigh whispered, looking down at the open Bible in his lap. "We were supposed to win. It was supposed to end..."

"Yeah, whose side do you think God is on in this war?" Allison quipped. "Cause he needs to find us some better generals."

"Don't let Kennedy catch you saying that," I warned. "He thinks Little Mac hung the moon."

"God has abandoned us," Jack muttered, slapping the rag against his thigh. We all stopped to stare at him.

I frowned. "You're a cheerful one, you are."

"That isn't true, Jack," Westleigh said softly. "The Lord said He will never leave or forsake us."

Jack's head whipped up, his eyes dark. "Tell that to Abigail."

"Jack!" I gasped, but he'd already stood and stormed away.

Westleigh lowered his head in his hands.

"Don't mind him, Wes," I tried. "He's having a hard time lately. And just stop thinking so hard about it all. We can't see the whole picture, can we? Just like we don't know what the generals are doing—"

"Nothing right now," Allison quipped.

I glared at him, still speaking to Westleigh. "We can't see what God sees."

Westleigh thumbed through the silky pages of his book. "I suppose you're right."

"Of course I am," I said with a wink.

Allison shrugged. "And I was only joking. For what it's worth, Westleigh, I believe in what we're doing. And I can't help but think the Lord approves, you know? After all, you prayed for guidance, didn't you?"

Westleigh grimaced and looked back down at his Bible.

I watched him read, feeling that fidgeting in my soul again. I couldn't blame Westleigh for his doubts, when I had more than my fair share of them my own self. But he was supposed to be the solid one. I didn't like to see this side of him.

"Whoa!" Allison exclaimed, breaking into my thoughts. "Will you take a look at that?"

We lifted our heads. Across the river, flames roared, and in minutes the whole sky was on fire for miles.

"That's that plantation across the way," Westleigh said. I glanced over and saw the flames reflecting in his spectacles. "The Cole House."

"Good riddance," Allison said, and spat on the ground.

Hoarse hurrahs came from the raw throats of our ragged

army as we watched that vestige of slavery and rebellion burn. I heard a band playing in the distance, and men singing closer by. It all reminded me too much of the fires that swallowed up Brookfield back home, but 'twas a grand sight to us now. Even Westleigh found a small smile, though he hoped aloud that no one had been hurt.

The flames lit up the dark night, and I could swear I felt the heat of them on my face all the way on Harrison's Landing. I did feel a presence at my shoulder, then looked up to see Jack watching them. There was a glimmer of life in his eyes and two thick lines of tears running down his cheeks.

'Twas a sign of hope if I ever saw one.

from the journal of Allison Robert Horner

August 10, 1862 — *Finally, we've been paid again. Westleigh gave all his to Aidan to hold on to, said he didn't want any "blood-money." Jack told him he had to actually shoot someone to call it blood-money. Westleigh wasn't amused.*

August 16, 1862 — *At last, we are leaving this mud-pit. I think I hate mosquitos more than the rebs, now.*

August 24, 1862 — *Back at Alexandria. Ellen and Lucy are here too, transferred to the new hospital. I tried to see her, but she was overwhelmed with work. Lucy promised us all a dinner together soon.*

August 26, 1862 — *New regiments are coming in daily. We wait on news of what's to happen next. In the mean-time, some of the fellas have found a man giving tattoos cheap for soldiers. Jack's already gotten one with Abigail's name. Aidan and Westleigh want nothing to do with it. I'm not sure I have the courage to get stabbed by a stranger with ink either. Jack offered to do it instead. I declined.*

August 29, 1862 — *Dinner with Ellen and Lucy will have to wait. We're moving out. Heard there was more action at Bull Run, and we're to cover Pope's retreat. We're getting really good at this retreating business.*

MACTAVISH

September 2, 1862—*Yesterday we stood behind cannons all day, but they did not send us in. It was a grand show. Would've been better if it hadn't been pouring down rain.*

September 4, 1862—*Word is Lee's army has invaded Maryland. Damn them, they've gone too far now. I take it back. I'd rather fight with mosquitos in a mud pit than sit idly by while those traitors march through Maryland.*

September 13, 1862—*The army's clashing with Lee at Harper's Ferry. We wait in reserve. They'll soon wish they never stepped foot on Union soil.*

24

WESTLEIGH

Sharpsburg, Maryland
September 16, 1862

What are they fighting so darn hard for, anyway?"
The youngest in our company, Lieutenant
Brown's son, asked as we stood lined up on the
field near Antietam Creek. He was hardly a day over
fourteen and could barely fit into his oversized sack coat. I
felt as old as my father by comparison.

"Slavery, of course," Saoirse said tiredly.

"Only the Republicans keep squawking about slavery,"
Kennedy grumbled.

"You're not Republican?"

"Democrat," he huffed, "like any self-respecting Irishman
should be. Doesn't make sense, you Irish abolitionists. Don't
you know the first thing'll happen when those coloreds are free
is they'll come up and take the only decent jobs we have—"

"I read the rebs say they're fighting for 'states' rights,'" the young boy piped up again as Jack glared at Kennedy and Saoirse rolled her eyes. "What's that mean?"

"Means they think their blessed Virginia is more important than the whole United States of America." Kennedy spat on the ground.

"States' rights?" Allison scoffed. "That's just their way of saying we can't tell them not to own people."

"It was in all their damned declarations of secession," Jack grumbled. "Honestly, don't none of y'all read?"

"Wasn't it the North shouting about states' rights when the Fugitive Slave Act came out?" I asked, though I full well knew the answer.

There were murmurs of agreements up and down the line.

"You can say all you want we aren't fighting to end slavery," Saoirse declared, lifting her chin defiantly. "But that's what's going to happen. It's inevitable."

"Radical," a soldier mocked behind me.

"Fine, then, I'm a radical." Saoirse winked at me. "And a proud one, too."

"Well, all I know is I'll be damned if I let one rebel stick a single sesech toe in Pennsylvania," Allison boasted, squinting ahead as the morning sun reflected in the fog that hovered over the fields and the lines of men that stretched over them for miles. "If they knew what's good for them, they'd turn around and go back to Virginia right now."

Saoirse laughed, a rare sound that morning. "Someone

better tell the rebs," she teased. "I don't think they realize it's General Horner they're about to go up against."

"I mean it," Allison huffed, straightening his shoulders. "They're bold, coming this close. They'll pay for it, I promise you."

"One can only hope," Jack said dryly.

I could almost hear Allison's teeth grinding together. He'd already woken in a foul mood. The sight of the Confederate army, this far north in Maryland, didn't help much.

Allison growled. "Traitorous snakes. If my grandpap were alive today..." He trailed off, too angry to finish his thought. He didn't have to. We'd heard it enough times since leaving the peninsula. Apparently, if Grandpap Horner were alive today, he'd have given the whole Confederacy such a beating they'd have dropped their guns and run all the way to Mexico.

Morale was low since we returned to Alexandria with our tails between our legs. The engagement at Chantilly didn't lift spirits either, though our regiment was spared the fighting. Instead we watched, waiting in reserve, as our men scrambled about fighting Lee's forces.

Now we waited again, near the town of Sharpsburg, watching as our men faded into the fog and smoke, marching in their long battle lines, as cannons thundered in the distance, rifle-fire cracked like lightning, while men shouted and horses screamed. A little white church stood out in the distance, beyond farmland and tall stalks of corn.

It seemed an odd place to have a battle.

Jack leaned around me to squint at Saoirse. "Aidan? How are you this morning?"

"I don't know what you're talking about," Saoirse said through her teeth. Jack seemed to accept her answer well enough, for he just shrugged.

"Fair enough," he said softly. "Just, watch yourself."

Saoirse glanced up and nodded her thanks. I fidgeted between them, and felt her eyes on me.

"Westleigh," she said, nudging my elbow. "Perhaps you'd pray for us?"

"Of course," I said, wiping my damp brow with my sleeve, trying not to look as shaken as I felt. I'd hoped by now that I would have found my bravery, like Jack, or Saoirse, or Allison. I'd *seen the elephant*, as the older soldiers said, faced battle several times now. And here I was still trembling like a leaf.

Saoirse and the others bowed their heads. We didn't dare remove our kepis, not when we were to march in to battle at any moment. I figured God would understand.

"The Lord is my light and my salvation, whom shall I fear?" I began to recite the twenty-seventh Psalm and gave Allison a wink. The Lord is the strength of my life, of whom shall I be—"

"FORWARD!"

We snapped to.

Saoirse leaned towards me. "Here we go," she whispered.

I suppressed the urge to grab her hand and hold it, and swallowed the swell of panic lodged in my throat. I forced a smile. "Here we go."

"MARCH!"

We moved in our great blue line, with the bugle urging us ahead. Officers rode around us on horses that danced and fidgeted. The animals had enough sense to understand what was coming and dread it. What was the matter with the rest of us?

Of whom shall I be afraid, I finished in my head, taking a deep breath.

There was an unholy noise ahead, the blast of rifle fire and the cries of our men, and our lines quivered. We halted some ways back from the battle, a small hill ahead. The enemy was on the other side.

Suddenly, over the hill, came men in blue scrambling towards us. Some were missing their rifles. Some cradled bloody arms or pressed a palm to bleeding wounds, and all of them wore faces white with shock.

"Steady!" the colonel barked at us as the men ran past to safety.

More Union soldiers appeared on the hill, their lines ragged but steady, falling back to our position. My heart plummeted at the sight of them.

A third of the brigade that had marched first into battle was gone.

"Poor devils," Allison breathed as they reformed their lines.

"Poor us," Saoirse muttered, shifting her rifle at her shoulder.

I squeezed my eyes closed, desperately recalling more of the psalm.

Though a host should encamp against me, my heart shall not fear: though war should rise against me, in this will I be confident...

Officers shouted orders and we began to move again, though the awful sounds of battle, mixed with the ringing in my ears, muffled sounds the way the grass muffled the sound of our marching.

As we topped the hill, the sight took my breath away. Hundreds of bodies already littered the field in front of us, not even three hundred feet between us and the enemy, who were fortified, waiting, in a sunken road at the bottom of a steep embankment. We were close enough I could describe in detail their young faces, which looked ever so much like the ones around me.

They fired at us before we even had a chance to raise our weapons.

The sound of the carnage made my stomach lurch. Men cried out and dropped around us in scores as we hastily loaded our rifles.

"Look sharp!"

I jerked my head up to see a dozen or so rebels come charging at our flank from the road. Fire poured into them from our lines to my left.

Not one of them remained standing.

I raised my weapon with the others, and remembered what Jack told me at Malvern Hill. Every one of them I shot was one less man killing one of us. His bloody logic did nothing to abate the anguish in my soul.

Sweat dripped in my eyes as the order came to fire, and I shot wildly, unsure if I hit anyone or not. Smoke billowed out, stinging my eyes more.

"RELOAD!"

The volley began in earnest, as we rained fire into their lines and they answered ours, a blaze of death and smoke. The roar was deafening, intolerable, a constant crashing in my ears. Saoirse said something beside me. We were pressed in, shoulder to shoulder, and still I couldn't hear her.

A minnie ball whistled by my ear with such a pitch that I cried out. It struck a man behind me. I felt the warmth of his blood spray the back of my neck. He fell at my feet and looked up at me with his mouth slack and one eye shot clean out.

"Westleigh!" Jack barked beside me, wrenching my eyes from the ghastly sight. "Keep firing! One at a time..."

I gasped, fumbling for my cartridges and loading as quickly as I was able. I fought for breath, concentrated on the mechanical steps of preparing my weapon. I fired with the rest, again and again, and found myself getting quicker, hands steadier, but my heart was pierced with each shot I made.

I saw their faces sometimes through the smoke, the ones I aimed for. The ones trying to shoot my friends. I whispered to them, begged them to stop. Pleaded with them, with God.

And then I'd fire.

I don't know if they fell or not, I was too busy trying to blink the tears and sweat out of my eyes as I reloaded. And no sooner did our bullets shred their lines, more rebels filled in to take the place of the fallen.

"Please," I begged. "No more."

But the battle kept going, they kept coming, and I kept firing.

Before I knew it, I'd run out of rounds. I shook my empty box, cursing.

"Your pockets, Wes!" Saoirse shouted at me in the midst of the fury. "Did you put any in your pockets?"

I fumbled with my coat and found the other cartridges we'd been urged to carry, though I never thought I'd have need of them.

Another rebel volley shattered our line, and Allison jerked with a grunt before sinking to his knees at my feet.

"Al!" I cried, nearly dropping my rifle. But Jack grabbed my arm before I could throw myself to the ground.

He nodded across the way at an old Confederate who was waving his saber and shouting, trying to rally his troops, and I felt a surge of fury at the sight.

Jack growled. "Aim at that sesech bastard."

I aimed with the others around me, and we fired. The man went down. Wounded, or dead, I didn't now. I wasn't even sure if it was my bullet or a dozen others from my company which took him down. All I knew is that I felt a sudden rush of triumph and joy, and that frightened me.

But our line withered under another shower of bullets, and we were pulled back to the hill to lay on our bellies and continue firing.

"That was close." Allison crawled in beside us, wheezing.

I threw my arm around his neck. "You're all right!"

"Yeah, but my canteen sure isn't."

"Where are our guns?" A soldier shouted behind me. "For heaven's sake, where's our artillery?"

"They wouldn't stand a chance once they came in sight," Jack said. "Careful with those rifles as you load them, boys, they'll be hot."

"Don't have to tell me twice," Saoirse muttered.

My arms and head ached, the hot sun sapped my strength. My shirt underneath my coat was soaked through, and could feel sweat carving its way through the dried blood on my skin.

The battle raged, while bodies filled the road. A red hot fury bubbled up inside of me. All of this death, and for what? For slavery? I narrowed my eyes as I took aim again. What sort of man died to preserve such wickedness?

What sort of man killed for it?

They claimed to fight for their states, their homes. Even if that were so, were their homes worth so many lives? How much hate did it take to make someone prize land, or property, or their own interests over the life, dignity, and freedom of your fellow man?

Peter would remind me that there's the same capacity for hate, and love, within each of us. That none of us were incapable of doing terrible things, just like no one was beyond redemption.

But then, Peter had never seen the sort of things I saw at Antietam Creek that day.

I hated them. I hated the pain they'd wrought, the families they'd destroyed on both sides, the evil they fought for. That fury inside me swelled and I wanted to beg God to unleash His wrath upon each of them.

But all I could do then was mourn.

"Look," Saoirse said, nudging me. She pointed down the hill to our left, smiling. "Look there, it's the Irish!"

I wiped my eyes and caught a glimpse of a green flag with a gold harp, and felt a twinge of pride. Meagher's brigade waded into the fight, with the sprigs of green in their kepis and their bayonets fixed as they charged. A cheer went up among us as they swept into the midst of the storm.

The sound of the firefight reached an impossible, earth-shaking roar, and our musket-fire poured relentlessly into the rebels as Meagher's men fought them in the road almost hand to hand.

Jack swore beside me and reached over to grab the cartridge box off the dead man beside him. He looked murderous as he aimed at the men below. I wouldn't doubt that he hit every single one of his marks.

"Damn it!" Saoirse cried out, dropping her gun. "The blasted thing's jammed!"

"Give me your ramrod, then," Allison called out over the din. "I accidentally shot mine at a Grayback."

"We're moving again," Jack said, and we started to all stand. He handed a discarded Enfield to Saoirse. "Take this, he won't need it."

"Merciful Father," Saoirse cried, grabbing the weapon.

We surged back down the hill, firing into a mess of rebels as their lines started to break. Some started waving in surrender while others stood and fought, and the rest broke and ran for the cornfield.

"They're running!" Allison shouted hoarsely, jabbing his fist into the air as he hollered. "Look at 'em go!"

But when I looked, all I could see was blue and gray… and red. So much red. Scores of men filled the once sunken road to the brim in straight lines, blood and gore and forgotten weapons strewn about them.

I bent over on my knees and retched.

Antietam, Maryland. Bodies in front of the Dunker church

25

SAOIRSE
Sharpsburg, Maryland
September 16, 1862

The fields moved like the waves of the sea. Only instead of water it was flesh and blood, men crawling and crying out, shrieking as they sought to find safety. Didn't matter whether they found friend or foe. So long as it was away from death.

Half our company was dead or wounded. And Lieutenant Brown's young son, Lewis, was missing. The lieutenant was near mad with worry.

We thought they might send us in to pursue the rebels, but I'm not sure a one of us could have made it much farther. Three solid hours of fighting, though it hardly felt like five minutes. We stood on the field near that bloody lane, watching the carnage continue at a distance.

Horses and mules littered the fields, too. As the

afternoon wore on, and the sun started baking everything, dead or alive, I could smell a stench rising up to mix with the gunsmoke that still filled our nostrils.

Westleigh collapsed on the ground next to me, head between his knees.

"Do you have your water, then?" I asked him.

He nodded.

"I could use some," Allison said, holding up his canteen. A bullet had pierced the side, and it leaked. Allison poked his finger in the small hole. "That's too close for my taste."

"God was watching out for you," I said, passing him my canteen. I glanced around at my boys, feeling an overwhelming wave of relief to see them whole. "Watching out for all of us."

"That's 'cause we got Westleigh here praying for us," Allison said, nudging Westleigh with his leg. "Isn't that right, Kavanagh?"

Westleigh groaned softly from the ground.

There we stayed, till the sun turned as bloody as the fields and dipped low in the sky, and the sounds of musket-fire slowly faded to small pops and ripples from skirmishes across the chaos of the battlefield. From our position I could see the cornfield—or what was left of it. Certainly not corn. The stalks had been sheered away by the men and bullets.

As night fell, the sounds and smells grew worse. I could hear the cries for help, for water, and in the dark I couldn't tell which voices came from who.

"Listen to them," Westleigh whispered, head still between his knees. "Why can't we help them?"

"Battle ain't over," Jack said gruffly. But even he looked shaken by the day's events.

"What are we waiting for?" Allison said, taking a seat next to Westleigh, who had yet to move.

"There's got to be a flag of truce," our sergeant explained. "Which means somebody's got to give in, and that hasn't happened yet. We'll likely be fighting again in the morning."

"Again?" Allison blurted. "We whipped their tails today—"

"And we got ours whupped good too," Jack said, gesturing around the ragged remains of our regiment.

Allison slumped.

"Are they saying how many yet?" I whispered, glancing sideways at Westleigh. Allison had his arm around his shoulders now.

"Nobody can say for sure," Kennedy said. "The Thompson brothers didn't make it. And I heard Company D is gone."

Westleigh's head snapped up, his face horror-stricken. "Gone?"

"Just two men left standing. Point is we're beat too, and the rebs know it."

"Oh, Athair," Westleigh moaned, gripping his hair.

There was murmuring behind us, and we got quiet as

Lieutenant Brown walked by with his brother, holding a lantern to search all our faces.

"Poor chap still hasn't found his boy," Kennedy said.

Westleigh stood suddenly. "Does anyone have another lantern?" He spun around. "Candle? Anything?"

"Got a lantern here, boy," Kennedy held it up. "But you can't go out there, not without a truce."

Westleigh didn't seem to hear him, taking the lantern and looking at me. "Are you coming?"

Of course I was. I leapt up to follow him.

"We'll find another lantern, go the opposite way," Allison said, pointing to Jack.

"Boys," Kennedy grabbed my arm. He held my eyes. "Be careful."

I nodded, then hurried to catch up with Westleigh.

We picked our way through the grim field, delicately stepping over fallen men as we swept the faint light over their faces in search of Lewis. More than once I wish we hadn't.

Westleigh paused, his hand over his eyes.

I touched his elbow. "Should we go back?"

"No," he said shakily. "I'm fine."

"You're not," I argued quietly. "And you shouldn't be."

I swept my eyes over the field.

"None of us should," I whispered.

"This—" his shoulders shook, and he bowed his head. "Is anything worth this?"

"Freedom is," I said quickly.

Westleigh shut his eyes. "Why must it be paid for so dearly?"

"Because men are greedy and cruel," I growled, looking around. "And their hearts are dead."

I tugged at his sleeve, and we continued our gruesome search, but there was no sign of Lewis. At least not that we could tell, I realized with a growing horror. There were men in such a state that their own wives or mothers couldn't recognize them...

"Saoirse?" a voice called softly. I looked up sharply at Westleigh, but he hadn't spoken. His eyes were wide too, and he cast the lantern light around. I heard the voice again at my feet. "Saoirse, is that really you?"

"There," Westleigh said, hurrying to a man laying against a fence rail. We crouched next to a tall, young rebel soldier with a stomach wound, and as Westleigh brought the light to his face, I couldn't believe my eyes.

I blinked more than once. "Henry Goodwin?"

The young man gave me a bloody smile. "Never thought I'd see you again," he said, and coughed painfully. "Why am I not surprised you'd sneak your way into the army?"

"Henry," I repeated, moving his hair out of his eyes. "What on earth are you doing here?"

Henry shifted and whimpered.

Westleigh held him still. "Don't move. Here, take this." He helped Henry drink from his canteen. Henry could hardly swallow, but thanked him anyhow.

"Why are you here?" I asked mournfully, fighting tears. "You should be back in Brookfield, helping your papa with his store."

Henry looked away. "Wasn't really my choice. Pa got into some trouble, and I—they said if I—" he blinked at me. "Your pa was there!"

A cold swept over me, and I shook my head. Henry was delusional. He'd lost so much blood... "Henry, my father died in the fire—"

"Not Mr. Callahan." Henry coughed violently, and I held his shoulders still while I waited anxiously for him to find his breath. "A man... with hair like yours... he played the fiddle..."

I met Westleigh's eyes, and they were as wide as my own. David was in Texas? He must have gone with Timothy and Eoghan after all! But, why Brookfield, of all places?

Henry was fading again, and I gave him a gentle shake. "Henry dear, stay with us. Was there another man there? A big great Irishman with tattoos?"

He tried to answer, but began coughing again. When he finished, there seemed hardly a wisp of life left in him. Westleigh looked at me and gave a small shake of his head.

I held Henry gently as he began to cry.

"Tell my papa—"

"I will," I choked, ready to promise him anything. "I'll tell him you were so brave."

Henry swallowed. "Don't much care about that," he croaked. "What's done is done. Just tell him I love him, if you ever get the chance."

"I will," I said again.

"You're the brave one," he said, smiling softly. "Always were. Had all those big ugly men in Brookfield scared to death of you, you know that?" His laugh turned into another painful cough.

"Henry," I said, swallowing hard. "About my father, do you know where he is now?"

"Saoirse Callahan." He didn't seem to hear me, settling in my arms with a contented sigh. He closed his eyes. "I was gonna marry you. I wish I'd been brave enough to ask…"

My chest tightened. I felt Westleigh's eyes on me, but he'd sat quietly back to give us privacy. Henry drew a few more ragged breaths, but he said no more before going limp in my arms.

He was gone.

I sat very still, holding him for a while before Westleigh gently placed his hand on my shoulder.

"Saoirse," he whispered, using my real name. I hadn't realized I missed it so much. "I'm sorry, we should get back before they send people searching for us, too."

I nodded, and let Henry lean back against the fence rail. I thought about looking for something to send his mother and father, but his own men would take care of him. At least I hoped so.

I let Westleigh help me to my feet, and we staggered back to our lines before anyone took any shots at us. Allison and Jack were already back. Jack looked ready to jump out of his skin.

"Where were you?" he demanded. "I heard shots a ways off, I thought—"

"I saw Henry," I blurted, unable to stop the tears that flooded my eyes. "From Brookfield."

Jack's eyes widened. "Goodwin's son?"

I nodded, unable to say more. Jack's gaze softened.

"He was a good kid," he whispered, shaking his head. "How'd he end up here?"

"He said his pa got into trouble," Westleigh said gently. "He didn't say what kind."

"What do you think we would have done, Jack?" I asked. "If we'd stayed in Texas? What if they forced you to fight?"

His eyes were dark. "I would've died before fighting for their rebellion." He looked over the field and shook his head. "No home is worth selling your soul like that. We left Texas. We would've done it then, too."

I winced, thinking of Henry. It was all so tragic. But what bothered me more was the news he gave us.

"He said David was there," Westleigh whispered, echoing my worry. "Do you think he's in trouble?"

Jack froze. "David. In Brookfield? Did he say why?"

I shook my head. "He was fading fast," I whispered.

318

Allison whistled. "Well, that would explain why David isn't writing. Have you seen the news coming out of Texas lately?"

Westleigh smacked him in the arm and shook his head.

"He could've told someone," I snapped. My chest hurt, and I felt a flood of anger I couldn't quite identify. "Lucy, Peter, George. Why won't he write!"

Westleigh mercifully changed the subject. "Did anyone find Lewis?"

Allison nodded. "Afraid so," he said, sighing. "He—he didn't make it."

"No," Westleigh whispered. "Oh no…"

My stomach did a flip, and I pushed my way past the others. "I'm—I have to go—"

I didn't stop to answer Jack when he asked if I was all right, or to explain to any of them that no, in fact, I was right awful, but I didn't want to speak to any of them. I ran away, back up the hill to a tree away from the others, and rested against it while I broke into ugly, messy sobbing. I staggered to my knees and clutched my arms around my middle.

"Oh God," I breathed. "God, why?"

Why little Lewis? Why Henry? Why the Thompson brothers or Abigail or Aidan or every poor miserable soul laying on that field?

Westleigh's questions were sticking in my brain. Why did it come down to blood? *Why* were men so cruel and greedy and full of hate?

"Please don't cry alone," Westleigh said as he came and knelt beside me. "You always think you have to be alone."

I stiffened, trying to wipe my eyes. "Honestly, I thought I was going to throw up."

Westleigh made a face. "You wouldn't have had any judgement from me."

"Thanks," I muttered. We sat together, quiet. I sighed after a while, feeling Westleigh struggling with his unasked question, and answered him. "No, I wasn't in love with Henry."

Westleigh's eyes widened. "I wasn't—I didn't—"

"Henry was the only decent lad in Brookfield," I admitted. "And I might have gone through with it, just to keep the peace at home. But I didn't love him."

"Why—" Westleigh tugged at his collar. "Why are you telling me this?"

I looked at him. "I reckon you can figure it out."

Westleigh coughed. "You," he said finally, "your heart is broken, I can see that plainly."

"I'm not heartbroken," I said flatly. "I'm angry."

Westleigh fidgeted. "Angry? At—Henry?"

"Henry, yes," I said. "I don't know, all of them."

"The rebs?"

"You know there's probably a good many more of them down there, dead on that field, that were decent men?" I picked at the grass in front of me violently, shredding blades between my fingers. "Fair minded fellows. Good hearts. All fighting for the wrong side because either they were too weak to stand up to the bullies, like Henry, or they bought into all their lies."

Westleigh nodded, biting his lower lip in thought.

"Point is," I said, "we killed them. Because they kill us. And nobody who's dead gets a chance to fix what they've done wrong."

"I wanted to hate them," Westleigh said softly. "There for a moment I did. And it felt so good. Just easier to hate them all. But it's—it's more complicated than that, isn't it? That's why I know there has to be a better way."

I turned to smile sadly. "And what's that?"

"Well, love your enemies, for starters." Westleigh shrugged a bit. "But I'm—I'm still figuring out what that means."

"Well, I guess for every Henry who's out there, there's likely ten of Nathan Reeves at least," I muttered. "So don't feel bad if you want to hate 'em just a little. They brought this on themselves. Hate begets hate. That's what makes me angry. What they've brought us to."

"Hmm," Westleigh said. I watched him, as he fiddled with the buttons on his coat. He looked so different than he had in battle earlier. I'd watched him then, too. Was in awe of the change that came over him, the way he stood straight and strong and the way his eyes would look so sure, so set. It took a good year, but he finally made for a decent soldier. More than decent. He'd been brave.

But as I watched him fiddle with his buttons, or thinking

of the gentle way he'd treated Henry, I realized I liked him better when he wasn't.

"Why are you here, Westleigh?" I asked again, softly.

He looked up at me in confusion. "But I've told you, I—"

"I know all that," I interrupted. "But why *here*. Why the army? You, of all people."

"Oh. Why *me*?" His smile had pain underneath it.

"That's not what I meant," I said, growling in frustration. I turned to face him. "Back in Dove Hollow, you said you were praying for answers. For God to show you where you were to go. Did He really tell you to take up arms and kill those enemies you think you're supposed to be loving? Is that the answer you got?"

Westleigh withered under my stare, and in the moonlight I saw his eyes were wet. He finally swallowed, and said, "No. Not like that, at least."

"What then?"

Westleigh rubbed the back of his neck. "I just knew I had to follow you."

I shut my eyes. 'Twas the answer I expected, but hearing it aloud made my stomach hurt all over again. "You did not join this army because of me," I said hoarsely. "Please tell me you didn't do this because of me."

He didn't answer, and my temper flared.

"Dammit, Westleigh!" I snapped. "You can't do that to me! Tell me the truth—you never got an answer to your prayer, did you? Don't you dare blame God for this!"

Westleigh looked away, breathing hard.

"That isn't fair," I croaked. "Do you realize what that means? If you die, then it's *my* fault. How am I to live with myself if anything happens to you?"

His jaw was tight, and I was shocked to see I'd angered him as well. He turned back to glare at me. "I assume you'll find a way," he said with an edge to his voice. He pushed himself to his knees.

"Wait!" I grabbed for his wrist, suddenly feeling awful.

He looked back at me with a hard expression I'd never seen on his face before, like a mask designed to keep back the flood of pain behind it. "We should get back," he muttered. "We need sleep if we're going to have to fight again in the morning."

He stood and walked down the hill without waiting for me. As I watched him go, I realized there weren't many feelings in the world worse than the sort that came from knowing you broke Westleigh Kavanagh's heart.

from the journal of Allison Robert Horner

September 20, 1862—*We camp near the battlefield still. Weather is miserable. The smell of death is overwhelming. Not much in the mood to do anything but sleep.*

September 25, 1862—*Escaped camp today with some of the other boys for a bit of foraging. Found a farm nearby, but the old lady there caught me trying to steal chicken eggs. She dragged me inside the house by my ear, and fed me pie. I'm never going back to the army.*

September 22, 1862

Important Proclamation By The President

THE SLAVES OF THE REBELS PROCLAIMED FREE

I, Abraham Lincoln, President of the United States of America, and Commander-in-chief of the army and navy thereof, do hereby proclaim and declare that hereafter, as heretofore, the war will be prosecuted for the object of practically restoring the constitutional relations between the United States and each of the States and the people thereof, in which States that relation is or may be suspended or disturbed.

That it is my purpose, upon the next meeting of Congress, to again recommend the adoption of a practical measure, tendering pecuniary aid to the free acceptance or rejection of all the slave States, so called, the people whereof may not then be in rebellion against the United States, and which States may then have voluntarily adopted, or thereafter may voluntarily adopt, the immediate or gradual abolishment of slavery within their respective limits; and that effort to colonize persons of African descent, with their consent, upon this continent or elsewhere, with the previously-obtained consent of the Governments existing there, will be continued.

That on the 1st day of January, in the year of our Lord one thousand eight hundred and sixty-three, all persons held as slaves within any State or designated part of a State the people whereof shall then be in rebellion against the United States shall be then, henceforward, and forever free; and the executive government of the United States, including the military and naval authority thereof, will recognize and maintain the freedom of such persons and will do no act or acts to repress such persons, or any of them, in any efforts they may make for their actual freedom.

26

WESTLEIGH
Downsville, Maryland
September 30, 1862

Allison plopped down on a crate and set a basket on top of the card table with a triumphant grin. "Look at that! Fresh out of the oven. No breaking our teeth on hard bread today, fellas."

Saoirse leaned forward to inspect the basket, pulling back the cloth. The smell made my mouth water. But she rolled her eyes at Allison. "You can't go charming nice old ladies to get bread."

"Well, I believe I just did." He winked. "Don't be such a sourpuss, Aidan. Jack's got that job already."

Jack stuck his hand in the basket and pulled out a chunk of bread, shrugging. "I don't see anything wrong with it. Especially if they were *lonely* nice old ladies."

"She said I reminded her of her grandson," Allison said.

"How am I supposed to deny her the pleasure of my company? You're welcome, by the way. And I grabbed us a paper, too."

Saoirse snatched it up before Jack had the chance. "Do you think they've said anything else about Lincoln's proclamation?"

"You mean his ultimatum," I corrected bitterly. "He's not going to free *anyone* if the southern states lay down their arms by January the first."

"And that's only the states in rebellion," Jack said around a mouthful of bread. "Slaves here in Maryland don't get any freedom. Or the other border states."

"Then what good does it do?" Allison rolled his eyes. "'Cept rankle the Confederacy?"

"That's certainly a bonus," Jack mumbled.

"It changes everything," Saoirse said, eyes bright. She looked at me, and I quickly interested myself in the basket to avoid her eyes. Ever since Antietam, I haven't had the courage to meet them.

She didn't seem to notice.

"It's what we've been saying all along—that we're fighting to end slavery!"

"That's not what that—"

"You *know* that's what Lincoln wants," she said, undaunted. "Just 'cause he has to measure his words all careful-like, with all those Washington politics."

"Hang politics," Jack spat. "Just say what you mean and get things done. I'm tired of all this dancing around."

Allison shrugged. "I don't know, it's kind of interesting to me. The strategy to it," he said. "Sort of like war."

"Then I definitely do not care for it," I muttered to myself. I picked up my notebook and pencil, content to stay out of the conversation, if it was going to be about politics *or* war. But then, we didn't seem to discuss much of anything else, lately. But I agreed with Saoirse. Lincoln's proclamation changed everything. For once, I felt like maybe God *had* called me here.

I frowned, recalling my conversation with Saoirse on the hilltop. What had she expected me to say? That the heavens opened up, a great light filled the room and the voice of God himself told me to become a soldier? I could hardly make sense of anything that night. I only knew the burdens on my heart, and that I begged God to guide my steps. I got just one answer from Him that night, after hours spent on my knees in prayer.

Trust me.

In the chaos that stormed around us, the madness that seized the country, I had only one anchor, that God reigned in Heaven and that no matter what evil men did, God's love would never fail.

As for following Saoirse into war, I thought with a flood of shame, I was following my own foolish heart, not the will of the Lord. Whatever that was. She was right to be angry at me, though I wish she'd never asked. But then, Jack warned me, and I didn't listen. I failed to guard my heart.

"Speaking of war," I heard her say to Allison, "did you

catch any gossip while you were out and about? What are the rumors now, do they know what we'll be doing next?"

"Don't trust any of that," Jack said. "None of them have a lick of sense and just want attention, that's all. Give me that paper if you ain't gonna read it—"

Saoirse tossed it at him, nearly smacking him in the head and leaned forward to listen to Allison. "Well, come on with it!"

"Nothing much," he said with a shrug. "Only that they caught a couple boys from Company G trying to desert."

"Damn cowards," Jack grumbled from behind the paper.

"I heard Kennedy say they were riled up about the proclamation," Allison countered. "Said they were perfectly willing to risk their lives for the Union, but not 'black freedom.'"

"Worse than regular cowards, then," Saoirse spat. "Selfish ones."

"They're not the only ones complaining. Though there's plenty admitting that if freeing the slaves makes this whole mess end quicker, they're all for it."

"At least that's something," Saoirse said. "But you've really heard nothing about when we're—"

"Jack Callahan!"

Our heads all snapped up to see Declan stomping towards us, his face crimson with fury. Jack leapt to his feet and stood in his path. Declan marched up to him, standing toe to toe without a care that Jack was a whole head taller.

"Give it to me," Declan seethed, "I know you've taken it!"

Jack didn't back down an inch. He folded his arms. "You're gonna have to back up there, runt, before I knock you on your ass. What are you talking about?"

Declan snarled. "Don't do this. I'll get the captain over here, and I'll—"

Jack gave him a small push. "I said get out of my face."

Declan stumbled back a step, fuming. He looked like a cat about to spring. "A letter," he spat. "They saw you in my things, I know you've taken it."

I noticed Saoirse shift nervously. What had Jack been up to?

Jack rolled his eyes. "I don't give two figs about your stuff, and I don't know about any letter. Now if you don't calm the hell down, I'll—"

Declan lashed out with his fist, catching Jack square in the jaw.

I winced. He probably should have hit Jack harder. It would've given him a few seconds of a head start.

Jack was on him immediately. He pinned Declan beneath his muscled weight. Declan didn't even try to fight back. He was doing all he could to just keep Jack from breaking his nose.

Jack lost himself to his rage, pummeling Declan as a crowd gathered by our tents. Saoirse and Allison hollered and I looked around in a panic. None of the officers were nearby, not yet.

"Stop!" I cried, leaping towards them. "Jack, stop it!" I reached down to try and pull him off of Declan, when he swung back and caught me in the gut with his elbow. I landed on the ground with the wind knocked from me.

Allison and Saoirse rushed in, and the three of us finally pried him away. No one helped Declan as he scrambled to his feet. Blood poured from his nose and he staggered as he raised his arm to point at Jack, who struggled in our hold.

"You—" Declan panted. "You'll regret this. The captain—"

Jack laughed cruelly. "You think that man actually cares about you?"

"I'll be back," Declan snarled. "And I'll find that letter. And we'll see what he does with you then!"

"Shut your trap," Saoirse barked. "Jack warned you, now get away, or I'll let him go and see what he does with *you*."

We didn't release Jack until Declan was well out of sight.

Saoirse swore at him. "What did I tell you?"

I blanched. "Did you really—"

"I didn't take anything," Jack growled. He wiped his brow. "I didn't find anything useful to take."

"Jack!"

"That boy is up to no good," Jack snapped. "And I got a feeling if we don't find out what it is soon, we'll regret it."

"He'll bring the captain back here," I said suddenly. "He'll search our things…"

Saoirse's face drained. "Do you mean—"

"What if he finds something to give you away?" I whispered. "Diaries, letters…"

"Not a chance," Allison shook his head. "We've all been real careful when we write, just in case."

I noticed Jack and Saoirse exchange a look. I swallowed when I thought of all my writings in my diary and had the sudden urge to cast it into the campfire. I made a mental note to keep the book on me at all times, from now on.

"Still," Saoirse said nervously, "I don't like this, not at all."

"He's bluffing," Jack growled. "Captain won't be bothered by this, not if—"

His eyes widened, and Saoirse gasped at the same time.

"A letter," she said, grabbing Jack's arm. "Jack, if *we* find it—"

"We'll have something on the bastard!" He grinned. "See? We did get something out of all that snooping."

"What are you talking about?" I didn't like where this was going at all. "Please, tell me what's going on?"

Jack and Saoirse looked at me as if finally noticing I was there. Jack's brow gathered.

"Forget about it, Westleigh," he said with that low rumble of his. "I told you a long time ago to stay away from Declan. It's high time you listened to me."

"Wait," Saoirse said, holding up a hand. "Maybe this would help—if we could get Westleigh *closer* to Declan, perhaps he could find out what he's really up to."

I shook my head. "Please," I said, doing my best to be patient. "Just tell me what you think he's caught up in. I want to help—"

A bugle call cut off my words. Whatever Declan was doing, I'd have to find out after guard duty.

Nothing made me feel more like a coward than being on the picket line. Every noise, every slight movement had my heart pounding and my eyes darting around like a frightened deer. Every time I stood guard, by the end of my watch, I sported a terrible migraine from the tension. At least I was never bored, like the other men complained.

And it gave me time alone to think, to pray. I'd stand with my back against a tree, my rifle a strangely comforting weight in my hands, and speak with God. Even if sometimes it felt more like complaining.

"Athair," I whispered into the quiet night. "Father, my spirit is too heavy. I'm tired, Lord. And my head is in such a fog... I try to hear your voice, but there's so much *noise*. Saoirse keeps asking if this is Your will, and I don't know! I try to have faith, I want to trust you, but..."

I leaned my head back against the tree trunk and took a shuddering breath.

"Every time I close my eyes," I whispered shakily, "I—I see those men filling the road. I hear their suffering and I smell the death..."

I fell silent. I had no words to describe the sorrow that rose up to fill me, and I let the tears fall freely. And I heard like a whisper the words of Paul. *The Spirit itself makes intercession for us with groanings which cannot be uttered.* I wept, the waves of wordless anguish rolling off of me were my pathetic prayers to Heaven.

I didn't hear anyone approaching until it was too late.

Before I could even cry out, a hand slid over my mouth and someone whispered harshly in my ear, "Be still!"

I startled, whirling around. Declan stood beside the tree, and I blinked in surprise. "What?" I lowered my rifle. "Why'd you sneak up on me?"

"You didn't hear me calling out? I was waiting for you to ask me the counter-sign." His brow arched. "Good thing I wasn't a rebel."

I rubbed my eyes. "I must be more tired than I thought." I looked back up. "You won't tell the captain?"

Declan shook his head, coming closer into view. I could see the bruises on his face from Jack's beating and felt a twinge of pity.

"Did you come from the camp?" I asked, squinting.

"No," he said, pointing off into the distance, but it was too dark for me to see. "There's a farm out a few miles. Captain had me call on the lady who lives there. Her son was killed at Antietam. Stevenson."

I winced. "Noah."

"That's his name."

I shook my head. "I had no idea he was from these parts."

"He'd been working in Pittsburgh when the war broke out." Declan leaned against the tree and pulled out one of his cigarettes.

"Did you know him well?"

Declan paused, holding a lit match between his fingers. "No," he said, the flame's light casting a glow on his face. "Just following the captain's orders."

"Right," I said, not daring to ask how the captain knew Noah. Too many questions and I'd scare Declan off, especially after the incident earlier.

He watched me, taking a long drag on his cigarette before speaking again. "I'm sorry for my behavior earlier. I don't know what came over me."

I turned in surprise. Declan, apologizing? And after such a display? "You threatened Jack."

Declan grimaced. "Like I said, I'm not sure what came over me." He took another sip of his cigarette and blew out the smoke in a huff. "It's all rather embarrassing, really."

I inched closer. "What is?"

His face reddened. "That letter, Westleigh," he paused, looking away. "It's—it's special. And a bit... sensitive."

My pulse quickened. "Sensitive?"

"It's from a young woman," he said quickly, cheeks darkening with color. "A girl I met in Pittsburgh. I'd rather not say more. I just need it back. If any of the other men see it—"

"*Oh,*" I said, suddenly understanding. "She's your sweetheart, isn't she?"

Declan nodded. "Her father's well known back in the city. And he doesn't much care for me. If anyone found out..."

"That's why you're so anxious to have it back," I said, almost smiling in relief. "Well, why didn't you say earlier? Jack—"

"He *was* snooping through my things," Declan said, eyes flashing. "I've every right to take issue with that. If he has that letter—"

"Fair enough," I said, raising a hand. "But you didn't do yourself any favors by riling him up. And besides, I don't think he has it."

Declan scowled at the ground, breathing out another long tendril of smoke. He sighed. "Could you find out?" he asked slowly.

"Find out?"

"Do you really have to repeat everything I say?" he said curtly, then took a deep breath. "Yes, just—he hates me, Westleigh. Not without reason, I reckon. But he'd listen to you. If you could just find out what he's done with it..."

I shifted nervously. "I—I could speak with him," I offered. "I'll let you know if I find out anything."

"Thanks, Cousin." He gave me a wink. "I'd best not distract you from your duty. Stay safe out here."

"Right," I said, gripping my rifle again. "I'll see you in camp."

Declan tipped his hat and wandered towards camp, and

I took my position back against the tree. I couldn't wait to return and speak with Saoirse and Jack. So, Declan had a sweetheart? No wonder he lost his temper. And perhaps this explained all of his other behavior, as well. If it was all just a big misunderstanding, that could be righted, easily enough.

I breathed a sigh of relief and settled against the tree. "Thank you, Lord."

from the journal of Allison Robert Horner

October 2, 1862 — *Old Abe visited the troops today. Saw him riding by on his horse. Tallest man I'd ever seen. Westleigh says Aidan and him got a closer look, when the president dismounted to walk the street down by the river. Aidan got to shake his hand. He spoke of nothing else for the rest of the day. The whole company was jealous, even Kennedy.*

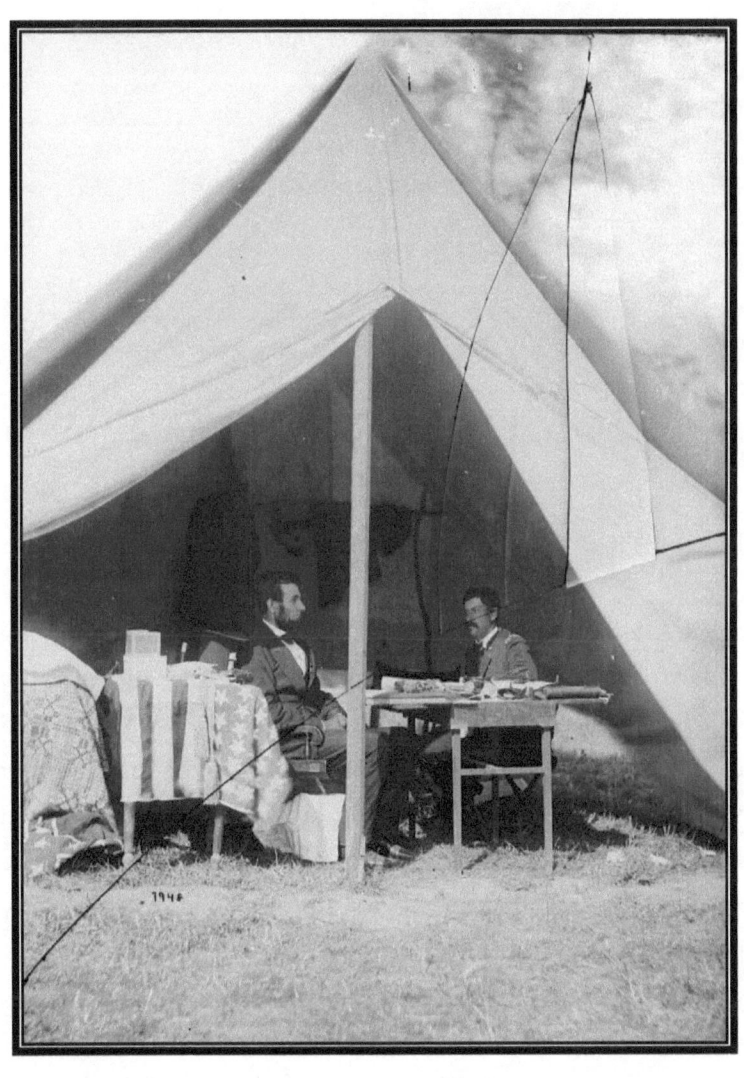

*Antietam, Md. President Lincoln and Gen. George
B. McClellan in the general's tent*

27

SAOIRSE
Downsville, Maryland
October 5, 1862

I knew I was dreaming as soon as I saw Aidan stirring a pot of stew at our campfire. The rest of the army snored around me, the midnight stars glittered overhead, and I sat up in my tent, just watching my brother who was supposed to be buried beneath the Texas soil. At first I thought Declan had invaded our space, but then he smiled at me. And sure, my dead brother was a more likely sight than Declan smiling.

Aidan was dressed in one of our uniforms, handsome as ever. His bright green eyes were cheerful, as though war never marred this land. As though he and I had never stepped foot on its cursed ground. As though he hadn't lost his life in that dark Galveston alley.

"What are you doing here, little one?" He gestured around

us and laughed. "'Tis the last place I expected to find you. Why aren't you at home, safe with your books, in your garden?"

I felt a stab in my heart as I crawled forward out of my tent. "Ireland is lost to us, Aidan. Remember?" I swallowed hard, and added with the softest whisper, "just like you."

Aidan stared at the campfire, brow furrowed. "Ah. I'd forgotten." He looked up again. "Where is Uncle David, then? Certainly he misses you."

The pain in my chest twisted harder. "I don't know."

"You should've stayed with him. He's lost without you."

"I know." I stared at my hands. "There are lot of things that should've happened. Or shouldn't. 'Tis the way it is."

"But why here?" Aidan asked gently, searching me. "Is it revenge? Justice? I hardly recognize you, *mo dheirfiúr*. Your eyes—"

I harassed Westleigh with the very same question on the hill at Antietam, and if he felt half as pained as I did then, I felt sorry for it. I forced a humorless laugh. "You're in *my* dream, I reckon you should understand why."

"I do," he said, and turned to face me fully. "But you need to say it. Why are you *here*, Saoirse?"

His eyes had gone hard, and they bore straight into my soul.

"Because *you* aren't!" The words burst out of that aching hole in my chest that I'd forgotten was there. If Aidan had lived, so many things would have been different. But he was gone, and I knew why, and so I had to make up for it. I dug my fingers into my shaking knees. "And it's my fault!"

Aidan lowered his head. "After all this time, that's what you still believe? That it's all on you to fix everything?" He squinted at me. "Remember what *really* happened that night."

I shook my head and placed my hands over my ears. "I don't want to talk about it!"

"Saoirse—"

"No! I cannot relive it, *please.*"

"You know who's really to blame, love."

"Stop it!"

I gasped as hands reached up and held my face. They were so warm and real that I wondered if I was dreaming after all.

Aidan wiped away a tear on my cheek. "If you must blame someone, blame *me.*"

"Aidan—"

"I beg of you—" his voice broke, "let go of your hate. Go home."

I swallowed. "Níl aon tinteán mar do thinteán féin."

"There's no hearth like your own hearth."

"I can't just leave." I shook my head, pushing his hands away. "I have a duty—"

Aidan leaned back and gave me a wink. "Whoever said your hearth was a place?"

"What's that supposed to mean?"

His lips moved, but I couldn't hear his response. I reached for him, trying to draw closer, but he seemed farther and farther away. I felt myself falling, and cried out for him again.

And then I awoke, eyes snapping open to stare at the canvas above me. Jack leaned over me with concern.

"Some nightmare," he said hoarsely. "Thought I was gonna have to smother you to shut you up."

I pushed him away and sat up, hunched over my knees. Jack sat quietly while I clutched the ring that lay against my fluttering heart, trying to fight away the uneasiness left behind. "Aidan," I managed to mutter.

"That's what you kept saying. Figured someone was going to wonder why you kept calling your own name in your sleep." Jack handed me my coat. "When you're good, Westleigh's got breakfast ready. We're gonna be late for the preacher's sermon."

I rolled my eyes and crawled out of the tent. "More like another rambling lecture, you mean."

Jack shot me a look over his shoulder, and I shut my trap.

We ate swiftly, and I didn't speak a word to the others. Pieces of my dream swirled about in my head. Disjointed, as dreams become, the edges of them dulling the more I awoke. All that was soon left was the image of Aidan's eyes and a feeling of *something* crawling 'neath my skin. I actually welcomed the spectacle of our regimental chaplain sputtering and ranting his way through some ill-prepared lesson to distract me.

It was a hot, miserable morning. Too warm for October, Westleigh complained as we sat to listen. Gnats buzzed around my sweaty neck, and I slapped them away with a growl. I tried to pay attention to the preacher, but I was suddenly aware of every bead of sweat, every speck of dirt and grime, and—

Good heavens, there was a louse crawling in my hair!

I shifted, wriggled, and scratched for the next hour, and by the end, I was half-mad and only knew one thing.

I wanted a bath.

NOW.

I hurried back to my tent to dig through my belongings for my necessities. Back in Washington City, Ellen had managed to send me a bit of soap that had some perfume to it without raising any eyebrows, and I'd hidden it carefully in my bag. I hesitated to use it. What if the other soldiers smelled the hint of lavender? But then, I'd noticed a couple of the more handsome, well-groomed officers had a sweet scent about them, sometimes. Not that I went around smelling them, or anything. But when everything around me smelled so strong of... well, *men*, it drew my notice.

I tripped out of the tent, clutching my belongings to my chest, and ran into Jack. He was fully dressed, weighted down with all of his accoutrements and checking his rifle.

"What are you doing?" His brow arched. "We got drills, kid."

"Blast it." I tossed my things back into my tent and scrambled to get my leathers. I wanted to sob. "I forgot."

Jack's brow arched. "How do you forget about drills?"

I scratched my head furiously again. "I'm going mad!"

"Coz, you got there a long time ago."

"Oh, shut up."

Soon as morning drills were over, I grabbed my belongings and raced for the creek. Sure, and it was risky to take such a dip in the daylight, especially on a warm day like today, but most of the fellas were busy setting up another ball game.

There was one spot in particular that was more secluded than the rest. Most of the boys didn't go there for privacy because someone spread a little rumor about some menacing sort of critter that made its home on the bank.

I was quite proud of the success of my little fib.

Unfortunately, I let my boys in on the secret so they'd know where I was sneaking off to, in case anything happened. And so when I heard Jack and Westleigh's voices before I broke past the thick bushes, I stifled a groan.

"I can't believe what I'm hearing." Jack rubbed his temples as he paced in front of Westleigh, who looked beaten, again. "Why on earth would you listen to anything that weasel says?"

"I just thought—"

"That I wasn't telling you the truth the first time?" Jack snapped. "I don't have Declan's damn letter, Wes! Why would I lie to you?"

Westleigh bristled. "You and Saoirse are up to something, you cannot deny that. You told me to forget about it, remember?"

"I certainly do. You seem to be the one having a hard time with that."

I shook my head. Oh, no. Not getting into that mess today. Not with my bath waiting. Nothing else mattered.

I spun on my heel and hurried away while they continued to argue.

Time to find a new hiding spot.

Thanks a million, boys.

I traveled farther down the creek, contemplating just throwing myself in, clothes and all, and staying there till the bugle called for lights out. Up ahead, a patch of trees with some glorious shade called to me. I half-ran, half-crashed into the bushes, and tripped onto the clear bank.

Just as the captain himself was buttoning up his trousers.

Olsen's eyes widened at the sight of me. "Kavanagh? You better be telling me rebs are overrunning this camp."

I gulped. "No, sir."

"Then why're you running full-tilt like you got the devil on your heels?" He squinted at the messy bundle in my arms. "What do you have there?"

I couldn't help it, I flushed bright red. My arms felt like jelly. All I could do was tell the truth. "I—I was just looking for some peace and quiet to wash up, sir."

Every 'sir' that passed my lips left me feeling even dirtier. I wish I'd shoved him in that creek then and there.

Olsen smirked. "What, too shy to dive in with the rest of the fellas? You ain't got nothin' they haven't seen."

I nearly fell over. "Too crowded," I blurted out before words failed me completely.

"It's the army, what did you expect?" Olsen paused, and stared at me. "Speaking of close quarters, I heard about a little row between that injun and Declan. Care to explain that?"

"What row?" I blurted before I could think. Of course Declan likely told the beast.

Olsen's brow rose. "Don't get smart with me. The one where he nearly beat my man senseless. Heard you were in the middle of that, too. You're both lucky I haven't court-martialed all of you troublemakers."

"Declan started it," I spat. "*Sir*. You'll have to ask him. He's the one who came in swinging, he was."

Olsen looked surprised, and I thought I saw a flicker of fear in his expression. "Really? He went after Jack?"

"I'm sure he didn't tell *you* as much."

Olsen's jaw tightened. "He didn't tell me anything," he growled. Then he seemed to catch himself, and waved me away. "Just stay out of trouble. This is your last warning."

He sauntered out of the clearing. "Carry on, Kavanagh."

I gave an awkward salute, what with my arms full and everything, and I held my breath as I waited for what felt like forever after he walked away. What if he hid in the bushes? I shivered in disgust. But then, he didn't seem to suspect me at all. And at that moment, I was too tired, too grimy, to care.

I carefully laid out a handkerchief on the mossy ground and arranged my things before peeling off my sack-coat. I slid my suspenders off my shoulders and peeled away the sticky cotton shirt—

"Aidan?"

"Mary and Joseph!" I held the shirt to me and whirled around to see Westleigh standing there, mouth hanging open in horror.

"Oh!"

"Turn away!"

He nearly fell on his face spinning on his heels. I yanked the shirt over my head. I hadn't gotten as far as my bindings, so the little fool didn't see anything, really, but you couldn't tell that from the way the color'd drained from his face.

He started to leave, and I called out to him. "Where are you going? Get back here!"

Westleigh inched backwards, daring a side-look over his shoulder. "Y-yes?"

"You can turn back 'round," I said. He did so, slowly. "Well? What's so important you interrupted my bath?"

Westleigh swallowed. "I—I'm sorry—"

"Ah, forget it. 'Tis a lost cause today, it seems. What did you want?" I froze, recalling the conversation I overhead between himself and Jack. "Westleigh, I don't know where Declan's blasted letter is, either."

His jaw tightened. "You heard me."

"You're lucky the whole army didn't."

"None of you are listening!" Westleigh threw up his hands. "You're so blinded by your pain and your hatred of him that you don't even *want* to see the truth."

"We're blind?" I balled up my fists. "When it's you yourself who's so determined to see the good in someone you'll just ignore every other rotten thing they've done?"

He scowled. "This is all a big misunderstanding. If the three of you would only—"

"You'll stop that sentence if you don't want to be punched in the mouth."

Westleigh's jaw clamped shut.

"I don't want to talk about that devil anymore. I'm weary of it," I said.

Westleigh shook his head, not meeting my eyes. "Then I guess I don't have anything else to say…" He turned, and I called out again.

"Wait!" Curse my own idiotic self, I was never going to get that bath. But little bits and pieces of my dream stitched themselves together in my mind, and I just felt Aidan urging me to say more. "I'm sorry, Westleigh."

He paused, but kept his back to me.

I swallowed. Damn boy would make me say it all, would he? "I don't want to fight you. And I'm sorry for what I said before, after the battle. 'Twasn't fair of me to mock your faith. You've always been the strongest of us."

Westleigh turned again. "But I'm really not," he whispered. "Because I don't know what I'm doing here, Saoirse. I don't know if I did the right thing, and that frightens me. Most days I don't even know if God is listening to me. But I do know this…"

He pointed back at camp and took a deep, shaking breath. "I

am convicted, beyond all doubt, that your brother needs us. Needs *you*. That he can and *will* find his way home."

"He *destroyed* our home," I growled.

"I'm not talking about a house." Westleigh's voice shook. "I'm talking about that place where you know you're loved and you feel safe enough to love in return. I'm talking about family, Saoirse! That's what Declan needs. And I will give my life to prove it, with or without your, or Jack's, help."

I rose to my feet with a rush of anger, ready for another shouting match, when Westleigh's words cut me to my heart.

"Maybe he's why I'm really here," he said curtly. "There. You don't have to feel burdened anymore if I die. It wasn't for you, after all."

Westleigh shoved his way through the bushes and left me standing there with an open mouth.

Self-righteous little—

"Hey Westleigh!" Allison's voice called out from beyond what would have been my sanctuary. "Seen Aidan around?"

I swore, about to kick my soap into the creek, and Allison's head popped through the bushes.

"There you are!" He bit his lip. "I um, could use your help with something, if you got a moment."

He swung his arm over his head, holding his trousers aloft. "I seem to have split my pants. Don't ask. But d'ya think you could help me sew them back up?"

I sat around the fire as the sun was starting to set, squinting at the seam I was sewing up in Allison's trousers with the dimming light. He was lounging about in nothing but his drawers, playing cards with Jack, Westleigh, and Michael Connolly.

Neither Jack nor Westleigh spoke much, they were both in too foul of moods. Allison and Michael were amusing enough to listen to, with their banter back and forth.

"I'm serious," Allison said, playing his hand. "I want to learn it. I already know a few swear words from Westleigh's pa."

Westleigh rolled his eyes.

"What would you be doing with Irish, anyhow?" Michael declared. "Sure and it does us no good, either. What little my da knew the English beat out of him while he was still a lad in school."

"I could teach you, Al," I said. "Though I think my time would be better spent learning you how to mend your own trousers…"

Allison winked at me. "Let's be honest, I'd only make it worse."

Jack and Westleigh nodded in agreement.

I went back to my task, stopping only when it was time for supper. We ate in near silence. Jack was in one of his moods, and Allison was trying to write another letter in the dim light. I choked down my rations. We needed to sneak away and go foraging soon, because the food was getting

scarce and what we had was getting old. Supplies have
been held up for weeks, Lord knows why. But we were still
better off than some of the new regiments. Heard around
camp that there was one outfit of Pennsylvania boys that
marched straight from Washington to Antietam and still
didn't have any tents, poor devils.

I'd just finished the mending when Sergeant Kennedy
walked up, looking like he'd just got off picket duty.

"Lads," Kennedy said quietly once he was standing in
the ring of our firelight. "Get up. Horner, get your trousers
on, for Heaven's sake. Orders from the colonel. We've got
ourselves a little assignment."

I threw Allison's trousers and hit him square in the
chest. Jack and I stood.

"Just us?" Jack's eyes narrowed. "Not the whole
company?"

"Get your gear on, and meet me at the edge of camp in
five minutes. I'll fill you in then. Get to it."

28

WESTLEIGH
Downsville, Maryland
October 6, 1862

Allison hopped on one foot, trying to shove his brogan on the other. Somehow he kicked it off and it smacked Michael in the behind. Allison tumbled to the ground in a heap.

Michael turned to glare at him. "Watch it, Horner."

"I can't help your big old backside was in the way."

"Both of you shut up," Jack said, tossing the shoe back at Allison. "Sergeant's coming."

Allison hurried to tie his laces. The shoe was a poor sight, worn so that his big toe almost stuck out the side. He must've had a hole in his sock, too.

Josef Haering helped him to his feet as Kennedy came up. The sergeant's face was red, even in the darkness, and as I saw the shadow over his shoulder, I understood why.

"What, him too?" Saoirse muttered.

Jack tensed beside her.

Declan didn't look any happier to be there than Kennedy was to have him at his heels. His expression was pained, and from the way he walked, he looked as if his feet were encased in lead. He kept glancing over his shoulder, looking anywhere he could but at any of us.

"That's everyone," Kennedy said after counting heads. "What's left of our squad, that is."

I winced, remembering the fresh news of Private Murphy's passing that morning. Another casualty of Antietam. It made my heart heavy.

"Sir?" Corporal Hastings asked. "What's happening?"

"Supplies are coming in." Kennedy spoke quietly so we had to crowd together to hear him. "Got some wagons, colonel says, coming down a road nearby. Trying to sneak 'em in before they get snitched like the others. We're off to make sure they come in safely."

Michael scratched his head. "I thought our lines were secure? Just a couple wagons off the main road? This is a Union state, after all—what's all this about?"

Jack leaned toward Saoirse. "Don't matter much to me long as I get my coffee," he muttered. "And better food."

"I didn't figure this was up for a vote, Connolly." Declan finally pushed his way into the huddle. "Do you always question your orders?"

Saoirse flinched beside me, gripping her rifle. "Why's he here barking?" she asked under her breath.

Jack nudged her.

"There's been rumors a local gang of ruffians are causing trouble for the lines," Kennedy explained tiredly. "Rebel sympathizers, not rebs. No cause to get the whole company out of bed. Now shut your traps and let's get moving. I want at least a few hours of sleep tonight."

Our march from camp was silent, and the night was oppressively dark. Thick clouds passed quickly over a starlit sky, mostly blotting out the moon, but for brief glimpses of light that peeked through. The wind was fierce and gusty, blowing in a chill that would've been a welcome change from the heat that day. But it cut through my wool uniform and hit the sweat trickling down my back, and left me shivering.

We followed Kennedy and Hastings in two columns. Josef and Michael were ahead, then Saoirse and Jack behind them, with Allison and me at their heels. Declan brought up the rear.

I could *feel* the fear rolling off him behind me, and I thought I could almost hear his teeth clattering together. I tried glancing over my shoulder, but it was much too dark to see him. Allison noticed my fidgeting.

"Don't," he mouthed. "Leave him be."

I shook my head. "Just a second."

Allison rolled his eyes, and I dropped back to Declan's side.

He kept his eyes ahead. "What?"

I glanced up, caught the worried look in his eyes when the moonlight peeked through the clouds again. "You all right?"

"Grand," he said through his teeth. "Get back in line."

"I am in line," I argued. "You don't look so good. Maybe you should head back—"

"You find my letter?" He looked at me so sharply I flinched. I shook my head. "Then I suggest you don't speak to me until you do, if you know what's good for you."

I swallowed back the fear and took a deep breath. "For what it's worth, I think you should just try talking to Jack without punching him."

"Quiet back there!" Hastings hissed from the front of our column.

I fell back in beside Allison and ignored the look of exasperation he gave me.

We marched for a little while, and none of the land looked familiar in the shadows. The farther from camp we went, the darker it became. We were far from the main road, or the supply line. The wind died down, and the clouds moved more slowly now, keeping us in darkness longer.

I knew we were lost when Kennedy stopped us, swearing.

"Callahan!" He motioned at Declan, who came to him with an audible sigh. "Well, boy? Where are the wagons?"

"How should I know?" Declan grumbled. "I'm not the officer here."

An odd look passed between Kennedy and Hastings. Our corporal shrugged. "Maybe they already got looted."

Kennedy took his kepi off to wipe his brow. His hands were shaking.

Allison tensed beside me. He leaned over. "Something doesn't feel right, Wes…"

I looked at the others, who were busy surveying the shadows and trees around us, all gripping their rifles tight.

Only Jack seemed steady. He moved slowly and kept watch with a solid, unblinking stare. But there was something about the resignation in his expression that didn't make me feel any more at ease.

I swallowed hard, holding my own rifle tighter. "I'm inclined to agree with you."

"Captain Oliver said you know this area," Kennedy complained. "That's why he sent you!"

"Then he lied," Declan spat. He looked ready to jump right out of his own skin. "I don't know where the hell we are!"

Jack swore softly, and stepped closer to Saoirse, backing her up against Allison and me, like he was shielding her from whatever lurked in the dark.

I held my breath and began to pray for a break in the clouds.

"There!" Josef pointed, and I saw a little light between

the trees. A moment later, we could hear the creaking of wagon wheels, the jingle of bridles.

Kennedy rushed forward, and he exchanged the signs with someone in the shadows. He motioned us forward, and we were all audibly relieved when we saw Union men on a dirt road, lit by a few dim lanterns.

"About time." A man with a grey mustache frowned from his perch on the wagon. "You boys here to see us to the camp?"

"Aye," Kennedy said, giving a small salute. "Though we have to question the wisdom of not using the main road. With bandits about, doesn't seem safe at all, at all."

The other man scratched his chin. "We were told there were trees felled on the path. Sent us thisaway 'til they cleared 'em."

"Let's get a move-on, then," Kennedy said. He turned to give us instruction, when a gunshot punctured the silence. One of the wagon-soldiers dropped and the lantern shattered on the road.

My heart choked my throat and the next thing I knew, we were hunkered down with our backs to the supplies, loading our rifles as Kennedy yelled at the other men to get rid of their lights.

No one spoke. We hardly breathed as we waited for the next shot.

Michael shifted beside me. The sound of his brogan grinding into the gravel roared in my ears.

Another crack, and I heard a bullet strike the wood of the wagon above our heads.

Michael gulped, and stayed still.

I searched for the faces of my friends. Allison was to my right. Jack and Saoirse were crouched together near the horses. I couldn't see Josef, or Declan, but I heard breathing behind us on the other side of the wagon. I peered into the darkness, but saw nothing of our attackers. The moonlight was completely snuffed out now. No glow to shine off the metal of our weapons. Or our hidden enemy's.

Suddenly Jack raised his weapon and fired into the inky black. There was a grunt, a thud, and quiet.

Then they returned fire.

"There!" Kennedy pointed at the wisps of smoke between the trees.

We all stood to fire at once, and the smoke muddled what little sight we had. Shots peppered our group while we ducked and reloaded, and the man atop the wagon fell with a cry.

I felt a hand drag me to the ground, and Allison pulled me backwards. We lay on our bellies under the wagon, peeking out to aim and fire at the phantom bandits.

I couldn't see the others, but I heard Jack talking to Saoirse.

"Can't be as many of them as us," he said. He spit out the tail of a cartridge. "Can you see 'em?"

"No," she replied, and gasped as another bullet whizzed overhead.

There was another shot in the distance—one of the other men from the wagons?—and I heard someone cry out from the trees.

Allison and I reloaded, and I squinted through the smoke. As quick as it'd begun, the firing stopped. We crouched still in silence, and I held my breath.

Kennedy was the first to stand. Then the corporal. One by one, we came out from our hiding places, still eyeing the edges of the road warily. Allison shook dust from his hair.

"Traitors," Hastings snarled as he dared to inch closer to the woods. "How'd we fare?"

"One dead, another wounded," Jack replied.

Michael whistled lowly. "That was—"

A deafening explosion of rifle fire drowned him out. I saw the flames shoot out from the barrels, not twenty yards from our position.

Michael went down behind me, dead before he hit the ground, shot clean through his neck.

We scrambled again for cover as another volley roared from the trees. Allison grabbed me by the collar and we dove behind the wagon, crashing into Declan and Josef.

"What's happening?" I cried, grabbing Declan's arm. "Is it the rebels?"

Declan didn't answer. He looked positively terrified, sweating and shaking and muttering in Irish under his breath.

From the other side of our cover, I heard our returning

fire, the back and forth popping of rifles. The officers shouted orders. There was no sense hiding now. They knew we were there, whoever *they* were. And we were pinned down.

"Those—" Allison panted, "those aren't bandits!"

More shots were exchanged as we gathered our courage. We began to crawl forward to get a better view, when Jack shouted again, leaping to his feet with his hands above his head.

"Hold your fire! We're Pennsylvania! Union boys!"

Josef gasped next to me, and Declan was pale as death. "No..."

After a terrible pause, Kennedy called out the sign, and was answered with the counter-sign.

Allison groaned. "Our own men..."

We crawled to our feet as soldiers crept from the trees. I felt my knees give way when I saw the blue of their uniforms. They looked as bad off as we did.

Their sergeant approached Kennedy, and the two got to arguing. We quickly found out they were Massachusetts boys from another brigade, also sent to look after the supplies. Only they'd been sent to the main road. By the time they came up on a firefight between us and the bandits, they thought we were rebs with stolen supplies.

"Ain't that just typical," a private with a strong Boston accent grumbled. "Can't they talk to each other? Officers got their heads so far up their—"

"Watch it, Ryan," his friend snapped.

We surveyed the damage. The supplies were fine. We'd lost nothing, and if there were any bandits left alive, they'd run a long time ago. We hadn't wounded any of the Massachusetts boys, thank the Lord. But we lost Michael. I watched Josef kneel down beside him and I cursed this terrible war.

Jack and Saoirse came to find us, looking shaken but unharmed. Saoirse watched Josef and Michael with tears in her eyes.

Declan found us too, seeking out Jack. "How'd you know?" he asked hoarsely. I passed him my canteen, and he nodded his thanks. His hands shook as he took a drink.

Jack glared at him, but didn't voice whatever thoughts I could see swirling about in his narrowed eyes. Finally, he shrugged. "You mean you can't pick out that accent from a mile away?" He looked over his shoulder at the Bostonians. "Honestly, I took a gamble. They weren't bandits, and didn't seem likely the rebs were all the way out here."

I breathed a heavy sigh of relief, until Jack spoke again.

"Why do you think they came out, Declan?" He inched closer, making our cousin stumble back. "Seems mighty odd they'd get the same orders as us, don't you think?"

Saoirse tensed, her eyes wide as she gaped up at him. "Jack—"

"I don't know what you mean," Declan snarled. "Why do you all keep thinking I know something?"

"Leave him be, Jack!" I begged, stepping in front of Jack as Declan hurried away. "Please, he couldn't know why the orders got switched up! He got sent along the same mission we did."

Jack's glare softened, and he looked at me sadly. "Westleigh, you poor stupid boy. I don't think he's even fighting the same war."

from the journal of Allison Robert Horner

October 9, 1862—Woke up with a fierce toothache. Jack practically dragged me to the dentist in company L. Guess I ought to thank him. At least he didn't look like he enjoyed watching me squirm too much.

October 12, 1862—Since Lincoln's proclamation and his visit, lots of the men have been doing nothing but talking politics. And by talking, I mean we've seen an increase in fistfights and men dragging around cannonballs. So a sergeant in company H started up a debating society, to keep things more civil. Aidan and I have been going almost every evening we can. That kid would make a great lawyer—well, if such a thing were possible.

29

SAOIRSE

Downsville, Maryland
October 15, 1862

Jack's hand slipped and he dropped his breakfast in the fire. "Dangit," he muttered, trying to reach for it. He pulled his hand away with a sharp hiss and managed to knock over his coffee by his feet. "Dammit!"

He kicked over the rest and stomped away.

Allison did his best to fish out the meal and set things right as Westleigh watched Jack head for the trees.

"What's the matter with him?" he asked, eyes sad.

I sighed. I'd woken in the middle of the night to hear Jack's tears. It'd been a long time since I heard him cry. I tried to comfort him. He turned me away, which wounded me, till I remembered the date.

"It's been two years," I said softly, picking at my own breakfast. I had not the appetite for it. 'Twas always so, whenever I knew he was hurting. "Two years today since he lost her."

Westleigh hung his head, and even Allison looked mournful. I imagined he was thinking of Ellen.

We ate in silence after that.

Just before drills, Jack came wandering back. His eyes were puffy, but no one said a word. Allison offered him a fresh cup of coffee, which Jack turned away.

As we geared up, Jack touched my arm and took me aside. I held my breath, waiting for him to speak, ready to offer up any words of comfort I could.

But then he spoke of my brother.

"Listen," he said quietly, glancing over his shoulder. "I been thinking about the other night, with Declan."

"What is it now?" I was tired of it all. Sure, and we had too much to worry about just trying to stay alive. I was trying my hardest to keep my disguise, which grew more exhausting every day. I didn't want to think about whatever my weasel brother had gotten himself tangled in anymore. "Shouldn't we leave this be?"

Jack blinked. "I'm surprised at you. Probably should be glad to hear you say that, but I don't think we can." He lowered his voice. "Don't tell Wes, but I think he's right. I don't think Declan knew what was going on. And I think that's worse."

"Worse?" I wondered just how little sleep he got the night before. "How exactly is that worse?"

"Don't you see?" Jack whispered. "I think it *was* a set up—but for Declan."

I rubbed my eyes. "You're not making any sense."

"No, you're not listening." He frowned as the drum rolled the call for drills. "Look, we'll talk after. I think it's time we spoke to the colonel about this."

"You're mad!" I felt a flutter in my chest. "You've only speculation, what if—"

"Not now," Jack said. "C'mon, we'll be late."

I scowled as I followed him. What the devil was in his head? And didn't he realize all 'twould take was one word from Declan, and they'd find *me* out?

Why was Jack so bent on uncovering something?

But I knew, soon as the little voice of doubt crept into my head as we started drills.

Jack was hurting. And 'twas Declan's fault.

The next thought took my breath away.

Was this about revenge?

I glanced at Jack. His gaze was fixed ahead, and his mind seemed far away.

What if Westleigh was right? Declan may have been a weasel, and Olsen had some sort of hold on him—but we hadn't a clue what any of that was about. And 'twasn't like Jack to jump to any sort of conclusions without evidence. For Heaven's sake, the clues could be staring him in the face and he'd ignore them out of pure stubbornness if it meant keeping out of trouble.

My eyes stung.

I missed Abigail more than ever.

We marched the morning away, and I did my best to occupy my mind with my steps.

Left, right, left, right, left, right.

Someone started a song, and we all chimed in cheerfully. Made me think of our days of endless drilling in Washington. How I missed the boredom of camp life before we'd set out for that disastrous campaign in Virginia.

Even Jack sang along to our marching song, but his heart wasn't in it. He didn't get all the words right.

Later we stopped for shooting drills. And if time moved slow in battle, it stood positively still the moment Jack's rifle exploded beside me.

I saw it all happen at once—the smoke and flame bursting, Jack falling, the soldiers around him scrambling out of the way as I was practically picked up and thrown aside.

Allison was rushing forward, while Westleigh held me fast by my shoulders. Sergeant Kennedy shoved through the crowd that gathered. I couldn't see Jack.

My ears were ringing. I heard someone speak, muffled, and felt a shake.

"What—?"

Someone spun me around. "Are you hurt?" Westleigh's mouth moved, but I could barely hear him. "You were close—"

I tried to shove him off me. "What's happened?"

"He's injured," Westleigh said, holding both my arms to keep me from knocking every single one of them out of my way to get to Jack.

I shook my head, clearing my ears a bit. "If you don't let me go, Kavanagh—"

"Out of the way!" Kennedy bellowed, making men scatter. "Get out of the way!"

He and Allison were lifting Jack's limp form, and I gave a sharp cry, cut short as Westleigh shook me, hard.

"Saoirse, please," he hissed in my ear. "The Captain is watching."

I stopped straining, feeling blood drain from my head. Westleigh let me go, and I watched Allison and the sergeant bear Jack away towards the hospital tents.

"Double-loaded?" someone asked, kicking at Jack's discarded rifle.

Another scoffed. "During drills?"

"Might've jammed and didn't know it."

Arguing overlapped.

"It's these shoddy rifles—"

"We'd only fired one shot—"

"He's a dumb injun, what'dya expect?"

I gritted my teeth. "I need to see him, Westleigh."

"So do I, but—"

"What?" I scowled. "Afraid I'll be a hysterical woman?"

"Hush!" Westleigh's brow furrowed as he leaned in.

"Listen, Olsen knows how much Saoirse Callahan fought to keep Jack alive two years ago. You think he's not already suspicious of how close Aidan Kavanagh is to him?"

I shook my head. "I don't care. Please, he's hurt, Westleigh—"

"All right, that's enough!" Our colonel rode up on his horse. "Get back in line! This isn't a holiday!"

I stood frozen, watching the direction they'd taken Jack, but I couldn't see past the rows of tents. "Jack—"

"Kavanaghs!" Olsen snapped. "Keep dawdling and I'll put you in the stocks."

Westleigh nudged my arm and we got back in line.

"I promise," he whispered to me. "I'll get you to him soon as we can."

But when we got to the tent hours later, we weren't allowed in. Allison had been pushed out, too.

"I couldn't see much," Allison said, looking pale. "He had his hands over his face—"

"God," I whispered as a prayer. I paced outside the tent. *Let him be all right, let him be all right...*

"Did you see the rifle?" Allison asked Westleigh.

"Couldn't get a close enough look, they say it was double-loaded."

Allison scratched his head. "That just doesn't make sense."

"Well, he was awfully distracted this morning..."

"Jack's smarter than that," I snapped.

Allison touched my arm. "We know he is. But you of all people know how distraught he's been."

"Those new rifles," Westleigh said. "Didn't we hear boys over in the Sixty-ninth complaining about trouble with them?"

"Shoddy work," Allison said, nodding. "You think that's what happened?"

"Well, he just got that one last week, didn't he?"

I kept pacing, trying not to wring my hands, trying to ignore the feeling of Westleigh's eyes on me.

Nobody let me see Jack until well after the sun went down. Allison and Westleigh were good enough to wait and let me visit him alone. When I saw him lying in the bed, time stood still twice in one day.

"No," I breathed, heart shattering. "Oh, Lord, no…"

His head turned at the sound of my voice. "Aidan?" he called weakly. "Is that you?"

I willed myself to move forward, until I was standing at his side, and forced myself to look down upon his marred face. His skin was burned, not terribly bad, but painful all the same. 'Twas the bandages around his eyes that made my heart stop.

"Jack…" I reached out and smoothed his hair from his brow. He flinched under my touch. I moaned. "Oh, Jack…"

He swallowed hard. "Looks bad, does it?" He winced at his own words.

"Are they—are you—" I couldn't bring myself to ask it.

Jack's chin trembled. He nodded, turning his head away. After a moment, he managed to say shakily, "I expect so. Nothing they could do. Might heal, they said. Maybe."

I sat heavily on the side of the bed, grasping his hand.

Jack forced a tight smile. "Guess it could've been worse," he whispered. "Just my sight, right? Lots of men lost worse..."

I wiped at my wet cheek. "Your weapon, they said—"

"Don't care what they said," he snapped. "I know that damn thing was unloaded last night before we all turned in. If it was double-loaded, wasn't me who did it."

My blood went cold. "You think someone—"

"Sabotaged it? Yeah, I do." He was trembling with rage. "And not *someone*."

I felt my breath leave my lungs.

Declan.

I clenched my teeth so hard I almost heard them crack. "I'm going to kill him."

"No, don't," Jack croaked, gripping my hand. "When I leave, forget about him. Forget about all of it. Keep Westleigh away from him. You're right, we should've left it all alone..."

He began to tremble, anguish twisting his face. "I'm frightened," he whispered. "Look at me, I'm a coward—"

"No!" I gripped his arm, resisting the urge to just hold him as I would've done before the war. "Oh, Jack, you are so, so brave... Abigail would have been so proud of you."

Jack laughed bitterly. "If you think that, maybe you didn't know her so well. I know what she'd say to me right now, and it ain't pretty."

"But you've been fighting for her," I said, more tears gathering in my eyes. "Jack, you've honored her memory…"

Jack turned his head towards me again. "You think that's why I did this?"

I blinked. "Why else?"

He worked his jaw, gripping the bedsheets in his fists. "To kill as many of those slave owning bastards as I could." He broke into a sob. "I'm sorry, I'm not your hero, you shouldn't think of me as such! But I'm sorrier that I can't protect you anymore, I'm sorry that I failed you, that I dragged you into this…"

"You did not," I said firmly, laying my hand gently against his scarred cheek. "I wanted to fight. Following you was just how I justified it to myself."

Jack gave a short nod, sniffing. He took a deep breath, calming himself.

"But you will always be my hero," I whispered, leaning close. "I don't care what you say."

Jack forced a laugh. "Stubborn mule."

"I learned from the best."

Jack's smirk faded, and his brow gathered again in pain.

"They'll be sending you home." I swept his hair again. "Peter and George will take good care of you. Wilberforce, too."

Jack chuckled weakly. "Well, as long as the dog is there..."

"I wish I could write to my father," I said. "If he knew—"

"Don't worry about me," Jack said. "I'll be in good hands. I worry about you three."

"We'll be fine," I assured him. "We'll all be home before you know it."

"I hope so," Jack said. "You're in charge while I'm gone, okay? I know you can take care of yourself, you never really needed me—"

"That's not—"

"Shut up and listen, you little fool." The corner of his mouth lifted, and the heaviness in my chest lightened just a little. "You gotta look out for those boys. Make sure Allison doesn't try to fight the whole rebel army by himself. Hide his pay from him so he doesn't gamble it all on cards. And go easy on Westleigh. That boy's heart is too big for his own good, but he means well. Be patient with him." Jack sighed. He looked exhausted.

"And me?" I wiped a tear away from my cheek. "Any instructions for me?"

He gave another weak smile and pulled me close to whisper. "Give 'em hell, sis." He gripped my hands tighter, and his voice cracked. "Then get your butt home. All y'all. Do whatever you can to get home."

Home. The word broke my heart all over again. Home was family, Westleigh said. My family was all in splinters. Lost, dead, or broken.

How could we ever come *home* again?

"I'll keep us all safe, Jack," I said tearfully. "I'll bring us home."

Whatever that meant.

I gave a quick look around us, and bent forward to kiss his cheek before anyone saw. I sang softly in his ear until his hand dropped from mine and he fell soundly asleep.

Rock of ages, cleft for me, let me hide myself in thee...

I walked away from that tent in a daze. The sun was gone, and there was a chilly mist in the air. I hugged my arms to my chest. I felt like those poor souls that left those butchers with fewer limbs than they came with, and Jack was my right arm. How could a soldier fight without her right arm?

Sergeant Kennedy stopped me when I returned to camp. His lips were pressed together in a thin line. "How is he?"

I forced back the sob rising in my chest and nodded curtly. "He's fortunate," I forced out. "His injuries were limited to his eyes."

Kennedy shook his head. "Poor lad. I like the cowboy, I do. 'Tis certainly a shame."

I looked at my feet. "Yes sir."

Kennedy patted my shoulder. "Well, get on and get some rest. No telling when we'll be marching out again."

"Are there rumors?"

"There's always those," he said. "We've done more waiting than fighting in this war so far, that's for certain. Now get on, your mates were asking after you."

I thanked him and started back towards our tents when the back of my neck tingled and I stopped dead in my tracks. Olsen stood outside his tent, staring at me with a pipe between his lips and a threat in his eyes. I tried to stand taller, to challenge him as we glared at each other across the street. But that tingling in my neck turned into a full-on shiver, and I withered beneath his stare. I scrambled out of sight as fast as I could, and ran all the way back to Westleigh and Allison.

I didn't see Declan anywhere, nor did I stop to look.

I came tumbling into our little space, and the boys jumped up.

"What's the matter?" Allison asked, steadying me as I almost tumbled into the fire. "You look—"

"I have to speak with you both," I said breathlessly, still shaking. "Away from here."

They didn't even argue or ask questions, but Allison kept his hand on my shoulder, slowing me down as we quietly made our way to the trees that bordered our tent row. I wanted to keep walking, for miles and miles until we were away from that place. But they stopped me just out of sight of the others and waited for me to talk. All I could do was burst into tears.

"Hey," Allison said, pulling me into a hug. "It's all right. He's going to be fine. Think of it this way, he gets to go home first, the lucky devil."

Westleigh frowned at him. "No jokes right now, Al."

Allison shrugged. "Sorry."

"It's fine," I pulled away, wiping my eyes. "I just—I don't know how to do this without him…"

"We're still here," Westleigh said softly. "We've all got each other."

I nodded, but I couldn't tell him that it wasn't the same. No one was Jack. He'd always been there, ever since the night Aidan died…

The memory brought a fresh wave of tears, and I had to sit down on the trunk of a fallen tree before I fell.

Westleigh and Allison knelt beside me, waiting in patient silence for me to compose myself.

I gulped down a final sob and blew my nose. I had to tell them, I had to warn them.

"Declan," I blurted, taking a shuddering breath. "Jack told me everything. What he's done—I—"

Westleigh squinted. "What has he done?"

"Jack says he sabotaged his musket." I wiped my eyes. "I didn't think he would stoop so low, but then I saw the captain watching me, and—" My stupid heart was pounding, and I felt a bit of blackness creep into my vision, so I paused to take a few deep breaths.

"No," Westleigh said firmly, shaking his head. "Jack

is family. Declan stood up for him at the ball game, remember?"

"He also almost razed an entire town," I growled. "He got Abigail killed. And our parents. He destroys *everything* he touches. And for some reason I cannot understand, you refuse to believe how rotten he really is."

"Of course I understand the pain he's caused." Westleigh's voice rose as he stood, and Allison begged him to shut his mouth. Westleigh ignored him, pointing at me. "*You* refuse to believe he can change."

"Because he can't!" I cried. "And now Jack might be *blind* because of him!"

Westleigh froze, his face ashen. "Oh, Saoirse. Oh, no..."

I wiped my nose. "Doctors said he might heal. We don't know."

Westleigh shook his head. "I can't believe Declan would—"

"I don't care what you believe," I snapped. "Jack's seen him sneaking around. He knew too much, and Declan saw to fixing it."

"Then it must have been Olsen," Westleigh protested. "He must have forced him to—"

"How is that any better?" I rose to my feet, and he stumbled back. "Men like Olsen have power because cowards like Declan give it to them! You've stood up to that snake before, haven't you? For Timothy? Why can't Declan do the same?"

Westleigh didn't answer, staring at the ground.

"I'll tell you why," I growled. "Because he doesn't care about anyone but himself. Not Jack, not me, and certainly not *you*."

Westleigh blinked and looked away from me.

Jack's plea came to me suddenly—to be patient—and I summoned every ounce of my strength to take another long, deep breath. When I finished, I softened my voice as best I could. "I want to believe you about Declan," I said hoarsely. "But you're a fool to think he'll come back. Both my brothers *died* the night we came to Texas. And now Jack is—"

I couldn't finish, breaking into a sob again. Jack, who sang to me and held me when Aidan died, who looked out for me, for all of us, when we were falling apart. Jack was hurting.

Westleigh's shoulders drooped, and if he had any argument left in him, he'd lost the will to fight. Finally, after a long moment, he turned from me and began to stagger away.

Whatever grip on patience I had slipped, and I shouted after him. "Westleigh Kavanagh, if you don't forget about Declan, I will never speak to you again!"

He stopped.

"Where are you going?" I demanded.

I finally caught sight of his anguished face as he glanced back over his shoulder. "To sit with my cousin," he said with a wretched catch in his throat. "And tell him how sorry I am."

30

WESTLEIGH

Stafford Court House, Maryland
November 2, 1862

I stood upon the ridge at the end of our row and looked out over the sea of white tents, and beyond, toward the river. Men milled about, now that drills and parades and inspections were over for the day. They were as busy as bees, lugging firewood, digging, building. Settling in for the winter months on a miserable piece of land that felt more crowded than Harrison's Landing. At least it was too cold for mosquitos.

Allison, Saoirse and I finished our makeshift structure yesterday, big enough for the three of us. We piled up mud and logs to make three short walls, used our tent halves for a roof. One of the washerwomen brought us some hay for our flooring, which made the nights a bit more bearable.

But the settling in only served to make me *un*settled. And as

I watched the rest of the camp dig in and carve out their little winter homes, I couldn't push down the rising sense of panic at the possibility of facing another long year of war. Especially without Saoirse to talk to. She and I hadn't spoken much since Jack was injured. She was still angry at me for defending Declan, though after I saw the damage done to Jack by his hand, I wondered for the first time if she was right. Maybe Declan couldn't change. But if that was so, what did that mean for the rest of us? Was there any hope for healing at all?

Those thoughts plagued me day and night, forming a dark cloud that hung above my head, and I didn't feel much like talking with anybody, anyway. Until the mail came that morning. I pulled a letter out of my pocket, just arrived from Peter.

David had come home to Dove Hollow.

Saoirse was struggling to clean her gun. She stood on her tiptoes, stretching as high as she could to fit the ramrod, the rag fitted around the end, down the barrel. I watched her, unsure if I should offer my help. I'd grown fast over the past year, inches taller. My trousers finally stopped covering most of my brogans. But she'd more likely spit in my eye than accept my help. Not sure I blamed her.

She chewed her lip, then brightened, before jumping up on a barrel and going back to work. I couldn't help but smile a little.

Suddenly her head came up, and she looked straight at me, her eyes squinting. I felt like ducking away, waiting till Allison

was around later to give her Peter's news. It was always easier
for us both when Allison was around. But she looked over my
head about the same time I heard commotion behind me.

Someone was shouting down the hill, where a large crowd
gathered. Men from our regiment were flooding out of the tent
rows to see what was happening. I shielded my eyes from the
sun, but there were too many people in the way.

"What is it?" Saoirse appeared at my side.

There was an energy in the air, but an agitation, not
excitement. Whatever it was, it was nothing good.

"Not sure," I said. "But I have a bad feeling—"

Allison shoved past a crowd of soldiers heading down the
hill, sprinting up towards us. He scrambled up the rest of the
way, coming to rest in front of us, panting hard.

"Don't go down there," he said, hands on his knees.
"Let's—let's get back to the tent…"

"And be the only ones not curious?" Saoirse asked.
"Whatever it is, we should—"

Allison grabbed her arms, his eyes wide. "It's a woman," he
hissed.

Saoirse staggered back.

"Not our regiment," he added quickly, pointing behind
him. "One of the Ohio outfits. Someone ratted her out this
morning. She's been with the army since Bull Run, they
say."

"Ohio?" she looked stricken, as if she'd known the
woman. She pulled her kepi down low over her head and

started fiddling with her handkerchief. "How'd they find her? Who is she?"

"Don't have all the details," Allison said. "Lots of gossip going around. Some say she came in with her husband, who died in Washington City. Others saying she's a prostitute who's snuck in, but that's probably a lie. Too many men say they've seen her in battle, fighting just as strong as the rest. But there's one other rumor… that she's a spy for the rebels."

I looked at Saoirse. She was as pale as the November sky.

"What are they going to do to her?" I whispered.

Allison wiped his brow. "That's the question of the hour."

Saoirse swore and began to pace.

"First things first," Allison said, stepping into her path. "Calm heads, all right? Just breathe, Kavanagh."

Saoirse stopped and nodded, but shoved her hands self-consciously under her arms.

Allison winked at her. "There, now nobody'll know."

"Shut up, Al," she snapped, and winced. "Sorry."

"No offense taken," he said. "Let's get down there, looking curious. Not scared. Got it?"

Saoirse shrank in on herself, facing down the hill towards the crowd, but her gaze was elsewhere.

"Hey," Allison said, turning her to face him. "One thing's for sure. One thing you have that she didn't, is *us*. And we aren't going to let anything happen to you."

Saoirse nodded, but stared at the ground. Allison and I moved to flank her as we made our way down the hill.

At the bottom, Declan came out of the crowd. When he saw us, his shoulders dropped with relief. He spoke in a low voice, and we leaned in to hear him over the crowd.

"You're here," he said. "I thought—"

Saoirse just glared at him.

Declan shook his head and turned to me. "What the hell have you come down here for?"

I looked back and forth between Saoirse and the crowd. "We thought—"

"Never mind that," he pointed back up to our camp. "Go! No telling what's going to happen down here..."

"Didn't know you cared," Saoirse spat.

Declan's eyes flashed. "I told you I didn't. But if your stupidity comes down on me—"

Allison and I nudged her back before she could pounce on him. I nodded. "We're going."

Declan growled and stalked off in the opposite direction.

We returned to our tent and sat in tense silence while the camp still buzzed with the news. Still no word on the fate of the woman, but just before dinner, our company was called together. We came out and lined up in front of our tents, standing at attention while Olsen and the lieutenant passed us each by in a silent inspection.

I thought Saoirse was going to faint when they lingered in front of ours. But they kept walking.

Olsen addressed us all. "By now I guess you fellas have heard the gossip," he said gruffly. "I'm going to say one thing, and one thing only—if any of you even thinks we've got a whore in this outfit, parading as a soldier, you will inform me *immediately*."

He passed by Declan, who swallowed hard and stared over the captain's head. Olsen didn't notice, too busy sneering with contempt as he delivered the rest of his speech.

"'Cause despite what you may be hearing, there's nothing brave, or romantic about what this *Jezebel* has done," he spat, walking by us again, meeting each of our eyes in turn. "It's deviant. Wicked. Against natural law."

Saoirse almost lost her footing, falling hard against me. I gave her a small push and she straightened.

"Dismissed," Olsen barked at our company.

We fell out of line, turned our backs to him and towards our campfire for dinner, but his voice made us freeze.

"Private Kavanagh," he rumbled, coming closer. "A word."

Saoirse breathed in sharply, but I turned first. Olsen squinted at me. "I meant the other one," he said, waving his hand.

Saoirse swallowed and turned to face him. They stared at one another, and out of the corner of my eye, I saw Declan hovering to watch nervously.

Olsen folded his arms as he scrutinized her. I cursed silently. I should have given her David's letter sooner. I should have taken her and fled as soon as the Ohio woman was found. I should have—

"Have you gotten any word from Jack Callahan lately?"

Saoirse's jaw tightened. "No sir, as he's no longer able to write to me."

I tensed, but Olsen only smirked.

"No, he can't, can he?" he said. "Apologies. Have you gotten word of him, then? Has anyone written on his behalf?"

I shifted on my feet, pressing my hand over the letter in my trouser pocket. What was Olsen on about?

Saoirse, thankfully, didn't have to lie. "No sir, I have not."

"Hmm," Olsen said, scratching his head. He placed his hands on his hips. "Shame what happened to him."

Saoirse held his gaze evenly. "You think so, sir?"

The captain's mask slipped a moment, and I saw the unbridled hate like a fire in his eyes. He turned his glare to Allison and I as well, before settling back on Saoirse. He inched forward, his shoulders raised as he made himself bigger, threatening her with his imposing form.

"You must be feeling his loss keenly," he said, his voice low. "I couldn't help but notice how much of a shine he took to you."

I marveled at how solid Saoirse stood, how even her chin was, the steadiness of her eyes. "War makes brothers of soldiers."

"Brothers," Olsen echoed. "There's lots of brothers killing each other in this one."

"Sometimes blood goes bad," she said. Her eyes narrowed slightly as she looked over Olsen's shoulder where Declan stood.

He scoffed. "Well put," he said. "So this brother of yours, he tell you why he was snooping through his cousin's things?"

I felt my mouth go dry. But why would Olsen care about some lost note from his errand boy's sweetheart?

Saoirse tilted her head. "I'm not sure what you mean."

"Brother," Olsen repeated again, nodding. "Loyalty. I can respect that."

He took a step back again, and I felt safe to breathe. But he didn't leave. He scuffed his boot against the barrel beside her, knocking the mud from it as he chewed the inside of his cheek. Finally, he looked up again.

"Be careful, Kavanagh. You're protecting someone who isn't here to protect you anymore." He clicked his tongue inside cheek. "Maybe you oughta consider why that is."

No! Jack's rifle... did that mean...?

Olsen whirled around and stormed away. None of us could move.

Allison swore. "Did he just threaten—"

"Don't talk, either of you, and walk away," Saoirse snapped, and whirled on me. "Do you believe me now?"

We had supper that evening in near silence. I gave Saoirse the letter from Peter, and in it, the note from David...

PALADIN

Mo thaiscí,

Please forgive me for waiting so long to send you word. I'm sorry to have made you worry. I cannot put to writing my experiences over this past year, and there is so much I want to tell you, but I promise that I will explain everything, one day. All you need know now is that I'm home again, safe, and am devoting myself to Jack's care. His spirits are low, but we all know the hell he has come through before, and how he came out stronger. He will again. He sends his love.
Be safe, my little ones. Watch out for one another. You are both so strong, so brave, so kind. I'm tremendously proud of you. May the Lord keep you and guide you, and bring you home again soon.

Tá grá agam daoibh,
Dáithí Caomhánach

She said nothing to me. Just handed the letter back, and went to bed. I lay there on my back, looking up at the faint moonlight that filtered through our canvas roof. Allison snored softly. Saoirse's breathing was slow and even. How she found the peace to sleep, after the events of that day, I'll never know. My own mind was too alive with fears and questions to rest.

Midnight came and went, and still no closer to sleep

389

than when I first lay down, I had to get up and relieve myself. I crawled out of our tent, shivering as the cool night air bit through my cotton shirt. I pulled on my sack coat and, quietly as I could, made my way towards the latrine trenches.

I wasn't surprised at all that I ran into Declan on my way back.

We both stood outside the tent rows, half-dressed and shivering, neither sure of what to say. He cleared his throat to speak, but I beat him to it.

"I have nothing to say to you." A burning anger coursed through my limbs, and I would've welcomed it, had it not left me feeling even colder than before. "I know what you did to Jack."

He tensed, but made no denial.

I shook my head. "Why, Declan?"

He swallowed. "Go home. Both of you. Drag her back, if you have to. I know you're in love with her. Run away, and take her with you."

My face burned. But I would admit nothing, especially not to him. "We're not going anywhere." I did my best to stand taller. "And if you even think of trying anything—"

"Neither of you ever belonged here anyhow," he snapped. "I'm saying this for your own good."

I felt the sting of his words and narrowed my eyes. "Don't pretend you're worried about us. You only care about saving your own skin."

Declan scoffed. "You sound like her."

"Why can't you stand up to Olsen?" I demanded, taking a step forward. "I know why you're doing this, Declan. You don't have to give him any power over you. If you'd only—"

Declan rolled his eyes. "Spare me your idiotic sentiment for once, please."

I stiffened at the sound of contempt in his voice. It put a crack in my heart to match the one that seemed to open between our feet. I sucked in an icy breath. "You're a selfish coward."

Declan winked at me. "Ah, now he gets it."

I immediately regretted my quick-barbed tongue. "Wait, Declan—"

He disappeared into his tent, leaving me standing there with an aching anger that threatened to shake me to pieces. I dragged myself back to our shelter, but I didn't go inside. I sat outside the entrance on one of our makeshift chairs, pulling my great-coat around me, and watched the stars.

"You're determined to drive me mad, you know that?" Saoirse stuck her head outside the tent flaps, startling me. "You daft boy."

"You're awake." I coughed. Maybe I was sitting out in the cold for too long. She crawled out, grabbing her great-coat too, and pulled it around her shoulders like a blanket.

"Couldn't sleep either." She sat on the crate opposite of me. "Nightmare."

I nodded. I heard her sometimes at night. "What about?" I asked quietly.

"Aidan. Telling me to go home," she said, looking down at her knees. Her face was drawn tight, and she fiddled with Aidan's ring on the chain around her neck as she struggled for her words. "I've been hearing his voice for months. And in this last one, Jack was there too. Telling me to run. I usually ignore them, but after this morning, their words feel a bit more ominous."

I shrugged. "They're just dreams."

"But what if they aren't?" she whispered. "What if they're warnings?"

"It's just your fears talking," I insisted, ignoring the echo of Declan's warning in my mind. "And it's all right to be afraid."

Her eyes were far away as she stared at the sky, deep in thought. "I feel so lost. Jack's gone. He's been at my side since the day Aidan died. I don't—I don't even know what I'm *capable* of without them."

I stared at her, dumbfounded. Saoirse, the girl who stood up to slavers and fought her way out of Texas. The girl who defied all convention and fought alongside men twice her size. Who charged a hill and rescued the colors and faced down rebel guns, all with a smile on her face? I laughed aloud. "Are you mad? You're incredible! Half the things you've done, you did with Jack chasing at your heels, yelling at you to be careful."

Tears brimmed in her eyes, but she smiled.

"If anyone's lost without Jack," I said, swallowing the sudden lump in my throat, "it's me. I'd be dead if it weren't for him. And it's my fault he's not here. If I'd only listened to you both about Declan—"

I coughed, and hid my face in my hands. Saoirse said nothing. Why would she contradict me? She'd been saying it from the start. Declan was worse than a lost cause, he was a threat to the people we loved, and I'd looked the other way.

I heard shuffling, then felt her sit next to me. She pressed up against my side. We both huddled there in our coats until the silence that had settled became a peaceful, comforting quiet. A kind I hadn't felt in a long while.

"I care a great deal for you, you know," Saoirse said a bit later. "Even when we fight. Even when you're being a stubborn fool."

My cheeks grew warm. "And I feel the same," I managed. I couldn't tell her how I really felt, not now. Not to risk having her flee from me again.

"Grand," she said. "Listen, it's not your fault about Jack. Even if you'd listened to me—which is not always advisable, anyway—how would that have stopped Declan?"

I dragged my sleeve under my nose. "Maybe."

She nearly nudged me off of my box. "Oh, stop it, you ninny. You can't fix every wrong in the world. And you can't save people who don't want to be saved. But maybe don't give up on him just yet."

I blinked. "Are you serious? After what he's done?"

Saoirse's brow darkened. "I don't mean he deserves it," she muttered. "And I don't have to like it. But you felt so strongly about it before. Maybe that means something. I just don't think you should lose sight of your quest. For your sake, not his."

We lapsed into a few more moments of easy silence while I wrestled with my unspoken doubts.

"So what does this mean, now?" I asked. "With everything that's happened today."

"Your words have been a great comfort," she replied, and took a deep breath. "If anything, after tonight, I feel even stronger than before. More sure of my decision than ever."

"I wish I could say the same about mine."

She studied me, her eyes sad. "I'm sorry if I ever made you doubt it."

"Ah, don't blame yourself," I said. "I've done enough doubting on my own. I'm a terrible nervous wreck."

"I don't think so," she whispered. "I think you're one of the strongest people I know."

My heart swelled, and I couldn't even hold her gaze

without falling apart in a stuttering awkward mess. "We should get back inside," I said, teeth clattering together. "It's freezing."

"That's the first sensible thing I've heard you say in *months*."

31

SAOIRSE
Fredericksburg, Virginia
December 11, 1862

A warm hand on my shoulder brought me out of a shallow restless sleep, and I buried my face into the arm of my coat with a groan.

"We're moving," Westleigh said hoarsely. He coughed. "They want us in line at the crack of dawn."

I shivered and drew my coat 'round me more, squinting at him as he cleaned his spectacles. "What in Heaven's name is the time?"

"Four," he said, and coughed again.

"You sure you're feeling all right?"

I could see a hint of his smile in the dark. "Just a cold this time, promise." He nudged Allison. "Rise and shine."

"Go away, Mother," Allison mumbled, pulling his coat over his face.

I propped myself up and raked my fingers through my short hair with a frown. These cold days made me miss my locks and bonnets. The tips of my ears were like ice.

Westleigh pulled on his brogans and tossed one of Allison's at his prone form. His stomach caught them with an *oomph*, and he sat up groggily, hair sticking out every which way.

"Get a move on," Westleigh said. "Hastings is taking care of coffee this morning, but it'll just be hardtack and cold salt-pork for breakfast."

"Lovely," I said. "Maybe a broken tooth'll wake us up, some."

"'Tis the wail that is heard in camp both night and day," Allison's voice squawked in an attempt at singing as he pushed himself up. "Tis the murmur that's mingled with each snore. 'Tis the sighing of the soul for spring chickens far away, O, hard tack come again no more!"

"Quit your whining." Westleigh threw Allison's other shoe at him. "Get dressed!"

By the time the sun rose, we were dressed and fitted with our leathers, and forming our lines on the parade ground. And we were almost awake. Allison's obnoxious yawning wasn't helping any.

Westleigh nudged him, nodding at his hair. "Aren't you going to do something about that wild animal on your head?"

"What for?" He yawned again.

I stomped on his foot. "Cut that out."

"Inspection," Westleigh said, fishing a comb out of his haversack. "Captain doesn't need any other reason to harass us. Here."

Allison grumbled and set about combing his hair, getting it somewhat tame just as the orders came for us to march. We were a few miles from a little old town, Fredericksburg, on the other side of the Rappahannock River, where our boys were busy trying to build bridges to get us 'cross the waters. We heard the firing. Shells starting early in the morning. The distant popping of rifle fire, probably aimed at our engineers.

The march was a hard slog through such thick mud I thought I might lose one of my shoes more than once. Mud crawled up our trousers and weighed down our ankles, cold mud that I could feel seeping through the holes in my worn brogans.

The march was quiet at first, most of the regiment too tired and grumpy from our early rise, the frigid air, and our soggy trek. But soon our regimental band started up a tune, and that got Allison singing and chipper in no time. The mood lightened considerably. Which was fortunate, for the march lasted a good three hours before we came to rest behind our batteries, which had begun to rain hellfire upon the town of Fredericksburg.

The whole earth trembled with the fierceness of the barrage, and we stood in silence as we watched the destruction unfold across the Rappahannock. I felt each boom of the cannon fire shake the very bones in my chest. The noise was near-constant.

I felt sorry for the poor town, squatting there on the banks of the river, unable to flee.

Westleigh shifted next to me, and I didn't have to see his face to know his distress, but for the longest time, he said nothing. Not till the sun began to set, and the haze from the guns and exploding shells mixed with the bloody sky, making a fantastic display of colors and smoke wreaths in an eerily beautiful scene. As we watched it with a bit of wide-eyed wonder, Westleigh, biting his lip, finally heaved a great sigh.

"The people," he whispered. "Do you imagine they got the people to safety?"

"Damn the seseches," Hastings growled behind us. "It's their own fault."

Westleigh's reply was softer than anyone but myself could hear. "But there could be children down there," he murmured. "Children don't get a say in this..."

"I'm sure they all got out, Westleigh," I said softly. "They probably left a long time ago."

His brow knotted. "What if they had nowhere to go?"

I sucked in a breath. To blazes with this terrible war.

They kept us there, waiting behind our big guns, those lead monsters, for the whole night and next day. Sleep was fitful on cold ground, and the bombardment seemed like it would never stop.

On the morning of the thirteenth, they awoke us again long before daylight.

The guns had stopped. It was time.

Westleigh was awake before me, again. I wondered if he'd even slept. He sat hunched over his knees, scribbling something on a piece of paper with a shaking hand. He paused to rub his cold fingers together, trying to warm them.

"What are you doing?" I said, leaning over.

He glanced up and held out the scrap of paper. On it was his name.

"In case—" he said scratchily, and stopped. He curled his hand around the scrap and looked away before he tried again. "In case…"

"Shush." I laid my hand on his arm. "Don't talk like that."

"After Antietam." He shook his head. "The things we saw. Some—some of those men, they weren't *whole.*"

I grimaced, trying to ignore the images that sprang to my mind. I slid my hand beneath my coat and felt the ring around my neck. Well, 'twasn't *my* name, but the ring would identify me, more or less. Though they might be in for a right surprise when they buried me…

Westleigh slid the paper into his pocket. "I just want someone to know what's happened to me," he said. "In case."

I shook my head. "Not going to happen," I said emphatically. I wouldn't let him talk like this. "You won't need it."

He didn't try to argue with me. He sighed, breath curling out in front of him like rifle smoke. "If something happens—"

"Please, just stop—"

Westleigh looked at me. "I was only going to say, you know everything I'd want to say to Da anyhow," he said softly. "Especially how sorry I am."

"Me too."

We fell in line as day broke again. The sun rose over our shoulders to shine on a thick blanket of fog, stretching out over the river and fields, snaking through Fredericksburg's streets. 'Twas the thickest mist I ever saw, and I wondered if it was due to all the smoke in the air, mingling and mixing to make a cotton-like haze that you could cut a saber through.

In the distance, we heard the sounds of battle. In the heights beyond the town, above the cloudy ground, I could just barely make out the rebel lines, squatting with their artillery.

After noon, when the mist had departed and the battle-noise had been clamoring for hours, the calls came for our regiments to march, and our column moved forward. I eyed the pontoon bridges with trepidation. Sure, and those wobbly planks and boats didn't look safe at all. Not that I doubted the skill of our engineers, but how grand a job can you do when you're being picked off by sharpshooters?

"Looks like you'll finally get to go swimming, Aidan," Allison teased me. "That is if you don't step carefully."

"You don't shut your trap and I'll push you in, I will," I muttered. I took a deep breath, wishing I'd learned to swim. What if I fell, and in this great heavy coat and all? But then the bridges had taken quite a bit of stomping from the rest of the army, surely it would hold us, too.

The rebels started firing at us.

The whole column flinched like we were the same animal, ducking as shells came over head. The officers urged us forward, double-quick, to get us 'cross the bridges before we had a chance to wonder just how cold the water really was.

We got across unwounded—and not a soul gone 'overboard'—though more than one shell had come sailing over a bit too close to our heads. They hurried us into the town, and we got our first look at the terrible damage our guns had inflicted upon the structures.

It reminded me of the first spring we spent in Texas, when a tornado had come roaring through Brookfield, a few years before the fires did their dirty work. I remember how Goodwin's store had a broken window and a few missing shingles, when the building next looked like someone sliced a wall clean away.

Broken wagons and toppled carts, glass and bricks littered the streets. Books and loose papers whirled about in the wind. A church steeple was splintered and hanging off the roof. I saw someone's parlor off a ways, their furniture tossed and cushions shredded, but not by cannon fire. There was a discarded stash of treasures out in front of one porch, looted out of a fancy home and left behind by whatever soldier had been scolded for taking it.

We paused to rest on the street by the river, and they made us lie down. Bullets and shells kept raining around us, so we crouched there, and waited.

Then we saw them, covered in mud and blood, the staggering, haunted Union men sprinting down the streets away from the fire towards safety. Some of them collapsed in the streets. Others ran inside abandoned houses and slammed doors, all of them seeking whatever cover they could find.

One poor soul was running straight for us, only to be taken down by a rebel ball. He landed face-first at the captain's knees.

Oh, but our brave men did not quake.

"Steady," I heard Kennedy say. "Steady on, la—"

A rifle shot rang out and I heard the dull thud of a bullet finding its mark.

I whirled around. Kennedy was slumped over. He would've looked asleep but for the red blooming at his breast.

The company began to scramble, shouting as another shot struck the brick building above my head. Bits of brick rained down, and we frantically searched for our attacker.

"That's too close," Allison panted, scanning the streets. "That's—that's not coming from up that way—"

Another shot, this one hitting the ground by the lieutenant's feet, who'd leapt up to search our surroundings.

"Get down!" Hastings cried, grabbing for him.

"There!" Someone shouted, pointing up at a blown-out window of the building across the street. "Her!"

I looked up and saw a woman duck back inside, reloading her weapon. When she leaned out again, I saw the wild look of fear in her eyes as she took an unsteady aim.

Olsen leapt to his feet and fired his sidearm. She ducked out of the way, out of sight. He growled and gestured to the lieutenant and Declan beside him. "Get in there and get her out!"

They rushed towards the house, holding onto their hats as they dodged the fire in the streets, and pushed down the door that was barely hanging from its hinges. We stayed prone in the streets, frozen in wait, and heard a scream.

Lieutenant Brown and Declan came out a few moments later, the woman kicking and screaming between them.

"Let go of me, you blue devils!" she screeched. "I'm a lady, put me down!"

"Mama!"

My head snapped up, and a boy—too old to be a child, too young to be in the army—came rushing out onto the porch. He had his mama's musket in his hands.

Olsen raised his gun.

I gasped. "No!"

A shot rang out, and the boy dropped dead.

I don't think I've ever heard a sound so terrible as that mother's scream.

Declan and the lieutenant released her, and she ran sobbing to her son's fallen form. Declan picked up the discarded musket, pausing to look down at the boy with a pained expression.

Lieutenant Brown ran up to the captain, breathless. "Sir," he said, brow gathered. "That boy, he—"

"Was old enough to shoot you in the back," Olsen said

dryly, holstering his side arm. He jerked his chin over his shoulder, and Brown came back in line.

I looked over at Westleigh. He had his head bowed in prayer.

We hadn't even got to the battlefield, I thought with an ache in my chest. And already we'd seen too much death.

*Street in Fredericksburg, Va., showing houses
destroyed by bombardment in December, 1862*

32

WESTLEIGH
Fredericksburg, Virginia
December 13, 1862

A r nAthair, atá ar neamh: go naofar d'ainm. Go dtaga do ríocht. Go ndéantar do thoil ar talamh mar a dhéantar ar neamh."

The words of the Lord's Prayer in my da's language warmed me inside, gave me more strength than any march of a regimental band, and ours was silent, anyhow. Of all the Irish words I learned, I committed those to my heart and mind the strongest.

"Ár n-arán laethúil tabhair dúinn inniu, agus maith dúinn ár bhfiacha, mar a mhaithimid dár bhféichiúnaithe féin," I murmured as we marched up the streets towards the raging battle beyond, gripping my rifle tightly, thinking of the boy in the street behind us with a twist of my stomach.

Oh, Lord, forgive us…

I felt my heartbeat in my throat. We passed by two privates, bearing their wounded captain between them, rushing away from the battle. They were each bleeding. I swallowed. "Agus ná lig sinn i gcathú, ach saor sinn ó olc."

Father, deliver us from evil...

Saoirse gave me an encouraging smile. "Áiméan," she finished.

Allison snorted. "I understood that word."

A shell hit the road beside us and showered dirt into the air.

I clamped my jaw together to keep it from shaking, and we were silent the rest of the way up the road.

They stopped us behind a small ravine and moved us from our columns to a line of battle. Our regiment was the second line. As I peered around the men in front of me to see the battlefield, my heart dropped.

The rebels were entrenched behind a long stone wall on the heights ahead, their artillery and muskets firing over open ground, where scores of fallen Union men and horses lay. The only cover was a small structure where I saw a group of soldiers huddled, seeking shelter from the death raining around them.

"This is insanity," Allison breathed beside me. "A slaughter!"

"Men!" our colonel ran in front of us, shouting, "our orders are to take that wall! Fix bayonets! Do not load your weapons!"

"What?" Saoirse blurted, looking at us. "What did he say?"

"Do NOT load your rifles!" Olsen shouted the colonel's orders, coming to each of us in line. "Fix bayonets!"

We did as instructed, and our line was brought to shoulder arms.

"Bayonets'll be the only thing that works against that," the colonel shouted, pointing to the wall. "Let's give those bastards hell! Forward!"

The command was shouted up and down line, while shells burst among us. Screams came from our left as a rebel ball blew a hole in our ranks, and the men scrambled to fill it.

"MARCH!" The colonel led the charge, shouting over his shoulder. "Double quick!"

Our lines moved, down into the ravine and up the other side, and we were on that open field. The regiment in front of us held their rifles out before them, the points of their bayonets gleaming in the sun as we pushed forward, a grand and terrible sight charging against Death itself. Hurrahs went up from the men in a great thunderous roar. A line of Tennyson's tumbled through my mind.

Half a league, half a league, half a league onward…

We pushed forward, unflinching, with the rest, even when the shells tattered our lines or musketfire dropped the men around us. I lowered my eyes from the enemy for only a moment, to try and gently step around the men who had fallen, while I frantically prayed I wouldn't be joining them. The colonel interrupted my petition with a shout.

"Never mind the obstacles in the way! Charge!"

Our pace quickened, and we rushed ahead, our roar as deafening as the cannonfire. Saoirse beside me joined in, her voice rising with them. I finally felt it build up in me, burn my chest, and loose itself from my throat in a raw, feral cry. Every stitch of me reverberated with it, every fear, pain, hope, and loss fueled it. We ran, reckless and gallant warriors, toward that stone wall.

Theirs not to reason why, theirs but to do and die...

The rebels stood and opened fire.

Bullets ripped the air and zipped over our heads. A man went down in front of me, and I nearly impaled myself on his bayonet as I tripped past.

A wild feeling overtook me, and I felt that weightlessness Saoirse described. I thought we might run straight at the wall, fly right over, and chase the rebels for miles away from here.

Then we came to where the last charge had been stopped.

Rows of men, alive and laying on their bellies, blocked our way. As if a row of blue dominoes had fallen over, they clung to the hillside and called to us desperately. Some dared to raise their heads or wave their caps, only to flinch and press themselves against the ground again as a bullet came cutting over their heads.

"Get down!" a captain cried. "Get down for mercy's sake!"

"Lie down you fools!"

"You will all be killed!"

Our lines stumbled and froze, and some of our men joined

them on the ground in confusion, hearing officers yelling commands. We tried pressing on, but our lines were crumbling. Saoirse and Allison were still pressed tight against my shoulders, so I kept moving.

Then someone grabbed my ankle, and with a force pulled me down to the ground.

"What are you doing?" I cried, readjusting my kepi. I looked around frantically. Saoirse and Allison had been pulled down, too. Our regiments joined the living and wounded and dead men on the ground, flinching and ducking as the bullets kept raining.

"Westleigh Kavanagh?" the soldier who had pulled me down stared with a slack jaw. "What on earth are you doing here?"

I squinted through the mud on his face and recognized him, my roommate from the college. "Oh, you know, Ted, just out for a picnic."

His chuckle was cut short by a shell bursting nearby, and he swore.

"Stand and fire!" I heard our officers call up and down the line. "Load your weapons!"

I flipped over on my back and scrambled to load my rifle.

Ted buried his face into the ground. "It won't work," he said. "Nothing's getting past that wall. Just stay down."

I glanced to my right, and saw Saoirse crouched and ready.

411

We rose together and fired a volley at the rebels behind the wall. I could hear the bullets striking stone with loud pops, but the rebels were stalwart, while our line was cut to pieces. Those of us left standing dropped down again to reload.

We fired half a dozen rounds like this, rising and falling, with fewer of us standing each time, in a constant barrage of musketfire.

"Cease fire!" I heard as I dropped to the ground again. Officers ran among us, some going to each man to relay the order. "Cease fire!"

"Do not waste your ammunition!" the colonel bellowed, standing with his saber raised. "Give them the bayonet, that's what these bastards want! Forward!"

Shaking but determined, our lines rose, somewhat less solid and grand than before. We stepped over the men still clinging to the hillside, ignoring their pleas as we advanced. The fire against us was stronger than ever.

I heard shouting to my left and saw the regimental colors wavering as the guard flinched and splinters flew. Bullets had shattered the pole of our flag, and they grasped desperately at the remains to keep it flying high.

The line in front of me disappeared as a shell burst, ringing my ears and sending blood, dirt, and metal flying. I felt the hot sting of it brush my cheeks and staggered on the uneven ground. The regiment before us crumpled, and still our commanders urged us on.

We were almost there, some fifty yards from the wall, kept moving forward by sheer will alone, when a whole host of rebels rose from behind the wall, their lines four or five men deep, and fired.

A force slammed into my midsection and I lost my feet, falling and landing hard on my back. I struggled to breathe. I felt as if someone had delivered a blow to my stomach, and I willed myself to look down.

There was a dent in my belt buckle from where the ball struck me, but I was unharmed. The sight of it made me laugh and cry at once.

"Fall back!" the colonel shouted behind us. "Fall back!"

I scrambled to my feet and ran with the others, and realized I'd lost sight of my friends. I paused only for a moment, whirling around to find them, when a hand pulled me down for the second time that battle.

"You'll get your head shot clean off, you eejit," Declan snapped, forcing me to the ground beside him. "Haven't you got any sense?"

"Saoirse!" I gasped for breath. "Where's Saoirse?"

His face paled as he looked around. A bullet struck the ground in front of us, and we inched back.

I dared lift my head. "Allison!" I called. "Aidan!"

"No use, they couldn't hear you over this din." Declan grunted, rolling a large dead soldier up on his side. "Help me with this poor chap…"

I swallowed down my nausea. We pushed him over till he

blocked our heads, and I silently begged the poor man's forgiveness, even if he wasn't there to give it. We huddled behind him, pressed together in desperation to stay alive. I flipped over on my back, breathing hard, as I gathered in what was left of our regiment.

Everywhere men huddled together among the dead. Some hid themselves between the legs of a fallen horse that was being cut to tatters by rifle fire. All around me was the sound of bullets striking flesh, and I tried to block it out with my hands.

I should have taken her away. I should have told her my heart, and begged her, with all my might, to leave. I should never have come here…

Declan gripped my shoulder.

We heard the sound of a bugle, and I looked past my feet to see flags waving brilliantly above the rise. Long lines of Union men, as gallant as all the ones who came before, marched forward with their bayonets flashing. They cheered, and hollered, as we had done. They looked fierce and brave, but with a groan in my heart, I knew. They were only marching toward their deaths.

"Take the wall!" came the cries of their commanders. "Charge!"

Their hurrahs drowned out the sound of the bugle, and they rushed forward towards us. I braced myself, trying to become as small as possible so they wouldn't trip over me.

There was a crack like lightning from the wall, followed by the murderous thunder of cannonfire, and the whole field shook. Smoke billowed out, filling my lungs and stinging my eyes. I couldn't see for moments as the acrid white cloud lingered. Finally, it began to dissipate, and I bit back a cry.

The charging brigade had vanished. Disappeared, as if it'd never existed. No colors to be found, no gleaming bayonets.

They were gone.

33

SAOIRSE

Fredericksburg, Virginia
December 13, 1862

I awoke in a ravaged graveyard. The veil was torn between the worlds, and ghosts and terrible spirits moaned and wailed around me. I squeezed my eyes shut in terror, lest I see lost souls hovering about the field. Darkness had fallen. Fog crawled over the field again and blotted out the stars. The mist was like a cruel blanket, smothering us with a chill and muffling the cries for help. For water. For our mothers.

I took a deep breath and opened my eyes. Spirits didn't cry out for water.

I groaned, trying to turn over, but my muscles were stiff with an ache from the cold and the fighting. I squinted to look around me and realized with a bit of annoyance that one of my eyes was crusted shut with blood. I rubbed at it

416

and felt my head scream in pain. I dropped back down, biting back a scream of my own.

With shaking hands I reached up and touched my crown, breathing fast and frightened. I was afraid to find some of it missing, but it was whole, and still sticky with blood, which matted my hair and had flowed down my face.

I hissed at the sting where I touched it, and recalled what happened in quick flashes. The rebels rising again to fire at us. The captain shouting at us to aim, his back to the wall. Smoke blinding my eyes as I threw myself at him, knocking us both to the ground as a hail of bullets rained around. I remembered the bite of the one that grazed my scalp. But I didn't remember much else after that.

I looked around. I lay among a pile of men, and I couldn't tell who was dead and who was sleeping. Everyone was bleeding. The captain wasn't there.

A crack came from the wall, and I ducked down as more bullets peppered the miserable forms around me.

I swallowed what felt like glass. I reached for my canteen, but it was gone. From the tear in my coat, I could only guess a rebel bullet cut the strap loose.

I forced myself to raise my head enough to search the men around me. "Westleigh?" I called hoarsely, but my voice was barely a whisper.

The cold was downright hateful, and the mist was like icy fingers around my throat. I shook to my bones, cursing that I'd left my overcoat back at the ravine with our knapsacks. 'Twas too heavy to fight in. Many of the other men had done the same, shucking what we didn't need before that fateful charge. And now we'd freeze to death.

I saw some movement, men crawling about the field, trying to get away. Some were shot for their efforts. They didn't move again.

Beside me lay a young captain from another company, his handsome face already grey with death. I looked him over. The bullet that claimed him struck his breast, from the dark stain on the blue coat.

The rest of the coat was intact.

It was a struggle, but I managed to get the poor soul freed from his overcoat and wrapped it around myself. I sighed, already feeling the wool hug my shoulders and soothing the tremble that had set in.

I had to find my boys.

I began to crawl, through mud and gore, with hails of bullets still striking around me, sharpshooters aiming at anything that moved. I went slowly, dragging myself only inches at a time, pausing in between to play dead.

I aimed myself in the direction of the line, desperate to find a face I recognized. A terror rose within me. What if they had retreated? What if the army had fled and left us behind for the rebs to sweep in and take us prisoner?

I swallowed my fear. They wouldn't still be shooting if the battle was over. I kept crawling.

Some of the men I passed over were alive and urged me to lay still. They huddled under their overcoats together, desperate for warmth. I lifted the corner of one coat to see a face stare back at me, stricken white with fear.

"Pennsylvania?" I rasped.

He shook his head.

I moved on.

I made it another yard when I felt something grab my ankle, and I twisted around.

Allison held a finger to his cracked lips, which trembled as he tried to smile. "Caught ya."

"Al!" I crawled beside him. He was huddled behind a rock, over which had fallen a sergeant. The man's coat was tattered by rebel bullets.

Allison grabbed my cold hands. "It's good to see you," he said, shivering. He swallowed. "Westleigh?"

"Still looking," I rubbed my aching throat. "Got your canteen?"

Allison nodded, holding it out to me. "Take what's left, I'm fine."

I fell over on my back and almost choked on a sob as I quenched my thirst.

Allison grinned. "You look awful."

Rifles popped, and we flinched as another shot struck the poor sergeant.

"I've been better," I admitted. "Where is everyone else?"

Allison lifted his finger, just barely, to point down past

our feet. "Saw most of the reg trying to make it back to the ravine. What's left of us. I've been trying to find you two."

"The captain left me," I said suddenly, shaking with rage. "I saved his life and he abandoned me!"

Allison grunted his disapproval. "Well, what'd you go and do a thing like that for?"

"It'll not happen again, it won't." I took a deep breath to calm my pounding heart.

"You all right?"

"Fine, I—" I pressed my palm against my breast, and stopped. My eyes filled with tears. "My ring. Aidan's ring, it's gone!"

"Shh," Allison said, grabbing my hand. "Maybe it's with your knapsack. Weren't you rummaging around in it earlier before the battle?"

I shook my head. "I don't know…"

"Come on," he whispered close. "Sooner we find Wes and get back, the sooner we can find out."

I felt ashamed for worrying about a piece of jewelry. "Oh! Westleigh—I'm sorry, my head—"

"Hey, no," Allison said, smiling softly. "I know what it means to you. Now, can you move? Are you well?"

"I can manage," I gasped, nodding. "Let's go."

"Down the hill," he said, pointing. "I've searched up here all I could, I think he fell back with the others before everything went to hell."

We started our slow, terrible crawl, stopping every time

we heard the angry snipe of a rifle. Soon we started to see familiar faces from our brigade, even a few from our regiment. But none of them were alive.

We came upon a grizzly sight — a pile of men, stacked upon each other like a small wall. An arm dangled down unnaturally. It was missing a few fingers.

Allison grimaced, touching my shoulder. "Come on —"

We heard the soft sound of crying coming from behind the macabre fortification and crawled towards it. Behind, huddled together for warmth, were Declan and Westleigh.

"Get down!" Declan hissed. "Sharpshooters are —"

Another pop made us scatter as it struck the arm of the dead man with a *thwack*.

We scrambled around to hide behind Declan's wall. Westleigh was lying on his belly, face buried in the crook of his arms.

I came along side of him and hugged him tight. "You're alive!" I whispered with a tearful laugh. He didn't raise his head. "Westleigh? We're here, everyone's safe."

He didn't respond, continuing to weep in his arms.

Declan frowned over him at me. "Are you injured?"

I touched the top of my head and winced. "Just a graze, but it bled something fierce."

Declan looked over me, expression unreadable. "Settle in," he said hoarsely, nodding over his shoulder. "Regiment's coming back. We might be at this again in the morning."

We shifted to make room behind the bodies, all curled around each other, with Allison at my back and my arm draped around Westleigh's trembling shoulders.

I settled my head on my arm, watching him as he cried. Not frightened tears, or tears of pain—he was unwounded, whole. Safe. I listened, and I heard tears of grief. Deep, heart-rending grief.

I held him tighter, tucking his head beneath my chin. An arm brushed mine, also hugging Westleigh's shoulders protectively, and I looked up to see Declan staring at me with an unreadable expression. There was something almost vulnerable in his eyes. For a moment, I thought I was with Aidan again.

The sharp pop of muskets awoke me with a start, and I squinted at the morning sun.

"Rise and shine," Allison croaked beside me. I turned my head to see him smile at me weakly. "Wish I hadn't let you finish off my canteen."

I shifted to lay on my stomach and looked to my right. Westleigh was beginning to stir beside me.

But Declan was gone.

I startled. "Where—"

"Don't know," Allison croaked. "He was gone when I woke up. Keep your head down, pickets are still at it. I even saw sharpshooters taking aim at some stretcher bearers, trying to get to the wounded."

"Bastards! What about the regiment?"

"Heard orders to lay low," he said. "Don't return fire. We're waiting."

"For what?"

"For them to stop shooting at us like turkeys in a pen, I reckon."

Westleigh coughed beside me, and I gave his shoulders a gentle shake. "Wes? You all right?"

He shifted to turn to us. His spectacles were gone, his eyes puffy and red. He looked in a daze, but managed a feeble nod before laying his head back on his arms.

I shifted uncomfortably. "Maybe it's good we can't get any more water," I mumbled. "I already feel like my bladder will burst."

Allison grunted, fishing around his haversack. "You two hungry? I have just a spare bit of hardtack."

I took some for myself and tried to pass a bit to Westleigh. He wouldn't look back up again.

I nudged him. "You need to eat."

"I cannot," he finally spoke into his arms. He took a shuddering breath. "The smells…"

I wrinkled my nose. I hadn't paid much attention to them before, but now they assaulted my senses and made me dizzy. The cold helped, but with the morning sun high in the sky, the putrid stench of death grew stronger.

I still choked down my hardtack, and after much coaxing, convinced Westleigh to do the same.

We lay there in silence for most of the morning, through the afternoon, listening to the pickets and the rebels exchanging fire. My head was growing weary again, and I might have dozed a few times, but Allison was there to wake me.

"Stay with me, Kavanagh," he said, winking as night began to fall again. "We'll get out of this yet."

I groaned. "I want a bath."

Allison laughed.

Westleigh hadn't spoken since breakfast. He was asleep, I figured, turned away from us and curled up under his overcoat.

Allison began to hum one of our marching songs behind me to himself.

I turned over. "What's that one?"

"Dunno, heard the Irish brigade singing it. Don't know the words."

"Hum it again, sounds familiar."

He cleared his throat and tried a few bars, but his voice wasn't keen on pitch when it wasn't dry and scratchy. He shrugged. "Not sure."

Westleigh's voice came from behind me, not singing, but reciting with no life in his voice, "'The minstrel boy to the war is gone, In the ranks of death you'll find him.'"

Allison wrinkled his nose. "Oh, figures. That's

depressing. What else can we sing?" He snapped his fingers. "It's almost Christmas. How about a carol?"

"I'm not sure singing is a grand idea right now," I said, pointing. "Sharpshooters?"

"Like they don't already know we're here," Allison said, and tried again. "God rest ye merry gentlemen, let nothing you dismay. For Jesus Christ our Savior was born upon this day—"

"'Tisn't Christmas day yet."

"Just let me sing a song."

"Who's the fool singing carols?" someone called out from the ground.

"Shush, let me hear him," another soldier said.

Allison grinned and finished the tune, then nudged me. "Your turn."

I shook my head. "I'm definitely sure that's not a wise idea," I said, sighing.

"Who's going to care out here?" Allison said. "Nobody'll know who's doing the singing."

"Oh Holy Night," Westleigh whispered beside me. "Do you know it? It's—it's my favorite..."

I swallowed. How could I refuse his request?

I started out sounding like a squeaking mouse, all wavering and pinched, but my throat loosened, and I lifted my song up to the heavens above me. "A thrill of hope, the weary world rejoices, for yonder breaks a new and glorious morn—"

"Shut up!" Declan appeared suddenly, throwing himself to the ground as a bullet whizzed by to smack a rock near us.

"Where have you been?" I hissed.

"I went down to find out what was going on," he whispered. "They're pulling us out, back into town."

"That took you all day?" Allison scoffed.

Declan glared at him. "I was kept behind," he growled. "I didn't have to come back, you know. Now you want to stay up here, that's fine by me, but I'm getting the hell out."

He slid back and started to quickly make his way toward the ravine. I moved stiffly, nudging Westleigh, with Allison giving me a little push. My joints ached, my head felt like it'd been stomped on, and there was a swollen knot on top of it. But the three of us crept down, and I could see other men on the field moving and doing the same.

Somehow we crawled our way back out of the ravine, and hurried down the road into Fredericksburg without ducking another blasted rebel bullet.

Our regiment was reforming the battle line on the main street. We fell in, hardly able to stand. My kepi and canteen were gone. We'd left behind our knapsacks, and I was wearing the dead sergeant's overcoat. But none of the rest of our boys looked much better. At least we still had our rifles.

We stood waiting for orders as ambulances clattered down the street, piled high with the wounded men they were able to retrieve from the field. There was a great deal of commotion coming from the building 'cross the street, which had been turned into a makeshift hospital. Men sat outside with bloody bandages or laid on unattended stretchers. A pile of severed limbs sat outside underneath one of the windows.

I staggered where I stood, feeling my world tip, but Allison caught me. "Do you need to—"

"No, thanks," I breathed, pressing the heel of my hand to my head. "I'm fine…"

I pitched forward, rifle falling from my hands to clatter in the street.

December 15, 1862

I felt the sun on my face and moaned.

"Amen to that," I heard Allison grumble.

I rubbed my eyes, and a hand touched my shoulder, helping me sit up. I squinted at Westleigh, who smiled tiredly at me. He looked a bit more like himself, though he still didn't have his spectacles. He must have lost them in the battle.

We were on the porch of a building, just off the street, still across from the hospital. Most of our regiment still sat nearby. Some rested, others ate what little food they had in their haversacks.

"How's your head?" Westleigh asked softly, hand still on my shoulder.

I touched the wound gingerly and found it to be clean. Even my hair was no longer caked with blood and grime, though it was a great deal messy. Not half as bad as Allison's, of course.

"I did what I could," Westleigh explained. "Didn't want to try and untangle it though, not while you slept."

"Thank you," I said, twisting my fingers through some of the knots. "It's much better."

"Have some water." Allison handed out a canteen and jabbed his thumb over his shoulder. "While you were out, some of us went back and got some supplies."

I drank greedily, looking around.

Westleigh was rummaging through his knapsack, checking on his books. I found myself smiling, glad to see he'd recovered them.

"Everything in order?" I asked, leaning over to peek.

Westleigh's smile was unsteady, unable to fully form, and then slipped from his face completely. He worked his jaw, nodding, and turned back to his books.

I leaned further over until he looked up at me.

"And how are you?" I whispered.

He didn't try to smile this time. "I'm alive," he said in a hollow voice.

I laid my hand upon his shoulder. "And for that, I rejoice," I said. The corner of his mouth lifted.

I took another drink and sighed. "How many?"

"Ten from our company," Allison said softly. "Three killed, seven wounded, not including ones like you that got scuffed up. Or poor Sergeant Kennedy, God rest him. We've a few others missing."

I winced. "Who did we lose?"

"Corporal Morrison and two of the Holl brothers." Allison scratched his head, trying to finger-comb his messy hair. "And they aren't too sure about Stewart, either. As for the rest of the regiment, they're still trying to find all the boys. Afraid some are still out there."

A quiet settled back over us for the rest of the day, like the day before. We were too exhausted, in body and spirit, to say much. Even Allison was more subdued that afternoon.

Men kept pouring into town, on stretchers, ambulances, or dragging themselves in with missing boots, coats, and some, limbs. Seemed the whole army was either broken or bleeding.

More of the boys from our regiment showed up, but nobody else from our company. We numbered only thirty-six standing and able-bodied souls. I prayed those that were wounded recovered and joined us soon. But if the growing pile of limbs outside the hospital was any indication, there weren't many who could call themselves so fortunate.

After a meager supper we tried to steal a few hours

more of rest, only to be awoken after midnight with orders to form up.

I nearly wept in relief. Finally, we were getting to leave.

The captain gathered us from Company C together to whisper our instructions. "Our regiment is to be part of the rear guard," he said. More than a few of us were crestfallen, but he paid us no heed. Though he did pause as he looked at me, a curious expression on his face. It was gone as soon as I saw it, and he went back to his orders. "We'll cover the retreat by the river. No one is to make a sound. Keep your tins quiet, too. No noise."

As soon as we got to the river, it started to rain. We stood at attention in the miserable weather, watching the rest of the army move as quietly as an army could, as they marched 'cross the pontoon bridges over the Rappahannock. At least the sound of rain somewhat muffled our steps.

It rained all the way back to camp. More than once, I thought I'd collapse in the mud and lay there till Christmas, but Westleigh and Allison, holding either one of my arms, pulled me along, though I know they were close to falling over, too.

I thought back on our very first march, our little parade out of that sleepy village that felt like such a lifetime ago. The people of Dove Hollow lining the streets, waving kerchiefs and little flags, the band striking up a tune, our chests puffed with pride as we cheered with them. Knights, David had called us. And we'd thought ourselves as such.

Holy warriors, off to vanquish a great evil. But there was nothing holy about any of this.

I'm not sure I'd ever felt in my entire life so utterly *beaten.*

We reported in at camp, and found our old tent, but we were too exhausted to sleep. We sat outside on our boxes, slumped over and drooping, as the rest of the army wandered around like the lost souls we all were.

"They cut us to ribbons," I whispered, looking at them all with a heavy heart. "How do we go on?"

Westleigh looked at me, his kind grey eyes so terribly sad. But there was a resolve in them. "We just do," he said quietly. "Our mission hasn't changed, has it?"

I took a deep breath. "It hasn't. But I can't see the end of it. I close my eyes... and I can't picture it all ending well anymore. I can't."

Westleigh nodded, looking at his knees. He gave a small shrug. "I heard another verse of that song, from the Irish brigade. The one Allison didn't let me finish. Would you like to hear it?"

I glanced over. Allison had fallen asleep sitting on his crate, his chin dropped down on his chest. "Please."

Westleigh's song began timidly—he never sang aloud for us in camp, which was a shame, for his voice was truly lovely. He sang the marching song like a slow ballad, and I hung on every word, lifted it like a prayer. So beautiful that, by the end, I had tears on my cheeks.

Tears of hope.

MACTAVISH

The Minstrel Boy will return we pray
When we hear the news we all will cheer it,
The minstrel boy will return one day,
Torn perhaps in body, not in spirit.
Then may he play on his harp in peace,
In a world such as heaven intended,
For all the bitterness of man must cease,
And ev'ry battle must be ended.

34

WESTLEIGH
Fredericksburg, Virginia
December 16, 1862

Allison's hand shook as he held up the letter, his face twisted in a funny mix of joy and fear. I looked quizzically over at Saoirse, who winked at me.

"I take it she said yes, then?" Saoirse asked with feigned boredom, preparing the coffee for our mess.

Allison's head snapped up, and he gave us a lopsided grin. "Ellen sent me her answer!"

"We can see that," I laughed. "And what was her answer?"

"She wants to marry me," Allison said, eyes wide. "I'm not so sure how smart a girl she is if she actually said *yes*."

"I'd say she's a lucky one," Saoirse teased, "but I think you're the one who's lucky."

"No arguments there," he said, looking down at the

letter, holding it like it was sacred. "She says every day we're apart feels like a year has gone by, and—"

"You don't have to read it to us," Saoirse said, swatting at his arm. She smiled at him. "Those are Ellen's words for you. Keep them there, and cherish them."

Allison blushed, folding the letter and tucking it in his coat pocket. He sat, his hands under his bouncing knees as he waited for the coffee. A moment went by, and he pulled the letter out and read it all over again.

I caught Saoirse's eyes and we grinned, but I held them too long, and looked away quickly.

She served us our coffee, and for once I was glad to have it, the way it warmed my insides.

Allison couldn't sit still any more, and he took his coffee and letter to go wander and pace around the camp.

Saoirse sipped her coffee with a small sigh. Her eyes snapped open. "Oh!" she pulled a note from her pocket. "I've heard from home as well. I'm not sure if you can read it..."

My spectacles had broken in the battle, and until things calmed down, I wouldn't be able to find suitable replacements. Allison thought this was hilarious and insisted on making faces at me when he thought I couldn't see him.

I held out my hand, and she passed the envelope to me. More than one page was stuffed tight inside. I held them up. "Seems the whole town is starting to write."

I shuffled through them. I could make out the words if I squinted hard enough.

"Peter sends his love," Saoirse said. "They're getting the whole town ready for the Christmas festivities."

I saw a stain on the paper, and laughed suddenly, holding it up. It was a muddy paw print. "Seems Wilberforce also sends his love. And what did Da have to say?"

"He reports that Jack is on his feet and adapting well," Saoirse said quietly, "though he tries to do more than he ought, right now."

"Sounds like Jack," I said.

"He spends much of his time at George's, insisting on being given some work," Saoirse took the letter back. "At night they often sit at home and read the paper, always looking for news of us. They are all praying for us night and day, and are pleased to know that we're healthy and whole."

"We'll write to them immediately," I whispered. "They'll hear the news of the past few days soon and will worry."

Saoirse held up a letter. "I started writing this morning. I left room, if you wish for me to add anything for you."

"Thanks."

"He still hasn't said why he had us worry," she said with a bitter edge to her voice. "Hasn't explained a thing. What do you think kept him from writing for so long?"

I bit my lip. "I have my theories…"

I saw Declan walking towards us and clamped my lips together.

Saoirse saw the change in my expression and turned. Her mood darkened instantly. "What do you want?"

Declan looked as if he was about to sneer, then thought better of it. In fact, he just looked tired. "Believe it or not, I wanted to see how you were." He shook his head. "But seems you're back to your pleasant self, after all."

Saoirse stiffened, folding her arms. "That all?"

Declan sighed, and pointed behind him. "Captain wants to see you. Says he wants to thank you in person for saving his life."

Saoirse's eyes widened, and she stood a bit wobbly. She started to make her way towards the captain's tent, and Declan stopped her.

"Whatever you think of me, doesn't matter," he said, brow creased. "But I just wanted to say—you have surprised me. In every way conceivable."

She blinked at him. "Are you—*proud* of me?" I heard, for a fleeting moment, a childlike tone of hope in her question.

Declan turned away. "I didn't say that," he muttered. "Go on, he's waiting."

She glared at the back of his head for a moment, then hurried away. I watched her go, wishing I could tell her how proud *I* was.

I felt Declan's eyes on me and glanced up. He was studying me sadly.

"And you?" he asked. "Are you better?"

The scenes of battle rushed through my mind, and a marrow-deep cold shook me. I shivered in my coat, but forced a smile. "I am, thank you."

His frown tightened. He didn't believe me. I couldn't fool a man who had been masking his own pain so well for as long as he had. But he didn't press the issue. He nodded over his shoulder. "Thought any more about what I said?" He narrowed his eyes. "You should tell her how you feel. Take her home. I saw the way she was with you, during the battle. You'd be a fool to think she doesn't care for you."

I swallowed, wiping my palms on my trousers. Of course I'd thought about it. It was all I could think about, it kept me up at night and drove me to distraction during the day.

Not only would I risk my heart, but our friendship. I would be asking her to abandon her dream, for me. To run away, like cowards. But we'd be alive. We'd be together. We'd go home, to Jack, to David, and find another way to make a difference in this broken, hurting world. I would follow her anywhere. But would she follow me?

I took a deep breath and looked up with a smile. "I didn't thank you," I said softly, changing the subject. "For looking after me, on the heights. I'm… I'm sorry I called you a coward."

Declan grimaced. "You weren't wrong."

"No," I said firmly. "I was."

He shrugged, half-turning away. "You know, I remember Aunt Maggie too." He paused. "You remind me a lot of her."

I felt my breath catch. "Thank you."

Declan gave a short nod, and wandered away, hands shoved in his pockets.

I massaged my temples, trying to ward away the headache

that was forming there, but I couldn't help the smile spreading on my face. I finished my coffee and set about arranging my books. I picked one of them up with a sigh. A bullet had torn through my knapsack and buried itself in the cover of *Idylls of the King*. I placed it back in the bag. It was just a book.

As I shuffled the others, one book tumbled out, falling open on the ground. I bent to pick it up with a groan, still stiff from our ordeal.

A fluttering caught my eye, a letter tugged loose by the wind. I plucked it from the pages, thinking it was one of Peter's I'd accidentally used as a bookmark. But the handwriting didn't make sense, and so I lifted it closer to inspect it, squinting so that I could read.

My dearest Declan…

My arms went numb. His letter. The one he thought Jack had stolen.

I grabbed the book from the ground and it suddenly made sense. It was the Collins novel I lent to him at Harrison's Landing. Declan must've forgotten he used the letter to mark his pages.

I almost followed after him, but curiosity made my heart race. It was wrong, so very wrong to read it… but after all the trouble that was made about this silly little thing, I had to know the truth.

It was a lady's handwriting, that was clear. She started the letter detailing some trip she'd taken with her mother to New York—hardly anything sensitive or scandalous. She spoke of how much she missed seeing him, and begged him to ask for a furlough to come and visit, since Maryland was not far.

I paused. Maryland? But hadn't Declan said she was from Pittsburgh? I kept reading.

I have worn father down, and I know he would be more than happy to welcome you here for dinner again. Only, don't mention any of this to my dear cousin. I know how he hates when I flirt with his business partners. Speaking of business—well, I should not speak much of it here, only to report that Papa says that the war has improved our situation far more than he could have dreamed, and he is very pleased with the work you and cousin Marek are doing. I'm glad this endears him more to you, but I would much rather this war was over, so you could come back to me. Be safe, and write me soon.

Forever yours,
Susanna Olsen

I dropped down to sit hard on the crate and read over the letter again, furiously. My mind raced to make sense of it, pulling out what facts I understood, and laying them before me.

Declan's sweetheart was Olsen's cousin. They were working for his uncle in Maryland. Somehow, they were all profiting from the war.

I felt a cold panic seize me, and the letter fluttered in my hand. If Declan found out I had it... There was no way I could return it now, without him suspecting I'd read it. What would he do to me?

I shook my head. No, no, this was all wrong! Declan cared about us, I knew that now. I could see it in his eyes, behind the anger and the hurt, a desperate need for his family. He'd watched out for me on that hill...

It was Olsen. He was the one trapping Declan. And the longer he stayed in his clutches, the harder it would be to break him free. I set my jaw tight. I could not leave him alone. Not now. There had to be more to his story.

I looked at the letter again. I couldn't return it, but neither could I keep it. And I couldn't tell Saoirse — she would never forgive him. And after today, I felt so close to reaching him, closer than ever before.

You can't have them both, Westleigh.

"Yes Jack, I can," I muttered aloud. And I would. I'd bring them all back together, just like I promised so long ago in Dove Hollow.

I glanced around quickly and stuffed the letter between the burning logs of our fire. The edges charred and curled, and it quickly turned to ash. Soon, Declan's bonds with Olsen would crumble, too.

I felt eyes on me and glanced up to see Saoirse returning.

I wiped my palms on my trousers again, and swallowed

hard, putting all thoughts of Declan and his letter out of my mind.

I smiled as she approached. "There you are. Did he give you a medal? He should, after saving his wretched hide."

Saoirse sat down across from me, slumping over to rest her arms on her knees. I wasn't sure she even heard me, the way she stared at her toes with a pale look on her face.

Something was very wrong. "Saoirse?" I whispered. "What is it? What did the captain say?"

A bitter, nervous laugh burst from her, and she shook her head, staring at her toes for a long time before answering hoarsely. "He knows, Westleigh."

She looked up at me, stricken with fear like I'd never seen before, tears streaming down her face.

"Olsen knows who I really am."

EPILOGUE

October 28, 1862
Dove Hollow, Pennsylvania

David Kavanagh stepped over the threshold and dropped his bag with a heavy *thump* that was swallowed up by silence. He stretched his chest and his arms, shrugging off a bit of the weight from his travels with a loud yawn. The house was still quiet.

He shuffled into the parlor and sank into his armchair, noticing how the dust didn't rise when he sat. He shook his head. Over a year since he'd left town, and yet someone was cleaning his home. He probably had the Bischoffs to thank for that. They seemed to never stop looking after him.

And David had done a poor job of repaying their kindness, he thought as he leaned his head back to rest his eyes for a moment. Running away with Eoghan yet again, as reckless as he'd been as a youth, even though Peter begged him to stay home. But he simply couldn't bear the silence, or the safety, knowing his children were putting themselves in peril far away. Besides, he doubted they'd even had the time to worry about him. He would make it up to them all somehow. Visit Peter. Write to his beloveds. Soon as he had a nap.

He tried dozing, listening to the quiet ticking of the mantle clock. He shook his head, chuckling to himself. They even kept his clocks wound.

Sometime later he heard the half-hour chime, and still David couldn't rest. He groaned as he sat up. It was simply too quiet, he thought with a grimace, realizing he couldn't recall the last time he was truly alone. The dog wasn't even there to annoy him.

Wilberforce. He was probably still at Peter's. Well, the least he could do was go ahead and take the mutt off the preacher's hands. Then he could rest.

David dragged himself back out of the house and set off walking down the road to the parsonage. Oh, how he'd missed his little town. It was still early morning yet, the sun was barely up, and aside from a few shop owners heading to the square to open their businesses, everyone else would likely still be eating breakfast.

He could smell Peter's cooking from the front porch as he knocked, and his stomach growled noisily. He sighed. If

Peter heard that, he'd make him stay and eat, when all David wanted was to sleep for a week.

The door opened, and the portly preacher scowled at him behind his narrow spectacles. "You look like hell."

"Thanks very much," David muttered, and Peter stepped aside to let him in. "Missed you too."

"You didn't write."

"I told you I probably couldn't when I left," David said. "Too dangerous."

"Which is the reason I told you not to go, if I recall."

David rolled his eyes. "Wilberforce?" He whistled sharply. "Where are ya, boy?"

There was a wild scrambling of claws on the wood floor, and the huge white dog came barreling into the foyer. He tried and failed to leap into David's arms, settling for wrapping his paws over his shoulders and frantically whining as he tried to climb up in his arms.

"Whoa there, look who's grown! I didn't think this beast could get any bigger."

Peter grunted. "Well, he's feeling forgiving."

"Least someone is," David teased. "I am sorry, Peter. I can explain—"

"Not now." Peter waved him away. "Breakfast is ready."

"I really need to rest," David protested. "I'll come back this afternoon, I promise."

"No," Peter said firmly, turning around. His eyes were

so stern that even Wilberforce laid down immediately. The preacher pointed down the hall. "There's someone here you should see. Maybe *you* can get him to eat."

Alarm bells rang in David's ears, his first thought of Westleigh. "Is everything all right?"

Peter shook his head. "Of course not, David."

He walked toward the dining room, leaving David to follow nervously. Wilberforce stayed on his heels. As he rounded the corner, he saw a broken young man sitting slumped at the table, hands in his lap, a bandage over his eyes.

David's heart dropped to his stomach. "Jack."

Jack lifted his chin as his jaw tightened but didn't turn his head towards him. "Mr. Kavanagh," he said roughly. "Thought that was your voice."

David slipped into the chair beside him, resting his hand on his shoulder. Jack's muscles were taut as he shrank in on himself. "Oh Jack," David whispered. "I'm so sorry."

"So, you're home."

"Just arrived." David studied his features, checking him for other injuries. Other than his sight, and the burn marks on his cheeks, he seemed whole. "I'm sorry I wasn't—"

"Save it," Jack muttered.

David swallowed. "Fine. No excuses. But you'll want to hear what I have to say."

Jack shrugged.

David looked up at Peter, who'd paused with David's plate in his hand, waiting for him to continue.

David cleared his throat. "I was going to write and tell you this afternoon, but seeing as you're here now... we went to Texas. I saw the farm, what was left of it. I'm sorry, I couldn't find anything worth saving. But we stayed, worked with a group of Union sympathizers. Till Reeves found us out and ran us out of town, that is. We barely got out alive."

Jack became very, very still.

"One of the men knew you," David said slowly. "Sam Goodwin. He wanted me to tell you—"

"David," Peter interrupted sternly, his eyes wide. "Perhaps we should eat first..."

"No," Jack said. His chin trembled. "Please, just tell me they gave her a decent burial."

"She's alive," David whispered. "Abigail. Sam got her out of town, and Kitty, and Brian."

Peter almost dropped the plate he carried. Jack began to weep.

"She's *alive*, Jack!" David repeated, sliding his arm around the young man's shoulders to hold him close. "And I swear to you, we *will* find her."

TO BE CONTINUED

Sarah MacTavish currently lives in the same small Texas town she grew up in, but dreams of one day moving to Ireland. She's also a proud Hufflepuff, incurable Star Wars nerd, and unapologetic cat lady. When she isn't writing, she's either working at her local library, gaming, or helping her mom with the family tree.

Connect with her online at www.sarahmactavish.com

www.ingramcontent.com/pod-product-compliance
Lightning Source LLC
Chambersburg PA
CBHW051205120726
47905CB00004B/994